LAWLESS GOD

NORTH SHORE STORIES BOOK FOUR

LOLA KING

*Cover art by Wild Love Designs
Editing by Mackenzie at Nice Girl Naughty Edits
Alpha reading by Lauren Pixley
Beta Reading by Ratula Roy*

Fuck around and find out
  Unknown

To all my girls who will have Stockholm syndrome by the end of this book.
Nate is manipulating you.
But you'll love it anyway.

CONTENT WARNING

Hello, and thank you for picking up this book.
Before going in, please note this book is a dark romance for readers aged 18+ only.
The subgenre of dark romance can vary in degrees of darkness. My books are very dark.

If you've read my books before - this one is just as dark, just as twisted, and just as toxic.
I will say this to you: **The MMC, Nate, is barely redeemable. He doesn't try to be forgiven, he just manipulates you into thinking you have forgiven him.**

It's important for you to know your own limits, and that what matters the most is your mental health and your wellbeing. Reading is fun, fiction is great, but you matter the most.
The heroine in this book is turned on by feeling like she is forced, helpless, and can't defend herself. If this is not something you like reading about, then this book isn't for you.

CONTENT WARNING

Please note the following possible triggers in no specific order:

Non con
Dub con
Descriptive violent (consensual) sex scenes
Police violence
Torture
Murder
Violence
Gang-related activity
Forced marriage
Near Somnophilia (she's not unconscious but almost)
Forced drug taking
Manipulation in a relationship
Toxicity in a relationship
Mention of child abuse
Mention of child sexual abuse
Night terrors
Mention of marital rape
Sex trafficking
On-page sexual assault
Non consensual piercing and tattooing
Branding
Kidnapping
Child witnessing a crime
Description of out of body experience when being sexually assaulted
Blackmail

Kinks include:
Blood play
Knife play

PLAYLIST

Bad - Royal Deluxe
Monster - Willecho
Kamikazee - MISSIO
Riot - Bryce Fox, Sam Tinnesz
Bury Me Face Down - Grandson
She's My Witch - Kip Tyler
Truth Comes Out - Willyecho
Riptide - grandson
i hope ur miserable until ur dead - Nessa Barrett
Fuck You - Silent child
Free Animal - Foreigh Air
Welsome to the Fire - Willyecho
Hypnotic - Zella Day
Celebrity Skin - Hole
AMERICAN HORROR SHOW - SNOW WIDE
Save Me Some Sunshine - Rafferty
How Villains Are Made - Madalen Duke
Victim - Halflives
Daddy Issues - The Neighbourhood
Something To Hide - grandson

PLAYLIST

APHRODITE - Ethan Gander

Scars - Boy Epix

Godlen Boy - Bryce Fox

Dangerous Game Klery Beginners

madhouse - Nessa Barrett

Joke's On You - Charlotte Lawrence

Obsessed - Royal Deluxe

you should see me in a crown - Billie Eilish

Babylon - 5 Seconds of Summer

Kiss Bang - grandson

I Wanna Be Yours - Arctic Monkeys

how will i rest in peace if i'm burried by a highway -
KennyHoopla

Coming Down - Halsey

Love ino a Wrapon - Madalen Duke

RUNNING - NF

Rain - grandson, Jessie Reyez

Godless - BANKS

I Found - Amber Run

Lost - Ollie

lovely - Billie Eilish, Khalid

Bodies - Bryze Fox

505 - Arctic Monkeys

Flames - Tedy

die first - Nessa Barrett

Unstoppable - The Score

Woke Up A Rebel - Reuben And The Dark

Soldier - Tommee Profitt, Fleurie

Teeth - 5 Seconds of Summers

PROLOGUE
KAYLA

Bad - Royal Deluxe

Four years ago...

A silence like I've never experienced blankets the cold courtroom as the judge returns. As we all stand, I can feel Samuel Thomas's eyes burning holes into my skull. His boss is going down, and now everyone knows it's because of me.

I could take Sam down too. Intimidation of a key witness. His words yesterday were spoken quietly, but I heard them loud and clear. He cornered me in the parking lot, his giant body pinning me against my car.

Don't do this, Kay. Go back tomorrow and tell them your testimony is a lie. You think he'll go away forever, but surely you know him enough to realize he will not stay in prison, no matter what his sentence is. The only person in danger if you go through with this is you.

Everyone sits back down, and I do my best not to turn

my head to the side. In my peripheral, sitting with his attorneys, Nathan White's presence calls out to me.

My entire life changed in a matter of weeks. Where I grew up, *snitches get stitches*. Or more often, they get shot in the face. Especially if they're lying about it.

But everyone comes to a point in their lives where they must choose whether they want to be the predator or the prey. Whatever little morals I used to have went out of the window when I was offered a chance at survival.

I have to get rid of the bigger fishes who try to take over my pound.

Or how can I be the biggest?

"Jury," Judge Falton says, as he turns to the foreperson of the jury. "Have you reached a verdict?"

"Yes, your honor, we have," she answers.

My hands tighten around my thighs to stop them from shaking.

"Is it unanimous?"

"Yes, your honor, it is."

Looking down, I watch as the letters tattooed on my right hand's knuckles move across my skin from my anxious gripping.

K.I.N.G.

I rub my thumb against the mouth of a skull on the back of my hand.

Did my life as a criminal impact their verdict?

Attorney Garcia-Diaz made sure to make me sound unreliable on the stand yesterday.

Miss King, is it true you are part of a group called the North Shore Kings and that this group exercises gang-related criminal activities on the North Shore of Silver Falls? Am I wrong to say your father is the leader of that group?

Nate fucking *smiled* at me when she asked that question. He pushed his glasses up his nose with his middle finger to tell me to go fuck myself. He knew exactly what I was doing on that stand, probably planning ten steps ahead.

Objection, your honor, Luton, the state attorney, said without a second thought. *Irrelevant.*

Garcia-Diaz snorted, her perfect figure turning to Luton. *I'm simply asking for an update on your witness's employment status.*

Sustained. Judge Falton pointed at the pretty defense attorney. *This witness isn't on trial, Mrs. Garcia-Diaz. Please. Kindly focus on the defendant.*

She didn't care, though. It wasn't what mattered. The jury heard her entirely true accusations. If anything, some of them already knew. The Kings might be a small gang for big criminals like Nate White, but the city of Silver Falls *knows* us.

Who would believe a criminal testifying against another one? Anyone with two brain cells to rub together would know we all have our own agendas.

And they would be right.

What if I went through all of this, showed myself as an essential witness, lied in court, all for the jury to realize I was just a big fraud?

Then Nathan White doesn't go to prison.

He walks out of this courtroom as a free man.

And I'm a dead woman.

"Please, pass me the form." Judge Falton's deep voice startles me as the foreperson gives him the form with the verdict.

Why is it so cold in here? I've got a headache from forcing myself to stare ahead of me. I'm scared Nate's ocean eyes have the power to kill me on the spot if I even glance at them.

The judge takes forever to read the verdict. I just want to fucking know if I'm going to die or not. Is that so hard to ask?

There's always been a war on the North Shore of Silver Falls. We're a desolate town, abandoned by anyone who ever tried to make it a decent place. All that's left there are abandoned developments, old streets that haven't been redone in decades, broken houses we can't afford to fix, a high school that only spits out delinquents.

And two gangs fighting for power.

Every few years, the balance tips. If my gang, the Kings, aren't ruling, then it's because the North Shore Crew—NSC—has stolen the town from us.

There are ways for us small gangs to gain more power. We work for bigger criminal organizations, sell their drugs, their arms. We kill people for them so it's not linked back to them. In the case of my father, he also steals women off the streets if needed.

Nathan White is part of those bigger organizations. Sharks who come to our small, desperate town and make offers we can't refuse. Nate works for the Cosa Nostra, the Bianco family, to be exact. Just under a year ago, he came to the North Shore and offered my father to work for him. In exchange, he would give the Kings protection from the law and from our enemies, NSC.

But my dad is a stupid fucking man. His pride doomed us all when he refused the offer. And Nate is cunning. He did the one thing that would make my father bite his nails. He took that exact same offer to NSC. Before we could blink, the town was theirs, and our crew, the people who relied on us, lost everything.

I did my best to fix the shit situation my dad put us in, but my best wasn't enough. Nathan White is not a forgiving man. In fact, he is a complete psychopath. There was no forgiving my family for my father's refusal.

Thankfully, the man is also a megalomaniac, and when Nate got greedy—and got rid of his boss, Mateo Bianco, to take his place—I had already made a deal of my own with the Cosa Nostra's worst enemies.

The Bratva Wolves.

They were happy to offer me the exact same deal Nate had.

They just needed me to do one tiny little thing in exchange.

Get rid of him. They wanted the guy who kept trying to steal their territories.

It was part of our deal. And it took me a few months to figure out how.

Then Vladimir Volkov, the head of the Bratva Wolves, tried to kill Nate, and got himself killed instead. The news of Volkov dying spread fast, and I already had my contact in the Wolves. He knew Nate didn't kill him, but that he was there that night. He wasn't killed by Nate, unlike what I testified in a court of law yesterday, but the man was involved, and the chance is too big to pass up.

The Wolves want Nate out. Death, prison, it doesn't matter. They've already started helping us take over the town. It's my turn to hold my end of the deal.

All I have to do is get rid of him, and God knows I could never kill him.

I struggle to breathe when the judge finally speaks. My heart is ringing in my ears, my life flashing before my eyes.

Am I about to die, or strike the deal of my fucking life?

"In the case of the State of Maryland vs. Nathan White,

charges for murder, possession of a weapon during a violent crime, and illegal possession of a firearm, the jury found the defendant"—I think my heart is going to explode—"*guilty on all charges.*"

I let out a sigh so loud, the people sitting in front of me turn around, a matching sympathetic look on their faces. They probably think I'm glad a murderer is being put away for life.

Nate is innocent of the crime he's being accused of, but he *is* a murderer. He should be sentenced today on many other accounts. Arms trafficking, racketeering, drug trafficking, extortion, obstruction of justice, conspiracy to commit crimes, and everything else he used to do as part of the Cosa Nostra.

He might not have killed Vladimir Volkov, but his sister did. And I'm sure even a psycho like him would rather take the fall than snitch on his own blood. He's stuck. Because I said I was there. I said he did it, and he won't let his sister go to prison.

And that's all that matters. He's going away for life.

The judge and defense attorney go through some more talks, polling the jury to make sure it was a unanimous decision, and my need to smile twitches my jaw. There's a new energy rushing through me. The North Shore belongs to my family again. The Kings are back, and we have the Bratva Wolves behind us. The only person linking NSC to the Cosa Nostra is about to go to prison. They have no one, nothing. They're dead.

I keep my mouth straight, the fear of being in the same room as Nate still weighing on my shoulders. Until I see him walk away in handcuffs, knowing he's never getting out, I won't be able to breathe properly.

Judge Falton gives Nate an unimpressed look over his glasses.

"I will add that, while you are not being charged for other crimes, the court is aware of your criminal past and suspicion of being part of a criminal organization. The jury did not take this into consideration for their verdict, and it does not influence your sentence, but I know who you are, Mr. White. It is my task today to impose a sentence. Nathan White, for the murder of Vladimir Volkov, I sentence you to a life of imprisonment without parole."

The gavel comes down hard against the wood, and power resonates deep within my entire being, ringing the bells of victory.

Nathan White has made my life miserable over the last few months. He is the only man who made me feel true fear again.

And now he knows that you don't fuck with Kayla King.

Despite my best attempts, the need to look at him as they take him away is too strong. This man made me discover things I didn't even know about myself. I can have one last look. Like a little gift to myself.

He's looking right back at me, his dark blond hair tied tightly in a small bun, his eyes piercing through my soul behind his black-rimmed glasses.

I will never see him again. He's going away forever. I will never feel his hands on my skin, his mouth on mine, his personal brand of torture coursing through my body. My soul is forever broken by him, and yet something in my heart hurts.

I will *never* feel the things only he can make me feel again.

He turns around one last time, shining bright white

teeth at me. His smile always looks like death. Like he has something up his sleeve.

But nothing happens. Of course not. He's cuffed, surrounded by four police officers who are about to take him to jail. There's nothing he can do about it.

But he still winks at me, knowing that even if he's rotting in prison, Nathan White will haunt me forever.

PART I

REVENGE

While seeking revenge, dig two graves - one for yourself.
Douglas Horton

1

KAYLA

Monster - Willy Echo

Today...

"*Kayla King.*"

The way my name reverberates in the room when he says it is like nothing I've heard before.

It's lifeless, and yet there is no threat to it. Almost like he's trying to attempt kindness.

I startle when his knuckles caress my cold cheek. I've heard what this man is capable of. Why is he being so gentle with me?

I don't know what force pushed me to follow what my dad asked of me tonight. Going to the NSC leader's house? Asking for a truce? Just because he fucked up and refused Nathan's deal and we're paying the consequences of having lost our town.

Or at least, I am.

There was a huge party when I showed up. A house full of NSC people who wanted nothing but to see me dead. The leader wasn't there, but his two daughters were. Emma and Billie

Scott. And his stepson, Xi, was there too. I was in their driveway, turning around, when he caught me.

Needless to say, the three of them and I have a tumultuous past. Hate is meaningless when you compare it to what the Scotts and my family feel toward each other. We're mortal enemies.

But my dad sent me there anyway. And I would probably have died, beaten up by a crowd of NSC, if Nathan White hadn't pulled me out of there.

What for? He's their boss now. We refused his deal, refused to work for him, and he took it to NSC.

So why the hell am I sitting on his kitchen island, holding ice wrapped in a cloth to my busted lip?

"Being brave has to be timed perfectly."

It takes me a few seconds to come back from being lost in the depths of his midnight eyes. The chant of a siren has nothing on the ocean that swallows you when you look into Nathan's eyes.

"Worried about me being killed?" I rasp. Talking out loud hurts my ribs.

I'll get over it quickly. It's not the first time I've gotten beaten up. The war between the North Shore Crew and the Kings started long before I was born. Being in trouble is the way I grew up.

"I just think it would be a shame for such a pretty thing to get hurt beyond repair."

He doesn't mean it. I can see it right away.

Still, my heart skips a beat, blood rushing to my ears, but I narrow my eyes at him. "Is that how you hit on girls? Save them from being beaten to death, bring them to your house, tell them they're pretty?"

A chilling smile curls his lips. It's not subtle, and he makes no attempts at stopping it. For a second, I wonder how long it'll spread. It ends up wide enough to be haunting.

"I'm an opportunist," he explains calmly, hiding nothing of his horrible personality. "I like to help myself before others jump on an occasion."

I snort and look away from him so I don't lose composure. "Sorry to break it to you, but many have jumped on the occasion to fuck me before you."

He reaches next to me, grabbing the tumbler of whiskey he helped himself to when we arrived earlier. He didn't offer me one, and I didn't bother asking. I'm not planning on staying here. The only reason I haven't run away yet is because of self-preservation. I know not to anger a big player.

Swirling his whiskey, the amber liquid sloshes to the side. He stares at it before looking up at me. "But did they jump on the occasion to fuck you when you were vulnerable? When you were ready to do anything to keep your family and your crew out of trouble? When you were in such a dire situation, you went all the way to your enemies' territories to ask for a truce?"

His eyes stay frozen on me as he talks. I'm trying to look for something in them, but I'm met with an emotionless presence. He's accusing himself of abusing someone vulnerable, warning me that's exactly what he's planning on doing, and his voice is as flat as someone ordering a meal at a drive thru.

I'll take a vulnerable woman with my burger, please.

When I don't answer, he tilts his head to the side. "Would you do anything to save your crew?"

It's always the most handsome ones who are the most fucked up. I see Nathan around town. I see him coming to check on NSC, making sure the territories he's acquiring for his boss are going to make the Bianco family richer.

Everyone *notices him*.

He doesn't look like any of us. He's a real criminal. The kind that walks around in a suit, always looking his best when he causes chaos. Tattoos peek above the collar of his shirt, on his *hands and knuckles, letting us all wonder how many more he's hiding under the black button-down.*

He's handsome; he wears glasses that make him look smart. He's not raw like us. We wear our misery on our faces. We make ourselves look tough. We show the tattoos of which crew we belong to. Because the tougher you appear, the less likely someone will come and look for trouble.

Nathan isn't like that. He wears a perfectly molded mask.

Real monsters hide under pretty faces. Or how would they get so close to their victims?

I bite the tip of my tongue as I observe him. Wondering if I'm going to have to fuck him to get out of here, or if I could just hop off the counter and walk out the door. I doubt the latter is an option. And I doubt the former would be that easy.

I bet Nathan White fucks like he kills. And I've seen him kill... It's terrifying.

"Yeah," I finally say. "But not the way you think."

He cocks an eyebrow at me. The only sign that he is potentially interested in my opinion. "Tell me what I'm thinking."

"You're thinking I'm going to drop to my knees and suck your dick. Offer you anything you want so that, in exchange, you stop NSC from unleashing their fury on the Kings."

I thought I'd see at least a spark of interest in his eyes, but nothing shows.

What the fuck is wrong with this guy?

Ignoring the fact that his lack of emotion makes me feel uneasy, I keep going. "I won't. My kind of despair makes me murderous." I lean toward him, my eyes roaming over his gorgeous face. "You get in my way, you die. Period."

He has no problem holding my stare. He even breathes me in. "Do it."

I feel a crease forming between my eyebrows. "What?"

"Do it, Kayla. I've got a leash on NSC tighter than a virgin's cunt. Trust me when I tell you all their power comes from me. Everything that makes your crew miserable is because of me. I am the one in your way. So do it. Kill me."

For the first time tonight, I see something on his face. I wouldn't know quite how to define it. Curiosity? Excitement?

Does he...really want me to kill him?

Shifting on his counter, I put the ice to the side. "Anyone ever told you, you're fucked in the head?"

"Many times. So, are you going to kill me or what?"

He takes a sip of his whiskey.

"If you manage, your whole crew will be able to take over the North Shore again. Although, I have to tell you the rules first. I'll allow you a fair try, but if you fail...then we'll do it my way. I kind of like the getting-down-on-your-knees-and-sucking-my-dick idea you mentioned." He smiles behind the rim of his glass. Nothing about it portrays happiness. It's pure mockery. "And once I have my way with you, I promise I'll think about reeling back NSC."

"You're—"

"Fucked in the head. I heard you the first time. Think of it this way: no matter what happens tonight, you'll be leaving tomorrow morning knowing your crew is safe."

"Cute that you think it'd take me until tomorrow morning to kill you."

In that flat voice of his, he states the facts. "You won't kill me. But I will fuck your pretty body until tomorrow morning, that's for sure."

I lick my lips, swallowing my response. I'm more than capable of killing a man. I'm just not sure I can kill this man. No one becomes the right-hand in a Cosa Nostra family by being an easy target. Plus, he's expecting it, ready to defend himself.

His brow furrows as he looks at me like he doesn't

understand what's going on in my head, my hesitation. "Are you wondering if you should do it?"

"Of course I'm wondering if I should fucking do it," I hiss.

"I see." He takes another sip of his whiskey, making me yearn for the burning liquid down my throat. "Don't bother. You don't have a choice. The only way you're getting out of this house is if I'm dead or you've been fucked thoroughly."

His lack of emotion is stark now. He doesn't care about pretending anymore. Pretending he can feel, that he might understand my own emotions.

Right now, I'm not totally sure he can. I slowly slide my body to the side, getting some space from him. He's not standing between my legs, he's next to me, and I feel the urgent need to move away.

"Why are you doing this?" I'm not more scared than I was. I don't think fear is something I experience that often anymore. But I want to understand his intentions.

With a shrug, he puts the glass down on the counter. "Because I can."

When you grow up on the North Shore, you quickly learn to understand when a situation isn't going to diffuse itself. You become friends with your gut instincts. The animal inside you knows when talking is over and it's time to fight.

I don't wait one more second. I grab the tumbler, slamming it against his face. Or so I think.

The fucker expected it. That's probably the only reason he put it on the counter, so close to my hand. He was inciting me to act, to grab the only weapon I have at my disposal. He takes hold of my wrist before the glass can break against his skin.

"It would be a shame to let you scar my beautiful face."

I don't talk back, saving the energy I'll need. When he pulls me off the counter, I strike my fist against his jaw. He shakes his head, wild eyes looking back at me as he releases my wrist.

"That's a strong hook you have."

To confirm that, I punch him again, forcing him to take a step back. I use the brief moment to make a run for it, hoping I'll find the front door in this stupid mansion.

The man lives in Stoneview. Of course. The billionaire town not far from Silver Falls. He wouldn't mix with the poor people on the North Shore. Not even with the middle-class families on the South Bank.

Organized crime truly pays well.

I'm sprinting through the entrance hall when he slams into my back, taking us both to the floor.

I grunt as I roll over, making sure I'm facing him as he pins me to the ground.

"I told you to kill me or suck my dick. I don't remember running away being an option."

"Okay," I pant.

"Okay?"

Biting my lower lip, I bat my lashes at him. "Okay." I link my fingers behind his neck, running them up to the back of his head. "You want to fuck me, Nathan?"

I don't even let him answer. I bring him toward me as I smash my forehead against his nose.

Then I shove him off me and jump to my feet, running back to the kitchen.

The man wants to die? Who am I to take that away from him?

For a second, I forgot who the fuck I was. I don't run. I fight.

I hear him coming closer as I yank the drawers open, one after the other, to find where he hides the kitchen knives. When I finally find one, I hold it tightly and run back toward the kitchen door.

As I plaster myself against the wall, I listen to his

*approaching steps. The second his shadow crosses the doorway,
I flip around, aiming for his neck.*

"Desperate to die?" I hiss.

*I do manage to get him. A shallow cut on his shoulder just
before he grips my arm. It turns into a slit of liquid red as he
twists my wrist, forcing me to drop the knife.*

*He catches it before it reaches the floor, and I feel my eyes
widen.*

Shit.

*"I think I've given you a pretty good try, wouldn't you
agree?"*

*My breathing accelerates, and my desperation shows when I
attempt to pull my arm back, frantic eyes searching around the
room for an escape.*

*"I asked you a question, Kayla," he repeats, his tone almost
bored.*

It's like he's disappointed I failed to end his life.

"Did I, or did I not, give you a fair chance to kill me?"

*"Fuck," I push between clenched teeth as I keep trying to free
my forearm from his deadly grip. "Fine! You"—I pull some more
—"did."*

"I agree. I play fair."

*He wrenches me closer, flips me around so I'm facing away
from him, and puts the knife under my throat. "Now it's your
turn."*

*I force myself to control my breathing as he walks me
farther inside the kitchen. "I know we mentioned my cock in
your mouth, but I don't exactly trust you with your teeth."*

*I gasp when he pushes me forward, believing for a second
that the knife is going to cut my throat open. But he pulls it
away swiftly, and I put my hands on the counter, so my head
doesn't smash onto the marble.*

"I hope you didn't tire yourself out too much, Kayla. Because

you've got a long night ahead of you. Now spread those pretty legs for me."

He palms my thighs, a touch so light I don't understand why my legs part. If he's not forcing them, then is it me?

Survival.

That's what it is.

With one hand, he lifts my black tank top, and with the other, he traces the point of the blade against my skin, making me shiver.

"Here"—he presses a little harder—"is the third costal cartilage. I can reach the base of your heart if I push all the way." He drags the tip lower and a little to the left. "Spleen." And lower again. "Kidney." He stops when the tip reaches the band of my black jeans.

When he presses his hips into me, I feel his hard dick through his pants, lodged against my ass cheeks.

"Tell me what you want me to fuck first, Kayla. Your pussy or your ass?"

"I don't want you to fuck me," I grit out. It's getting harder to control my breathing with my chest crushed against the island, and his knife at my back.

"I've been told the Kings are liars, so I think I should check for myself."

He doesn't rip my jeans or hurt me. I'll only learn later that when Nathan White uses violence, it's calculated. Justified. At least to himself.

Nothing is violent now, only the calm, lingering threat of a knife against my lower back.

My black jeans end up just below my ass.

He doesn't even need to take off the lace covering my pussy to feel my wetness. His fingertips graze along the sodden material, forcing me to squeeze my eyes shut and look for an excuse.

There's a low chuckle in my ear, making me stay in the present. "So NSC was right after all. Kayla King can't be trusted. Such a wet liar."

My lips part when he pushes the lace to the side and presses a finger at my entrance.

It hurts.

That's not right. My first night with Nate didn't hurt. It was just pleasure. Being brought to heaven by the devil for a taste of paradise before he dragged me back down to hell.

But this...

Something feels wrong.

Fight!

I sit up in bed so quickly, my eyes aren't even open when I grab the gun under my pillow and point it at whoever is close to me.

I aim at the shadow I now see.

Safety off.

Finger on the trigger.

Whoever is here is going to be dead in—

"Babe! What the fuck are you doing?"

My boyfriend is right between my legs, his head popping out from under the covers.

"What are *you* doing?" I hiss.

Rolling away, his hand shoots across the bed and to the bedside table. He fiddles with the wire connecting the lamp to the wall before a yellow light illuminates the room.

"You were having a nightmare," he rushes out. "I was trying to...you know"—he waves his hand toward me—"make it better."

"By fucking me against my will?" I grunt, throwing the covers away from me and turning my back to him as I sit on the side of the bed.

I still haven't released the gun. The letters tattooed on

my knuckles are taut from how tightly I'm holding it. They're scarred, disappearing slowly over time because of the street fights and teaching people not to fuck with me.

"I'm pretty sure being fucked against your will is the only thing that makes you wet at this point," he mutters from his corner of the bed.

With a huff, I run my free hand over my face. I don't know what I hate more. That he tried to test that theory, that he knows me well enough to have come to this conclusion...or that he's right.

My mouth opens, intent on saying something helpful, but my brain has clearly given up on my relationship. "Don't do this again, Ivan. I might not stop myself from shooting you next time."

I finally put the gun back under my pillow, but I give up on going back to bed. I look at the time on my phone. Six thirty-three a.m.

"I'm gonna call my mom," I mumble to myself, maybe a little for him too. So he doesn't feel like me leaving the bed is just because I don't want to be next to him.

Ivan and I have been together for four years, and I always wonder how I've let it last that long.

I should really let him go. We don't share the same feelings. I can't even have sex with him anymore without having that voice in the back of my head that screams I hate it.

I met Ivan when I was looking for the Bratva Wolves. The organization seems to have always had two goals in mind: money and discretion. Meeting a Wolf is about as likely as finding a rare diamond in a mine. It's about as dangerous too.

Who would be crazy enough to look for an organization that goes by one motto.

A Wolf's face is the last thing you see.

Me.

But I wasn't crazy. I was desperate.

I did many things in my life that should have resulted in my death. And yet here I am. Still standing, unbreakable and unbeatable. And dating a Wolf.

Mine and Ivan's meet-cute wasn't exactly out of a romantic film. It was calculated.

Every night, for two months, I waited outside Vue Club on the South Bank of Silver Falls. The side of the city where North Shore trash like me doesn't belong.

The place seems like a normal club on the upper levels, but the underground structure hosts a BDSM club where some Wolves meet. A place where they do business discreetly while enjoying themselves.

I had no chance of getting in. I knew that. And even if I did, I knew no important player really went to that place.

But any Wolf would do. I just needed to meet one of them.

Until Ivan and his friend stumbled out drunk one night. Drunk enough that the friend had forgotten to button up his shirt after their night of enjoying women, and his tattoo of the seven phases of the moon—the Wolves tattoo—showed beautifully under the streetlamps. They walked to their car, and I took my chance.

You shouldn't drink and drive, I said carefully.

It took a minute while I waited for their "compliments" about my body to stop. But then they realized I was right.

Where do you need to go? I'll drive you.

It was my luck that they were too far gone to clock how strange it was to have a random woman offer them chauffeur service. I drove them back to a mansion they were staying at in the neighboring town called Stoneview. Where the one percent lives.

Where the Wolves do business with politicians and CEOs. The kind of business I would never even dream of.

They offered me to come in. I refused. The next night, I was waiting at the back of the club again. I drove them back home again.

On the third, I told them I was looking for a job and they needed to compensate me for my services. They did. In a matter of weeks, I was part of a dangerous gang by day, and Bratva chauffeur by night.

And guess what kind of private place the Wolves talk business in?

Their car.

I learned a few things from spending time with the two. First, they weren't that important, or they would have had their own chauffeur to begin with.

Second, they were both terrible at math.

Third, the friend was truly not important, but Ivan was the kind of useless that matters to the Wolves.

Family.

The Wolves have a very specific hierarchy. When the father, Vladimir, died, his sons took over the organization. Viktor Volkov, as the eldest, became *Pakhan*. The boss. And Aleksei, his brother, was left with the only thing Viktor did not want to deal with; kidnapping, selling, and abusing women. Human trafficking seemed to be a line Viktor did not want to cross himself. He didn't stop the flow of money, though. He just tried to clean his conscience by giving it to someone else.

Just below Viktor and Aleksei are Viktor's right-hand man, Mikhail; Viktor's accountant, Stanislav; and the man I like to call Viktor's little bitch, Aaron Williams. Others call him the messenger.

I know that now, but I didn't back then.

No, what I learned in that car was even more important than the people I will never get a chance to see.

Ivan is Vladimir's bastard son. A third, younger brother, who was not allowed to have an important part of the business because he was the result of Vladimir Volkov sampling products of his sex trafficking ring. A first, apparently, and something too important for him to throw away. So, he killed the mom, kept the kid, and gave him some random shit to do in his organization. Nothing too important, nothing that would make him a target or get him killed, but something that would keep him close.

Ivan's job was to bring drugs to different areas owned by the Wolves and deliver it to their dealers. They wanted to start a serious business on the North Shore. To take advantage of the desperate people here who don't see the light at the end of the tunnel and need drugs to make them feel alive. And guess who else wanted that territory too?

The Bianco family of the Cosa Nostra.

Or Nathan White, to be precise.

But on the North Shore, dealers either belong to NSC... or to me. Back then, to my father.

The Kings were in a bad situation, but Ivan and his friends didn't need to know that. All they had to know was that they had a smart woman with influence driving their car. A direct link to North Shore dealers. And that a deal between the Wolves and the Kings could only bring them more money.

We'd ask for them to be our direct supplier of pure, uncut quality, that we would take care of cutting and selling. We would do any dirty work for them, make people disappear if they gave us police protection that would allow us to get rid of some NSC enemies without repercussions.

That's the kind of deal I wanted. *Needed.*

I even added a bonus to my offer.

I'll get rid of Nathan White. The Bianco family won't be in your way.

In the end, my luck wasn't that I am a math genius who explained to them the kind of money they could make off the back of my crew if they let me offer a deal to Viktor Volkov. It wasn't that I am smart, and they were so dumb they could barely handle the current job they had let alone explain to Viktor what I had to offer.

No. In the end, my luck was that Ivan thought I was beautiful. In his own naïve mind of a person who never really asked to be part of this, in his rose-colored version of the world, he saw in me a woman he genuinely fell for.

Ivan wasn't built to be part of an organization as deadly as the Wolves. He's just a kid whose mom was killed by her rapist.

Ivan should have been a teacher, or a nurse. Someone who's given the chance to care for people. Because I know how much he cared for me back then. I know he brought my deal to his half-brother, Viktor, not because he understood it, but because he wanted to make me happy.

Like the cold-hearted bitch I am, I used that to my advantage.

I would have never dared asking him to take it to Vladimir. His father, the head of the Wolves, was inaccessible. But Viktor? I managed.

I got my crew a fucking deal with the Bratva Wolves. I put the man who was in my way in prison. Almost two years later, Aleksei, Ivan's other half-brother died. That brought him closer to me. Even if he wasn't on good terms with him, in his heart, he didn't feel as close to the Wolves as he did when he was alive.

Then it was my dad's turn to lose his life to our criminal wars.

I didn't even shed a tear, but Ivan *feels* a lot of things. My dad's death brought him even closer to me because he wanted me to feel loved despite losing a member of my family. I wish he understood that my father never dished out love. Only punches. To me, he was the only man still standing between me and being the head of our gang.

And now, here we are. Four years after my deal. Four years with Ivan by my side. Four years of the North Shore Kings ruling our town like royalty.

And I'm about to lose it all because NSC has decided to fight back.

I squint when the harsh bathroom light hits me.

Every day that passes, it becomes harder to look at myself in the mirror. I dislike the woman I've become.

I know my traits have hardened over time. There's a constant scowl on my face, eyebrows as black as my hair always pinched to show not to fuck with me. It's usually enhanced by heavy makeup and by the 'HELL' tattooed along my temple.

I open the vanity above the sink without a second look at my face. Since Ivan last talked with the Wolves and told me I had officially lost their protection or any business with them, there's a constant headache banging at the back of my head.

Like someone is hammering just above my neck.

Bang. Over a hundred people rely on you.

Bang. They won't be able to feed their families.

Bang. Your closest friends are unsafe.

Bang. Your crew will run out of money.

Bang. People will die.

I huff for the second time in less than five minutes of being awake.

My entire life is a shitshow.

Popping two pills in my mouth, I swallow them before getting in the shower.

Two months ago, I was at the prime of my success. I didn't care about angering the Wolves because I was planning the biggest job of my life without their involvement.

I didn't care when the Wolves decided to let me go, because I knew everything I had put in place to secure mine and my crew's future was going to go perfectly fine.

With three of my most trusted soldiers, closest friends, I robbed ten million dollars from the Bank of Silver Falls. And we fucking got away with it.

There was no reason for us not to because I planned it all myself.

But there was one thing I didn't calculate.

My lifelong enemy, Emma Scott, the head of NSC, waiting at the place where we would hide the money with three of her guys, guns ready.

They took it all. Ten fucking million dollars. My future, my safety net, my pride. All gone in a matter of minutes.

While Emma had spent months securing a deal with a new family from the Cosa Nostra, while she planned to rob me, I was being careless and throwing my relationship with the Wolves away.

Now I have nothing. No big organization backing me. No money. No new plan.

And she has all the leverage she needs against me.

My lips part when the freezing cold water hits my skin.

I've been driving myself crazy thinking over and over again how the bitch found out about my heist.

She's tough, street smart, an opportunist. She grew up on the North Shore, in the family that built NSC. Emma Scott knows an opportunity to take power when she sees one. But she's not intelligent. At least not like *me.*

She's a follower, still taking advice from her dad when it comes to leading NSC.

I'm a leader. I would sacrifice myself time and time again for my crew. I quite literally threw myself at the Wolves to secure our future. I would risk anything to keep us in power.

She and I aren't the same, plain and simple.

Lately, my right-hand, Elliot, has noticed she got a new car. A Range Rover she certainly can't afford.

Then she had the occasion to threaten me with some secrets I kept from the Wolves. Things she should have never known in the first place, like the fact that one of our girls was hiding with us while someone from the Wolves was looking for her. Someone who has paid a lot of money to have her.

When Emma stole my money right after the robbery, I knew something was off.

Someone has been tipping Emma off about my plans, my struggles, everything about the Kings. I just don't know who.

I turn the water off, stepping out of the shower and grabbing my towel.

I can't get it out of my head.

Who the fuck is close enough to me to be able to give an advantage to Emma?

Who the *fuck* would dare betray me?

The bathroom door bursts open.

"Calling your mom without your phone, then?" Ivan shoves my phone against my chest. "It won't stop ringing."

Elliot is written on the screen, and I pick up right away.

"Good morning, sunshine." His cheery voice already pisses me off, but he is my best man, and I wouldn't be where I am today without him.

"Why the hell are you calling me at seven a.m.?" I grunt.

"Trust me, I wish I had gotten more sleep too. Bennett turned up at my door this morning. Shot."

"Shot?"

"There was a late night..."—he looks for the right word to control the damage—"commotion. Bennett and a few friends ran into some NSC guys on their way back from a house party."

I take a deep breath as I walk back to my bedroom. I need to get dressed. "Which territories?"

"Ours. NSC is feeling invincible since Emma stole our money, and our guys aren't exactly the tamest people I know."

I put the phone on speaker as I slip on a pair of jeans and a sweater. "So it was a bloodbath."

"We killed two of them. They killed two of ours."

I take a step back from the phone. My hand automatically coming to my face, I rub my lower lip with my thumb.

"Fuck." I say it levelly, but Elliot knows me well enough to guess it doesn't mean I'm not pissed the hell off.

Death is not a daily occurrence on the North Shore. Despite the war going on, we have rules in place. Rules that keep us all alive. Respect the crew in power. Don't wander in territories that don't belong to you. Don't start useless drama.

But the tables are turning, the power balance tipping, and our crews are becoming restless. Four deaths in one night prove that.

My phone beeps. Another call. *Ashley* is written on the screen. She owns a garage in our territories. She's one of ours, but she never calls me.

"Hold on, Elliot. Ashley is calling me."

People don't call unless it's an emergency. Over time, my phone has become a bad news line. Cries for help, threats, death announcements. That's all it's about.

All day. Every fucking day.

I don't say *hello* when I pick up the phone anymore. I say, "What's wrong?"

"*Kay.*" Her panicked voice kicks my fight-or-flight response into gear. I'm already pacing the bedroom. "*They destroyed everything! Fuck,*" she pants down the line. "*The repair shop...it's all* fucked."

Instead of letting fear take over, I feel my heart harden. Another layer of concrete surrounds my already tense organ. Ashley was keeping stuff for me in there. *Emergency* kind of stuff.

"The powder," I say, trying to sound calm.

There's a pause that already tells me everything I need to know. "*They took it all.*"

The fucking assholes.

I keep emergency coke there for this exact case. If I don't have money, if I don't have the Wolves, then at least I have enough kilos to sell and survive until I find a solution.

"*I'm so sorry,*" she whispers. That's when I hear the pain in her voice.

"Are you okay?"

"*They knocked me out good,*" she rasps.

The fuckers didn't even break in overnight. They

waited for her to show up so they could hurt her in the process.

"Your brothers," I add in a hurry. "Where are they?"

"*They...*" I hear her gulp even over the phone. "*They went after them.*"

"Call them back right the fuck now." My order is stern, and she's already apologizing again.

"*I'm so sorry. They were fuming. I told them to wait for me to call you and see what you say.*"

"Ashley," I hiss into the phone. "If your brothers kill them, I swear to fucking God, I'm going to shove my gun up their asses. Call them. Get them back. No more deaths. Especially not on our side."

I hang up on her, back to calling Elliot right away. I don't even wait for him to say hello.

"Emma Scott is out of her fucking mind. She's become the kind of bold that either means she's got everything in place to take over us, or that she's suicidal. I'm going to go with the former." My teeth could break with how hard my jaw tightens. "We're not ready for a war. We're so fucking far from ready we would get annihilated."

"*What happened?*"

"We've got no fucking money, no suppliers, and they just stole the emergency bricks of white I was keeping at Ashley's."

There's a pause while Elliot swallows the shock. "*The bitch is weakening us before they attack.*"

"They're going for a full-on war," I confirm.

I run my thumb back and forth over my lower lip as I flip through options in my head, and in none of them do the Kings come out on top.

I can hear my dad from beyond the grave.

I told you, you weren't fit to run this crew.

"*That's when you come up with a genius plan, Kayla,*" Elliot says, in a way that shows he's counting on me. That I'm the one who always comes up with solutions.

"I will," I say simply. Anxiety bubbles in my stomach, but I refuse to let it win. There's a solution.

There is *always* a solution.

"*Now would be a great time for you to spit it out. A plan, Kay. Any plan.*"

"I will," I grit out. "Give me a fucking minute, will you? I'll come to yours. I'll have something by the time I get there."

I hang up immediately, ready to start a day that already feels too long.

Ivan is dressed, ready to go. "Let's get this sorted."

I sigh when he wraps his arms around my waist.

His soul is too pure for the things we do. My heart pinches. Guilt. It mixes with the unease of the uncertain future that awaits me.

"I'm here, babe. No matter what happens. I promise you, I'll be by your side."

"You're a good man, Ivan."

He chuckles. "Or maybe I'm just trying to show you there is some good in our broken world. Even for a guy like me, who is the product of the worst crime that can be committed."

I guess we have that in common.

I turn around in his arms, looking into his ice-blue eyes as I bring a hand to his soft, blond hair. "You're beautiful," I murmur.

It's true. He's a handsome man who, despite his good heart, has a tough look from the Russian blood in his veins. He's a kind man to me because he loves me, but he will easily crush a life in his hands.

He's been raised and trained by the Wolves, after all. He might not have a cunning mind, but he is as tough as they come.

Tipping his head down, he brushes his lips against mine. "We're going to go to Elliot's, sort this out, and then I want you to come home with me and let me make you feel good."

His words are like a cold shower. I turn my head to the side. "Ivan," I huff.

His hands grip my waist tighter. "I know how you feel. I know the reason you hate having sex with me. Because you think I'm weak. That I can't give you what you want."

He pulls me closer against him. There's a violence in his gesture that cuts off my breath in the best way.

"Just because I'm nice to you doesn't mean I'm a nice guy."

"You have no fucking idea what you're talking about," I snap back.

I don't know why it angers me when he shows he knows me. Like the answers to my problems are so evident to him.

"I respect you, Kay. I respect that you're a self-made woman who knows what she wants in life and isn't afraid to get it. But I can show you what it's like when I don't. I can show you what I'd do to you if you were just another bitch the Wolves have power over."

My face must show how I'm suddenly turned on by the man who's had no effect on me for about two years because he chuckles.

"It's okay to like it the way you do, Kay. Let me give it to you."

What he doesn't understand is how hard it is for a woman like me to *let him* give it to me. It would be so much easier if he didn't give me the choice to agree. Because how can someone who has built an empire on being the strongest out there admit that she wants a man to dominate her? To not give her a choice? To make her shut up and take it?

I wish Ivan hadn't cared about my gun in his face this morning. I wish he'd taken it from my hands, pointed it at my head, and told me to lay back down and be quiet while he uses my body.

But I'm Kayla King. I would never admit this to anyone.

Shaking my head, I shrug out of his hold and turn back to the bed to grab my phone. "Let's just go."

"You were wet, you know?"

I look behind my shoulder, eyebrow cocked at him. "Excuse me?"

"You were wet when I started touching you this morning. You might have been half-asleep, but your body liked that I didn't give you a choice in it."

I was wet because I was dreaming of the night Nathan White didn't give me a choice. I was wet because I was dreaming of the last man in my life who gave me an orgasm.

I turn around and pin him with a death stare. "Well, I guess you're fucking right, then, aren't you? I'm a weirdo in bed. Bite me."

I don't even care to carry on the conversation.

Ivan told the Wolves he didn't want to work with them anymore when they dropped me. His only current goal in life is to be by my side. His worries are to make sure our relationship is fine and that it's going to last. My worries are to keep my crew in power.

We don't have the same priorities and probably never

will. I don't give a shit about my sex life when I wake up every day wondering if the North Shore still belongs to me.

Emma Scott is trying to ruin my fucking life and I'm not going to stand back and wonder if my boyfriend is happy enough with my sexual prowess.

I have a town to rule.

A war to win.

2

KAYLA

Kamikazee - MISSIO

"I'll come up with something," I say to Ivan as we step outside. Probably to convince myself.

"I know you will, babe." He opens the passenger door and helps me in before going to the driver's side.

This is my car. It's a nice Mercedes. I bought it for myself at the prime of my success. A gift to myself for everything I achieved. I'm the one who usually drives, but today I let him take the wheel.

I have given everything I have to keep this crew in power. I have spent days and nights scheming to keep NSC weak enough that they would never try to take over.

So where the fuck did Emma get the courage to fight against me?

My phone rings as we drive the dilapidated streets of the North Shore. An unknown number.

I've had an unknown number try to call me every few days for months, but I haven't picked up. Unknown never means anything good, and they haven't left a message. But maybe I should get it over with. Just as I'm about to pick up, Ivan snatches my phone away from me and declines the call. He puts it on silent and throws it onto the backseat.

"Ivan," I groan. "I know you're trying to be helpful right now. But this is my job. I need to handle this situation."

He shakes his head. "You need a minute to calm down so you can think clearer. Stop answering your phone for half an hour at least, then we'll see."

I let my head fall against the seat and allow my boyfriend to drive me around for what feels like hours, but I suppose isn't long at all. He parks in front of a convenience store and turns to face me.

"I'm going to get you a cherry soda because you like unhealthy shit like that in the morning. You wait here and don't check your messages." He's about to open the door, when he stops and brings playfully narrowed eyes to mine. "Do I need to take that phone with me, or can I trust you?"

I snort, shaking my head, because I'm surprised he can still bring a smile to my face. "Promise I won't check my phone."

My fingers twitch to grab the device in the back seat as I watch Ivan walk into the store, but I decide to close my eyes and ignore reality for a second.

That's until the driver's door opens again.

That was quick.

Too quick.

My eyes fly open just as the sound of the backdoors being opened kicks my heart into a crazy beat.

I sit up straight, but I keep my cool as I observe Logan making himself comfortable in my car. He's slowly becoming Emma's right-hand, and I don't think I want to know why he's here.

Gaze flicking to the mirror, I catch the two people sitting in the back. I've already seen the last man blocking my door from the outside.

"Awesome," I huff.

If I die surrounded by NSC because my boyfriend wanted to get me my favorite drink instead of letting me handle my shit... Fuck, I'll haunt Ivan forever.

My eyes keep going to the glove compartment where I keep a gun. I have one at the back of my jeans too, but I don't think I'll be quick enough since one of the guys is already pointing his at my head.

Way too fucking close for my liking.

The muzzle grazes my temple, and I lock my muscles not to flinch away from it. NSC will have to try harder if they want to see me scared.

What the fuck do they think I've been through to become the leader of the Kings? Knit my dad pretty scarves? I've been through hell and back to earn my place. A bit of intimidation from these guys isn't even purgatory.

Logan leans close to me, observing my face like I'm some fucking abstract painting or something.

"Your boyfriend is going to get jealous if you get any closer," I tell him. "How's Racer, anyway? No concussion, I hope, since he got knocked out while you were robbing us."

Logan and Racer were with Emma when they stole the money we'd robbed from the bank. Elliot's stepbrother, Ethan, knocked him out cold the second he could. It was a while ago, but I like reminding him.

Ignoring my attempt at taunting him, he presses his index finger against the tattoo on my face.

"Hell," he reads, then hums to himself. "I've always wanted to see this thing from up close." He leans back, finally leaving my face alone. "Crazy how hard it is to get close to you."

"Yet here you are."

He nods slowly. "I've been trying to get you alone for a few weeks. That boyfriend of yours never leaves your side."

I fake a smile. "Love, what can I say?"

"Sure," he snorts. "You're Kayla, *the ruthless* King. You wouldn't know what love is if it hit you right in the face."

I look around the car, at the two men behind me, and the back of the one leaning against my door.

"Are you here to talk about my very boring love life, or is there anything else you want?"

He changes topics quickly, aiming to shock me. "Ashley's brothers are dead. They followed our guys who robbed their repair shop. Ran right into our ambush. Stupid move, really."

I nod as my stomach tightens, already wondering how I'm going to break the news to Ashley without telling her *I told you so.* People piss me off when they don't listen to me.

"Not their smartest move," I agree.

"Emma thinks it's time you two meet to talk about the future of the North Shore."

I keep my face blank, even though I'm not even looking at him. "Of course. That's the next step in her little plan, isn't it? Try to get me to agree to a fight in the Death Cage."

Our gazes cross when I feel him tense. "My idea was to kill you. It would solve a lot of our problems." His nostrils flare from fury, and I don't blame him.

Men in my crew—Ethan and Elliot, to be precise— killed his best friend last year. Logan has a personal vendetta against the Kings.

That's his weakness.

Revenge makes you stupid, volatile. It makes you

unable to think straight. This is business. Plain and simple. He's too dumb to understand that.

He looks away. "But Emma's the boss. So she's extending an invitation to her house. Today."

We both watch as Ivan walks out of the convenience store. His eyes widen, his hand automatically going to the back of his jeans.

I shake my head and lift a hand to stop him as I turn to Logan. "I'll be there sometime this afternoon."

"He's not invited, by the way." Logan nods once, stiffly, and calls his guys to all get out of the car.

Just like that, I agreed to go to my enemy's house. I just have to hope she doesn't shoot me on sight.

3

KAYLA

Bury Me Face Down - grandson

"So much for leaving it all behind," I mumble as Xi Benhaim pats me down.

The guy promised his girl he was leaving NSC after finding love and all. But here he is, checking I don't have any weapons on me as I stand in Emma Scott's living room.

Xi's brother, Lik, is here too, and he's sitting on the sofa next to Emma's dad.

"I'm not here because I want to be, and I'm not here to participate in this shit." His blasé voice tells me it was probably Emma who begged him to be at the house for this.

"I guess you're just the welcoming committee, then."

He grunts a barely understandable *yes* and nods to Emma, standing right behind him as he steps to the side.

"Kayla." Her taunting smile deserves a punch to the face just to see how it would look without her teeth.

"Emma," I answer sharply.

There's always been nothing but hate between us. We

grew up side by side, living in the same town, going to the same school, learning the tough life by being part of two opposite gangs. In another world, we might have been best friends, or we might have been two bitchy girls who hate each other. In our world, our crews fight. Often to death.

I don't know how our relationship would have been if we hadn't grown up with hatred toward each other's last names. We did, and that's all that matters to me.

In this life, in this world, in this town, our confrontations have always been akin to a boxing game. With a stupid fighter who barely uses their brain, but struts around like a peacock, taunting and threatening the other with empty threats. And a smart fighter who works hard and thinks twice before any move they make.

I'm the smart one, of course.

I tilt my head to the side, observing her as she bravely turns her back to me to go sit down on her sofa. She doesn't offer me a seat, and I don't take one.

"Who is it?"

I don't need to explain my question. Emma isn't acting on her own, and I don't need anyone to tell me to know that. She has never made such bold moves against me. If anything, Xi used to be the bravest one of their crew, always going hard at my men to teach us a lesson despite the Kings being in power. Emma was the one trying to keep him on a leash because she was too scared of repercussions. Not anymore. Xi left this life, and Emma somehow has been the one making moves to take me down.

She rolls a blonde hair extension around her index finger and unrolls it, watching me dying for an answer.

"Is it the Lucianos? Has Vito been spilling info on my crew?"

"Vito Luciano doesn't know shit about what your crew has been up to."

Her evasive answer makes me want to curve my back and hiss in her face like a frustrated cat.

"So who is it?" I grit out.

She shrugs, so cocky and proud of her plan. "Did it ever occur to you that maybe I don't need anyone? Maybe I have the right people in the right places? Or that you weren't that discreet about the robbery? That NSC has been putting up with your shit for too long and we've been planning our takeover for a while behind your back? The Kings' reign of this town is over, Kay. I've got your money, I've got your products, and my people are more than ready to kill yours to take over the territories you stole from us. Be a good sport and accept the fight so NSC can take over the town the right way. We wouldn't want a bloodbath. At least, you wouldn't."

The gangs of this town have put rules in place for as long as I can remember. We respect no laws other than ours. When the power balance starts to tip, we have something in place to avoid an all-time war.

A fight in the Death Cage.

Both crews send a fighter, and only one gets to come out alive. Whichever crew that fighter belongs to, they get the town.

That's how us Kings got back the North Shore four years ago. We grew stronger and stronger, and NSC knew they had to have a fight before we ate them alive. The Bratva sent one of their fighters for us, and we absolutely annihilated whoever NSC sent.

Emma has been asking for a fight for months. I've been categorically refusing because we were still in a place where we could defend ourselves. That was before she stole all my money.

Now...I have nothing to fight back with. Now she's got me backed into a corner and I have no fucking choice. If I don't want the streets of the North Shore to run red with blood—Kings' blood—I have to take the fight.

My hands curl into fists. Next to Emma, Lik and her dad look at me with bored gazes. Like they already know I don't have a choice. Xi leans against the back wall, watching us, but clearly unwilling to participate in this conversation.

"Kayla." Lik's smooth voice forces my gaze to him. "We have everything in place to take over. The fight is for you. To give you a fair chance. To save your people's lives." He talks in a way that almost sounds reassuring next to Emma's threatening tone.

"Who says you'll win? You don't know who I'm going to send. You could be shooting yourself in the foot here."

Emma snorts, sending her hair over her shoulder before leaning forward. "Why don't you fight and see? Here's the deal, Kay. Get someone in that cage against NSC. If we win, as the rules go, the town will belong to us. But here's what else I'm throwing in for you. Call it a gesture of goodwill. If the Kings win, I will admit defeat. That my plan didn't fucking work. I will not only let you have the North Shore, but I will give you back the ten million you and your boys stole from the bank. How does that sound?"

In usual situations, I would be sharper than this. If Emma is willing to bet that much on the fight, it's because she has a plan in place that is probably hard as steel.

But this isn't a normal situation. She's put me between a rock and a hard place. She holds all the cards, and I'm left with no choice but to send my very best fighter into the Death Cage and hope for the fucking best.

With teeth gritting so tightly my jaw is bound to dislocate, I eye them all one last time before digging my gaze into Emma's pale blue eyes.

And I nod.

She catches her surprise quickly, pretending to be a tough girl who knew this would work all along.

"Tonight," she finally says. "I won't wait another day for this town to belong to me."

"I'll see you there."

That's all I can muster before leaving. I close the door quietly and stride to my car, calm as the sea on a beautiful day. I sail through the streets, open my door, and look ahead of me as I grab the steering wheel with a white-knuckled grip.

Ivan is right here next to me. He was waiting for me in case this was a trap.

It was a trap. Because while it wasn't violent, I came in owning the North Shore, and walked out in some sort of limbo where these streets don't really belong to me anymore. At least not until I win that fight.

"So?" Ivan asks softly as he puts a hand on my thigh.

"Fuck," I whisper. "Fuck. Fuck. Fuck. *Fuck!*"

I hit the wheel so hard a honk resonates down the empty streets. It's bordered by dilapidated homes with front yards that look like dumpsters. Broken cars, broken windows, broken lives. That's what this town is. *Broken.* And yet we all fight to make it our own.

My phone rings the second I put the car into drive. This time, I ignore it on purpose. I need to go to Elliot's house and tell him what happened.

I'm haunted by my dad's bored voice as I drive. He had

that way of putting you down so low yet still acting like he didn't care about it.

You lost the deal with the Wolves.

You lost the money from the robbery.

You're going to lose the North Shore.

Someone is going to die tonight. Either from NSC or the Kings. And only one crew will keep control of the North Shore.

One life lost to save many others.

When my phone rings again, I grunt in frustration.

"Do you want me to take that?"

"No," I snap at Ivan.

I park in front of the brothers' house and walk in without knocking.

"Please, come in," Elliot says from the sofa, sarcasm thick in his tone. "What took you so long to come over?"

"Three minutes earlier, and you'd have caught us naked," Jade, their girlfriend, laughs, sitting between the two brothers.

Jade is the girl who chose the Kings over going back to the man from the Wolves who used to pay her to keep her. She chose us. She didn't want to go back, and in exchange for protecting her and keeping her, we lost our deal with the Bratva.

She's wearing her nasal cannula, which means that sex session was pretty intense because she barely ever needs to use her small oxygen bag anymore. Girl got shot in the chest by NSC a few months ago. She's yet another reminder of my failures to protect my crew.

"What's up?" Ethan asks. The quieter of the two brothers who live in this house nods at Ivan and stands up, grabbing two chairs for us and putting them next to the coffee table.

But I'm unable to sit.

"I have news."

If there's one thing I hate in life, it's disappointing my crew.

"What's wrong now?" Elliot sits straighter, forcing Jade's head off his chest where it was resting.

I look at my feet. "You guys know I'd do anything to protect you. But things are getting out of hand. The Kings' grip on the North Shore is...pretty much non-existent." I lick my lips and look up. "I agreed to a fight in the Death Cage."

"What?" Jade gasps. "When?"

"Tonight."

"When I said find a solution...that is not what I meant," Elliot says mockingly. He's never liked taking anything too seriously.

But I do, and I have no response.

There's a stretched silence that makes me shift on my feet before I get my shit together. "I need help choosing our fighter."

Elliot designates himself without a second thought. "I'll do it. Whoever they send, I can assure you I'm bigger than the—"

"No," Jade cuts him off.

"I'm crazier," Ethan adds. "I'll rip their fucking heart out. Send me."

"No!" she insists with a rapid shake of her head. "Are you two crazy? I'm not losing either of you."

"You won't lose us. Whoever goes will win," Elliot explains, like it's so simple.

"You're not going," I interject. "You guys are like my brothers. I can't send you to your death." Elliot and Ethan have been with me for long enough that I consider them family.

"You have to send *someone*, Kay," Ethan says softly.

"Caden would destroy anyone," Jade murmurs. The mention of my younger brother kicks my brain back into gear.

Jade isn't wrong. Caden is as unhinged as they come. But he also had dreams of leaving this place behind, and he did. It's not my place to drag him back and even less to the Death Cage. I'm not taking that kind of risk.

"No. No, no, no. If I'm not sending you two, I'm not sending my *brother by blood*."

"I'll go."

We all turn to Ivan.

"I'm a Wolf," he says with pride. "The kind of training we get isn't found anywhere else." He shrugs. "I'll kill him, and then it's done."

My mouth twists. "Emma said she'd give us the money back if we win. We keep our hold on the town, we get the money. All our problems will be gone."

I did have strong feelings for Ivan once, but they've left with time, and I don't know if they'll ever come back. Our relationship started because of what I needed from him, and while my heart knows this is wrong, my scheming brain understands what I need to do. That man is our best option for the fight.

"I'll do it, Kay. I have no doubt I'll come out of there alive."

Something pinches my heart. Maybe I do have remnants of love for him.

"Promise?" I whisper.

He smiles at me, cupping my jaw. "I promise."

My phone keeps ringing as I walk into the warehouse. This abandoned area of the North Shore has two of them. One for our casual fights. One for the Death Cage.

I walk in through the south entrance, reserved for the Kings. The same way I know Emma will be coming in through the north entrance for NSC.

We all keep separated in here. Rules are rules, and each crew gets their side.

That's until someone dies, and one half of the crowd goes hunting for the night. All is fair after a fight in the Death Cage. The night is bloody. Enemies die, vendettas are settled. Then the winning crew takes over officially the next day.

My phone has been going off all day. Kings' members, unknown numbers. The only one I picked up was when my girls called. Everyone else, I was too anxious to talk to.

I walk through the crowd, heat hitting me in the face as I ignore everyone who tries to stop me.

No time. The fate of my fucking crew is on the line. I can't talk.

I'm texting Ivan as I stand at the front, right by the cage. I've got a front-row spot for the show, ready to face death, like I have many times before. I wish him good luck, asking him if he knows who he's fighting against, but he has no idea.

I'm typing quickly on my phone as it rings again, and answer by accident.

"Fuck," I mutter to myself.

I might as well fucking listen now.

"Hello?"

"*Miss King?*"

"Yeah?"

"*Miss King, hi. This is Pamela Phillis, I was the prosecutor in the case of The State of Maryland vs. White. I've been trying to call you for months. The case had been reopened after some new evidence was found.*"

My heart drops to my stomach.

"*You were a major witness to the trial, and I wanted to get you to testify again.*"

Oh. Fuck. For a second, I thought she was going to tell me the guy got out. I take deep breaths, calming myself.

"Of course," I tell her. The crowd becomes rowdy, people getting louder as the fight is about to start. "Look, I'll testify again, if needed. Honestly, anything you need."

I'll lie in court a hundred times if it means he stays locked up.

"*Well, actually, I was calling to tell you—*"

Someone shouts next to me, and I miss everything she says. I snap at them to shut the fuck up and press my index finger against my ear as I turn away from the cage.

"Sorry, I'm in a busy place. Could you say that again?"

"*The defendant,*" she repeats. "*I wanted to let you know he was released from prison five months ago. I've been trying to tell you by all means, but you're very hard to reach. I called and sent letters too. I've been trying to get you to testify again since January. When you didn't show up, I at least wanted to tell you he was released. I'm glad I finally got through to you.*"

My heart doesn't drop to my stomach this time. It completely stops.

My hand falls to my side, numb, my phone slipping and crashing on the floor.

Five months?

I don't need to wonder anymore who was feeding information to Emma. Who gave her the brand-new car, who tipped her off about the bank robbery, who gave her fucking *courage*. I know exactly who helped her take back power over this town.

"Kayla," someone calls from behind me in a way that practically sing-songs my name.

I don't want to turn around. I want to run away. But the crowd is right there, and the presence behind me has a threatening edge.

My lower lip trembles as I shift on my feet, slowly moving until I face the cage again.

I'm Kayla, *the ruthless* King.

I rule the Kings. I rule the North Shore.

I'm not scared of anything.

I'm not scared of anyone.

My eyes fall on him. He's inside the cage, his fingers hooked through the fence. He's topless, with his hundreds of tattoos on display. Dirty blond hair, eyes a blue so deep the ocean doesn't compare.

And just like that, I know Ivan will be dead in a few minutes. I know I'm going to lose my town tonight.

I can't move, captivated by a dangerous smile only the devil knows how to wield. Terrifying and tempting at the same time.

I'm Kayla King.

I'm not scared of anyone except one person.

"Hello, little sunflower. Did you miss me?"

Nathan White.

4

NATHAN

Riot - Bryce Fox, Sam Tinnesz

Only one thing could make this moment more perfect. A camera.

Anything that could immortalize her reaction.

It wasn't always easy for me to read people. I had to memorize feelings and human reactions like someone learning a new language. When you don't understand something, you study. Otherwise, you're at a disadvantage. I have mastered the understanding of feelings. Basic human emotions aren't that complicated when you put effort into reading them.

I can read the average person like an open book. I observe what make people tick just for the fun of it. I'm pretty sure I would have made a great detective. Maybe a special unit or something. I can imitate feeling empathy for people if I try hard enough. When I really put effort into it, I'll even shed a tear or two if necessary.

There's something about Kayla King I always found

difficult to read, though. That's the problem when someone has made an effort to put up a front.

But there's one thing she was never able to hide from me.

Her fear.

Because that's something she rarely feels, and when she does, she doesn't know how to hide it.

The woman has faced death more times than the people around her combined. She's been threatened, had guns pointed at her head, knives under her throat, and been cornered by enemies in dark alleys. She's seen it all.

She hasn't needed to hide fear because she genuinely rarely feels it anymore.

She hasn't learned to control the trembling of her lower lip, or her darting eyes. She can't stop the slight flaring of her nostrils and the line that creases between her eyebrows.

A beautiful deer caught in headlights.

The mix of shock and terror on her face is an image I will probably be touching myself to later. Because fuck, if there's something that turns me on, it's seeing the one and only woman on the North Shore everyone calls fearless, scared for her insignificant, pathetic life.

Scared because she knows she risks no one's wrath but mine.

Scared because she's always prepared for anything, but she couldn't have been prepared for this. I made sure of that.

But mainly, she and I both know the reason she should fear for her life is because she took something from me no one else had before. Something I would never allow anyone to take.

My freedom.

And God only knows I'm about to do the exact same to her.

I'm going to pluck my little sunflower and cut her off from the world. I'm going to put her in a beautiful crystal vase, and I'll be the one in charge of her fate. Even now, seeing me in the flesh, she doesn't seem to realize I'm about to end her time as a free woman.

I smile at her, my fingers tightening around the links of the cage. She didn't answer my question, whether she missed me or not. I think she did. She wishes she didn't. She wishes the relief of knowing the man who owns her was far away, locked somewhere he couldn't torment her anymore, came with peace. But I bet her body didn't allow that. I bet her tight little cunt longed for me every fucking day of the three and a half years I was away.

But then again, my siblings always told me I was a delusional psychopath. So maybe she didn't.

Her terrified gaze flicks to the side of me, indicating I should turn around. I must have missed the call to start the fight. It's not like there's a referee and some rules. They don't call it the Death Cage for no reason.

Bare knuckles, anything allowed.

My version of Disneyland, if you ask me.

Kayla realizes too late that her glance gave away that her little boyfriend was coming behind me.

I turn around, avoiding his arms that were going for my neck. Straight to a chokehold, I see. This fight is going to be quick. Very quick.

Ivan Volkov might be a Wolf, but deep down, he's ashamed of it. All he's ever tried to do is to get away from the criminal organizations. That's why he never mentions the last name he shares with his now dead dad. I know a lot about the Wolves. The family I grew up in were their direct enemies, and I was sent to the Silver Falls area in the first place to make sure they didn't take over too many territories. To make sure the Bianco family of the Cosa Nostra had a hold on the city they wanted for themselves.

I have never let anything get in my way. Not the fact that I was born with something missing—something that allows humans to connect. Not my own siblings when they tried to convince me to leave the Cosa Nostra. Not the Wolves when I moved here. Not even Mateo Bianco, the old boss of the Bianco family. I was his right-hand man. The person he trusted the most. And I got rid of him to take his place.

Just before some sneaky little sunflower sent me to prison.

I let him attempt to hit me a few times. His fists fly toward me, but I'm too fast for him to come anywhere near touching me.

He steps back to take a breath, his guard up as he jumps from one foot to the other. I use the space to observe him further. It's not like I haven't had a chance to do that in the last five months, but never this close. While Kayla was flying too close to the sun, attempting a robbery she planned to a T, I was making sure I knew every little thing she was up to. That included how often she was with her useless boyfriend. Too often was the conclusion I came to.

I take in his strong body moving. He's big. Someone who clearly works hard to keep in shape. I was always on the lean side—made of pure muscle and zero body fat—rather than like a bodybuilder. I got a bit bigger in prison, but I'm far from looking like a gym bro on steroids.

I sigh to myself. I still haven't put my fists up, and I can hear the NSC crowd insulting me. My eyes cross with Emma Scott's and she shouts at me to fucking do something. I've never been one to follow others' plans or orders, though. So I focus on my victim again.

"Seriously," I say casually. "Did she actually go for a guy like you?"

His eyes narrow, probably wondering if he knows me from somewhere.

"What?" Clearly, he can't place me in his memory.

"How was she, Ivan? Did you ever get her wet enough to actually stick your dick in her? Or are you going to die without having found what she really likes?"

A low growl rumbles past his lips, and he comes back charging. The moment he goes for my face, I grab his wrist, flipping him around and wrapping my forearm around his neck. I keep him close, his back to my chest.

"If you give me your last words, I'll pass them onto her. Don't make it too cheesy, though."

"Fuck...you..." I press harder against his windpipe, making him cough as his cheeks redden.

Those are some disappointing last words, but I don't insist. I wasn't really going to tell Kayla anyway.

"Well, this has been only mildly entertaining," I admit in a flat voice. "Do me a favor, will you?"

Shifting quickly, I place a hand on his chin and one at the top of his head. "Say hi to your piece-of-shit dad for me."

Then, I snap his neck, dragging gasps from the crowd. For a few seconds, the warehouse falls silent, questioning if I really just killed the guy by *breaking his neck*.

That's until I let him go and his limp body falls to the floor of the cage. I turn back to Kayla, knowing exactly where she's standing.

Just because she's watching, I make a show of lifting my fist in the air to make sure everyone around knows I've won. To make sure Kayla is well aware that she lost everything she's worked so hard for. That the North Shore now belongs to NSC.

And would you take a wild guess at who NSC belongs to?

I'll help.

Me.

5

KAYLA

Bury Me Face Down - Grandson

The sound of a dead body hitting the ground is deafening. Especially when it announces the end of your reign.

For the few seconds of silence that surrounds us as Ivan's body falls to the floor, I imagine the way kings felt when they saw their empires fall.

In the silence, I only get a few seconds to mourn the death of my rule over the North Shore of Silver Falls.

Three.

Two.

One.

The crowd wakes up. Screams reach me. The north side of the warehouse cheers loudly enough to pierce my eardrums, making my ears ring. I'm aware I don't have long before they breach to our side, starting their purge for the night.

I need to move. I need to get to a safe place far from this warehouse.

Because while some members of NSC have personal

vendettas against my people, most of them only have one clear face in mind.

Mine.

But I can't move. Nathan White has a hold on me just as strong as before I sent him to prison. His ocean eyes keep me in place, victory shining in them. He doesn't say anything, doesn't call for me, or threaten me.

He walks closer to the edge and squats on the raised floor or the Death Cage. He doesn't need to ask me to come over. My feet move of their own accord, taking me to within his reach, only a small barrier protecting me.

"My beautiful sunflower," he says softly. I don't fall for it. I've learned a long time ago that anything soft that comes out of Nate's mouth is a lure to bring you closer so he can hurt you harder.

His fingers reach through the fence, and all he does is pinch a thick strand of my ink-black hair with his fingers. "Survive the night for me, will you? I have better plans for you than dying at the hands of NSC."

He tugs the strand before letting go and standing up.

I'm not ready for the interaction to be over, too shocked to process anything, but he decides that for me when he turns around and joins Emma and her close circle.

All that's left in the Death Cage is Ivan's dead body.

I run a hand across my face, and it ends up hovering over my mouth. I used that man for everything he could give me.

All for nothing.

He deserved better than that. Better than me.

Someone bumps into my back, startling me out of my self-pity. I swing around, ready to kill the first NSC motherfucker who dares come for me, but to my surprise, it's Nyx.

"Kay!"

"What the fuck are you doing here?" I hiss back at her.

The kid is seventeen, and every time she's begged to become an active member of the Kings, I refused. She's a good kid. Great at school. Practically a genius. She has a better future in life than to be part of a stupid gang.

"I had to come see the fight. It was too important to miss."

"Yeah? Glad you're out now?"

She shakes her head. "Now isn't the time to scold me. I'm sorry, okay?" There's a panic in her voice that I'm sure everyone feels.

Everyone but me.

Defying death will bite me in the ass one day, but I spent twenty-five years escaping it despite the number of people trying to get to me. It's only natural to start feeling invincible.

I look around us, something feeling strange. NSC isn't here anymore. As far as I know, the warehouse is only full of Kings.

Nyx notices my sudden reaction, and she wraps her hands around my upper arms, shaking me. "They're blocking the exits, filtering whoever comes out. If they've got an issue with them, they're pulling them to God knows where."

"What?" The next beat of my heart feels like a struggle, but nothing shows on my face.

"I just ran to both gates, Kay. They're surrounding us. Some Kings are fighting them at the south entrance. They pulled one of us into a car when he tried to leave through the north entrance."

"Who?"

She shrugs, shaking her head again. Her half black,

half bleached, wavy hair slides over her shoulders. "I don't know his name."

Emma and her friends are gone. Nate has long disappeared.

"This was planned. They all rushed out when Ivan..." She hesitates, her eyes darting to the cage on our side, not even finishing her sentence.

"Nyx," I scold her. "You weren't supposed to be here tonight. Now you're just one more life I have to worry about."

"I'm sorry," she moans again.

I'm barely eight years older than her, but the girl doesn't have a mom anymore, and I've always had a soft spot for the little brat. I can relate to your mother leaving you behind.

"Just stick with me, okay?"

The first person I call is Elliot. He's smarter than to stay in a full warehouse on a Death Cage night.

"What are you doing and where?" I snap as soon as he picks up.

"*Just waiting for your orders, boss. Ethan and I are watching this fucking mess from his car. They're blocking the north and south gates. Do you know any other exit?*"

I look around, taking in the state of the anxious crowd around me, waiting like lambs for the slaughter. A teenager runs to me, pushing people out of the way. I recognize him instantly. He's the little brother of one of my soldiers.

"They took him!" he cries out. "They took Postman. I tried to run after the car, and they pushed me right back in here. They're fucking butchering us!"

Motherfuckers.

Of course they'd go for my strongest guys. We didn't

nickname the guy *Postman* for no reason. When you ask something of him, he fucking delivers. Often bodies.

His brother is about to talk again, when someone else bumps into his back in his hurry to get to me.

"Kay—"

I cut him off. "I'll take care of it." I go back to my call with Elliot. "On the side of the warehouse that faces the woods, there's a door Emma uses. I'm pretty sure she thinks we don't know about it. Go check if anyone is there."

This warehouse isn't a simple rectangle of four walls. It's an old, dilapidated building that has many alcoves within different walls, other rooms, old offices. It even used to have a second and third floor, but they're not accessible anymore.

"Go through the woods, Elliot. Be discreet. Every single NSC member knows who you are. And tell Ethan to bring a crowbar to the windows facing the highway."

"*The windows?*"

"They're boarded up. Tell him I want those fucking boards gone."

I hang up, turning to Postman's brother. "We'll get you guys out of here. Don't worry."

"What about Postman?" he asks, wide eyes begging for an answer I can't give him.

Time to throw life's realities at him. Time to show him there's a reason his brother and his friends call me a ruthless bitch.

"We'll get Postman when NSC decides to give him back."

My phone vibrates, and I look down at Elliot's text.

Elliot: No one is watching that door.

"Alive?" the kid asks. I look up at him, feeling my brow furrow. Who asks such a stupid fucking question? "*Alive?*" he repeats.

I put a hand on his shoulder and point at a door on the NSC side of the cage. "See that door over there? It leads to back rooms and old offices. Start gathering some people and follow the main hallway. It'll lead you to a back door. You know Elliot Pearson? He's waiting for you there. Just go there with as many people as you can, stay quiet, and as soon as you're outside, run through the woods."

He nods numbly, so I slap his cheek without strength. Just to bring him back. "Listen to me. When you're in the woods, you run. No hero shit, no looking for your brother, no avenging him. You run for your fucking life. Clear?"

With a stern nod, he turns around and starts gathering people.

Wasting no more time, I take Nyx's hand and drag her with me in the opposite direction, pushing through the crowd. The moment people see me, they let me through.

"What the fuck are we meant to do?" someone calls out.

"Don't worry," I throw back.

I stop by the window of the dilapidated warehouse. If NSC are at the south and north entrances, they shouldn't be watching this side. If they are, Ethan will let me know. I pull out my gun and use it to break whatever is left of the window that used to be here. I can already hear Ethan working at the board that's stopping us from exiting.

There's a loud *crack*, the sound of wood splitting, and I finally see a familiar face.

"There's no way you can walk back to our parking lot from here," my friend says calmly. "They're encircling Kings' cars, waiting for us to get there. I'm parked under the highway bridge. Everyone is going to have to abandon their cars and walk that way."

"Can't we reach the woods from here?" Nyx asks. Her hand is getting colder in mine, her body clearly in fight-or-flight mode.

I shake my head. "Not if they're guarding the main gates. They'll see us trying to access the woods."

"I don't know the way back home from the highway," she says, frantic. "Should I go through the other door?" Turning her head to me, she grips my hand harder.

"I won't let you go home alone, don't worry."

I spend twenty minutes making sure no one is getting caught as they escape through the window.

Keeping Nyx near me, I check with Elliot that others are going through the back door. I don't have much time before NSC notices not many of us are trying to go through the main gates anymore, but I can't escape while I still have people here.

"Kay," Ethan calls out from outside. "You need to fucking go. They're going to come after you and you know it."

I ignore him and help Nyx climb over the ledge. "Listen. You take her to her trailer, okay? Her dad must be worried sick. Then you go home with Elliot and lock your fucking doors."

He grabs Nyx, setting her on the ground outside. "You're being an idiot. Come with us."

"I'm not leaving Kings behind."

"Then Elliot and I are staying too."

A gunshot resonates in the warehouse, making us all duck down. NSC is coming in.

"Kay!" Nyx screams past the ringing in my ears. "Oh my god, I thought they shot you."

"Fuckin' hell. I'm fine." I cock an eyebrow at her. "I'm not made of fucking glass, am I?"

It seems she is, though. She's trembling like a leaf, her face paler than I've ever seen.

I turn my gaze to Ethan, his hard eyes narrowed on me.

"Don't sleep tonight. I'm serious, Ethan. NSC knows how important you and Elliot are for our crew. They know where you live. Do not fucking close one eye."

"We won't," he mumbles as he grabs Nyx's forearm. He's already walking away when he shouts back. "And don't you fucking die."

I smile to myself. Of course I won't. I never do.

I run to the other side of the warehouse, following the last Kings getting out as NSC comes after us. They were casually waiting for us to go back to our cars, grabbing whoever they wanted. They didn't expect they'd have to chase us through the fucking woods.

"Kayla!" someone shouts at my back as I sprint to the back door. "You're not escaping NSC tonight, bitch!"

I don't recognize the voice. I know the most important people I should be worried about when it comes to NSC. Their soldiers know me, but I don't know them. They're just little ants to crush under my boots.

As I bump into a few Kings trying to fight back, I try to stop them, telling them to go back out and to safety, that we're not fighting tonight, we're retreating. But some people don't give a shit about battle tactics. They only care about their pride.

"Fuck." I almost choke on my own breath when I stop dead in front of a girl holding a knife.

She's not scaring me, but she did fucking surprise me, coming out of nowhere.

I don't need to wonder who she belongs to. She's got

their tattoo on her neck, a dagger with the letters NSC on the hilt.

I snort when she comes at me without thinking. I point my gun at her chest and, without a doubt, I shoot.

Kill or be killed. That's what I grew up hearing.

"Did no one ever tell you not to bring a knife to a gun fight," I mumble as she falls to the ground.

Apart from the people I couldn't bring back with me, it looks like I'm the last one out of the back door. I push the heavy metal, ready to breathe in some fresh air.

But I barely have time to notice the moon shining on the shadow at my side, when something hits the back of my head.

I stumble to the ground, tightening my grip around the handle of my gun to make sure I don't lose it. I twist, doing my best to land on my shoulder and roll onto my back so I'm not in too weak of a position.

Feeling the dizziness engulf me, I try to focus my vision through the pain at the back of my head. A boot lands on my wrist, crushing it to the asphalt and forcing me to release my gun. I want to fucking laugh when I notice who just hit me.

"Logan," I chuckle. "I thought Emma specifically told you not to kill me."

There are two other men with him. An NSC member called Law, and one other I don't know, but I don't really give a shit. Logan is my main problem.

"Yeah. She told *me* not to kill you." He nods at the two men with him and they're quick to each grab me by the upper arms, lifting me up.

The world tilts for a few seconds, and my vision goes black. Shit, he got me good. I try to look around, but my head is heavy, and I feel warm liquid running down my neck.

Logan grabs my chin when it falls to my chest, making me look up at him. "She won't know it's me if you're just another casualty of the night, will she?"

"Motherfucker." My voice usually sounds much fiercer than that. The pain pounding at my skull isn't helping.

"Let's take her to the woods," he tells the other two. "She can die with the rest of her cowardly crew running away from us."

I can't keep up with their pace, my feet giving up and dragging behind me as they bring me to the dark woods that take up most of the North Shore.

The light of the moon can't even make it through the thick branches when they finally drop me to the forest ground. A mix of pinecones, needles, and moss welcome my fall. This time, I don't even have the strength to turn around, landing on my stomach. My cheek against the soil, I smell the earthy dampness of the forest.

With every second that passes, I feel less awake. The pain has taken over my entire head, and the nausea coursing through my body tells me I've got a serious concussion.

I groan when a foot presses on my back, but I know I'm not going to die. There's no way this is how I end. Not me.

Logan squats next to my face, his weight heavy on my body. "This is going to take a while. You don't deserve a fucking bullet to the head, believe me."

I'm aware. The day I really die, it'll be slow and painful. People like me don't pass away of old age. They die because they got caught by the enemy. If I'm lucky, I'll get hit by a car when I cross the road on a random Tuesday.

"Logan." I smile at him, my eyes fluttering closed from

the pain it brings me. "Don't make the mistake all your dead friends made. Kill me now before I kill you. Don't waste any time."

That does it to piss him off. His punch to my nose is strong enough to push my face harder against the soft ground.

A split second later, his two friends are kicking my back and my sides, forcing me to curl into a ball and protect my already injured head.

The position allows me to slip a hand under my hoodie unnoticed and grab the gun I taped to my body before coming to the fight.

What kind of delusional person would I be if I showed up to a Death Cage night without multiple weapons?

I get a few dangerous hits that threaten to make me pass out before I can finally grab the handle safely enough that I know I won't drop the gun the second I shoot. One of them hits me hard in the kidneys, making me cry out as I finally go flat on my back.

"Three guys, one woman. Exactly what I'd expect from NSC," I groan before aiming my gun at the nameless guy.

I shoot him right in the chest. I would have aimed for the head, but my vision is blurry, and I needed a bigger target.

The other two take a step back as a survival reflex, giving me enough space to stand up. Even though I'm swaying, I can see Logan pulling out his own gun, and I'm quick to shoot his way. I miss, but it gives me enough time to run.

"I told you to fucking kill me," I rasp before sprinting the other way.

Well, not sprinting. I'm hobbling as fast as I can

through the thick woods, doing my best not to hit a tree or trip on a root.

I hear something whiz past my head before a bullet lands in a tree trunk not far from me, sending splinters flying everywhere.

Holy shit, I need to hurry.

I accelerate despite the pain in my back, my stomach, and my head. Without looking, I aim my gun behind me, hoping for the best without being able to stop and aim properly. I have no time to waste. I do it again, and again, making sure they don't dare follow.

I'm out of breath before I reach the tree line, but I think I lost them. It was too hard for them to follow without taking a bullet, and with the darkness of the woods, they must have lost where I was going.

As I lean against a tree, my lungs constrict from my injuries and the need for oxygen. I tap my pockets for my phone, but it's not there anymore. I must have lost it while they were dragging me to the woods.

Looking up at the black sky, I smile to myself. Another day of surviving the North Shore.

I feel more alive than ever as I slowly make my way back to my house. Territories mean nothing tonight. Tomorrow, the map of the North Shore will be drawn again, and we will lose everything we gained while we were on top. My stomach twists. It would have been easier to accept my fate if losing my town didn't come with the news of Nate being out of prison. Knowing that this wasn't Emma's plan, it was his. She didn't manage to weaken us. He did.

Five fucking months.

He's been out since February. Long enough to plan his revenge, to spy on me, to know exactly what I've been up to. The prosecutor said she sent letters to let me know he was out, but I never received anything.

Is there any point thinking about this now? The real problem isn't why I didn't know, but the very fact that he's out and here...and that he said he has things planned for me.

I didn't only put Nate away for my deal with the Wolves. He had control over me I couldn't fight. He liked to play with me and taunt me.

Once a week, for four weeks, he'd call me to his house. Once a week, he had one night when I'd let him do whatever he wanted to me.

In exchange for being at his mercy, he held back NSC in their violence against the Kings.

I put him away because I couldn't take the hold he had on me anymore. I knew I wouldn't survive it. The fear, the torture...the pleasure. It was all too much.

Now he's back with a plan, and I have no idea what's coming for me.

The walk is long, and more than once I have to hide in a bush as members of NSC in loud cars drive down the streets, looking to feast on Kings.

By the time I reach my front door, my head pounds harshly, and I can barely hold myself up as I grab the keys from my bra. It takes me a few tries to get them in the lock, but I finally manage.

My entire body is begging me to just rest my back against the door and drop to the floor, but I need to at least make it to the bathroom and check my injuries. I can't rest until I'm sure I will actually wake up tomorrow.

Tomorrow. It seems so far away on this never-ending night, but the responsibilities I have will arise again very soon. Finding my people, making sure they're okay, preparing for survival...counting the dead. It'll come too fast.

I drag myself to my bathroom. There's a constant smell of burn in this house. It's the same house I grew up in, my father's. We were a family of four before my mom fucked off, escaping her abuser and leaving my brother Caden and me behind. Then it was up to us to deal with him. Until NSC tried to burn us down. Literally. I was unconscious when Caden dragged all of us out. By the time he went back for my dad, it was too late.

Caden lives in New York City now with his fiancée, and I sent my girls to live with my mom for their safety. I only found her again after my dad died. I barely knew her when she agreed to help. So it's just me. My bedroom burned down, and so did my dad's, so I live in Caden's old room.

I haven't been here in a couple of weeks. Ivan got a small house on the edge of town when we started dating, and I've been staying there for a while.

It's strange being back in this shithole. The carpet is worn down and stained, one of the windows in the living room boarded up. It smells of cold ashes when I walk into the hallway, and the light there doesn't even work.

I push the bathroom door open, and it creaks on its hinges. The main light doesn't work here either.

Wonderful.

Hobbling to the sink, I leave my gun in it, feeling for the switch on the wall for the light above the mirror. I squint my eyes the moment it turns on, the reminder that I got hit at the back of the head a little too brutal.

When I feel for the back of my head with one hand, matted hair sticks to my fingers from the blood there. A groan escapes me when I accidentally press on the growing bump.

"Shit," I hiss.

I grab a bottle of painkillers, some disinfectant for the cuts on my body, and a lot of cotton balls. My nose is blocked and something warm is still running down my face. I haven't seen myself, but I already know I've got a bad nosebleed.

I have to use my hand, now covered in blood, to hold the sink as I feel the dizziness come back. Everything is tenfold now that the adrenaline is running out. I can barely breathe from the hits on my ribs, and the muscles at my lower back are frozen.

My breath comes in short bursts as I finally close the vanity, but my gasp is loud when I see a shadow behind me.

I instantly reach for the gun, but he's much quicker than me. In a split second, he's at my back, his own hand twisting mine to grab the weapon himself. And when he leans closer to me, his mouth just above my ear and his face finally lit up by the vanity light, I know tonight is far, *far* from over.

Before prison, his dirty blond hair was always tied in a tight bun at the back of his head, but it's shorter now. Long enough that it's brushed back, as if he ran his fingers through it. Only one rebellious strand falls just at the corner of his left eye, resting on the rim of his glasses.

He smiles at me. His beautiful, wicked smile that promises pain. Any kind of pain. Mental, physical, emotional. As long as it hurts me.

The gun points at me, the barrel against my throat and the muzzle just under my chin.

"Well done for not dying out there. Three guys against you. Tsk, cowards."

I struggle to swallow, feeling my throat move against my own gun. He's not wearing a suit as I remember he always did. I can't quite see his jeans, but I notice he's wearing a simple black t-shirt, showing the countless tattoos that cover his arms and all the way to his fingers. He fought, he followed me to the woods, and he came here.

"You were watching," I rasp.

Our gazes lock in the mirror. His night eyes brighten, as his free hand fists my hair, making me wince from the already unbearable pain at my skull.

"Of course I was. What if they broke my toy before I even got to play with it?"

I glance at the black weapon against my pale skin and look up at him again. "Kill me."

This is the best outcome I can hope for. For him to end this now. I sent him to prison. I testified against him, lied through my teeth in front of the jury. Almost four years of freedom was enough. I would rather die than go through the punishment he's had years to plan.

A rumble starts in his chest before he laughs loudly in my ear. "Are you kidding me? Kill you?"

"I'm not doing this again with you," I hiss, stupidly attempting to move in his hold and making the pain worse. "Fucking kill me, Nate, because I'm not going back to playing your games."

Leaning even closer, his lips graze my ear as he whispers, "You're doing whatever I tell you to do, Kay. So if I say you live, then you fucking live until I order otherwise."

He leaves a kiss so soft below my ear, my eyes flutter shut. It takes all of me not to let a sigh breeze past my lips. I vaguely feel a release at the back of my head, his hand leaving my hair. When I open my eyes again, he's got a needle pointed at the side of my neck.

"No," I whimper, but the needle's already pricking my

skin, inserting whatever is in there into my veins by the time more words tumble out of my mouth. "What is it?"

"This?" He pulls his hand away and throws the injection in the sink. "Just a little something to help me carry you to your next destination."

He releases me, and I stumble back, my body suddenly heavy.

"Nate," I groan, attempting to catch myself on the sink.

But my hands feel lifeless. I might as well be a ghost with the way they refuse to grip the ceramic.

Just as I feel myself falling to the floor, two hands catch me. His arm slides under my legs as he picks me up, the other holding my waist.

"I got you." His words sound as freeing as if metal handcuffs were closing around my wrist.

"No," I moan as my head falls against his chest.

"You'll be spending a bit of time with me now, little sunflower." I hate this nickname. I fucking hate anything that comes out of his mouth.

I hate it all because it makes me weak. *He* forces me to be weak.

"You're as beautiful as I remember, Kay. Especially when you're helpless."

I try to shake my head, denying I'm helpless even as my heavy eyelids seal my eyes like an unstoppable gate.

"Don't do this." My slurred words barely come out. "Nate, don't...don...d..."

I still hear his response as I blackout completely.

"I forgot how much I love when you beg."

6

KAYLA

Truth Comes Out - Willyecho

The pounding in my head is unstoppable. I'm sitting down, but I might as well be lying on the floor in a doorway with someone repeatedly banging a door on my head.

Chin to my chest, I can feel blood slowly dripping from my nose, making it impossible to breathe. It tastes coppery on my tongue, and my throat is dry from having to breathe through my mouth.

Despite my entire body being in pain, some parts are clearly becoming numb. My hands and feet, for example. I'm barely conscious, but I can tell it's because of the ropes around my wrists and ankles.

My hands are tied together behind the back of a chair, and the fact that my head is drooping in front of me pulls painfully at my shoulders, but I don't have the strength to lift it up. In a herculean effort, I attempt to move my legs to feel for wiggle room, but my ankles seem tightly bound to the front two legs of the chair.

Even I have to admit this doesn't look too good, but it wouldn't be the first time I'm in this position.

I can't place myself in what seems like a completely dark room, and I'm not even sure if my eyes are open or not. I attempt a deep breath, but my muscles are tense from the beating, refusing to let me breathe decently. It's cold in here, but suffocating. The air is damp, tickling my body every time oxygen passes through my lungs.

There's a dull sound in my ears, mixing with ringing. It hurts every single cell in my brain until I realize it's music.

Oh, the motherfucker.

I'm in a pitch-black room, bound to a chair, barely able to keep myself conscious longer than a few seconds at a time...and *"She's My Witch"* by Kip Tyler is trying to make itself a space in the already asphyxiating air.

Nate likes his rock songs. He's got his favorites from every period since the fifties. He'd always say *"She's My Witch"* reminds him of me.

Nathan White is back, and he wants to play games.

The thought only drags me back to the darkness, and awareness leaves me again, my muscles slackening as I slip back into oblivion.

It's the thirst that wakes me up. The song still plays. I could almost hear it starting over and over again in my pain-induced sleep. I can tell my body is trying to protect itself from the agony I'm feeling in every single one of my limbs, and the new attempt at lifting my head is met with so much aching in my skull and stiffness in my neck that I faint on the spot. All I feel is my head dropping forward before totally blacking out.

. . .

I want to scream when I become aware of the music notes again. Same song, same old rock and roll beat and fingers smoothly pinching an electric guitar.

Little sunflower, do you have any idea what everyone in this town thinks of you?

The words he said back then echo in my suffering skull.

Kayla, the ruthless King. Ready to follow in her father's footsteps. Ready to paint this town red, for her crew to be on top.

I grunt, wanting his voice out of my head while knowing perfectly well it comes from my own memories. He'd played this song back then too while I was tied to his bed, and he was circling it with a kitchen knife in his hand.

Kayla King is a cold, heartless woman. She doesn't feel anything, only the need for power. She'll do anything to rule the North Shore.

I cough, my throat so dry I feel like I'm choking on sand.

Kayla King. Do not get on her bad side. She'll slit your throat without a single thought.

I squeeze my eyes shut, my chest tightening so much I can't breathe anymore. I need this fucking song off.

Look at me, Kayla. My eyes open. Despite the darkness, I could swear he's right here, calling my name. But it's just the memory of that night. *Everyone fears you. And you? You only fear me. Everyone fears Kayla King, while I have her in my bed, at my mercy, scared for her fucking life.*

I drag in air, coughing some more as a whimper escapes me. As if it wasn't enough for Nate to haunt me in my sleep for four years, the vivid memories now torture me during my waking moments.

Lost in my anguish, I forget about reality and startle when the music stops suddenly. I feel deaf, like leaving a concert and all that's left is a lingering hum and the feeling that everyone speaks too quietly.

I can only tell there's a door somewhere in front of me because of the line of light that appears underneath it. It forces me to lift my head as much as I can—which isn't much. Quickly, it's followed by a block of light spreading in the room when the door opens only long enough for a tall form to get inside before it closes and the light disappears.

There's a flash, and I hiss as my eyes squeeze shut, my chin meeting my chest again. My eyes burn despite being protected by my eyelids. That fucker turned on the light as if I haven't spent God knows how long in a pitch-black room. The pounding in my head is unbearable, and I feel like I'm going to pass out again. Except I force myself not to this time.

One should not lower their guard when they're in a room with the devil.

"Rise and shine, little sunflower."

The simple clicking sound of what I know are perfect leather Oxfords advancing toward me is enough to make me want to disappear into the darkness again.

There's no stopping the fear making my body jump when his hand threads into my hair. I hiss when he pulls, forcing my head to lift. My neck screams, my skull ready to explode.

Breathing becomes nearly impossible when he tilts my head back, my neck now in the exact opposite position it's been for many hours.

"Open your eyes and look at me, Kayla."

I tremble at the gratification in his tone. Nate doesn't feel. Not happiness or love. Not fear or sadness. He has two modes. Satisfied. Frustrated. That's it.

He likes a challenge, and he likes when the reward is high.

I have always been a challenge to him.

He saw similarities between me and him, and he wanted to play with that.

What can hurt Kayla King?

What can make her feel?

What can make her cry?

What will make her fear for her life?

I know better than to play tough when I'm in an impossible situation. There's nothing I can do to defend myself right now, and it's better to give him what he wants. To keep him appeased.

It takes me a long minute to blink my eyes open. The light is white, harsh, and my eyes are watery on top of a dizzy vision. All I can see past the blurriness are two beautiful, empty, midnight-colored eyes.

So. Fucking. Empty.

A chill runs down my spine. Slowly, everything becomes clearer. Especially the pain. My body is begging me for a way to let it all out. To cry and scream. It needs an outlet for the agony. But my mind has always been stronger. So I swallow past the horrific dryness, I toughen my stare, and I look straight into the devil's eyes, awaiting my sentence.

"There she is." There's no change in his tone, no smile on his face. He doesn't need to pretend when it's just the two of us.

Nate is smart enough to know it would be dangerous for the world to discover who he really is. He puts on a perfect act even to his closest allies. He is a better leader if people think he can relate to them, or that he understands them.

But I know the truth.

Everything he does, he does it because it will reward him. Every move he makes is to lead him to more power. Everyone he surrounds himself with is a step on his ladder to success. Whatever that means in his fucking psychopathic mind.

He observes me silently for a long time, forcing me to move things forward if I want to ever get out of here.

"Where are we?" I would speak with a stronger voice if I wasn't speeding on the highway to death. My desperate rasp will have to do for now.

"Is that what you want to start with? Not what I want? Not to beg for a glass of water? Not how long it's been?"

Fucking bastard is having the time of his life, isn't he?

His eyes narrow for a short second before it hits him. "Ah. I see. Where you are is a priority because if you manage to escape, you need to know which way to run."

I make sure he can't see it in my eyes that he got it perfectly right.

"Well..." I wonder if he knows his grip tightens on my hair. "Rest assured, you're not going anywhere until I say so."

It's the effort of my life to stay quiet. Many people who have told me *"you're not going anywhere"* were quickly proved wrong, but I don't put it past Nate to literally chain me to the floor to keep me here.

"But if you insist." He shrugs. "We're in the very same house you wanted to buy for yourself."

My heart stops.

If he's been out for five months, then he was around while I was planning the bank robbery. He was out when I planned to buy this very house with the money I was going to steal.

A house in Stoneview.

The billionaire town right next to our city is an unattainable dream for every single person who grew up on the South Bank of Silver Falls. For us on the North Shore? It doesn't even cross our minds. People are too busy surviving to dream.

I didn't want to buy this house to have a nice place next to the dirty politicians and owners of conglomerates who live here. I wanted to wash my money. After his arrest, his house was seized, and it was going to be sold again. It's easy in Stoneview to pay enough for people to look away and not check where the money comes from.

This house would have been mine if Emma hadn't stolen the money from me. Of course, it wasn't Emma. It was Nate.

"Kayla," he chuckles, knowing perfectly that I'm connecting the dots. "You can't be mad at me for sending Emma to steal the money you were going to use to buy my own house after you put me in prison based on pure lies. I am only playing fair here. Or, at least I'm playing by the rules you set by lying in court."

What am I even meant to say to that? *Yeah, Nate, you're right. Why don't you ruin my life, steal my town, and tie me to a fucking chair?*

"Hey, at least you got what you wanted. You're back in my house, little sunflower."

This time, I can't stop my upper lip from curling in anger. He knows this isn't what I wanted. I wanted clean money. At least part of it. I wanted to use the other part to find my own suppliers of drugs without having to go through the Wolves. I wanted to become a big player in the game. What a joke.

A knock on the door startles me. He releases my hair,

giving my neck a much-needed break. I don't have the strength to hold myself up, and my head drops again, starting a new chain of throbbing within my entire body.

Nate walks back to the door, opening to no other than his closest man. Samuel Thomas.

My anger comes back double. I did him a favor in the past. He owed me, and he promised that, in the impossible chance of Nate getting out of prison, he would keep him away from the North Shore.

Sam eyes me, guilt flashing in his gaze before he focuses on his friend again. "Emma and her guys are here."

"What?" A flash of adrenaline explodes in my body at the name of my lifelong enemy finding me in this position.

Is that his plan? Let her fucking kill me while I can't defend myself?

Nate glances back at me, talking like this is the most obvious situation. "Isn't that how it works in your shitty town? The day after the fight, the leaders of NSC and the Kings meet to discuss the new map of the town and how to restore order. That's what I was told."

"I'm not discussing shit with Emma Scott while tied to a chair in your fucking basement," I grit out.

He looks me up and down, not caring about the distressing state I'm in. My brain could be bleeding right now, and he couldn't give less of a shit.

"It looks to me like you don't have a choice, Kayla." The way he points it out, like I'm the crazy stupid one, makes me want to scream.

That's what he does. He makes you lose your mind slowly, but with a steady intensity.

"Untie me, Nate."

He doesn't acknowledge my half-assed demand. "Remember, little sunflower. I have big plans for you. How you and Emma split the North Shore has zero importance to me, but she's been doing good work for me for months, so she deserves her ridiculous reward. You, you be a good girl and nod your head when I tell you to. Once this is over, we can move on to more important things."

"I'm not agreeing to any demands Emma makes. Not until I think about the impact it has on the people who count on me. I'm not going to give my entire town away."

He cocks an eyebrow at me, probably surprised at my surge in energy. The fucker doesn't know I would rise from the dead if it meant fighting against Emma Scott.

"Did you not hear me the first time?" There's no irritation in his tone, he simply can't seem to understand why anyone wouldn't listen to what he orders. "I said you nod when I tell you to nod. You don't need your voice for that, so don't make me gag that cute mouth of yours."

Narrowing my gaze at him, I stay quiet.

I will die before I let Emma think she can get more than she's allowed. I will give back what we took, but I will not risk my people's safety.

And Nathan White can go fuck himself.

7

KAYLA

Riptide - grandson

Being tied to a chair, at anyone's mercy, while Emma Scott's smug smile looks down on me is a humiliation I never thought I'd go through even in my worst nightmares.

I groan when she grabs my hair, her long claws scratching my skull as she forces me to look up at her. "Oof," she sniggers. "That's a nasty hit to the nose, Kay. Who got you so good? I'll send them a thank you basket."

I think hard to stay calm. I think of all the times I told my soldiers to act pragmatically rather than with pride.

And I fail.

I spit blood in her face, hitting the corner of her mouth.

"Stupid bitch," she hisses, wiping herself with the sleeve of her leather jacket.

I try not to flinch when she pulls her fist back, ready to bring more pain to my already battered body.

"Emma." Nate stops her right before her blow. Her angry eyes stay on me when he continues. "Be kind and don't damage her."

Emma's eyes narrow on me, quietly promising this isn't over.

"Can we move this along?" Nate's bored tone makes mine and Emma's feud seem pathetic. And that's what it is to him.

But now that I know he won't let her hurt me, I'm going to get inside her fucking head.

I look at the men standing behind her, one on each side, as if she needs bodyguards. Logan has always been close to her. The other is Law. His real name is Lawrence, but they like to think he lays down the law for Emma. They say that, but he's just come back from a year of forced sabbatical after Ethan had butchered his face in a fight. Now he bears some nice scars done by my crew. I'm looking forward to humiliating her in front of who she clearly considers her most trusted guys.

"Remember the last time your crew had me tied to a chair, Emma?" I speak barely above a rasp, but it's the words that count.

She stops moving for a few seconds, her eyebrows drawing close, as if wondering if I'm really going to bring this up. It wasn't a good position for me, but I still believe it was worse for her.

"What the fuck are you talking about?" There's a warning in her voice that matches the look in her eyes.

Doesn't she understand I've never been scared of her? Never been scared of NSC. Especially not when a bigger predator is in the room, holding her back.

"Come on," I snort. "Your dad and his friends wanted to see if you deserved to be a full member of NSC. They took me after school, and they tied me to a chair in your fucking living room. Surely, you can't forget *that*."

She rolls her eyes, faking annoyance. "You think I

remember every single interaction I've had with you, Kay? Please, stop thinking yourself more important than you really are. All I know is if I kill you right now, I won't have to deal with you ever again."

I nod, which brings a sharp pain to the back of my head. My eyes flutter closed before I can focus again. "Right. So you don't remember when they put a gun in your hands and told you to kill me to prove yourself?"

I smile wickedly. "And you don't remember when you started shaking and crying. Poor girl couldn't even hold the thing in her hands, let alone keep it pointed at me. *'Dad, it's too much. Please, I can't do this.'*" I imitate her voice.

Her hands curl into fists at her sides, and it's all she can do to control herself. "I was fucking twelve," she hisses at me, taking a threatening step closer.

Looking up at her, I fight back the screams from my body. "And I was eleven. *Still*, I was stronger than you. I didn't flinch one bit when your dad pointed his gun at me. I didn't cry when you ended up beating me up because you didn't have the balls to end me. And I'm still here. Bet you wish you had killed me now, bitch, because I'm still *fucking here* and I'm still standing."

Her whole body is shaking; she can't hide it. She's about to lose her shit, ready to pounce on me, when a hand lands on her chest.

Sam's.

He doesn't say anything to her. A simple look from his black eyes is enough to make her step back. She takes a deep breath, and the high might have been short-lived, but it was enjoyable. Now I feel ready to negotiate.

She clearly is too, because she stands taller in her platform shoes. The girl is fucking tiny. She's wearing a pink leather skirt and a top that could be a bra under her jacket. I bet she'd love to gouge my eyes out with those acrylic nails she always sharpens into claws.

"You're not still standing, Kay," she sneers. "You're tied to a chair in a basement the day after your crew lost a fight in the Death Cage. I don't think you can fall any lower than that. Now, if you don't mind, I only came here to tell you the spots NSC will take over so you can relay the information to your soldiers."

Her eyes dart to Nate. I know he's standing right behind me because his mere closeness brings goosebumps to my skin. He must give her a silent go-ahead because she continues with renewed confidence.

"We'll take back the road through the woods and the convenience store by the highway." Those are always stolen back and forth between the two gangs, so I'm not surprised she's reclaiming them. "You can't deal at the Silver Moon Motel either, or send any of your girls there."

Nate's hand comes to my shoulder, assertive. He puts pressure there as he says, "That's fine."

"What the fuck?" I snap. "That's not fucking fine. The motel has never been a one-crew zone. It's for sex workers who want a safe place to work."

"It is now." Emma's voice hardens as she crosses her arms over her chest. "If you have women who want to work there, they'll pay us a fee."

"You're losing your fucking mind," I bite back. "I'm not agreeing to this shit. I'm not going to send my girls on the streets to get snatched up by the Wolves or whoever will send them to be sex trafficked."

She shrugs, her bleached blonde hair shifting on her shoulders. "Then I guess tell them to pay the fee."

"They're independent workers, Emma." Could this girl

give me a bigger fucking headache? "They don't pay cuts. It's the whole fucking point of them not having a pimp."

"They pay *you*." Her disgusted tone makes being tied up a million times worse. I could really decorate her face with a few punches.

"They pay me for protection, you fucking idiot. I don't take a cut on the jobs they do. They could have a million clients a month, and I'd still take the same amount to protect them."

"Look at you. A fucking angel. Well, they can keep paying you for protection. They'll pay me to work in my territory. Unless they want to switch crews." She shrugs. "NSC girls won't have to pay to work from the Silver Moon Hotel. So, I guess it's up to them."

"You're a cunt."

"I'm a businesswoman. Just like you."

I open my mouth to talk, but Nate's grip on my shoulder tightens, forcing me to bite my lower lip so I don't cry out from the pain it causes.

"I said it's fine. Move on."

Emma nods at him before addressing herself to me again with even more audacity this time.

"Your dealers can't deal at North Shore High. Even if they go to school there." I open my mouth, but she cuts me off. "Yes, that was a neutral zone. Not anymore. Xi had enough guys there to control the whole place anyway. You may take your shit-ass dealers somewhere else."

"Fine." Nate's agreement makes me want to set his face on fire and drag my nails through the burns.

"This is not how the exchange works!" I pull at my binds, because only one woman can make me lose my patience and it's her. I vaguely feel Nate's hand leaving my body, but I'm too angry to think more of it.

"You can't just take everything. People need to eat, they need to live. There'll be riots if I go back to my crew, telling them they have nothing left."

A smile tips at the corner of her lips. She knows exactly what she's doing. "Aw, no. Riots in the Kings' ranks." She pretends to shudder. "How terrible."

"Emma, I swear to fucking god—" I choke when something soft is pushed inside my mouth. It pulls from behind, tugging until I feel it being knotted at the back of my head.

He gagged me.

The bastard gagged me with some sort of rag. Both corners of my dry mouth split open from the material now keeping my lips slightly apart. My desperate need to drink is enhanced, and I groan behind the gag, incapable of talking anymore. Unable to believe what he just did, I fight in my binds, but my battered body doesn't let me do much moving before it gives up.

For the first time since this ordeal began, I feel myself flush from the humiliation. Nothing, and I mean nothing, could have been worse than being tied up and gagged in front of my worst enemy and her bitch boys.

I would rather die a painful death than witness the mocking cackle that is now leaving Emma's throat.

Nate's hand now wraps around the back of my neck as I feel him lean down. "I think I gave you plenty of chances to simply nod like I told you to. You are not here to fight for your case, simply to make things official. Clear?"

His thumb presses at my pulse point, his fingers on the other side, and his palm hot on the back of my neck. My cue to nod.

But how can I? I'm witnessing someone destroy my lifelong work, and he expects me to be quiet and agree. I had to fight NSC and my own family to end up at the top. I had to jump through every single fucking hoop, and all for what? So Emma Scott can steal it all because she and Nate found a common enemy in me?

The enemies of my enemies are my friends. That's what this is. Pure and simple. She's a fucking opportunist who jumped at the first occasion to put me down.

And she succeeded.

Nate's grip tightening makes me cough. I want to refuse. I want to put all my mental strength into this. But my body is giving up, the agony too much to take anymore, and before I know it, I'm nodding silently, my head falling forward, my eyes stuck on Emma's pink platforms.

I have to hold back a whimper when he releases the pressure. His hand stays there, but I can feel blood flowing to my head again.

"You may carry on, Emma," he says calmly. Because hurting me and making me live my own personal nightmare has no impact on him whatsoever.

"Anything you want to sell will have to go through us. We can provide you with stock..." She keeps going with a joy in her voice that kills me a little more with every word.

The rates she offers me are laughable, a cut that means they'll keep getting richer and keep my crew completely dependent on them.

But Nate presses on my neck, so I nod.

And when she starts naming streets of the North Shore where Kings are now forbidden to go, it takes all of me not to scream behind the gag. Instead, I nod like a puppet on a string whenever Nate tells me to.

That's until she says, "...and Willow Close."

I freeze. Not that I was moving much anyway, but I feel every single one of my muscles locking tight.

It takes all of me to lift my head when Nate pushes on the nape of my neck to make me nod. My eyes cross Emma's self-satisfied stare.

I shake my head, incapable of agreeing to not set foot in Willow Close.

I twist, craning my neck to meet Nate's stare as I move my head from side to side. They can't do this.

They can't make me give up my own street. My house. The place where I grew up. I might hate the shithole, but it's *my* shithole.

But all I need to understand that he had planned this is Nate's blank stare and the way he nudges his chin in Emma's direction.

He knows exactly what he's doing when he makes me nod again, agreeing to give up on ever setting foot in my own home again.

Which begs the question: Where the hell does he expect me to live?

8

KAYLA

i hope ur miserable until ur dead - Nessa Barrett

"We should tend to those nasty wounds of yours, shouldn't we?"

Emma has been gone for what feels like forever, my lifelong work with her, when Nate walks back into the basement. He didn't leave me in the dark this time, but the harsh light has been forcing me to keep my eyes shut anyway.

"You let her take my home." I force myself to look up at him, my eyelids becoming heavier by the second.

I don't know how much longer I can stay conscious. I'm exhausted, mentally drained, body battered, and my adrenaline has run out completely.

The corner of his mouth tips up as he crosses his arms over his chest. "Well, pretty Kayla, you didn't really live there anymore, did you?"

I don't even say that he let her take Ivan's street too, and I can't go back there either. That's not his point. His point is to show me he knows what I've been up to.

Reality hits me in the face, my chest tightening. Flashes of Ivan's body falling to the ground, mixed with all the times he's made me smile and laugh, all the times he took care of me, showed me how much I meant to him.

"You killed him," I rasp.

Squatting in front of me, he takes my chin between his thumb and forefinger. "Think really hard. Are you sad because I killed your little boyfriend? Because you loved him? Or are you sad because the things he provided are gone?" His blank voice turns smug. "You're not the kind of woman who gets attached to the nice feelings a boyfriend can give you, little sunflower. You were with him because you're a smart woman who would do anything to get to the top."

He caresses my cheek, making me wince, but I don't have the strength to try to get out of his hold.

"And I don't want you at the top, do you understand? I want you weak and deprived of everything you've been wanting for your entire life. You took everything from me, and I'm taking everything from you. That's how the game works. I took away the money from the robbery, I took away your dealing spots, I took the power your crew had, your town, your streets, your fucking house. And I took away your useless boyfriend."

Comparing a human life to the lifeless things he stole from me is exactly how Nate's brain works. *A plate, a jacket, a man…*it's all the same to him.

He shakes my head slightly, like he's disappointed by my lack of reaction. A cat can't toy with its mouse when the mouse plays dead.

But I need time to process. The pit in my stomach is infinite. I'm drowning in the realization that he's back and intent on making me suffer.

For how long?

What are my chances of surviving this?

I've escaped death many times, but there are things worse than death. Being in Nate's clutches is one of them.

"Come on, Kay." He gently shakes my lifeless head again. "You and I get to play again." There's a slight intonation of excitement in his voice when he talks about ruining me. "It's fun." He cocks an eyebrow. "Plus, it's not like you and Ivan were crazy in love. You fucked twice a month, at best."

My heart drops as my eyes search his. "H-how long have you been spying on me?"

"Me personally? Five months." His honesty is brutal. "Sam? A little bit longer. I had to make sure you weren't getting those letters from the prosecutor asking you to come testify again. Or the ones telling you I was out."

Panic seizes me unlike anything I've known before. It's something only Nate can make me feel.

Pure, unadulterated fear.

I pull at my wrists, my heart ready to jump out of my chest. This is perfectly planned. I can't win when he's God-knows how many steps ahead. He said it himself, there's more to come. All that happened till now was simply what he needed to get out of the way.

I shift my legs, desperate to find any way out of this fucking nightmare.

"What do you want?" I pant, my skin raw from the ropes. "What do you fucking want?" I finally move my head out of his hold, eyes darting around the room for anything that could help.

There's nothing but gray walls and concrete down here.

"Let me go, Nate." My lungs freeze, and I gasp my next breath. "Fuck...fuck...*let me go!*"

His head tilts to the side, observing me clinically like I'm some fucking lab rat he's testing shit on.

"But you've got no home, little sunflower. If I let you leave"—a smirk spreads on his mouth from the satisfaction engulfing him—"where will you go?"

The room starts to spin, pain shooting through my body as I'm forced to give up on trying to get out of the ropes.

"I think you're fainting," he tells me flatly.

No. No, no, no.

Shaking my head, I refuse to admit my vision is darkening as my eyelids grow heavier.

"I'm not...fuck...you..."

It's a complete blackout until he's the one to wake me up again. I'm lying down this time, but when I finally manage to open my eyes, I don't recognize the bedroom. I've been to his before, so I know this isn't it.

He's got a bottle of water in one hand, the other on my forehead. "You've been here for almost twelve hours. You need to drink."

I suddenly become too aware of the thirst again. My hand shoots for the water bottle, but he pulls it away, and my weak arm flops back beside me.

He laid me down on top of the covers. I notice I'm still wearing the same dirty clothes as last night, muddy from my run through the forest, my jeans ripped at the knees. Blood has dried on my face, and I feel disgusting.

Mainly, I'm thirsty.

I can't even take in my whole body, my vision still hazy.

"Get in the bath and I'll let you drink."

My eyes flutter shut, and I shake my head in the slightest. It's all I can do.

"No," I finally say, though it burns my trachea and my throat. I have to swallow the little saliva I have left before I can talk again. "No, we're not doing this."

He cocks an eyebrow at me. "What is *this* exactly?"

I lick my dry lips. "*You do this, I'll give you that*," I rasp. "I'm not bargaining with you, Nate. I'm not playing your games. Give me the water."

"Let me bathe you and I will."

I have to bite my lip to not scream and beg for the bottle. They're so chapped that they split right away, sending the taste of blood on my tongue.

"No," I repeat sternly.

I'm not going to get naked in front of him. I'm not going to do what he says. I'm not going to follow his orders like a little bitch.

He'll start with small things, and before I know it, he'll own me.

If I don't fight now, I've already lost.

And I don't fucking lose.

He sighs dramatically and steps away, putting the bottle on a dresser not too far from the bed. "So stubborn."

I narrow my eyes at him. "Please, forgive me that I like to decide for myself," I spit out as he walks out of the room, but leaves the door open. "Motherfucker," I mumble to myself.

It takes me multiple attempts to get up. My sides are stiff and bruised, and my legs shake as I put my feet on the floor. I can still feel the pain from the ropes at my ankles, the left one still heavy from not being able to move freely for so long.

I'm sitting on the edge of the bed, when I catch

something. Blinking down at my feet, my breath stops in my throat.

No, he fucking didn't.

No wonder my left ankle still feels heavy. It's wrapped in a leather shackle, attached to a chain... My eyes follow it...

Attached to a chain and bolted to the *fucking floor*.

Panicked, I shoot into a standing position, swaying on the spot.

I must get out of here.

My body feels like I weigh a million pounds as I stumble toward the dresser. I need to hydrate if I'm going to think straight. Fuck, I need to hydrate if I don't want to faint again.

I'm just about to get to the dresser, reaching for the bottle, when the chain clings. I stupidly step farther anyway, tripping and falling to the floor.

"You're joking," I snort. "You're fucking joking!" I scream at the empty doorway. The scream rips my insides, but I needed to get it out.

I extend my body, reaching as far as I can, even though it feels like someone is hammering my ribs.

In the end, I give up. It's clear he did it on purpose so I can't reach anything he puts on the dresser. I want to go back to the bed, but I don't even have the strength to stand up again, so I just bring my knees to my chest and drop my head onto them. My fingers snake to my ankle, and I blindly play with the lock holding the leather in place.

I don't even lift my head when I hear his steps coming toward me. His presence is suffocating.

"Look at me, Kayla."

I grunt as I do, the room spinning and him with it.

"What's wrong?" he asks, a genuine curiosity lifting his voice.

"You know what's wrong," I rasp, blinking up at him. Everything feels too bright, which only enhances the headache that still won't leave me.

"Is it that you want to take a bath, maybe?" he suggests.

I would do anything for the chance to wrap my hands around his throat and squeeze. His calmness irks me. His casualness of waiting for me to break with his hands in his pockets and his head slightly tilted makes me nauseous.

"Do you?" he insists, pushing his glasses up his nose. Black rim. Square top and rounded bottom. They make him look kind, *compassionate*. What a fucking joke.

My *yes* is barely audible. I can't get myself to truly answer him. Unable to look at him without puking on his shoes, my eyes drop.

"Then why don't you ask nicely?"

As my eyes snap up again, I'm hoping they can annihilate him on the spot.

"Nate," I growl, but it's more like a whisper

And since he's not getting what he wants, he grabs the bottle of water, cracks it open, and takes a sip. "Yes?"

I press my lips together.

Pick your fights. Be smart about this.

I inhale as much as I can through my stuffy nose and slowly exhale out of my mouth. "I'd like to take a bath."

He cocks an eyebrow, waiting for something I don't know I can give.

It seems to last forever. My eyes are stuck on the water contained within the plastic when I grunt, "Please."

His response is instant. "What a sweet little sunflower. Of course. Let's get you in there."

9

NATHAN

Fuck You - Silent Child

"Strip."

Her jaw tightens, muscles bulging by her temples. I had to help her move from the bedroom to the en-suite, and she already hated that. She can't stand needing anyone's help.

I get rid of my suit jacket, hanging it on the hook attached to the door, and unbutton the sleeves of my white shirt before rolling them up.

She's still standing when I open the bath tap and adjust the temperature.

"I said strip, Kayla."

"I'll strip when you leave the room," she snaps back. She attempts to make it harsh, but she sways, putting a hand on the wall so she doesn't fall.

There was probably no need to chain her to the bed. She's so weak she couldn't take two steps in a row.

Her eyes lose focus for a few seconds, and I wonder if she'll faint again.

The three men who beat her up yesterday damaged her more than I thought, and she's clearly got a bad concussion based on the number of times she's fainted.

That's honestly annoying.

"I'm not leaving the room," I explain calmly since she decided to act like she doesn't get it.

"Then I'm not stripping." The frustration in her voice is yet another form of denial.

She needs to get it through her little head that there will be no more negotiating what I ask, and that she needs to execute my orders without hesitation or questioning.

I drop salts into the bath and look back at her as I straighten up. "I'm making it nice for you. You can thank me later. Now get in there."

When she doesn't, I look her up and down, completely unimpressed by her childish behavior. I bring a finger behind my ear, caressing the skin there, right at the tip of my glasses' branch, while I think of what I could say or do. It comes easy.

Grabbing the bottle of water, I unscrew the cap and throw it to the floor before holding the water above the bath.

"What are you doing?" she panics.

Slowly, I tip the bottle until water pours out.

"Nate..."

"I'll stop when you're in the bath. You can drink whatever's left."

Eyes wide, she acts quicker than lightning. "Okay... fuck, okay." Her hoodie is already on the floor. "Fuck, I'm doing it. I'm getting in the bath...*stop*."

I slow down, wanting to laugh when she's finally naked and trips over herself before hurrying into the tub.

I stop as she hisses, the hot water probably too intense for her cuts and bruises.

"This is highly amusing," I tell her flatly.

She's still lowering herself as she bites back, "Fuck you. Give me that bottle."

Because I'm true to my word, I hand her the half-empty bottle. She snatches it from me, drinking like she's been in a desert for three days.

"Not too quick."

She ignores me.

I shake my head and grab a loofah and shower gel on the side of the bath.

I don't like the sound of the bottle as she crushes the plastic. My head twitches to the side, but I guess the woman isn't really happy right now.

"What do you think you're doing?"

I press the loofah against her shoulder, making her wince, and point out the obvious since she doesn't want to accept it. "I'm washing you."

She raises a hand, ready to rip the thing from my fingers, but I snatch her wrist with my free hand. "Do you know what I love, little sunflower?"

She eyes me suspiciously, and I'm surprised she doesn't know the answer. It's not like I ever tried to hide it.

"Hurting you."

My eyes roam over her naked body, at the way she brought her knees up. Only her lower stomach, hips, upper thighs, and intimate area are submerged. She's hiding her pussy by keeping her legs tight and her knees to her chest.

"And I'll hurt you, Kayla. I'll hurt you a lot." When my grip tightens on her wrist, I love the way she grits her teeth so her mouth doesn't twist in pain. "So don't give me any reason to do it more than I already will."

Her lips flatten, and she takes a deep breath before relaxing her shoulders. I let go of her wrist, and her arm falls numbly into the water.

I nod at her because I'm not sure how else to tell her this is what I expected. She sits there like a lifeless puppet whose strings got cut as I wash her shoulders and neck. I move on to her back, and she silently rests her chin on her knees, her gaze lost.

Pushing her long black hair over one shoulder, I focus on scrubbing. She'll talk eventually. In the meantime, I observe her back, then her stomach as I move her to start working on her chest. I do her breasts, but I make sure to keep it clinical.

She needs to understand I am just establishing control. I am not bringing her pleasure yet. That will only come if she behaves.

She drops her head back against the tiles behind her and squeezes her eyes shut when I move down her stomach.

I ignore the way her nipples have hardened, but my dick doesn't.

My dick fucking loves Kayla. Always has.

There's something about her body that makes her so... alive. Even more so now that she has black and purple bruises all over her stomach and that she tries to stop herself from whimpering when I go over them with the loofah.

I observe her body from head to toe as steam billows around her. She has makeup running down her damp face, and a black bruise on her cheek. Her nose is slightly swollen, dry blood still sticking below her nostrils, and her lips are cut and chapped.

Goosebumps litter her pale skin as I drop the loofah

and caress one of her tattoos with my thumb. This one just below her right breast is a noose one would use to hang themselves. It's small, a bit thick and gray from how old it is. She's got plenty of them. Some done too young, some covering scars. The Kings' crown at her neck is a statement of her pride. To the family she was born into and the reason she is so one-track minded.

Kayla thinks her ultimate win is to be at the head of her pathetic gang. To own the North Shore. Silly dreams of a silly girl. Why reign over a kingdom when you could rule the world? Why be a queen when you could be a goddess? I could give her that. I would have if she hadn't sent me to prison.

Not because I enjoyed fucking her more than I enjoyed fucking other women. And I really did. Not because I felt anything for her, but because she is useful, resourceful, intelligent, and a great person to have by your side.

Sadly, for her, she ruined that by trying to outshine the master. Big mistake.

I caress one of her many scars. Proof that she's been through much more than anyone else around her. Proof that she's powerful and people have tried to take that away from her.

Emma Scott was wrong. Kayla *is* still standing. Except now, she'll be standing by my side. At all times.

My hand goes lower, finding a new scar. I trace my thumb just above her pubic bone, where the line of her underwear would be if she was wearing any.

"This is new."

Her hand plunges under the water, seizing my wrist.

She doesn't hesitate one second. "This is NSC trying to gut me alive while you were away."

"And you survived?"

She snorts, her eyes opening to meet mine. "I survive everything, Nate. You, more than anyone, should know that."

That's true. "Let go of my wrist and spread your legs."

She shakes her head. "No. You're not touching me."

"I am touching you right now." Isn't that obvious?

"You're not touching me...*there*."

"What are you, fifteen? You can't say *don't touch my pussy*?"

She eyes me silently for a few seconds.

"Will you stop if I tell you 'don't touch my pussy?'" she bites back.

"No." And to prove my point, I put one hand on her knee, pulling her legs apart, and cup her pussy with the other.

"Nate..." she gasps. "Stop." I push past her lips and press threateningly against her entrance at the same time as I bring my other hand to her hair, holding her in place.

"No. I think it's about time we talk about your future, or lack thereof, if you don't start behaving."

She twists, but there's nowhere for her to go, and she freezes again when I breach her entrance with a single finger.

"Stop moving or I'll make it hurt. And then it'll make you wet and you'll end up enjoying something you don't want. That'll be hard on your conscience, you know it."

"What the fuck do you want from me?" she grunts.

"I'm glad you asked. And before I tell you, I think we should rewind a little bit. Remind ourselves why you're in this position in the first place. Because once you know, you'll think I'm a bastard, Kay. But I want you to remember exactly why I'm doing it, and that you're the one who started this. That all's fair in love and war. You proved it four years ago, didn't you?"

I pull harder at her hair, making her wince in the process and hardening my cock. It is so deeply satisfying when I know she's in pain, no matter the degree of it. As long as I'm the one inflicting it.

"Kayla," I start, in all seriousness. And I know that angers her. Especially when I tip my mouth into half a smile on purpose to provoke her. "Why are you getting wet already?"

She's incapable of replying, especially not when I push farther inside her.

I shake my head, tsking her for being a silly girl. "Don't blame me for your own way of being fucked up." I pull out my fingers, pressing them against her clit and rubbing languid circles.

"What did you do to me, little sunflower? Why do you deserve what I'm about to tell you?"

Her lips part, as if to say something, inhaling sharply, but then she shakes her head. She doesn't want to talk because she doesn't want to moan.

"What did you do when you lied in court, pretending you saw me kill Vladimir Volkov?" Since she wants to play dumb, I'll narrow the questions until she gives me what I want to hear.

I keep playing with her clit, feeling the way it swells against my fingers, then I pause for a few seconds so she can refocus. Stupid girl can't even multitask.

She gasps, her chest trembling. "I did what I had to do to stay on top. You would have done the same. In fact, *you did.*"

Her little reminder of me working with the feds to send Mateo Bianco to prison does nothing to make me lose my focus. I couldn't care less how the man disappeared, as long as the throne was free for me to sit on.

I push two fingers inside her, watching as her eyes flutter shut before she takes control of herself again. She bites her lower lip when I start moving.

"What did you take away from me, Kayla? Say it. When you sent me away for almost four years, what did you take. Away. From. Me." I punctuate the end of my sentence with sharp pressure on her G-spot.

That finally gives me what I want.

"Your freedom," she moans, letting her head fall slack against my hand in her hair.

"Say it again."

"I-I," she pants. "I took your freedom away."

I nod, keeping my gaze on her as she slowly opens her eyes again. "And now I'm going to take yours."

When she tries to deny my words by shaking her head again, I tighten my grip in her hair, immobilizing her while I keep thrusting my fingers in her pussy.

"You can't... You can't keep me here forever."

"Keep you here? You don't think that's the only thing I'm going to do, do you?"

I had four years to think of what would make Kayla King hurt the most. For a person who fought tooth and nail to get what she has, for a woman who's always taken care of herself and thrives on independence, there's only one thing I could come up with that will truly make her feel the way I felt.

"You're going to marry me, little sunflower."

10

NATHAN

Free Animal - Foreign Air

Her entire body freezes, going into shock. She opens her mouth to talk, but I think it's about time she gets a taste of how I think my wife should behave. At least if my wife is Kayla King.

With a harsh movement, I pull her head underwater, holding her there with two fingers in her pussy and a hand tangled in her mane.

Her hands shoot to my arm, her nails cutting into my skin as I watch her struggle. Bubbles float to the surface, and she splashes me as she starts flinging her legs too.

I tilt my head to the side, wondering if she can see me from underwater and how I look.

Does she feel like I'm in control now? Does she understand that her freedom is mine? Has it hit her yet that I hold her pathetic life in the palm of my hand, quite literally?

Hundreds of bubbles become dozens and then a few. I guess I should let her breathe.

Pulling her back up, I give her a few seconds to gasp air into her lungs and cough. I release her hair, but I want to keep playing with her, so I move my fingers inside her again.

"S-stop," she coughs before gasping some more.

But why would I stop if she's getting wetter? And why would I stop if I'm the one in control? Why should I care what she wants?

She starts getting her bearings again and wraps her trembling hand around my wrist between her legs. "Nate..." She's still heaving for air, but I don't think it's for the same reason anymore.

The little slut who gets off on fear and pain is about to come.

Oh, how fun it's going to be to play with her. Kayla has always been a very entertaining toy.

I feel her soft walls contract around my fingers, and her legs start to shake, so I pull my fingers away.

"Orgasms are not on the agenda," I state blankly as I release her entirely. "Not until you can prove what a sweet, obedient wife you can be."

Her body slackens in the water, and she blinks up at me, drops of water falling from her lashes.

She tries to calm her breathing, but it takes her a few attempts before she can talk again.

"I am not marrying you," she rasps.

I stand up, taking a towel from the side to dry my arms and hands, and look down at her.

"We can talk about why you will over dinner. I've got a hint for you. It's the same reason I'm not in prison anymore." I wink at her and drop the towel. "Wash your hair and meet me downstairs. You need to be fed and hydrated."

I don't look back when I leave, and I don't lock any door. She can make herself at home here. She can even try to leave. I'll enjoy the thrill of chasing her.

My lifelong friend and enforcer, Sam, is eating a burrito at my kitchen island when I walk in. He stops mid-bite, his obsidian eyes looking me up and down, then keeps on eating quietly.

Sam and I are friends because life put us in each other's way from a very young age. His dad worked as an enforcer for my foster dad. And my foster dad happened to be the head of one of the most powerful Cosa Nostra families. The Bianco family.

Of course I've developed an attachment to him over time. Not over love or the good times we've spent together, but because it was simple. When you can practically read each other's mind from how much you know someone, evolving together is only natural.

When we realized we were stronger together, we became inseparable. Survival of the fittest and all. Plus, he's come to love me over time. If I died tomorrow, the guy would be devastated.

And because we're so close, I don't need him to talk for his eyes to ask what the fuck I've been up to with Kay, so I answer him.

"I proposed to her." Or as close as it gets, I guess. I grab myself a bottle of water from the fridge and take big sips as I eye the empty shelves. "And all I have to offer my bride-to-be tonight is takeout."

"I still strongly believe this is a terrible idea."

Closing the fridge, I turn around and lean on it. "But you will go along with it anyway."

He takes another bite of his burrito, nodding as if this didn't need an answer anyway. Of course, he will.

I check the paper bag on the table, noting there are another two wraps in there. "You're so thoughtful."

"I'm going to tell Rose."

My head snaps up. "Not yet."

He swallows his last bite, drinks from the glass in front of him, and crushes the now empty foil wrapper in his fist.

"Nate," he groans. "You've been out of prison for five months and still haven't told any of your siblings. Jake lives in this very town. Rose lives with *me*. She's going to cut my fucking balls off already for keeping the truth from her for so long. Don't make this harder on me."

"You're the one who chose to be with her despite my multiple warnings. Now you deal with it. What kind of best friend fucks his friend's sister while he's in prison?"

I would say my friend's only flaw is that he started dating my sister while I was in prison. And while I did hurt him for what he did when I got out, that doesn't seem to have deterred him. Of course, because he's a greedy man, he ended up dating two other people too, and now they all love each other, like that makes any sense at all.

"Stop being petty and let me tell her," he huffs, unaware that I'm debating his lifestyle in my head.

"No."

The second my sister learns I'm back, she'll be all over me to tell me to leave the Cosa Nostra behind. Hell, she'll come to Kayla's rescue, for all I know. She likes protecting women and all.

He runs a hand across his face, fighting the anger rising. Calmly, he grazes his tattooed knuckles against his jaw, observing me, before he repeats himself. "This is all a terrible idea."

"Or so you said. I don't understand why you think that."

"Of course you don't," he snorts. "It involves

understanding a human being with fully functioning emotions."

"I can do that." I point at the two lines between his eyebrows. "I can tell you're worried for me right now. See?"

He looks at me, deadpan. "No," he says sharply. "You've learned about emotions, and what they look like, people's tells, but you do not understand them, Nate."

"I don't think that matters. What I understand is Kayla is made of fifty percent independence and fifty percent fight, and by clipping her wings and making her unable to fight back, she will be nothing." I tilt my head to the side. "Do you get that?"

"I'm not an idiot," he mumbles.

"You sound like one."

"There are repercussions to clipping someone's wings, especially a woman like Kayla King. Trust me, I've got one of those at home. You weren't here in the last four years when her crew was on top. That was because of her. Fuck, the girl put someone like *you* in prison for a deal with the Wolves. You think she won't fight back, but she will because you can't kill someone's will to fight. It's inside them. It becomes everything they feel and crave. They don't call her the ruthless King for no reason, Nate. She is brutal. She is merciless. And she is fucking smart."

He takes a deep breath. "You want your revenge? Kill her. Because when she kills you, you'll be just another name on a list of people who *wish* they had killed her when they could."

I watch him for a few seconds. He truly believes what he's saying. Kayla has built herself a reputation so strong, even my hitman of a friend wouldn't mess with her.

But that's because they don't know her like I do. They

haven't seen her weaknesses or witnessed how beautifully I can make her break apart.

"Do you know what I love?"

He slowly blinks at me, unimpressed with my response, but he doesn't say anything.

"A good challenge."

His eyes dart over my shoulder, as the hint of a smile pulls at his lips. "Is that right? Well, here's one for you. Your future wife is sprinting across your front lawn."

I spin around, looking out the window. In the dark of the night, I can barely see Kay as she climbs the brick wall of my gated yard. The last thing my exterior lights illuminate is her long black hair as she jumps off, and I assume, starts running down the Stoneview street.

"Huh." I scratch the back of my head, mentally adding this to my list of things to do. "I'll have to deal with that."

"Before she comes back to kill you, if possible," Sam adds.

I wave a hand dismissively. "The girl has a horrible concussion, and someone just tried to drown her."

"Could that someone be you, maybe?"

"Well, not all proposals are done with flowers, Sam. My point is, she's going to need some rest over the next few days before she plans anything."

As he stands up, his massive body makes the stool next to him look miniature. "I'm going home, then."

Grabbing my phone out of my pocket, I keep talking to him as I look for Emma's number.

"I just need you for one last thing, then you're free to go back to your football team of lovers."

I press call without even waiting for a reaction from him that I know won't come.

"*Nathan,*" Emma says sharply at the other end of the line. "*What can I do for you?*"

"The two guys with you this morning."

"*Logan and Law.*"

"Bring them to my house. Now." I hang up before she can come up with any excuses.

Sam's black eyes cross with mine, already knowing what our late-night meeting will be about.

When Emma walks into my office, she's alone and with a scowl on her face. I'm sitting behind my glass desk, a tumbler of whiskey in my hand and a ton of documents in front of me. Attorney Garcia-Diaz doesn't really care what I'm up to. Legal or not doesn't matter to her, as long as she can make it look legit on paper.

"Before you say anything," she starts. "They're right outside. I just wanted to talk to you first."

I take a sip of whiskey, letting the liquid soothe my throat.

"I've had a rather long day, Emma. Why don't you make this quick?"

"What...is your plan for the North Shore? I know you won't give it to me for free, Nate. Even after I helped you."

Her eyebrows pinch, and she starts biting the nail of her thumb. She is obviously anxious to be here.

"My plans don't concern you. I gave you the North Shore. You have police protection, thanks to me, and I will be supplying you with drugs and weapons." I take another sip of whiskey. "Congratulations, you're officially a big fish in what I consider a puddle. Now bring your little fishes in before this conversation gets even more boring."

Her jaw works from side to side for a few seconds

before she nods. She opens the door to Logan and Law, and they walk in, followed closely by Sam.

"Wonderful." I stand, undoing the buttons of my sleeves so I can roll them up. As I do, I walk around my desk, standing in front of it.

"We're all here to learn a lesson tonight, and I don't always feel in a teaching mood, so make sure you pay attention."

Emma is the first to eye the door and the way Sam stands in front of it, turning my office into a room without an exit.

"This is mainly for you, Emma. So you understand how to run a gang. Watch and learn, will you?"

I draw my gun from my holster and aim it at Law.

"Nate," she hisses with fury. "You said you would keep my most useful men alive. These two are the ones I need the most. You can't just come back and kill whoever you want."

"Well, here's your first lesson. I *can* come back and kill whoever I want. And what you say or don't say makes no difference to me at all. Your lesson is as follows: You need to start keeping your boys in check. Because when they suggested ending Kayla, and I specifically said I wanted her alive, and when on top of that, you gave a direct order not to kill her, I would expect them to follow said order. Instead, they caught her outside the warehouse and chased her through the forest to make her a casualty of the night."

"You fucking what?" Emma shouts at them. "What the fuck went through your head?"

"A bullet," I answer. Then, I shoot Law directly in the head, unfortunately painting my wall in blood and brain splatter. Splashes of it land on Logan too, and he takes a few steps back as he starts retching.

Emma closes her eyes for a few seconds, before staring daggers at me, but she stays quiet because she knows her place.

And then I shoot Logan in the thigh.

His scream is pathetic, before he falls to the floor and screeches like a banshee. He presses his two hands on the wound, blood gushing out from between his fingers.

"He needs a hospital," I tell her flatly. "And *you* need to make sure when I give an order, I won't have to worry about some people in your crew not following."

I put the gun back in the holster I keep around my shoulders, take my tumbler of whiskey, and lean against my desk. "Any questions?"

The whimpers of *fuck, fuck, fuck* from Logan are complete background noise as I look at Emma and wait for her answer.

"No questions," she says in a low voice, barely able to contain her rage.

"I'm glad. You may leave." I walk back around my desk, ready to sit down. "Oh, and Emma?"

She looks up from where she's crouching next to Logan. "Take Law with you."

It takes them a while to leave, even with Sam's help, but the second they're finally gone, I reach for my phone again, calling an old friend of mine.

"You've reached Martinez."

"It's Nathan White."

"At this time of night, I thought so. What can I do for you?"

"Kayla King, you know her, right?"

"Sure do."

I turn around to face my window, thinking of my little sunflower out there, probably thinking my promises in the bathroom earlier were just threats. Probably believing with all her being she can escape me.

"Pay her a little visit. Start with her house. If she isn't there, I'll send you some addresses to try."

"*Tomorrow's my little girl's birthday. I took the day off.*"

"And you should enjoy that time with your kid. Give Kayla two days."

The woman is about to be legally mine for the rest of her life. I'm a fair man, I can give her a few days to prepare.

11

KAYLA

Welcome To The Fire - Willyecho

I burst through the door of Elliot and Ethan's house, everything around me feeling suffocating.

My vision is so blurry I think I hit a wall before I can right myself.

"Kay!" The feminine gasp grabs my attention, and the small form hurrying toward me leaves no doubt that it's Jade. "Elliot, Ethan!" she screams to the rest of the house. "Come here!"

I feel myself swaying, and two arms catch me at the waist. "No shouting," I rasp. "My head is..." I don't even bother finishing my sentence, my words too mumbled anyway.

"Holy shit." Elliot's worried voice annoys me. I'm not that bad, am I? "Kay, what happened? Where were you?"

Jade's arms are replaced by his. "I'm fine." I try to shrug him off, but the step I take on my own is a failure, and I'm starting to fall when he catches me again.

"You say you're fine because you can't see your fucking face," Elliot bites back. "Let me carry you."

I snort, shaking my head. "What am I? A damsel in distress or something?"

"No, but you sure as fuck are a stubborn bitch in distress."

"Fuck, Kay." This time, it's Ethan entering the room.

"Help me get her to your bed," his brother orders.

"I need water," I croak. "And a gun. Give me a gun and I'll be on my way."

Jade runs to their kitchen, as the guys force me to hook my arms behind each of their necks. They lean down to help me walk and guide me to Ethan's bedroom.

I bite back a whimper when they lay me down on the bed, the simple act of resting my head making my headache worse.

"What the fuck happened?" Elliot asks, crossing his arms over his chest as he stands by my head. "We looked everywhere for you."

"Logan and Law caught me last night. Tried to kill me. I managed to get away, but then—" I lick my lips. I don't know if I have the strength to get into the last twelve hours with Nate, so I keep it short. "Then Nathan White wanted his revenge too."

Jade runs in with a glass of water, and I down it, so she heads back to the kitchen.

"Yeah, everyone's saying he's back. And *we* know who put him away, Kay. You need to lay low. Stay here for a while."

Like I have a fucking choice. I gave my own street to Emma Scott. But I'm not cowering from Nate.

He's a threat.

Threats get eliminated.

I shake my head. "Listen. I met with Emma. Nate is the one who has been supporting her. They fucked us over completely. She took everything from us."

I go over the talk I had, telling them everything I was forced to agree to.

"That's bullshit," he barks. "How the fuck are we meant to survive?"

"For now, I need you to pass the word around. Make sure everyone respects those fucking rules. Look out for the rats who will change sides right away. Especially the guys who left NSC to join us in the last few years. Trust no one, Elliot."

Ethan takes a step closer, joining his brother by my side just as Jade walks back in. I down another glass as he observes me. "You sound like you're about to do something stupid. Something that might get you killed."

"Not stupid. I'm putting an end to this before it even begins. I need to kill Nate. If I don't, he'll kill me."

"The guy is a psychopath," Elliot says, almost to himself, running a hand through his blond strands. "He won't kill you. He'll make you suffer."

"Yeah." I nod, the memories of earlier all too clear. My stomach twists and my thighs tense. "Yeah, I know. That's why I need to get rid of him now."

The brothers eye each other.

"So, give me a fucking gun." I try to sit up, but Elliot presses on my shoulder, making me wince as I lie back down.

"Yeah, you're going to fucking sleep first."

"But—"

"Kayla," he says sternly. "You're my boss, and I respect you. I know our hierarchy, and I would never give you an order. But I'm talking to you as a friend, as your family. You *need* to heal before doing anything insane that will most certainly turn against you."

When I'm about to argue, he smiles in that fake charming way he always does. "Don't make me call Caden."

My mouth snaps shut, eyes narrowing on him. "Leave him out of this. He can't know shit, or he'll come running back."

I might tease my brother, Caden, for leaving the North Shore, but ultimately, I know that was the best decision for him. Being unhinged made him a great member of the Kings, but I want my family safe, not at risk of dying every day.

"Sleep." He gives me a pointed look. "Do that for us and I won't send your overprotective baby brother on you."

"You're a dick." But my voice lacks real accusation as my eyelids flutter closed.

"Sweet dreams, boss."

I spend almost forty-eight hours in and out of sleep. Jade wakes me up every now and then to make sure the concussion hasn't gotten worse and brings me ice for the bump. Elliot tends to my nose, checks the cut at the back of my head, and gives me creams for the bruises.

On the second night at their house, I finally feel well enough to get out of bed. When I walk into their living room, Jade is asleep on the sofa, her legs on Elliot and her head resting on Ethan's lap.

"Long day at work," Elliot tells me as his gaze drops to his girlfriend. "She's always dead when she comes back from the garage." He looks back up at me. "Do you want anything? I made mac and cheese, or we've got frozen pizza—"

"A gun and a lot of ammo."

The brothers exchange a look, and Elliot is the one to get up since it's easier to without waking Jade.

He walks up to me, and I grit my teeth as he observes me from his insane height.

"What did he do?"

I cock an eyebrow at him, feeling my body tighten from the mere memory of Nate. "What do you mean?"

"Come on, Kay," he snorts. "I've known you for over fifteen years. You're not a reckless woman. You've never been. Even before leading the Kings, you always thought things through before acting."

My jaw tightens, and I lick my lips, finding it hard not to drop my stare. But I have nothing to say, too loyal to lie to my most trusted man.

"You're scared," Elliot tells me, like he struggles to believe it's the truth. "You're scared and you want to get rid of the person who is scaring you. But if you rush things, you'll be putting yourself at risk. And maybe even us." He takes my hand and squeezes reassuringly. "Talk to us, Kay. We might not have absolute power over this town anymore, but we're still your crew. We're still here. We'll fight with you."

"Elliot," I rasp, not feeling so confident in the face of his unconditional support. "Nathan White is a vengeful psychopath who has spent the last four years scheming how to make me suffer. I will not take any of you down with me. I'll deal with this on my own, even if it kills me."

"What did he say?" he insists. "What did he do?"

"If I tell you, you can't get involved, and you absolutely cannot tell Caden under any circumstances."

His eyes search my face, unable to construct the reality of the situation.

I take a deep breath. "He... *God*," I scoff. "This is fucking ridiculous. The maniac wants—"

A sharp knock on the door startles all of us. Jade sits up suddenly, rubbing her eyes as we all glance at each other.

Another knock and we know. Because no one else knocks like this on the North Shore.

"Police, open the door!"

"*Motherfucker!*" I hiss. I know this is Nate because the North Shore pigs rarely dare to come to our houses. Unless they're raiding us, but we've given them no reason to lately.

"Back. Out the back, *now*," Elliot tells me.

He reaches behind him and pulls out a gun from his jeans, shoving it in my hand.

Ethan is up in a split second, grabbing Jade's hand and dragging her to the kitchen, and I'm assuming to the basement.

I'm only wearing Ethan's pair of sweats and a tank top, but I don't have a fucking choice right now, so I run to their back exit just as the police kick down the door.

Definitely bribed. They would at least have given us the chance to open if this was a legit arrest.

The cops run into the house, two of them grabbing Elliot, forcing him to kneel and put his hands behind his head. He knows better than to fight back in this situation.

I snatch the door open, ready to run, when I bump into a strong body. Stumbling back, I look up at Captain Martinez.

As dirty as they come.

"Kayla King," he calls in his loud voice. "We've got a warrant for your arrest." He shoves a document against my chest that I can't even grab since he's already getting a hold of my wrists. I'm facing Elliot again as he twists me around.

"How much is Nathan White paying you, Captain?" I grunt as he manhandles me and rids me of the gun on me. "Let me meet the price."

He ignores my accusation. "You've got the right to remain silent..."

I zone out the rights I've heard a thousand times, instead focusing on my friend as Martinez cuffs me.

"Elliot," I hiss, the metal cuffed too tightly around my wrist. "Get me the fuck out."

His eyes focus on me, a thousand questions in them. I've never so desperately asked him for something. Especially not when we know I usually get arrested for a night or two in a holding cell before I throw a random alibi at them that people in my crew will confirm.

"Listen to me." I try to stay calm as Martinez pulls me away, but I can't when I know what's waiting for me. "He's going to force me to marry him. Don't... Don't let him come get me from the station. *You* need to get me out first, Elliot!"

I can't even see his reaction, pulled away through the back door and to the alley at the back of their house.

"You're a desperate fucking bitch, Martinez," I spit at him as he opens his car. "Always switching to the winning side with no fucking morals."

He ignores me as he forces me inside the cop car. Leaning in, he makes sure no one can hear me when he says, "If I had morals, I wouldn't have accepted your bribes in the past, King. Now don't make this worse for yourself and shut the fuck up."

He straightens and slams the door in my face.

"Fuck!" I scream in the empty car, just before he and his partner sit in the front.

.   .   .

It's the longest, most excruciating night I've ever had in the Silver Falls Police Station holding cell. I've been here many times, but in the last few years, I've always had special treatment. That's what happens when the Bratva Wolves donate enough money to the right people. Like a well-constructed charity benefiting the Kings.

But there is no more deal with the Wolves.

No more owning the North Shore.

No more fucking special treatment.

My stomach drops when Martinez advances toward the overcrowded cell. I already had to punch an NSC bitch's lights out when I arrived, and the anxiety of who is coming to get me out of here has been eating me alive.

So, when he smiles and calls *King*, I know Elliot didn't manage.

"You're being interrogated," Martinez adds, as he cuffs my hands behind my back.

"Ah, of course. I hope the night wasn't too long while you were making up something you could pin on me."

With a shove between the shoulder blades, he forces me to advance. "You fucking wish I spent that kind of time on you."

He makes me sit down in an interrogation room, facing a two-way mirror, and cuffs my hands at the front, to a metal bar drilled into the table.

I narrow my eyes at the mirror, wondering if Nate is behind it, laughing at my predicament, having the time of his fucking life.

Martinez leaves the room. It's just me under the harsh light, between three gray walls and that mirror. I know he's watching me, so I stay strong. I keep my face tight, my eyes hard.

I sit back, pretending to relax in the chair, and I wait.

For. Fucking. Ever.

Multiple times I wonder if he's there or if I made it up. How long can he just stand there watching me? How long will he wait? Until I break?

Maybe he went for a coffee with Martinez, leaving me to simmer in my own rage and fear. Neither of which I will show him.

But what if... What if he isn't there? What if this wasn't even his call? What if it was, but he doesn't care past teaching me a lesson? He doesn't even care enough to come himself and watch me suffer. As long as he knows I do, that's enough for him.

And then what?

Why does it make me feel weird to know I'm not worth enough to him that he would torture me himself? That his attention isn't completely on me. That he has other people who betrayed him, and who he cares more about.

I'm starting to believe he was never behind that mirror in the first place, when the door opens again.

Nate saunters in like a king in his throne room. Martinez isn't with him, and when he closes the door, I know the cop isn't coming.

"Kayla," Nate chuckles to himself. He drops a folder on the table and stands with his hands in his suit pants.

Midnight blue that matches his eyes. White button-up. Hair combed back. It barely looks blond on his side of the room that isn't directly illuminated by the white bulb. In the shadow, his eyes are dark, the angles of his face hard, and when he smiles, his teeth are bright and sharp.

I am fucked.

I lick my lips, trying to keep a semblance of pride in the way I hold myself.

"Watching you slowly believe I wasn't right there observing you for nearly four hours has been the highlight of my day, little sunflower. You badly love my attention. It's dangerous."

"Why is it dangerous?" I bite my lower lip the second the words are out, and he catches my regret, his mocking stare sending a wave of shame crashing into me.

Like an idiot, I didn't even think to deny his claims.

"Because Kayla." He opens the manila folder he put on the desk. I can see black-and-white pictures, but I can't make out what they are exactly. "That means you're already mine. That means whatever pretend fight you have in you will be gone soon. A part of you fell for me a long time ago, and the second I manipulate you to believe I reciprocate that, you will give me everything. Every single thing that makes you *you* will be mine. You're powerful, Kayla, but you're no match against me."

He presses the palms of his hands on the table, and his handsome face comes into the light as he leans forward.

"You think your punishment is to be stuck with me, but it's worse than that. It will be hard at first, but you'll fall for me eventually, and then...that's when I'll truly hurt you. When I take everything from you, when I turn you into a docile little housewife with no dreams, no wants but to please me. When you'll do it because you love me, because you think it makes *you* happy, when you're truly a shadow of the mighty woman you used to be, *then* I would have achieved my goal. Then we'll be even."

My lips tremble when I part them to take a breath. I can feel the truth of his words ringing throughout my body. The dread makes me speechless for a minute, but it doesn't bother him. He stands there, observing me with a blank face. Pushing his glasses up his straight nose, his eyes roam over my body. His tongue darts to his lip in a discreet yet captivating way.

The man is reading me with steel focus, and I'm too shaken to do anything to fight back. His description of my worst nightmare comes with the fear that I know he's capable of anything.

My dad had a spin on the expression *if you don't have anything nice to say, don't say anything at all.*

His version was *if you don't have anything* smart *to say... shut the fuck up.*

And as much as I hated my dad, I should have taken his advice in this instant. I know it the moment I say, "Your plan is destined to fail because you cannot force me to stay by your side. You can't keep me to yourself." I snort. "And you sure as fuck can't make me marry you."

He straightens up again, grabbing the first picture in the folder. "I'm glad you brought this up," he says matter-of-factly, like he's the attorney in my unfair trial. "In the last few days, how many times have you wondered how I got out of prison?"

Not nearly enough. I was too busy escaping his house and recovering so I could kill him.

Without waiting for my answer, he puts the picture in front of my cuffed hands, and my gaze leaves him, dropping to the paper.

It's a CCTV picture of me. I'm not doing anything wrong, just walking through the Silver Falls streets on the South Bank. I'm wearing a tiny tank top I remember I could barely breathe in.

Nate tilts his head to the side, looking at the picture too. "Your boobs look huge in this picture."

I look up, staring daggers at him.

The problem isn't what I'm doing, the size of my fucking boobs, or anything in this picture. Nothing except the date and time.

April fifteenth.

Four years ago.

The exact night Vladimir Volkov was murdered.

Time? 11:31 p.m.

"This one is from an ATM camera. The Kings won the fight in the Death Cage, and a few hours later, Kayla King is strolling through the South Bank."

He puts another picture in front of me and keeps on talking like a bad voice actor documenting a true crime show.

"At thirty-six past eleven p.m., she enters this burger place called Dirty Good Burgers. It stays open late. Do you know why? Because there's a club across the street, and they want money from all the starved drunk kids who leave in the middle of the night. This is the CCTV from the club."

He taps my black-and-white figure on the paper. "Caught in the act of eating burgers with your dad and Sawyer. Probably to discuss the meeting your dad will have with Emma's dad the next day."

For the second time, I look up, wishing my eyes could annihilate him.

He picks up the last picture. "I know you were with them because at two thirty a.m., you leave the restaurant with both of them." He adds it to the others in front of me.

I press my lips together. I had no idea those CCTVs were there, no idea those photographs even existed. Who did he hire while he was in prison to find them?

I'm not surprised they weren't found before. The trial

was swift. The city wanted to take him down, and they didn't question my testimony. They jumped on the chance to put Nathan White, known Cosa Nostra criminal, away for good.

I struggle to swallow past my dry throat.

Even before he talks, my fate is sealed. Nate knows I would do anything not to be sent to jail. I have more enemies there than on the streets of the North Shore, and I would have no protection from people who want me dead. No weapons, no allies. My crew has spent the last four years under police immunity, theirs hasn't. Anyone from NSC who committed a crime and got caught was sent straight to prison. Joining them would be signing my death warrant.

I hold my hands together, entwining my fingers so Nate doesn't see them shake, but I'm pretty sure that exact gesture is already a tell of my mounting anxiety.

"Tell me, Kayla," he purrs. "What period of time did the coroner estimate Vladimir Volkov's death?"

My eyes flutter shut, my mind refusing to accept I've already lost against him.

I hear him round the desk, and the next thing I know, I feel his hand in my hair, pulling so I'm forced to look up at him.

"Go on."

"Between midnight and two a.m.," I grit out.

"Huh." He pretends confusion, pointing at the time on the picture of me coming out of the burger place with two members of my crew who are now dead. "Then how did you see me kill him in a warehouse on the North Shore of Silver Falls if you were eating burgers on the South Bank?"

"If a judge saw this, then why am I not being tried for perjury?"

With a scoff, he releases my hair and leans on the table to face me again. "Because I paid a lot of money to punish you myself. This whole release was done under the table. The only one who caught us was the prosecutor, but she only knew I was being released, not what the evidence was. She did her best to stop us, but she simply didn't have the power against old, established judges who like extra money and protection, and who have been working with the mob for as long as they can remember anyway. That's why she tried to get you to testify again. To fight the real bad guys. She had no support to send you any official letters or get any help from authorities."

I shake my head. "So that's what you've been doing for almost four years? Finding out where I really was that night so you could prove I lied, and planning what you'd do to me once you got out?"

He looks at me, deadpan. "The other prison activities weren't for me."

He reaches inside his pocket again. "You lost, Kayla. You lost the moment you put me in prison. You lost before you even tried to play, believe me."

Pulling a black velvet box out of his pocket, he puts it on top of the pictures.

"Choose your punishment, little sunflower. Prison"—he opens the box and pushes it closer to me—"or marriage."

I shake my head, unable to talk. This can't be true. This can't be the only two solutions I have. Without a word, I stand up, pulling violently at the cuffs. I'm becoming stupid, attempting to defy physics because I refuse to accept my predicament.

"No," I grunt, pulling harder. "No, no. Martinez!"

Nate stands back, giving me space to lose my mind as he observes me with curiosity.

"Martinez, let me out!" I scream at the mirror.

"There are minimal chances of Martinez letting you out when I pay for his son's college funds." He explains this in such a practical voice, like I'm truly not understanding rather than denying the truth.

"Don't do this." I turn to him. "Don't. Just kill me."

He looks like he wants to roll his eyes. "We've been over this. Now make a choice. Should I bring those pictures to a judge that will put you in prison, or should I put this ring"—he plucks it out of the box—"around your finger."

It takes me another full minute of cutting the skin around my wrists with the cuffs before I give up, panting as I sit back down on the metal chair.

"I can't breathe," I wheeze. "I—"

"Shh." He moves behind me. Him suddenly massaging my shoulders makes me tense even more. But before I know it, his hands slide down my arms.

One travels all the way to my wrist, pressing my pulse with his thumb. I can feel he's still holding the ring. His other hand slides under my tank top from the neckline. He places it just below my left breast, his fingertips at my ribs and his thumb between my boobs.

He applies pressure against my heart, whispering in my ear, "Calm your heartbeat, little sunflower. Take a deep breath." He squeezes me in his arms, then releases me. "Again."

I follow the rhythm of breathing he's forcing on me, feeling myself able to let air in my lungs again.

"That's good. Keep going."

He repeats the same process, until he can sense my heartbeat balancing again.

"Good. You can cry if you want to."

I shake my head. Of course I want to. I want to cry and

scream. Deep down, I want to beg with all I have. But over my dead body will Nathan White get a single tear out of me.

"Now tell me." He brings his lips near my ear, kisses the side of my head, and says, "Will you marry me?"

There's a certain despair that takes hold of me. Death's cold claws wrap around my throat, choking me, dripping ice into my stomach. But against my skin, Nate's hands are warm, his grip almost reassuring rather than possessive, his hug supportive like he isn't the one who is forcing me into this situation.

The answer is right there. I have no choice, but a single word has never been so hard to utter. The feeling of the ring stuck between his hand and my wrist is grim. I don't even know what it looks like. I saw it, but it didn't register.

He gives me time. He might have given me forever had I needed it. But I can't die in this interrogation room. I have to get out. I have to start planning how to escape my jailer.

"Yes." The word barely exists in my raspy voice.

I feel Nate's smile spread against my skull. "You're making me the happiest man on earth, Kayla."

"I don't want to make you the happiest man on earth."

He ignores my retort, letting me go entirely. It's an out-of-body experience when he slides the ring around my finger. I can't pull my hand away, still cuffed to the table. I can't say anything. Any word would just get stuck in my throat and drown in my inner tears.

It's okay.

It's a ring.

A ring means nothing.

I can take off a ring. I can throw it down the drain when he forces me to go back to his house. I can bury it in the woods. I can make him choke on it.

A ring means nothing.

He walks into my field of vision and caresses my cheek as he looks down at me.

"Do you know why I call you sunflower?"

My heart twists at the sound of his softened voice. He's putting it on. I know he is because anything coming from him that sounds real is an act he's spent years perfecting.

But it's still disturbingly soothing.

I shake my head. I never cared. He wanted to give me a stupid nickname, and I didn't have a say in it. So I just went along with it.

"Because I always saw you lighting up when talking about something that was important to you. Your focus is incomparable when you set your mind to it. Your only objective is to follow your goals like a sunflower follows the sun. Or else you wither and die. Back then, your independence was your sun."

I search for something true in his gaze while I try to calm my heartbeat. But there's nothing to see, no emotion to catch. Where is he going with this?

"Now listen to me and listen really closely, Kayla."

He leans closer, his thumb pulling down my lower lip before letting go and pressing against my mouth. The gesture feels...almost loving. A lie if I've ever seen one.

"I am your sun now."

12

KAYLA

Hypnotic - Zella Day

I refuse to look at the ring. Refuse to see what the band is made of, if it's a diamond, which cut. No. That would make it too real.

I'm looking out the window of his Range Rover, watching trees and buildings pass by as we leave the city of Silver Falls, and he drives onto the highway.

He gave me his suit jacket to leave the station. It smells of him and there's only one way to describe it. Elegant. That's how he smells. Like a man in a well-pressed suit who holds the door for you, cherishes his loved ones, works hard to spoil his wife. Like someone who hugs you when you cry and kills the demons that haunt you.

Like a lie.

My arms are wrapped around my stomach, not crossed over my chest like I usually do. I'm in protect mode. Not defense or attack. *Protect.* Protect my soul and my body at all costs. I need recovery, and I have spent less than twenty-four hours dealing with him. I feel cold, and I'm shaking.

My teeth would be clattering if I wasn't clenching my jaw so tightly, grinding my teeth to the point of breaking.

As I watch other cars driving past, I put a shaking hand on the window. I feel like a little girl who needs saving. I feel like hitting the glass and screaming for someone to help. Is that what he's already reduced me to?

I can't be Nate's captive. What about my family?

What is going to happen when the girls don't get their calls from me? It's hard enough to only see them once a month. I will not live without them.

On my left hand, all I can feel now is the band around my skin. All I can notice is that it fits perfectly.

Cold sweat gathers at my lower back while I wonder how he knew my size. I'm starting to suffocate again, my freedom slipping through my fingers just because of a piece of metal touching my skin.

"Not even in your wildest dreams."

I startle at Nate's impassive tone, not understanding what he means until my eyes look down. Subconsciously, I started taking the ring off with my thumb. It's around the second knuckle now.

"That ring stays on you. Day and night. Sunshine or rain. Is that clear?"

His eyes are on the road, and I wonder if he notices me nodding. There's no way I'll agree to that out loud.

"I've got a song for you." He accelerates on the highway as he presses play on the car screen.

I look away again, and this time, rage overtakes the anxiety.

Motherfucker put on "*Highway To Hell*" by AC/DC. I could kill him with my bare hands if I wasn't in such a state of shock.

. . .

When we arrive at his ridiculous mansion, my heart kicks into a panic again. The perfectly white building could fit my house four or five times in there. I don't dare ask any of the questions plaguing my mind.

Is he really going to keep me here? How long? Will I really not be able to leave the house?

Surely, he can't expect me to stay here twenty-four seven.

I get my answer the moment we cross the main double doors. In the marble hall with ceilings so high every single step resonates, he stops, and I do too. He turns to me, cupping my cheek in that fake reassuring way.

"You escaped through the living room windows last time, so I thought I'd warn you that all downstairs windows are locked with a key. They key is on me." He smirks. "So unless you want to undress me, just know there's no way out."

There's the front door, I don't tell him. My eyes do it instead when they dart to the exit behind him.

"There'll be a guard or two at the front door at all times. This isn't really for you, though. I have a lot of enemies, and sometimes I have better things to do than kill people who are stupid enough to come for me, but I thought you should know they have orders to not let you through without me." He continues walking without any further explanation. "Come."

I realize I'm not following. Not because I didn't know he wanted me to, but because I can't. I physically can't let him explain how I'll be a captive in his house, forced to marry him, without at least minimum resistance. Not following him to the grand staircase is resistance, right?

"Kayla," he huffs. "I have a big day ahead of me and it's already ten thirty a.m. This whole convincing you to marry me took longer than I wanted it to. Will you be a sweet girl and follow?"

I narrow my eyes at him, crossing my arms over my chest. I feel completely ridiculous in a tank top with a suit jacket.

"This is kidnapping."

His eyes widen, and his mouth drops open as he gasps before bringing a hand to cover it.

"No? Oh my god, no. Call the police." With a dramatic shudder, his face goes blank again. "Kidnapping? Do you think that's the worst thing I've ever done? Stop wasting my time, will you?"

I'm about to take a step, when his fingers snap, making me freeze on the spot.

"Do *not* snap your fingers at me."

"Then follow, or you'll be following naked with a red and sore ass."

I'm practically vibrating from anger when I walk his way. The long hallways are interminable.

"What is it with rich people and long hallways," I mumble. "Did you really need such a huge house for yourself?"

"For ourselves, little sunflower. What's mine will be yours once the papers are signed. And what if we decide to have kids? They'll all need their own bedroom."

My gaze drops, stress eating at me again. He makes it all sound so real. Marriage...kids. I gulp.

"I need a phone," I finally say, as we turn into yet another hallway. "I need to be able to contact my family." I need at least that to contact the girls.

"Caden?" he asks, knowing him as my only living relative.

Instead of telling him the truth, I go for a vague answer. "My crew is my family. They'll need me."

He stops in front of a light wooden door. "Can you imagine every single bedroom door came all the way from Italy?" He turns to face me. "But you probably knew that. You criticize wealth because you don't currently have anything to your name, but when you thought you were going to be rich, you wanted to buy this very house."

Pinching a strand of black hair near my cheek, he pulls like a bully in elementary school. "I like your hair."

Does he, though? Because his intonation could mean he's talking about any other thing that makes him feel no specific way whatsoever.

"Sounds about as creepy as everything else you say," I answer. "So, about that phone? I lost mine when Logan and Law chased me through the woods.

His eyes twitch slightly, and he cracks his neck. "Yes, that was annoying."

"To say the least."

Ignoring my sarcasm, he adds, "Every time you please me, you'll get something you want. I'll put a phone at the top of the list."

"What? What do you mean, *every time I please you*? Not only are you keeping me captive, but on top of that, I have to be at your fucking beck and call at all times?"

He snorts. "What did you think this was? A vacation? You're being punished, remember?"

Cutting the conversation short, he opens the door, and I follow him inside the same bedroom he had kept me in a couple of days ago. He walks straight to the bathroom, and I hear the water running while I take in the space. It's luxurious but simple.

Opposite me, the dark hardwood floor is covered in a huge light gray rug in front of the bed. It's a simple king-size bed with a soft, black velvet headboard and a duvet that looks like the most comfortable thing I've ever wanted to bury myself in.

"This isn't your room," I voice out loud without looking at him. "Why not?"

"No sex before marriage, my dear bride. I need to keep you in a different room so you don't jump me. Plus, it has everything I need."

I round the bed, wondering what he means by *everything he needs here* and, as I feared, I find a chain bolted to the floor. The same chain that was attached to my ankle a few days ago.

I startle when I hear his voice right next to me again. "I won't always put it on you," he purrs, clearly loving the fact that he will. "Only as long as I know you need it. Then you can come sleep in my room."

"I don't care about your fucking room, but I don't need the chain." My swift reply only shows my panic, not my strength.

"We both know you do for now, little sunflower. But that's okay, it won't be that way forever."

I turn to him, realizing he's much closer than I thought. Tilting my head back, I sear my desperate gaze into his. "How long, Nate? How long are you going to make me pay?"

"How long was I in prison?"

"Practically four years," I huff. We both know that. He didn't need to make me repeat it.

"I guess we'll start with four years, then. Who knows, you might be the one who decides to stay after that. Stockholm syndrome is a wonderfully complicated thing."

I try to be discreet, but I don't control my small step back.

"It's okay," he says softly. "You won't realize it. All you'll feel is happy and in love, and you won't believe anyone who tells you otherwise."

He takes hold of my wrist, pulling me with him as he makes his way to the bathroom.

"Now let's get you cleaned up. Take a shower and I'll get you some food up here. I'm a fair man, Kayla. I'll give you a few days to make peace with your situation. To remember that there isn't just a chain and locked windows that keep you in this house, but the fact that you chose your sentence and that, if you leave, those pictures will go to a judge quicker than it'll take you to run out of this town."

His detailed explanation makes me feel like a kid facing an adult who is trying to make them understand something for the tenth time in a row. It's rushed, barely articulated enough to catch the words. He says them, but he's done repeating himself.

"Now in you get." He points at the huge shower in the corner of the room that could probably fit three to five people.

"No bath today?" I ask as I ditch the suit jacket.

"Why? Do you want me to make you come while I hold you underwater?"

He takes a step back to let me through to the shower and ends up just past the doorway.

"You didn't make me come," I snarl. "One could wonder if you're even capable of it." I slam the door in his face, not caring if this is part of the things that *don't* please him.

As promised, by the time I come out, he's brought me food. On the dresser standing opposite the bed, he put a platter with some scrambled eggs, crushed avocado, toast, and bacon.

I eye it suspiciously. "I feel like you're about to take a picture for socials or some shit."

"My cook, Daniel, likes to make aesthetic plates. He's got a cooking Instagram or something. I don't know." He points at a silk nightgown on the bed. "This is for you. Put it on." Then he checks his watch. "Before the end of time, if possible."

To reward his unnecessary comment, I take as much time as I can putting the nightgown on. I drop the towel, standing naked in front of him, and lazily grab the silk before slipping it over my head.

He looks at me, unimpressed, but I pretend I don't notice.

"Sit on the bed."

I do, and it goes against all my instincts not to fight back when he kneels before me and wraps the cuff around my ankle. The sound of the chain skimming the floor and the edge of the bed makes me twitch.

But I *can't* fight back, right? He said it himself; it's not the chains, or the locked windows, it's not even the very fact that he could easily overpower me. It's the documents. It's three life-destroying pictures.

Simple pieces of paper that keep me still when the *click* of the lock slotting into place resonates loudly in my head.

"What's that face you're making?" His hand grazes up my calf, caressing my skin, raising goosebumps along the way.

When a devastatingly beautiful blue-eyed monster hides under your bed, ready to eat you whole, are you meant to let your body react to him?

And if not, what am I supposed to do to stop him?

I refuse to let my eyes leave the shackle around my ankle, as it's a reminder of my predicament. A reminder that his hand, now caressing the back of my knee, is a lure to get me to talk and open myself up, only so that he can destroy me better. That he's not asking *why* I'm making that face so he can find what's upsetting me—and isn't it obvious what is? No, he's asking *what* that face is. Because he has no idea.

"Wouldn't you like to know?" I snarl. "Isn't it such a lonely life being incapable of reading what someone is feeling? Being unable to share their joy, their sadness, their excitement?"

I lean closer and my gaze darts to his impassive face. "Having to rely on others to let you know what they truly feel makes you powerless and *weak*."

Still on his knees in front of me, he puts his other hand on my other knee, spreading my legs apart. The silk slides up my thighs, stopping just at my mound and revealing a fact we both knew. That he gave me a nightgown but no underwear.

He kneads my muscles, both hands now moving under my thighs.

"What is it?" he repeats. There's an undertone of frustration in his question, and I can go through today knowing I got to him.

He pushes up, sending me backward. My back falls onto the mattress, and his hands now ride to the junction of my legs and my hips as he drags me to the edge of the bed.

"Nate," I pant, a sudden warmth flooding my veins. "What are you—"

"What is that face?"

I look up, but he's not even looking at my face anymore, his mesmerizing eyes are locked on my pussy.

He licks his lips, a challenge crossing his gaze.

He's excited.

He's excited because he can't read me, and he wants to confront the issue at hand.

His head drops as he immobilizes me, locking his forearms around my legs, keeping my ass at the edge of the bed. He kisses my inner thigh, and there's nothing I can do to stop the electricity that leaves his soft lips traveling to my clit.

"Don't..."

I feel him smile against my skin. "Remember, little sunflower." He kisses my skin. "That word isn't included in our marriage."

I shake my head as his fingers dig into my flesh. He's holding my legs apart, his shoulders between them, his hands harshly gripping the apexes of my thighs.

He presses harder, a bruising hold that tears a whimper out of me as my head falls back on the bed. I squirm, my hands flying to the only thing I can grip, his hair. The second I pull, he holds harder.

"Fuck," I hiss. "You're hurting me."

"I know," he growls against me.

The pads of his fingers feel like blades as he ups it to another level. "Ow—Nate," I cry out.

"How much pain does it take to make you desperate for me to eat this beautiful pussy?"

"I don't—I won't. It-it doesn't—aah! It hurts!" My sudden rage is subdued by the realization that my hips just pushed forward. That I just fucking tried to get my pussy closer to his mouth.

"That's it," he purrs. "This little cunt is getting

desperate." I feel his mouth on my inner thigh again, and the sudden sharp pain of his teeth biting my skin makes me jump.

"Fuck!" I shriek. I slap the top of his head, knowing it won't change anything for him.

"Put your hands flat on the mattress, Kayla, and I'll consider not making you bleed."

My palms slam onto the bed so quickly it feels like he's the one controlling them.

"Very good." Another bite of my flesh, higher this time, makes me squirm under his hold.

When he releases me, he licks the wound and asks again, "What was that face?"

"Despair!" I scream urgently. "It was fucking despair because you're holding me here against my will. How can you not see that?"

He doesn't answer. Instead, I feel his head moving, and the next thing I know, his tongue licks a trail from my soaking entrance to my clit, making me shudder.

"No. Don't." But instead of taking hold of his hair again, I fist the sheets with both hands. Another lick, and I gasp. "Don't!"

"Don't make it feel good?" His deep voice rumbles against my clit, blurring the lines between good and bad in my head. "Would you like me to make it hurt some more?"

I try to speak, but he unleashes his devilish tongue on me again, turning my words into whimpers.

"Don't—don't touch me. *Stop*."

It's the fact that he keeps doing it after I asked him to stop that sends another wave of pleasure through my body. There's this poison in my veins that blackens my soul. There's this broken part of me that wants to keep screaming *no* louder so that he can force me harder.

But there's also the part of me that fissures every time he refuses to stop.

He pushes his tongue inside me, in and out, again and again, until the word *no* disappears from my lips completely. Until I push against his mouth, and he buries his face completely between my legs, marking it as a new territory he's conquering.

When he attacks my clit again, my eyes flutter closed. No matter how much I try to accept this passively, to not participate in the madness, he pushes harder, dragging moans out of me, thrusts of my hips, pants of pleasure. And those are the things he *sees*. He doesn't know about the floods of bliss flowing through my body or the coil tightening in my lower belly.

He can't feel my pleasure so close to exploding into a thousand stars.

Or maybe he can.

Because I'm lost in the decadence, twisting my fingers in the sheets, grinding against his tongue. When sweat pearls at my hairline from focusing on reaching my high, and when I realize I'm so wet the slickness trails all the way to my ass cheeks...he stops.

I gasp in oxygen, and it swallows the *no* I'm trying to scream at the same time.

"Would you like to come, my sunflower?"

I bite my lower lip, but the hopeless *yes* still comes out. I attempt to wrap my legs around his shoulders, and he stops me with a deadly grip, keeping them wide open.

"Would you like me to give this needy pussy what she needs?"

I nod slowly, throwing an arm over my face. "Yes."

"Why don't you show me how good you can beg, and I'll see if it deserves an orgasm?"

I loathe the spark his words ignite in my body again. He grazes his teeth against my needy nub, and I shiver all over again.

"Pl—" I lick my lips. This is so hard. "Please."

The tip of his tongue plays with me again, sending sensations through my belly, up my spine.

"Please, Nate," I whimper.

"Keep going." His breath against me could set me off. The flicker of a flame near gunpowder.

"Make me co—" A shaky breath breaks my word flow. "C-come, please."

"Getting better. Carry on."

"Please!" I twist my hips. My calves rest on his shoulders, and I tense them, trying to pull myself closer to him. "Please, Nate...please. I need this."

I whimper when he shrugs my legs off his shoulders, pulling away from me. He stands up, wiping his mouth with the back of his hand. My feet fall to the floor, chain clinging, and I gaze up at his towering form.

He observes my face for a minute. Tilting his head to the side, I watch helplessly as he learns every curve, every dip, everything that shows how desperate I am for him to bring down the guillotine over my neck and let me fall over to the darkness.

"Yes, I see it now. It's beautiful." The corner of his mouth tips up. "The despair."

Squeezing my eyes shut, I do my best not to let another whimper breach my lips. "Nate—"

"No need to embarrass yourself further, little sunflower. I don't require any more begging."

I fight past the trembling in my limbs to sit up, and he cups the back of my head "Don't move. I want to talk about what you said before your shower. About wondering if I could make you come."

Before I know it, he's plunging two fingers into my swollen pussy. My back curves, helping to accommodate the assault. He pumps them in and out, shattering my breathing all over again.

"Look at me."

My eyes snap to his, letting him suck the soul out of my body as he brings me near the brink of orgasm again.

"Open your mouth."

I'm already panting, opening my mouth barely takes any effort. He pulls his fingers out, shoving them so far into my mouth I would have fallen back if he wasn't holding my head in place. I choke around him, on my own taste. He pushes farther and I gag, my eyes watering.

He leans down.

"Kayla," he murmurs in my ear. "Does this taste like I can't make you come?"

I shake my head and squeeze my eyes shut, trying to breathe through my nose.

"No?"

"No!" I shriek against his hand.

"I'm glad we agree. Now you know that every time you doubt my capabilities, I'll prove you wrong."

I fall back on the bed when he lets me go, panting and sweating, but mostly fucking turned on.

"I'll be out for the rest of the day, and then out of town for two. I've now made the chain long enough for you to reach the bathroom and even the door if you need to open it and call for anything. Daniel will be bringing you food and there is a guard staying here called Enzo. He's very nice, but don't bother him if it's not urgent."

"Wait, wait...you're leaving me here? Chained to a fucking bed?"

I sit up again.

"I'm coming back late tonight and leaving early tomorrow morning. You'll probably be sleeping."

"You can't leave me!"

He huffs. "Kayla, I've put everything in place for you to be comfortable. You need to recuperate from the night of the Death Cage fight, and you need a few days to accept your situation. I am giving you that. Papers will be drawn by the time I come back, and we've got a date booked to sign at the town hall."

"Surely, I need to sign a marriage license before that," I say bitterly.

He waves a hand in the air. "According to the clerk at the Circuit Court, you already did."

My mouth drops open. "Did you forge my signature? How did you get my I.D.?"

"Your I.D. was at your house. While you were resting at your friends', I took it and sorted our marriage license. My good friend at the Circuit Court didn't mind your absence, nor the few missing info."

I narrow my eyes at him. "That's illegal, Nate."

"Yes, and as we both know, I hate doing anything illegal."

I grit my teeth, standing up to pull at the nightgown and give myself some sense of privacy now that he can't see my pussy directly anymore.

"Don't worry, little sunflower. Our license is perfectly valid. We can get married in three days when we have our appointment."

He grabs me by the waist, lifting me so quickly and easily, it makes me dizzy for a second. Then he sets me down on a chair by a vanity and puts the breakfast plate in front of me. "Now eat. I've got work to do."

Dropping a soft kiss at the top of my head, he leaves like this is a normal Monday morning. Like we're a normal engaged couple, and he's my loving fiancé going to work.

I eye the plate, then the room.

This can't be my life...it just *can't.*

13

NATHAN

Celebrity Skin - Hole

The water turns pink as I wash my hands. I lather my skin with soap for the third time, making sure to get the crimson liquid under my nails before I rinse again and turn the cold tap off. Grabbing the cloth Sam hands me, I turn back to the mess behind us.

The woman gagged and tied to a metal chair is still crying. She's silent now, though. Her whimpers have quieted. Her husband is doing a lot worse. His chin to his chest, he struggles to breathe, and I can understand he's been through a tough couple of days. They both have.

"Mr. Campbell," I say casually as I walk toward him. Sam is still standing by the sink, observing us. "I apologize our meeting had to take such a complicated turn, but I did warn you to accept my first offer."

He manages to lift his head, bloodshot eyes going to his wife. "You got what you wanted. Let my wife go."

"Of course." I nod toward Sam.

While he undoes the woman's binds and helps her pull

away the tape from around her face, I use my cloth to clean Campbell's right hand of blood.

I made sure to cut off his pinky from the left hand so he could still sign with his right, but some blood splattered when I was beating up his face.

"Here you go." I put a manila folder on the nearby table and drag his chair for him to face it. Opening it, I grab the pen in the pocket of my button-down and hand it to him. I undo the cuff holding his right hand to the arm of the chair.

"Take your time," I tell him.

He looks down at the documents Garcia-Diaz drafted for us.

"They'll kill me," he sobs. "Please...they'll kill me."

Mr. Campbell's chain of hotels has been very successful over the years. Of course it was when the Bratva Wolves were using it as an investment to wash dirty money. Then they'd take fees from Campbell's profit.

I will keep its luxurious reputation going when I own the five East Coast hotels and wash my money with it. Unlike the Wolves, I don't need a stranger as a third party between me and washing money. Whereas they had to go through Campbell, I can own the business and reap the profits. I have a little secret weapon for that.

First, I'm taking the businesses the Wolves have, making sure they know the biggest Cosa Nostra family is back and not fucking around.

I wasn't meant to be part of the Cosa Nostra. Technically speaking, I have no idea how linked I ever was to them when I was born. I was too little when I was abandoned, barely a toddler. But there's a reason Mateo Bianco, the head of the Bianco family, took me and my siblings in. He didn't have kids, and he wanted a legacy. I was the eldest, followed by my younger sister and brother. Twins. I was responsible for following Bianco's steps.

And I did exactly that. I did what I was taught when I put Bianco away. Cut off the head, kill the people who are too loyal to accept me in power, and take over the kingdom. Or, in this case, the Bianco family. I'm such a good student. It's too bad some sneaky little thing put me in prison before I could enjoy it. But I'm back now, and business is booming.

Once I take over the Wolves, I'll show the Cosa Nostra families—the Lucianos and the Rossis—that if I can take on the Wolves, they'll have to step away from Stoneview and its surroundings. Leaving me to control the area.

Easy.

When Campbell keeps crying instead of signing, the frustration gets to me. Why does everyone have to waste my time?

"Mr. Campbell." I'm calm, but the undertone of annoyance in my voice tells Sam to bring his wife over by the hair. Her whimpers make him shiver.

"Michael," she cries as Sam pulls out his gun and presses it against her temple.

"You don't understand," he tells me, voice trembling.

"I do understand," I say flatly. "Drying tears, snot, the redness of your cheeks. Your pulse is beating so hard that the skin at your throat is moving along with it. Your hands are shaking, your shoulders hunched, your leg bouncing. You're terrified."

I turn to Sam, proudly showing him how good I am at this.

He rolls his eyes. "Rach and Lik hate when I'm late to dinner. Will you move this along?"

I shrug, turning back to my victim. "See? I understand.

Now sign. We wouldn't want Sam to be late for dinner. I don't care about his other two partners, but he won't make my sister wait for him." I make sure to throw a deadly look his way before tapping the papers again. "Go on, Mr. Campbell."

"You don't understand," he repeats. "The W—The Wolves, if they learn I signed the hotels away...you don't understand."

"For fuck's sake," Sam growls. "I'm going to be so late."

I scratch behind my ear, looking down at the shaking man in front of me. Tilting my head, I try to squeeze my chest, to put pressure against my eyes, forcing myself to feel something. *Anything.*

It doesn't come. All I feel is irritated that Sam might be late for dinner with my sister. All I feel is excitement that the *Cascade Hotels* chain is about to be added to my portfolio of riches.

"Mr. Campbell, I thought our two days together made our agreement very clear. Sign the transfer of ownership." I release a huff, pretending to actually care. "Because, do you know what I would really hate?"

He shakes his head, avoiding looking into my eyes. "Bringing your daughters into this."

"Oh god," his wife whimpers next to me.

I notice his eyes shining with tears again, and in a swift gesture, I grab his hair, pulling his head back. "Don't you cry on that contract. No blood. No tears. Now sign."

"O-okay. Okay."

"Atta boy. Let's move this along."

I let him go and watch him put his signature on the document.

"Here. I signed. Please let us go. Please. My...my daughters."

I close the manila folder, making sure to pull it away safely and into the briefcase we brought.

"It truly was a pleasure doing business with you, but I have to say, your greed will keep bringing you trouble. My advice? Stop dealing with mobsters. You don't have what it takes."

I uncuff him, and Sam frees his wife.

"I'm sure your daughters will be delighted to come home to two very alive parents. Have a lovely evening."

It takes forever to drive back to Stoneview. The evening traffic on the way from Washington D.C. slows us down, and when Sam's phone rings, my eyes stay stuck on the car screen.

Lovebug.

That's his nickname for my sister.

"I want to kill you," I say simply.

He hangs up on her, and a laugh bubbles in my throat. "Good luck when you get home."

"I told you I couldn't be late for dinner. There are rules to make a polyamorous relationship work, Nate. Having dinner together is one of them for us."

"So what? They let you get away with being a hitman, so long as you wash the blood off your hands before you sit down to eat?"

"Precisely."

I shake my head as my thoughts go back to my sibling, Rose. "You should have left this life behind. My sister deserves better than a man who works for me."

His jaw clenches, his hands tightening around the steering wheel. "I *tried* to leave it behind."

"It's disappointing that you failed."

"Nate," he grunts. "Put a filter on and keep your blunt comments to yourself."

"With you?" I snort. "I don't think so. If you can date my sister, you can take my comments."

"For fuck's sake," he huffs.

"Why don't you find a good job? Something legal?"

"Because you would be nothing without me," he snaps back, hard British consonants clipping. "You need someone to keep you in check, so you don't kill every fucker that gets in your way."

I cackle, lowering my sleeves that I bunched around my elbow to beat up Campbell. I grab my cufflinks in my pocket and slowly button my cuffs again.

"I was in prison for almost four years, my friend. You had all the time in the world to do something legal without my influence. You didn't have to take contracts. No one forced you to kill people, especially not me. Now, of course, I'd rather you work for me. But I'm selfish. You shouldn't *want* to work for me."

"Fine," he snaps. "You want the truth?"

"I know the truth, but I think it'd do you good to voice it."

"I didn't even make it past freshman year in high school. I have learned nothing in my life but how to kill and work for selfish criminals like you. Who is going to hire a man who can't rub two brain cells together unless it's to figure out the quickest way to off someone?"

"You are very intelligent. Don't underestimate yourself."

"But I have no education. I know where my strengths lie and killing pays well. I need money. Who do you think invested in Rachel's bakery? Who pays for Lik's lavish lifestyle, when all he wants to do in life is be taken care of?"

Traffic comes to a standstill, and he turns to me, black

eyes flaring with anger. "Who do you think pays to put Rose through college? And who will pay for her to go to law school?" He looks me up and down, upper lip curling, and goes for the jugular. "Her family wasn't exactly there to take care of her."

It's not that it upsets me, but I still want to grab the back of his head and bash it against the wheel.

Technically, I understand why. Because when it comes to taking care of my sister, he hit me right in the gut. He went for my ego. He criticized how I take care of something that belongs to me. But while I can understand the reasoning of the fire it starts within me; it doesn't mean I can muffle the flames.

I smile at him. "It's going to hurt both of us if we use our fists. You're big and strong. I'm furious, plus we're in a car. It's not exactly practical."

"You dish it out, but you can't take it," he answers, his voice trembling with anger.

I nod, taking in the criticism, thinking of how I can punish my best friend and make him hurt for what he said. He opens his mouth when the phone rings again and *Lovebug* reappears on the screen.

"You keep quiet," he orders in his low voice as he presses the green button.

"A bit busy. Anything urgent?"

"*Uh, yeah,* dinner," my sister answers in her raspy, no-nonsense voice. "*Since when are you too busy to talk to me?*" Her unimpressed tone twists something in my stomach.

We're alike, except she can feel so strongly it almost creates jealousy in me. My sister is a genius. Too smart for her own good, and I'm surprised she still hasn't figured out that Sam is hiding something. Something being me.

Love made her stupid. She trusts him blindly.

"*Where are you?*" she asks. "*And how long until you're home? Because Rach made homemade sushi, and she said I can be the serving platter. You'll be missing out on—*"

"I have to go," he snaps, cutting her off just as I'm about to grab my gun and fire at his head. He hangs up on her, his eyes wildly moving between me and the road.

"I'm going to kill you. I'll make it hurt too."

He huffs, running a hand across his face. "Pretend you didn't hear that."

"Pretend you're not bleeding to death once I stick a knife in your jugular."

"Nate." He takes a deep breath to calm himself down. "Let's just stop with the Rose topic. I'm sorry I said you didn't take care of her, okay? It wasn't your fault you were in prison for so long. Let's just..." He waves a hand my way, completely done.

"Don't worry." I can see he's sick of talking, and I'm sick of the topic, anyway.

The traffic picks up again, and I look at the other side of the highway, moving slowly too. My thoughts automatically go to business, because that's all I've ever been taught to do. At least I'm smart enough to be aware of it.

Sam doesn't come out of the car when he drops me off at my house. Probably in a hurry to go home to his band of partners.

I shrug my jacket off, nodding at Enzo as he rushes to stand up from his seat in the foyer. "Boss." He straightens his suit.

I haven't seen Kayla since giving her breakfast two days ago. As I thought, she was asleep during the short time I was back at the house, and then I was torturing Campbell for two days.

"Attorney Garcia-Diaz dropped this off, sir." He hands me a brown envelope, and I open it right away, eyeing the prenup.

"Great. Has everything been alright? Did you talk to Kayla?"

He shakes his head. "She didn't need anything, sir. I've just been here. Daniel has been the one going up to feed her and that's it. He's up there now."

The way he says his last sentence triggers something in me. It didn't sound like he just brought her food two minutes ago. It sounds like my cook has been up there for a while.

"How long ago did he go up?"

Enzo shrugs. "About thirty minutes ago."

I feel my eyebrows meeting my hairline before I get my surprise under control. "Has he been staying up there for thirty minutes every time he brings her food?"

He shrugs again. "I guess so, Boss."

With a smile, I tilt my head to the side. "Enzo. Shrug one more time and I'll break both your clavicles."

I appreciate the man for supporting my coup d'état against Bianco when I decided to become the head of the family, but I'm going to need him to start acting smarter than that.

"Yes, sir. He has. Nothing malicious. I think she just needed the company."

"Have you been up there?"

"I checked twice without them knowing. They were just talking."

"Thanks."

I stop by the first door to the left, throwing the envelope

on my desk before making my way upstairs. I force myself to slow down my walk when my feet insist on hurrying, but when I get to Kayla's room, I think maybe I should have run.

She's laughing on her bed, wearing a large white button-down and nothing else, her hands holding a plate with a burger and fries.

Daniel is taking pictures of her with his phone. Her gaze focuses on him, eyes small from laughing genuinely. His back is to me, so he has no idea I'm in the doorway.

Kay notices me first. She must have felt a presence. Startling, she drops the plate on her lap, fries flying off it and onto the sheets as the tower of the burger crumbles down.

"Nate," she gasps.

Daniel whips around, practically jumping on the spot from fear. His eyes round, his hand holding the phone drops by his side.

"Boss," he squeaks miserably.

I extend my arm, palm up, and he takes a split second to come to me, depositing the phone in my hand as excuses bubble up his throat. "I was just... I was just. I c-can explain. This isn't what you think."

"So you're telling me you weren't taking pictures of my fiancée half-naked on her bed, laughing like a burger and fries are so fucking hilarious."

"We can't see her face!" he justifies. "L-look at them. It's for... It's for..."

"Oh, so the teenage giggles really were specifically for you."

"No!" He eyes Kayla, panicking some more. "Oh my god."

"Nate." Kay's stern voice feels similar to what I'd

imagine someone grating chalk with a cheese grater would sound like. Fucking irritating.

And why? Why am I even getting so frustrated at this situation?

I stop for a second, focusing on my thoughts. Possession, of course. My objects belong to me, not my cook. Jealousy? Because she was laughing with him, when all she throws my way is anger? No, that sounds too strange to be correct. I don't care how Kay feels about me so long as I can hurt her and get what I want out of her.

"Nate," she repeats, louder so she can get me out of my thoughts.

My gaze snaps to her, and my hand wraps around the phone in a deadly grip.

"He was taking pictures for his socials. You said it yourself, he makes those really cool plates, and he thought having someone holding them would get him more likes on his account."

I take a step toward her, not really surprised that it doesn't make her flinch in the slightest.

"I'm sorry, is this an influencer bootcamp or my house?"

"You left me here for three days chained to a fucking bed. I've been keeping myself busy however I could." She crosses her arms over her chest, still sitting on her bed, and cocks an eyebrow at me.

I observe her disheveled hair, the undone buttons of the shirt. Tilting my head to the side, I ask, "Did you two fuck?"

"What?" she snorts.

"Your hair," I simply say.

"I was napping before he brought me food. I have nothing to do here but sleep."

I turn my head to him, keeping my tone even. "Did you not notice the engagement ring on her finger?"

"Boss, I promise, I would never." He shakes his head like a crazy man, his face now drained of blood.

"You sound fucking insane," Kay mocks me. "He's a kid."

"A kid? He's twenty-two, and he knows exactly what he's doing, just as he knows who he works for."

"Oh." Kay purses her lips as she observes him, clearly not attracted to him. "He looks like a teen. Plus I was only using him so I could ask to borrow his phone."

Little manipulative vixen.

"What about you?" I ask Daniel. "Were you doing this hoping you'd fuck her?"

"I would never," Daniel repeats, terror making him tremble on the spot. "I would *never.*"

I smile warmly at him. "Okay, Daniel. I believe you."

"Thank you," he squeaks. He joins his hands in a prayer motion. "Thank you, Boss. I'm so sorry about the misunderstanding."

I stroll to the bed, grabbing a fry from Kay's plate and taking the whole thing in my mouth. It's delicious. Perfectly crispy outside and soft inside. Just the right amount of salt.

I take the fork from a wooden platter on the bed and stab a bunch more fries before sticking the deliciousness in my mouth, moaning to myself.

"This is so good, Daniel."

Walking back to him, I tap his shoulder as I swallow. "Such a shame you won't be able to use your right hand anymore."

His eyes barely have time to widen that I've already taken hold of his right wrist, slamming his hand flat on the dresser. A split second later, I'm violently forcing the fork through his hand, impaling him to the furniture.

His scream is piercing. It would truly be heartbreaking to someone who gives a fuck.

"Holy shit!" Kay gasps, falling back from the shock as I turn to her. Catching herself on her hands, she crawls backward on the mattress until she hits the headboard.

"Get up," I order smoothly.

"You're insane!" She scrambles to the side opposite me, but before she can go anywhere, I grab the chain attached to her ankle, pulling her right back.

"What is *wrong* with you?" she cries out as I drag her across the bed. "You fucking kidnapped me, forced a ring on me, and keep repeating how much you want to punish me, but now you want to act like a jealous bastard?"

"This isn't jealousy," I explain as I grab her ankle, pull some more, and then take hold of the shirt, pulling her into a standing position. "This is an assertion of ownership."

I take the knife from the platter with me, drag her to the wall next to the bed, and push her face first against it.

"Can you see alright, Daniel?" I ask, worried about his view of the show.

"Please," he whimpers, voice raw from crying. "It hurts...it hurts, please take it out!" His free hand hovers around the handle of the fork, but he can't get himself to touch it.

"Answer the question," I insist. Kay tries to shrug me off her, but I pin her to the wall with a hand at the back of her neck. "You stay still, my darling sunflower."

"What the fuck are you doing?" she barks back at me. "Let me go."

"Don't make me tape your mouth shut. Put your hands flat on the wall."

She's incredibly predictable when she doesn't, and instead tells me to go fuck myself. I press the knife at her throat and repeat my order. Everyone is always set on making me waste my time.

"Kayla, hands on the wall. Now."

Left without a choice, she places her hands on either side of her head. They don't even shake, what with the brave little thing she is.

"Now, Daniel. Watch." With the knife, I point at the diamond shining around Kay's finger. "See this? This means I own her ass."

I tighten my grip on my fiancée, having to remind myself how this whole thing started. My heart is beating a little faster than usual, and I'm finding it harder to think, as if the control I have on my feelings is slipping through my fingers. My thoughts are like trying to grab a fistful of water.

Oh, yes. The picture.

"That means no spending time with her more than necessary. That means no taking pictures of her. I don't care if she's wearing nothing or a ski suit. I don't care if her face is in it, her cunt, her little pinky. *No. Pictures. Of. My. Fiancée.*"

Turning back to Kay, I make sure to talk in her ear. My frustration turns to anger, and it shocks me when I hiss, "I own your ass, is that clear?"

"You're hurting me," she grunts back, just so she can avoid answering.

I don't doubt I am with how hard my hand is pinching the back of her neck and the way I press her throat against the wall, forcing her face into an awkward angle.

"I know." I smile brightly at her. "Try not to get too wet."

I slide my hand down, fisting the shirt so the hem lifts all the way to her lower back. "I see you found the underwear drawer. Keep your hands on the wall."

With the hand holding the knife, I drag her silk thong all the way to her mid-thighs.

"Stay still, little sunflower. I would hate to make this worse than it has to be."

She attempts to look back, neck straining, and I watch her eyes round as I press the tip of the knife to her left ass cheek.

"Nate!" she shrieks. When blood pearls on her porcelain skin, a sense of relief washes over me. This is already feeling better.

I drag the blade down, relishing the peace it brings me.

"Nate, *stop.*" She doesn't dare move now. Not even a millimeter. She stays completely still, too scared of the knife causing irreparable damage.

I release her and kneel behind her. Still, she doesn't move.

Pressing harder, I feel lucky my initials are so easy to write. She hisses when I start the last bar of the N.

"Please." Her legs tremble, and I notice she's holding herself on her toes.

"You're going to exhaust yourself," I say softly. "Put your feet flat on the floor."

I pull the knife away for a second, giving her just enough time to drop her heels to the floor, and I finish my N.

"What are you doing?" she whimpers. "Stop."

"You should cry," I suggest. "It'll help with the pain."

"*Fuck you!*"

I shrug, starting the W. "As you wish."

"Just stop!"

Unlike what I recommended, she doesn't cry. It's stupid, really. I'm only trying to help.

She whimpers again when I'm halfway through the W, and I drop a kiss just below the wound. "I have to make it deep," I explain. "Or it'll go away instead of scarring."

"You don't *have* to do anything." The shakiness of her voice starts to get to me. And by that, I mean my dick is getting rock hard in my suit.

It's been two long days and seeing the wetness gathering between her pussy lips as I hurt her is giving me a burst of energy.

"We're going to be the perfect couple, Kayla," I whisper against her skin, just to anger her some more.

"Nate, *please*."

Despair.

I can hear it so clearly now. Her tone when she's begging always takes on higher notes.

"I'm almost done, little sunflower."

"No," she whimpers. "Nate..." Her forehead falls against the wall, completely giving up.

I finish the second letter and pull away to admire my work. It's right where her beautiful bubble butt curves, only an inch above her upper thigh. It's going to be painful to sit down for a while.

"It's beautiful," I tell her honestly.

There's too much blood right now to see it clearly. It's dripping from the cuts, spread from my wrist when I went over again.

I don't know what goes through my mind when I lean forward and lick her wound. A strange mewls escapes her, her hands closing into fists against the wall, and my cock strains against my pants.

I wholeheartedly plan to stop now. But her soaked

pussy is right there, her shameful pleasure practically dripping out of her.

I drop the knife to the floor, and before I can stop myself, I'm spreading her ass cheeks, burying my face into her pussy.

Her cry isn't lost on me, and she fights back until I get the chance to force my tongue inside her, licking her addictive taste.

"Fuck," she pants. "I hate you... I h-hate you."

As I twist my body, one shoulder hits the wall so I can go under her and lick her clit with ease. There's no taking my time. I'm a monster devouring its prey and said prey moans so beautifully, I can't do anything but keep going.

I nibble at her clit, filling myself with a sort of warmth I haven't felt in a while. It's the sounds she makes, the way she squirms, pressing against me, moaning with her mouth against the plaster.

"I can't do this." She's hopeless, and it feeds my hunger.

This is what I wanted. *This* is what feels good. Kayla King at my complete mercy, unable to tell if she wants pleasure or pain, unable to decide if she needs to live or die.

I have her fate in the palm of my hand, and I could crush her in a split second.

When I take a break, her body shudders. "Nate... please."

This is different.

This doesn't sound like despair.

I freeze, my mouth hovering above her clit, my hands moving from her ass to her thighs, digging in the flesh, keeping them apart.

"What is this?" I ask.

"What?" She's panting, shaking, her voice has an edge to it I don't fucking understand and it's driving me mad.

"What are you feeling, Kayla?" I insist sternly.

"I-I don't know!"

I press my mouth to her wet pussy, growling against her soft, slippery skin.

"Just *think*." I pull away again, and she whimpers. "Tell me what you're feeling, and I'll let you come."

I had no intention of letting her come whatsoever in the next few days. Especially not before we're officially married. But I want—scratch that. I *need* to know what she's feeling. The excitement of understanding Kayla so I can hurt her further burns through my veins.

"I-I'm not sure."

"It's not despair." I know, because I learned despair from her. It's not that. She's using *please*, but it's different.

"No, it's not. I—" I lick her clit slowly, gently, showing her what she could get if she's a good girl.

"Name it."

"Shit," she hisses. "Anticipation."

"No."

"Yearning," she squeals as I bite her clit gently. "I need to come. Please, I don't know..."

I lick her again, teasing her so lightly, she tenses, muscles locking beneath my touch.

"*Craving!*" Her desperate scream fills me with dangerous electricity.

Craving. Yes, that's it.

"Very good," I mumble against her clit.

As I promised, my satisfaction comes with a reward. I hold her still, licking her over and over again at the exact same pace, draining any remnants of sanity she had left.

"Fuck," she moans. "Fuck...fuck."

Curiosity gets the best of me, and I bring my middle finger to her entrance. I barely push in, her pussy tightening and dragging me inside. I'm the one who has to hold back a groan when I press my mouth harder, and her walls contract around me.

"Nate," she pants, her voice a crescendo toward oblivion. "Nate...*Nate!*"

She yells, a mix of a rasp and her soul leaving her body. Her forehead hits the wall three times before she relaxes, and her knees give up. She falls to the floor, and from my position, I can barely catch her. I manage to grab her waist and flatten my legs as she falls on my lap, pressing my back against the wall. She ends up straddling me, her face in front of mine.

Her flushed cheeks aren't what pulls at something inside me. It's the stars in her green eyes. The shining mist that gives her the look of a fairy. Her black hair counters that, and that awful tattoo along her hairline reading 'HELL' shows who she really is. A demon with beautiful eyes that hide a broken soul. A soul now shattered by an overwhelming orgasm.

"Tell me."

She takes a staggered breath, lets her head fall against my shoulder, and whispers, "Satisfaction."

"Mm." I bring my right hand to the back of her head, scratching her scalp in a soft gesture. "Good to hear."

Because for every single emotion I understand from Kayla, it's a new weapon in my arsenal to destroy her.

"Please..." The pained voice makes me look up, and I'm suddenly reminded of Daniel and his hand impaled on the dresser.

I reach inside my pocket, and while Kayla is lost in her own world, her head resting on my shoulder, I undo the cuff at her ankle.

I tap her thigh. "Go shower. I need you in my office

afterward."

Instead of getting up, she bucks her hips, pressing her hot core against my hard-on. She doesn't look up from my shoulder, only uttering a pathetic whimper.

"I'll return the favor," she whispers, ashamed of what she's offering. She's clearly still horny and her brain clouded from the orgasm.

I chuckle. Fisting her hair, I pull her head back so she's looking at me. She winces, her beautiful features twisting.

"I'm not like you, Kayla. I'm not weak to the person I hate just because they can make me come. Now get your desperate pussy off my dick and go shower."

I pull her off me by the hair, sending her flying to the side. She gasps when she crashes against the floor, but catches herself flat on her hands at the last second.

Standing, I dust off my pants, smiling at myself when I see the wet spot on my crotch.

I turn around, looking down at her. "Dirty girl."

Then I'm back on my way to Daniel. I yank the fork out of his hand with more strength than I thought I'd need, and to his credit, he holds back another scream.

Damn, I was angry when I stabbed him. I can't even remember why. Now that I have Kayla's taste lingering on my tongue and her desperate form looking up at me from the floor, my violence seems like it was unnecessary. I guess that's what happens when Sam isn't here to stop me.

"You're fired." He doesn't wait to be told twice. He's out of the room in a split second, cradling his hand to his chest. I walk after him, not giving Kayla a last look.

I want to make sure she knows she is still less than nothing.

This is her own personal hell.

And she fucking belongs to me.

14

KAYLA

AMERICAN HORROR SHOW - SNOW WIFE

I wipe the mist on the mirror with my forearm and barely hold back a groan. I don't like how I look. It's not as bad as three days ago. The eye bags are gone, my nose isn't swollen anymore, and the bruise on my cheek is greenish rather than black and purple.

But something is wrong and it shows in my gaze. The green is still sparkling from the orgasm Nate gave me, and it's only lessened by my self-loathing.

I turn around, looking at the initials on my ass cheek, and I bite my lower lip to not let out a desperate whimper. It's red, burning, a part of the W still bleeding. A mark from the devil himself.

How did I let this happen?

No matter how much I want to put this on the threat of the knife or Nate's overpowering strength, I know it's not. It's my own weakness. He's right; I'm weak. Desperate. I let the person I hate the most in the world make me feel good. I feel like a deer that approached a hunter for petting.

What I need is better control over my body. What I need is to stop getting aroused every time he hurts me or forces me. Because that's fucked. It's completely suicidal. Nate has enough advantages. I can't give him more ammunition to make me bend to his will.

I take a deep breath, holding it in my lungs as I search the mirror for the strong woman I know I can be. My shoulders shrink when I huff, so I try again.

How many times have I had to get back up when I was down? How many times did I keep walking after people tried to break my legs? I am not weak. My body knows that like it knows how to breathe. It's instinctual, ingrained in my very soul.

Another breath. Another block. Finally, I watch my face harden, my expression fortifying. The brightness in my eyes dims. *Finally*, I look like Kayla King, queen of the North Shore.

I'm so out of place in a white marble bathroom lined with gold. Gold taps, gold shower head, gold handles. Pure, angelic white countertop. I belong in my half-burned house. I belong in the dilapidated streets of my broken town.

And I'll fight with everything I have to leave the gilded cage Nathan White is trying to put me in.

I square my shoulders, tighten the towel around my chest, and walk back into the bedroom. The bastard left a white satin robe on the bed, so I purposely go to the walk-in closet and grab a pair of underwear, a bra, a large t-shirt, and some sweats. I discovered all the clothes the morning he left. A closet full of outfits my size. Apart from the sexy underwear I'm sure he made a point of picking, there's a bit of everything. Clothes I'm happy to wear. But there's also a section I don't want to look at. A section of dresses and suits the first lady would own. Types of clothes I wouldn't be caught dead wearing.

I'm grateful for the thong when I put it on, knowing I couldn't stand anything touching the wound on my ass cheek right now. It's still throbbing like hell, and I'm glad it's nowhere I can see.

Fucking asshole.

Marking me like fucking cattle.

I'm going to ruin his life. I'm going to bury him so deep, even the worms won't be able to reach his corpse.

I don't care to brush or dry my hair. I put on what looks like running shoes. The expensive kind that would make me want to put them in a glass box rather than go on an actual run with them.

Just for the sake of it, I open the window and throw out the see-through satin robe. I look down, not for the first time since I've been here. The first thing I checked when he left was if I could jump out should he ever take that fucking chain off. The answer was no. We're too high and there's nothing to hold on to, nothing to catch my fall. Just a twenty-foot drop because rich people's mansions are dumb like that. They love their high ceilings on the first floor.

For a second, as I watch the robe get caught in the late summer breeze and land farther down, I imagine my broken body on the ground. What's better? Marriage with Nate or a painful death?

With a huff, I step back. Neither. I'm going to find a way out. My girls are waiting for me on the outside. They need me, and I won't give up. Every single fight I put up will be for them.

Nate isn't smarter than me, he's just been planning this for longer. We have to leave the house at some point to go to the town hall. I will be gone before we marry. That's a promise.

Never again will he chain me, mark me, hurt me.

Never again will he bring me pleasure.

I stop by the kitchen before I go to his office. I look at his set of knives, blades held by a magnet strip on the wall. Taking the smaller one, I put it in the band of my underwear. Then I grab the biggest one in my right hand.

Time to have a discussion with my dear fiancé.

When I cross the foyer again, I hear a toilet flushing. Shit. His guard. I hurry toward his office, not knocking before I walk in.

Nate is at his desk, sitting back, relaxed. His gaze is glued to his phone as he types. Eyes blinking slowly, his face stays as passive as ever. He's got his glasses on. Thick black rims framing his beautiful eyes. He looks like a handsome geek with his sandy blond hair brushed back, a soft strand falling at the corner of his glasses.

"Sit down." He doesn't even look up, calmly finishing his text.

I don't. Before he can see me, I pinch the knife by the blade, pulling my arm back. I take a gulp of air, block, and throw, exhaling sharply.

He grunts. That's all he does.

The phone clatters to the ground, and his hand shoots to his shoulder, where his white shirt is now colored a deep red. His surprised stare digs into me, but I don't waste any time. I sprint toward him, sliding across his desk and landing on him. His chair tumbles back, and we both fall to the floor. He takes the hit, air freezing in his lungs as his mouth drops open. Leaving the large blade in his shoulder, I reach into my sweats, seizing the small knife and holding it to his throat.

I'm straddling his stomach. Since we're still on the chair, his thighs are stuck between my back and the seat, now perpendicular to the floor. The first thing he does is kick the chair from under us so he can lie flat on the floor. I slide lower, sitting on his hips. It gives me a better grip on him.

"You want to mark me, Nate?" I hiss in his face. "I'll mark you back."

He blinks up at me, and a smile spreads on his lips. "That hurt, little sunflower."

He can't move his left arm, the pain in his shoulder probably too intense. But his right hand snatches my wrist, holding the knife closer against his skin, pressing, dragging red liquid to the surface. He bucks his hips, pushing into my core.

The motherfucker is hard.

"You're fucking sick."

"It turns me on to know you can fight back. It's like you're begging me to go harder on you next time."

I shove my knees into his ribs. "There is no next time. Let me out of this fucking house."

"But baby, look at us. We're so compatible." The worst is, he probably believes those words.

"Nate," I bark. But my threat is empty when he's the one holding the knife to his throat. His hand is wrapped around mine, and I lose any sort of power if I'm not the one menacing him.

"Harder, Kay. Show me how far you're willing to go."

"I'll kill you."

"Do it."

My eyes narrow on him. What kind of fucked-up game is he playing?

"Kill me and go handle NSC. Kill me and let your pitiful crew get eaten by your enemies. Only one person has a leash on Emma, and that's me."

"I can handle Emma Scott."

"Without money? With a weakened crew? After giving her the entire North Shore? Please, think before you speak."

His words hit me right in my pride. I would rather die than ever admit defeat against NSC.

"I can *fucking* handle Emma Scott."

His knowing smile makes my palm sweat around the hilt of the knife. "Then *kill. Me.*"

He tightens his grip on my hand. Three deep breaths later, I still haven't killed him, and I can't find a single reason why. But that's about as long as he decides to give me.

I was wrong when I said he wasn't moving his left arm because of the pain. Suddenly, I feel his left hand under me. I startle, but I can't get off him. Then he'd be free of me, and I'd be in a weak position. Even on top of him, with a kitchen knife perforating his shoulder and another at his throat, I'm in a weak position.

He doesn't touch me, and I wonder what he's doing until I hear the zipper of his pants. When he shifts again, I feel his hard dick against me.

"You fucking sick bastard." I'm furious. Not even at him, at myself. Because after that tough-love self-talk in the bathroom, I feel myself getting wet again.

What was the point of trying to find the strong woman in me if she disappears the second Nate touches me?

"Don't move, little sunflower."

He pulls at my sweats. It's almost painful because of the way I'm sitting. He has to use strength, violence in minimal movements, until they finally give, and he manages to lower them just enough to pull my thong to the side and press his hard-on against my soaking entrance.

He chuckles, so satisfied with himself I could punch him.

"Stop this, you fucking maniac."

He shakes his head. "Kill me."

He doesn't even have space to rub the length of his dick against me, so he can't prepare me or himself. Our bodies are too close together already.

No, all he can do is spear into me without mercy.

My mouth falls open, my eyes fluttering shut. "Shit." The hiss I intended is a desperate rasp.

"How are you feeling, Kayla?"

"*Fuck you.*"

"You don't mind if I fuck you first, do you?"

He pushes inside me, ripping a moan from deep within my chest. He can't thrust all the way out and back in, not in this position. Instead, he fucks me deep, with small movements.

"Stop," I whimper. "This is fucked. You're fucked. I hate you."

But I'm the one who presses my knife against him and rolls my hips. I'm the one who searches for friction against his pubis for my clit to get some drunken satisfaction.

Instead of answering, he uses his left hand to rip the kitchen knife out of his shoulder. He doesn't even make a noise. Throwing it to the side, he then puts a hand at my hip.

"I think you've had enough fun for today."

He flips us around before I can even take my next breath. Before I know it, the knife is at my throat, his hand still around mine. The fact that I should have killed him is a reality hitting me right in the gut.

He now has plenty of space to thrust into me like a madman. His movements pin me to the floor, stopping me from taking a proper breath. His violence pulls guttural noises out of me, cuts my breathing, turns me beastly.

I can't even scream. I can't fight, I'm too taken by his intensity.

The insults I want to throw his way are cut off by the pleasure spearing into me. Instead of fighting back, my head falls against the floor. With the knife digging into my throat, I feel the thickness of blood sliding around my neck. Worse, his shoulder wound is dripping onto me, the drops soaking his shirt slowly trickling onto my chest. Using his free hand, he spreads his own blood against me, painting me with the pain I caused him.

"What angered you, Kayla? That I marked you?"

He grunts, forcing his hard dick against my cervix and making me lose control. A shriek escapes me, pain and euphoria mixing. "Did you want to show me you're still your own person? Did you want to show you could still fight back?"

I can't answer, my lungs are too tight. They're crushed by the pleasure leaving my lower stomach and consuming my body. It locks my muscles, making me incapable of defending myself.

"Keep fighting. Keep showing me how strong you are. It feeds the fire I have to destroy you." Pulling back, he leaves only his tip at my entrance. "Every time, I'll show you who you belong to." He thrusts back in. "I'll show you there's nothing you can do. You can't escape."

He brings his bloody hand to my face, roughly pressing his thumb against my lips and pushing it inside my mouth. The coppery taste of his blood makes me gag, and yet I tighten around him, and I feel more delight taking over my senses and dizzying my mind.

"You're marrying me tomorrow, and it'll only get worse from then on. I'll use you. I'll destroy everything you are, and you'll be nothing but my *docile little wife.*"

I try to shake my head, but his grip on my face hardens. His face twists into a sick smile, the demon he truly is showing.

"And do you know what a good little wife does, Kayla?"

I whimper when I feel the gunpowder lighting up. There's nothing to stop it now.

"She comes on her husband's dick."

A scream tears from my lips, ripping me apart when my orgasm shatters me whole. He lowers himself, pulling the knife away, and licks the wound at my throat. It's not fatal. Of course not. It hurts just enough to remind me of my place. To show me the consequences of fighting back.

His thrusts accelerate, and when he comes inside me, fear washes away my momentary high. I pray to God my contraceptive shot doesn't let me down. Because nothing would be worse at this point than something else attaching me to Nate.

I close my eyes as he gets off me, stupidly thinking this is over. That's until I feel him kneel between my open thighs, his fingers at my entrance. Like the insane man he is, he's pushing his leaking cum back inside.

"I wonder what you'd look like pregnant."

My eyes fly open. "I'm on the shot."

He tilts his head to the side. "These things run out."

"I don't want kids."

I don't tell him the truth. I don't show anything. If he knew the truth, everything would spiral. Worse than it already is. I can't even imagine it.

"Did you know twins run in my family?"

Yes.

My eyes dart around his face, noticing the way he's trying to read my mind.

Scared he actually might, I talk to move things along. "I know your siblings are twins."

Shoving his fingers deeper, I tremble, the overstimulation too great. He presses a hand on my lower belly. "You'd swell so beautifully."

He moves his fingers, fucking me slowly. A torture of intensity and softness.

"Stop..."

"Give me a little more, little sunflower."

A shuddered breath leaves me, wrapping around the words I'm trying to utter. "I c-can't."

"You can. Think how stuck you'll be once I make you have my kids. Imagine our beautiful little family. The mother of my kids, married to the man who kidnapped her."

"No," I whimper, my eyes squeezing shut as the pleasure doubles from his fingers curling.

"Amuse me. Feed my imagination. Come on my fingers from thinking of your entire life by my side."

What he doesn't understand is that my imagination is twice as vivid as his. I can picture my fear of having him around them. How he would never *ever* let us go.

And for the third time today, I explode from his touch, hating myself, hating the situation, *hating him.*

Wiping his drenched fingers on my cheek, he stands

up. "I had other plans in this office tonight, but I think you need some rest."

Strength leaves me, the will to fight dissipating as he looks down at me.

This torment will never end. Exactly like he wanted.

15

KAYLA

Save Me Some Sunshine - Rafferty

"I don't understand."

My eyes skim the document he just put in front of me before going back to the title.

Prenuptial Agreement.

I would never admit it, but it's an enormous amount of pressure to be sitting at his desk, in his seat. The same one that makes him look so big and impressive. With a pen held tight in my hand, and all my focus on stopping said hand from trembling, I feel like a kid at her dad's desk.

A kid who doesn't get the big, complicated adult words.

This is why math is so much better. It always means the same thing. Anyone can understand it.

Words are difficult, and Nate is using that against me.

"There's nothing to understand," Nate says for the fifth time. "However, we do have to be at the town hall by eleven a.m., so I'd appreciate your pretty signature on the paper, Kayla." There's no impatience in his tone, only in the words he chooses.

Looking down again, I turn the page around. Even with my eyes on the paper, his hip is in my field of vision. I can see his thigh pressing against the desk. He's standing right next to the bloodstains on the floor where he fucked me yesterday.

The memory enhances the stinging pain on my throat, and sitting the way I am burns the mark on my ass.

This is fucking ridiculous. I'm not about to sign a prenup with the man who is holding me against my will and spreading blood on me when he fucks me.

And when he makes you come.

Fuck.

"I..." I hesitate, hating the stark difference between the educated asshole next to me, who probably had private tutors, and the minimum knowledge I got from North Shore High. When I showed up.

"This." I point at a clause. "I th—" I cut myself off from saying *"I think."* I need to at least pretend I know what I'm talking about. I read the sentence over and over again, squinting my eyes, tilting my head, trying to make it make sense. "It says you'll get everything if we divorce or if I die."

Unlike how long it took me to string my sentence together, he's quick to reply.

"You have no one else to give it to if you die anyway, and the more I get to play with you, the less likely I am to let you divorce me. So we're good."

I do my best to stay focused despite the wave of anxiety rolling through me when he talks about divorce, or lack thereof.

"I have family." He doesn't need to know exactly who I mean by family, and I purposely keep my gaze on the document.

But it seems he's sick of chatting. His hand wraps

around my jaw, forcing me to look up at him as his fingers dig into my skin.

"You have nothing to your name." Couldn't sound more unimpressed if he tried.

"Exactly." My eyes narrow. "What I want to understand is why you would want all my shares of nothing."

"See it as another way to have complete ownership over you."

"I'm not an object, Nate," I hiss. "You can't *own* me."

For a second, I see the confusion in his eyes. It seems object versus human is still a concept he's finding difficult to wrap his head around.

Shrugging, he finally says. "It's as close as I can get. All of you and everything you have will belong to me."

I feel like there's something I'm still missing. There is *nothing* that belongs to me.

"What if it's the other way around?" I ask. "If we divorce, or better yet, if you die, what do I get?"

"I don't know how much clearer I can be, but let me try again. It is very, very unlikely we'll ever divorce, Kayla. Even after four years, even if you beg me on your knees. The only way it would happen is me getting bored, but again, I don't see that coming. Seeing you suffer feeds me with new energy every time. So, don't worry about what you're signing."

Jaw tight, I'm forced to take a breath through my nose. "What if you die?"

The answer comes so fast there's no doubt in it. "If I die, everything goes to my siblings."

"And I'm free?"

He licks his lips, a smile spreading on his face. "Why? Thinking of trying to kill me again? Yesterday was already a failure, and every day you're going to grow closer to me.

Chances of falling for me are getting higher by the hour. Time is against you when it comes to Stockholm syndrome."

"I'll kill you right fucking now."

I can't, of course. His grip on my face is so unforgiving I can barely feel my cheeks anymore, and even if I tried to go for the gun in his holster, he'd have it out of my hands in no time. It would be a stupid mistake to forget Nate used to be Bianco's right-hand man. And he got rid of his boss like it meant nothing to him. He is a Cosa Nostra criminal. He is as ruthless as they come.

Underestimating his power would be deeply detrimental to my survival.

"Still waiting." His voice startles me, and I realize my eyes must have been darting around, looking for something to put my threat into action.

I close my eyes for a few seconds, trying to think clearly. I can't do that when his ocean eyes dig into mine, daring me to drown in them.

So, instead of thinking of the long run, I think of what I need now.

When I open my eyes again, I soften my stare from the one I'm used to giving, and I ask, "Will you give me a phone if I sign this?"

A slight line appears between his eyebrows, disappearing just as quickly.

"You said if I did things you liked, you'd give me things I need in exchange."

I try to read his reaction, but it's impossible. Trying is like attempting to predict which way to swim when you're stranded in the middle of the ocean.

"Ah, yes. You wanted a phone."

"My crew needs to know what to do," I lie. "I don't want

them to be in trouble because I can't pass on what Emma and I agreed to."

"And you didn't do that when you hid at Elliot's house?"

I gulp, feeling caught. "I did, but not everything. I was hurt, too. Concussion, remember? I just want to make things clear with him."

"Sign the prenup," he says calmly. "And then if you beg really nicely, I'll give you that phone."

My thighs press together. I know what begging looks like to Nate. I'm quick to feel the dampness between my legs, even if it's discreet. I'm not wearing anything but a satin robe. The same one I had thrown out of the window. He put me to bed naked yesterday, left it on my bed, and locked the walk-in closet. So this morning I didn't have a choice.

He lets go of my face, giving me what I'm sure he believes is a choice. I hold the pen tighter, draw my signature on his stupid prenup, and slam the thing on the desk.

"Here. Done."

I thought I'd see a smile on his face, but there's only entitlement. Because to him, there was no other way this was going to go.

"Very good. There's an outfit on your bed. Go put it on, we need to leave soon."

"The phone." My voice is stern because that's my default setting, but when I see the disapproval on his face, I repeat my request meekly... As much as I hate it.

"Um, the phone, please? I really need it."

He straightens, pushing away from the desk. Grabbing the armrest, he swings the chair around so I'm facing him and leans down to face me. "Is that what you call begging, little sunflower?"

LOLA KING

I always find it strange the way he adds *little*. I'm not little. Not physically and not in my behavior. I guess next to him, I am. I guess next to him, I'm nothing.

"Please, Nate," I huff. "A phone is a basic need."

"Food and water are basic needs. A bed is a basic need. I'm providing you with that. Anything else will come with begging on your knees."

This is it, isn't it? A taste of what every day of my fucking life will look like by his side. This is his revenge. This is what I knew would happen if he ever got out.

This is the risk I took by sending him to prison. By attempting to take him down.

"We will be running late to our appointment if you keep stalling, Kayla. Do you want a phone now?"

My eyes drop to my lap, my teeth gnawing at my lower lip. My pride is about to take the hit of its life, but I would do anything to get in contact with my family again. Even if it's only been a few days.

I hold my breath as I get to my knees in front of him, sitting on the heels of my feet. I keep my eyes on the floor, my hands on my thighs, and my voice is barely a whisper.

"Please." I gulp, my throat narrowing and choking me. "Can I have a phone?"

I ignore the sound of his buckle and squeeze my eyes shut when the zipper of his pants makes a loud noise as it lowers.

I feel him shift and sense his boxers lowering. A wave of heat from his skin hits me in the face, and in the next second, his fingers are pinching my chin, making me look up at his hard length in front of me.

"This is what seeing you on your knees does to me."

He's gripping his cock with his other hand, making it swell even harder. When he grazes the velvet tip against my

194

lips, my body shudders. He must feel it at the tip of his fingers holding me because a slow smile spreads on his lips.

"I don't need words for you to beg, little sunflower."

The scent of his body wash mixed with the warmth of him against me makes me heady. There's nothing more intoxicating than his attention. I have a sudden urge to open my mouth wide, to take him in and taste him. And the voice that should be telling me to wake the fuck up and not enjoy this is suddenly horrifyingly quiet.

"I have a burner phone in this very drawer." And I'm sure he means the one right to the left of my head.

What starts as a need to lick my lips ends up with my tongue caressing his crown. It's a mistake. A huge fucking mistake. My body fights against me, mouth watering, thighs clenching.

What the fuck is wrong with me?

The phone. You want the phone.

A simple graze with the tip of my tongue turns into licking his tip, then his length. When I touch his fingers gripping himself, he moves his hand, sliding it into my hair instead. I keep going, flicks and swirls of my tongue that I can't stop until I've gone all the way to his base and savored my way back to the tip.

Fuck, I hate myself. I hate how wet I am, and I hate the way my thighs strain from tightening to ease the ache. I hate that he tastes so fucking good to me, so addictive.

"Kneel up and put me in your mouth, Kayla. You're clearly starved for me."

Starved? He has no fucking idea what it's been like to not feel pleasure and satisfaction for four years. To fake an entire sexual relationship with a man who could not make me come even if he tried his hardest.

He doesn't understand me coming three times since he's been back is a record.

Moving up and placing my weight on my knees, I squeeze my eyes shut as I take him in, doing my best to ignore the fact that Nate is the man attached to the dick I'm sucking.

I relish the space it takes in my mouth. I'm so full of him, and I push harder until I'm gagging around his tip at the back of my throat. Even then, I don't need pressure from his hand on me, and he gives me none. It's out of my own free will that I choke myself on his length. I want to feel more of him. I want to feel his presence deep inside me and know that there's no escape from it.

"That's it, beautiful girl. Take every inch of my cock down your throat."

Before I can think clearly, I take masochistic pleasure in forcing myself closer, in swallowing his impossibly hard and thick cock. My eyes water, and my breathing stops as I push myself so far that my nose presses against the coarse hair at the base of his dick. I flick my tongue, and I'm too gone to stop myself from moaning around him. It makes him hiss, and his hand tightens in my hair. I feel his knuckles against my skull, the pull so delicious it doubles my wetness. I move my tongue again, as much as I can with the pressure of him against it. Tilting my head up, I pull away, all the way to the tip, and he releases a groan. I watch his mouth drop open, his eyes alight with need. Spit dribbles down my chin, and I don't even care as I take him in again. I'm not sure what I'm begging for anymore. The phone, or to fulfill a sick need inside me.

"Shit."

This time, instead of letting me torture myself, he thrusts into my mouth, down my throat, making me gag.

He pulls out and does it again. He fucks me relentlessly until his thrusts shorten, until I hear his teeth gritting, and until he throws his head back with a grunt.

He explodes in my mouth at the same time as he pulls out the slightest and some of it spills on my lips and chin. I gasp, mouth full of his cum. It's thick and sticky. It should make me gag and taste disgusting. Fuck knows I barely gave Ivan a one-minute blowjob, never mind letting him come in my mouth.

So, believe me that I surprise myself when I lock my gaze onto his and swallow. I don't recognize myself when I let him run his thumb up my chin, gathering his cum and pushing it back into my mouth.

I wrap my lips around his finger, my eyes fluttering shut as I lick it clean.

"It's good to see that you're learning your place, little sunflower."

The words twist my gut, and reality slaps me so hard in the face I fall onto my ass and swat his hand away from me. Crawling back, my head hits the seat of the chair.

"The phone," I rasp. "Give me the fucking phone."

It's hard to give an order with the taste of him on my tongue and my knees burning.

He takes his time putting himself back in his pants. His face is blank, only his breathing showing me he just had an orgasm. As he buckles his belt, I use the desk to bring myself back to a standing position.

Without a word, he opens the drawer and brings out the phone. He hands it out to me, but just as I'm about to grab it, he wraps his arm around my waist, bringing me closer to him as the phone presses against my ribs. Sliding his other hand beneath the satin robe, his fingers find my pussy lips, moving lower. He doesn't enter me, though. No, he just makes a point. That I'm so fucking wet I'm practically dripping.

"Remember," he murmurs. "I can take back privileges at any time. Don't use this phone to try to get out, Kayla. You don't want to see what I'm like when I'm truly angry."

"Truly angry?" I grit out, vaguely attempting to step away and certainly in vain. "What the hell was yesterday if not angry? You impaled a man's hand to the dresser."

He shrugs. "I had to make a point. But you don't want to know what I'll do to you if you use this phone the wrong way. It might not hurt as much as what I did to Daniel, but it will feel worse, believe me."

There's no point trying to suppress the shiver coursing through my body. He feels it too, and the corner of his mouth tips up. "I'm glad we're on the same page. Now go get dressed. We really are going to be late."

He releases me, giving me the phone, and I don't wait one more second to escape his vicinity. I stride to his office door, and as I open it, come face to face with a blonde woman, her fist up, as if ready to knock.

She's about my height, although completely different. Bright blue eyes, high cheekbones. She's got an arrogant look about her. An I'm-better-than-you highbrow bitchiness that contrasts with my rough don't-fuck-with-me bluntness.

I hate that I'm in a simple robe, disheveled, the phantom feeling of Nate's cum still coating my throat. It makes me feel vulnerable, and that's not a good look when you first meet someone. At least not in my experience.

She cocks an eyebrow at me, looking down her nose. Taking me in from my toes all the way to what I don't doubt is messy hair, I catch her eyes stopping at the tattoo of a crown on my neck, and then the one at my hairline.

I know what she's thinking.

Trash.

It's written all over her judgmental face. I've seen it many times on South Bank bitches who think they're so smart for recognizing a girl from the North Shore by her looks.

Proof of her already formed opinion, instead of addressing me, her eyes go to Nate, probably still standing by his desk at the back of the room.

"Mr. White." A bright smile suddenly appears on her lips, her face softening. "If you don't need anything else, I'll be making my way."

Only now do I notice the medical bag hooked to her forearm. It looks like real leather. I could probably pay a few months of my rent with it.

I turn around to see Nate's reaction. Does he know her well? Is she his doctor?

With the performance of a lifetime, Nate offers her a smile and a grateful nod. "Stitching is all fine. Thank you, Marcie."

My eyes narrow on him, hating the sweet words coming out of his mouth, hating that it's a side of him I don't get to see. Why do I get the psychotic bastard and *Marcie* gets a smile?

Why do I get chained to the bed and she gets a *thank you, Marcie.*

Why do I get—

"Well, if you need anything else." Her sultry purr makes the hairs at the back of my neck rise. "You know how to reach me."

He only nods at her before his eyes go to me, hardening again. He taps his watch with his finger. "Why are you still standing here?"

If only I had a gun. Just a simple handgun. Things would be so much simpler.

I shoulder Marcie as I exit his office, holding the phone tightly in my hand and reminding myself there are more important things than fighting with him about the way he talks to me. That's not going to get better, so I might as well get over it.

I'm walking farther into the grand foyer when I hear her behind me again. "Excuse me," she calls out.

I turn around, cocking an eyebrow at her. Can't she see I'm already barely holding myself back?

"That's the way out." She's pointing behind her with her thumb. Right at the front door. As if I'm too dumb to notice a gigantic double door.

"I can see that. So, why aren't you walking through it right now?"

My no-nonsense tone makes her eyebrows rise to her hairline. Her arm tightens on her bag before she shakes her head a little, finding her footing again.

"I was trying to be polite." Said in a way that shows I'm not. "I believe Mr. White expected you to leave."

"I believe you have no fucking idea what you're talking about."

"Look, if you're heading inside the house hoping to steal something after your night, I suggest you don't. He is not the kind of man you want to steal from. Leave with what you've been paid and be happy with that." She looks me up and down, pity transforming her features. "And maybe you should think of not coming back to work here again. The men who come to this house are not all as respectful as him."

Respectful?

Did she just fucking use *respectful* to describe Nate?

Wait. What did she mean by working here again?

My muscles freeze for a second before my entire body powers up once more. I take a threatening step toward her, forcing her to take one back.

"I'll scream," she panics, her eyes wildly roaming around the room. Maybe she's checking if her *respectful* friend is coming to save her.

"Did you just insinuate I got paid to sleep with the guy? Is that what I look like to you? You see a North Shore girl and you automatically assume I'm a sex worker? And on top of that, you think every sex worker is a thief?"

"Y-you're not?"

"What the fuck do you think we all do on our side of the river? Sell our bodies to rich fucks like Nate? Go around Stoneview looking for the first billionaire who'll stick it in us for a few bucks?"

She flinches when I raise my left hand, probably thinking the North Shore trash is going to hit her. I would have under any other circumstances. I was never one to stop myself from punching a bitch. I hate letting anyone step on my toes, but I hate proving a South Bank cunt right even more.

She raises her hands in front of her, eyes squinting.

"See that?" I wave my fingers in front of her.

And for the first time, I *really* look at the ring Nate forces me to wear. It's white gold, the round-brilliant cut looks elegant, and the diamond is big enough to not be missed, but not big enough to look like I'm trying too hard.

My nostrils flare in anger when I realize it's fucking perfect. It's classic, timeless, *beautiful*.

Marcie is looking at the ring with fear in her eyes, probably wondering what the hell I'm on about and why I'm suddenly silent.

"I'm his fiancée." Oh, the words hurt. They do. They rip me apart from the inside, shred my dignity to pieces.

But it feels nice to watch her face fall and realize she isn't going to be fucking *Mr. White* any time soon.

Call me possessive, but if the fucker is going to keep me here, I promise on my life he is not going to touch another woman.

"Marcie." Nate's stern voice startles her. She turns to watch him exit his office. "As much as I'd love to invite you to stay for coffee, your services aren't needed anymore. Kayla and I have an appointment in less than an hour and, as you can see, she's nowhere near ready."

As he turns to me, something flashes in his eyes that I can't describe. It's fire and ice. He's annoyed, but there's something else.

He walks past Marcie, his expensive shoes clicking against the marble as he strides to me. Before I understand what he's doing, he leans down, his shoulder hitting my stomach, and the world tilts as he flips me over. My head ends up by his gorgeous ass, and he wraps an arm around the back of my thighs.

"How many times do I have to tell you to get ready, woman?"

I grip the phone tighter with one hand, and with the other, I slap his back. "Put me down!" I rage.

When I look up, Marcie is heading toward the door, not questioning Nate's request for her to leave or the fact that I'm being carried away by a fucking caveman.

As soon as the front door is closed, I hit his back again. "Did you know she wants to fuck you?"

His back shakes when he laughs. "Of course she wants to fuck me. I don't know many women who don't, and this one has seen me topless more times than I can count."

Instead of tearing down his ego, I blow it up without even thinking. "What? Why? Who the fuck is she? Why was she here?"

I feel sick when he walks up the stairs. Suddenly scared he's going to drop me, I fist his shirt with my free hand.

"She's a doctor who works for me. She was here because my fiancée stabbed me yesterday, and it turns out that the wound was a lot deeper than I thought. I needed stitches."

"Good."

He slaps my ass so hard I shriek. "Don't make a habit out of hurting me or you'll see a lot more of Marcie. This might be news to you, but you're not very good at hiding your jealousy."

"I'm not fucking jealous," I hiss.

"*I'm his fiancée.*" He imitates my voice a little too well to my liking.

"She said I was a sex worker!"

"She was trying to rile you up. She's very possessive over me."

"She needs to fucking die."

It takes me a few seconds to get my bearings when he puts me down again, back in my room.

There's an entitled smile on his face when I look at him. "What?" I snap.

He shrugs. "I think I always wanted to marry someone possessive. It makes me feel special." With a wink, he turns around, hands in his pockets as he casually walks out of my room. "We're leaving in half an hour."

I slam the door behind him, but when I look at the bed, my rage dissipates, and panic takes over.

It's a silk suit. A perfect white. I run my hand over the pants, feeling the softness. The jacket is a little long, the pants too, but there are heels next to the bed. Along with a strapless lace corset. It's so delicate that it's see-through at the waist and the boning is visible.

I pick it up with a trembling hand before dropping it like it's burning my skin. Turning my back to the bed, I type the only number I know by heart on the phone he gave me.

The three rings take forever, and when my mom's voice finally comes through, I feel like crying.

"*Where the hell have you been?*" She sounds like she's already smoked two packs of cigarettes. And she's really fucking mad.

There's no love to be found when it comes to my mother. She saved herself by escaping my dad before my brother and I could even defend ourselves from him.

He did unspeakable things to her, but no matter how much I tried to understand her in the past, I don't think I'll ever be able to. Who leaves their kids behind? She never came back for us. Didn't leave an address or a phone number. We found her contact info in my dad's phone after he died. I needed her, and I told her she owed me for abandoning me and leaving me with an abuser. Now she helps me, but we can't even say we remotely like each other.

"Doesn't matter where I've been. I'm calling you now. How are—" I cut myself off, eyeing the door. What if he's right behind it? What if he's wondering who I wanted to call so badly. "How are they?"

"*Fine.*" I hear her pull on her cigarette and exhale. "*They're confused, though. Keep asking questions about you. Well, the one who talks does. That's what happens when you disappear.*"

I roll my eyes, ignoring her dig.

"I didn't *disappear*. Shit has been going down here. NSC—"

"*I don't care about North Shore drama, Kayla. I left a long time ago, and I don't want to hear about it.*"

"Don't I know it," I say flatly. "Put them on the phone."

"*It's almost ten-thirty on a Tuesday. Ever heard of preschool?*"

"*Fuck*," I snap. Fuck. Fuck. Fuck. I fall back onto the bed, a hand combing through my hair. I let my head fall forward.

I don't know when I'll be able to call again.

"Mom..." I hate the way my voice wobbles.

"*What is it, Kayla?*"

I can't deal with her annoyed tone. She's already so fucking sick of me. I'm like a kid who keeps making mistake after mistake. I wasn't even good enough to save when I was a child who had done nothing wrong. What about now? What will she think of me if I tell her what happened?

My throat tightens, and when my eyes prickle with the need to cry, I swallow everything back. It physically hurts to do so.

"*Kayla?*" Her voice isn't softening, but there's a tinge of concern there now.

I hear her smoke some more.

"*Listen to me. If it's a man, just run. You hear me? Run the first chance you get. It won't get better.*"

I nod. I know she can't see me, but the ball of tears is so big in my throat I can't utter a word.

"*Don't worry about them. They're with me. They're safe.*"

"O-okay," I squeeze out. I will worry. There's no doubt about that, but she's right.

She huffs. "*Kayla.*"

"Yes?" I sniffle.

"*Run to me. I'll take you in.*"

I hang up. I can't listen anymore. She's breaking down my defenses, and I have to stay strong.

The first thing I do is delete the call log. I don't want Nate to find out who I was on the phone with. I hurry to put on the white lace thong he provided, the corset, and the suit. I don't bother with the makeup pouch he left on the bed. I don't have to make myself look any different for him.

As I check myself in the mirror, I hate that the suit fits perfectly, that the silk embraces the shape of my body so beautifully. The corset adds a sexy touch and breaks the formality of the suit.

Taking a deep breath, I brace myself to see Nate again.

He's waiting for me in the foyer, looking down at his phone as he texts. When he hears my unsteady steps going down the stairs, he finally looks up.

His eyes widen for a split second before he strides toward me. As I make it down the last steps, he grabs my hand, helping me.

"I'm not used to heels," I grunt. I rearrange the corset around my boobs. "Or clothes that include lace and bones."

Instead of entertaining my complaints, he drops a tender kiss on my forehead. "You look beautiful, little sunflower. Radiant."

My eyebrows pinch closer, face hardening. Not because of his words, but because of the reaction I'm suddenly experiencing. There's a dangerous warmth spreading through my belly, and I swallow hard. Maybe I should drink acid to remind my body of the way it's meant to feel around Nate. He's manipulating me, and I'm being stupid enough to go along with it.

He keeps a hold of my hand. It's delicate. He's not forcing me out of the house. He's not dragging me by the hand. He's helping me walk in stupid heels.

As soon as he opens the front door, I notice Enzo standing there, and I freeze.

"Holy fuck."

"Enzo, point that away, will you?"

The huge man makes sure the tip of his automatic is on his right shoulder as we walk by his left.

"Sorry, boss."

"That's an AK-47," I hiss. "What do you think I'm going to do?"

"It's not for you. It seems the Wolves are officially aware of me being back. I've had a few threats coming my way."

"Huh. Who knows, with a little chance, they'll kill you before we get to the town hall."

He chuckles, letting go of my hand to open the passenger door of his car. "Chance doesn't exist in our world, little sunflower. Only strength and intelligence. Lucky for you, I have both."

He leaves me alone during the drive. He doesn't taunt me, and he doesn't make this harder than it already is. He stays silent, listening to "*Save Me Some Sunshine*" by Rafferty. His window is rolled down, his elbow resting on the windowsill. His head bobs as the singer asks for his sunshine not to be taken away, and my stomach tightens.

I am your sun now.

Biting my lower lip, I look at his handsome face. He must have traded his glasses for contacts because he's not wearing them. His gaze stays focused on the road, strong jaw softened by the relaxed features of a completely blank face.

There's nothing that could show what is possibly running through his mind. Is he thinking about his revenge? Or if this is a good idea?

"Nate." His name slips from my mouth before I can stop it.

With his eyes still on the road, he says, "Yes?"

I scratch my throat, unsure what the best way to approach him is. "You know that...that by marrying me, you're punishing yourself too?"

His eyes flick to me for a split second. "Are we really back on the topic of questioning whether this is happening or not?"

"I have to try," I huff. "Please, Nate. Don't you see that you're punishing the both of us? You're locking yourself in a loveless marriage. What? Forever? To hurt me? You're going to hurt yourself down the road. I'll hate you. I'll make your life miserable. You'll never be happy."

"Will you?"

"What?"

Switching hands on the steering wheel, he rests his palm on my thigh. "Will you be happy, Kayla?"

"No! Of course not."

He squeezes my thigh softly. "Then that's all that counts."

My head falls forward. I don't know why I thought I could reason with him. Maybe it's the way his hate becomes so passive that I could almost mistake it as something else. It's the sex. The lust we have toward each other made me believe that there was a side of him I could talk to. A side that would understand me.

"You'll be my wife in less than half an hour, sunflower. Stop overthinking it."

"I can't do it."

"But you will."

He stops at a red light and wraps a hand around my jaw, forcing me to look at him.

My chest tightens to the point of aching. My breathing becomes ragged.

"Don't freak out. Just go along with it. Be good and you'll adapt to this life in no time."

I won't. I know I won't. But I shut up because I have no way to say anything remotely agreeable.

His decision is made, and so is mine.

16

KAYLA

How Villains Are Made - Madalen Duke

Sam is already inside waiting for us. There were about a billion stairs to the entrance and my calves are burning from walking up with these heels.

Nate puts a hand at the small of my back, guiding us toward his friend. The second Sam sees us up close, his eyes go to my neck, then Nate's. I suddenly feel too aware of the long, red cut that practically looks like a choker. Nate sports the same, maybe even deeper. I doubt either of them will scar, but it currently looks like we both almost had our throats sliced. Which we did.

Sam huffs, running a hand against his face.

"Nate?"

The concerned smiles brightly. "My bride and I had a small disagreement last night. Nothing to worry about, it's sorted."

Sam shakes his head, but I'm not looking at him anymore when I notice Emma Scott walking out of a room.

"He's ready for us."

My head snaps to Nate, but he already has a hand up. "We both need a witness. Don't make a scene."

"Don't make a scene? Do you know how many other options you had for a witness?"

"Yes, and only one is aware of what I'm doing. I own a lot of people in this town, but we *are* talking about a forced marriage here. It's not exactly easy to make something like this happen. Let's go."

This time, he grabs me by my elbow, harsher than he has been until now.

It's a small room. Nothing too fancy, nothing that looks official. A man walks in, holding some paperwork. He's middle-aged, his brown hair peppered with gray. Wearing an expensive suit, he strides to the desk at the back of the room. Nate hurries me along as the man speaks.

"I don't have much time, Mr. White. This isn't how I'm meant to officiate weddings."

"I appreciate the favor."

He knows. That man knows this isn't something I've agreed to. It's obvious. Nate was in a rush because our officiant is doing this under the table, probably for a lot of money, maybe threats, could be both.

"Alright, I need signatures here and here from the bride and the groom." We're skipping the *I do's* then.

We don't even sit. Nate signs first, then shoves the pen into my hand. I'm shaking so strongly I can't even put the ball of the pen to the paper.

"Kayla." His voice is soft, his breath warm on the skin of my neck. He slides a hand along my right arm until he's gripping my wrist and pressing his thumb against my pulse. "Breathe, baby. This is almost over."

Don't call me baby. I'm not your baby.

The word itself doubles my panic.

"Please." I have never sounded so pathetic in my entire life. "I c-can't. Nate..."

"Take a deep breath." He's right behind me now, cornering me against the table. His thumb presses harder, hurting me, showing me how fast my heart's beating. "Calm your heartbeat. Control your emotions. Accept that this is happening."

I whimper when he starts pressing my wrist against the table, forcing the pen to paper.

"Mr. White..." The officiant hesitates. "This... She needs to sign herself."

His other arm wraps around my waist and all I feel is him. His warmth, his scent. I feel his breath, his heartbeat against my back. "Do it, little sunflower. Be mine."

My hand moves.

He releases my wrist but not my waist. The pen glides against the paper, black ink sealing my fate to his. A drop hits the paper right on my name, wetting the ink and thickening the *K* of King.

That's when I feel it, the tear that ran down my cheek and all the way to my chin before dripping onto the paper.

I drop the pen like it's on fire, wiping my face before anyone sees it.

"The witnesses, please." The hurried voice of the town hall bureaucrat makes everything even worse.

Nate helps me step back, and Sam steps in. He signs under Nate's name. Next is Emma. She grabs the pen, looks at my name, and I know she can see the wet spot.

Her head snaps around to me, her eyebrows pinched. She observes me, a prisoner of Nate's hold, helpless to the marriage I'm being forced into, and for the first time in my entire life, I see something that looks like sympathy in her gaze. For the first time, she sees us as what we truly are.

Two women who did our best at surviving, and yet kept playing the games men around us had set up for us. The wars they started, the vengeance they upheld. And today, she witnesses me lose the ultimate game Nate organized.

She hesitates, looking at Nate, then me again, and before she turns to sign, I read her words loud and clear on her twisted features.

I'm sorry.

The officiant practically rips the paper from her hold. He nods toward Nate, skipping anything he's supposed to say and instead muttering, "You're officially Mr. and Mrs. White. Now, please leave."

There's no kiss, only his hand in mine as he drags me out of the room. Only the hurried steps of our witnesses behind us.

"You did good," Nate murmurs as he takes me down the outside stairs and to his parked car. "It's done now. You're okay."

I'm not okay. I'm numb. I'm petrified. I'm like a lifeless doll as he opens his car and pushes me inside. He puts my seatbelt on, leaving a kiss on my forehead before rounding the car and taking his seat.

We're driving before I can even register that we're not in the room anymore. In my head, I'm still holding that pen. I haven't signed yet.

It's when I see the Stoneview woods that it finally hits me.

He did it. He forced me to marry him.

Run to me. I'll take you in.

My mom's voice resonates in my head. That's what she did. She ran to survive. She left it all behind so she could see another day.

The car slows down. There are no other cars on the

road, just us. But I think Sam wasn't far behind. We're heading back to his house. It's now or never.

But if I *run,* he can catch me. If I run, he'll still have access to those pictures.

If I kill him however...

His eyes are on the traffic light, and I look at his one hand on the steering wheel. The other is loosening the tie around his throat. He doesn't look worried in the slightest, doesn't mind that he just forced a woman to marry him.

I do. I mind.

Because I would do anything to get back to my family. And if you get in my way. You die.

The light turns green, but before he can accelerate, my hand shoots for his tie. He rears back in surprise, but he's too late. At the same time as I pull at his tie, I grab his hair with my other hand and push until his nose hits the steering wheel. The honk resonates loudly, covering his grunt, and I do it again until I see blood bursting out of his nose.

"Fuck, Kayla—"

Finally reacting, he tries to grab me, but I've got the advantage this time. I wrap the loose end of the tie around his neck and pull him toward me. His upper body ends up on my side of the car with all the strength I put in, and his head is on my lap.

"Don't you know who you just married?" I grit out, adrenaline rushing through my veins at the possibility of pulling this off.

His face gets redder by the second, and his chocking eggs me on. It's satisfying like nothing else.

"Don't you know *my fucking name*?" I hiss. I feel my biceps bulging as I pull harder. "I'm the ruthless King. You don't get to keep me captive, Nate. No one does."

He taps around with his hands, his eyelids drooping as he tries to reach for me, but he gives up and instead helps me pull at his tie.

Confusion twists my stomach until I feel the material rip.

Fuck.

But I'm quick to react. Before he can get away from me, I reach inside his suit jacket, grab his gun holster, and pull out the weapon. He's quick too. The second it takes me to point the muzzle to his forehead is enough for him to have pulled out the other gun and point it at me.

Silence falls heavily on the car. All that can be heard is our panting. Him more than me since he's still catching his breath, but I'm struggling to breathe too. It took a lot of strength to subdue him. The man is made of nothing but muscles.

So here we are, two guns pointing at each other, muzzles less than an inch from our foreheads. He licks his lips, clearly fucking excited by the situation. I might be known as the woman who isn't scared of death, but he's different. Death makes him ecstatic.

"Little sunflower," Nate chuckles, his face finally losing the redness, the skin going back to the sun-kissed color it usually is. "This is not exactly how I imagined our honeymoon."

I narrow my eyes at him. "You picked the wrong victim, Nate. I will never bow to you. I will *never* be your wife, no matter what the papers say. You'll die before you can ever make me yours."

He smiles that wicked smile. "You're already mine, Kayla." He bites his lower lip as he looks me up and down. "No more ruthless King. Only *Mrs.* White."

The door behind me opens before I can say anything. A

gun presses against the back of my head, and my eyes flutter shut, taking in the new situation.

"I told you this was a terrible idea," a British voice says from behind me.

Sam.

I knew he wasn't far. I was too slow.

Despite the threat of both guns, I don't lower my own weapon. I don't fucking care. I'll shoot. Let them kill me. Let my girls know I died trying to get back to them. Let the whole North Shore know it took two of them to bring me down.

All I see is the surprise on Nate's face as I press the trigger.

Click.

My eyes widen at the sound, my mouth dropping open.

"*No*," I push past a clenched jaw. I hit the barrel with my open palm. "You have *got* to be kidding me."

"Sam," Nate says casually, his smile coming back to his face. "Remind me to get that gun checked. I can't walk around with a weapon that jams in life-or-death situations."

I feel hope being sucked out of me, like death itself would steal my soul. I'm helpless as I eye Nate's fingers shifting on the gun. The barrel disappears as he puts his weapon away and softly takes the one I was holding.

My fist curls, and I'm ready to fight again. I'm going to punch him, beat him to death.

"Kayla…" The pity in Sam's voice is almost reassuring, like he's got my back. He doesn't, but he clearly doesn't want to see me hurt. "Stop fighting. It's useless."

"Listen to the wise man," Nate confirms. Not even looking at me, he grabs something from the inside pocket of his jacket.

As Sam shifts behind me, his gun presses a little harder one last time before it disappears. I see something flash at the corner of my eyes, and a cold, metal cuff is forced around my right wrist, where my fist still hasn't relaxed.

I fight. Fuck, I fight with all I have. I manage to get one last punch in Nate's jaw with my left hand before Sam cuffs them both behind my back.

The devil in front of me works his jaw from side to side before he turns to me.

A smile tips the corner of his mouth when I tremble. My eyes flutter shut, then snap back open, and nothing has changed. I'm still held hostage by a man who wants nothing but my suffering.

And he's now pointing a syringe at me.

Before I can even get my lips to part, he pushes the needle into my neck. The same way he did a few nights ago in my bathroom.

He's too weak to fight me. He does this because I'm a worthy opponent.

I blink a few times as my vision blurs. Nate holds me delicately as I faint. I can feel the way he cups the back of my head, helping me to lay back against the seat as he caresses my cheek.

"Oh, little sunflower." His free hand tugs at a strand of my hair like a little boy crushing on me. "You're in for a very long day of punishments."

"I hate you," I growl as the world goes dark.

17

KAYLA

Victim - Halflives

There's a ringing in my ears. That's the first thing telling me I'm still alive. I can't open my eyes, but I can slowly make out what the ringing is. Words.

"Huh?" That's Nate's voice.

"What?" I croak. Talking suddenly makes me aware of my own body.

I'm not sitting or lying down. I'm standing, or rather hanging, my toes barely touching the floor but enough so that the entire pull isn't on my shoulders.

My wrists ache from what feels like leather cuffs around them. They're high above my head, probably attached to the ceiling.

"I said, how many times do you have to wake up in my basement before you learn your lesson?"

I almost want to ask *what lesson*, but I think that'll just get me into more trouble. When I open my eyes, I know instantly that his promise of punishment is going to be more than I can handle. Because no matter how gorgeous

Nate is topless—his abs prominent below his countless tattoos and his shoulders already flexing from the excitement of hurting me—I know that it announces nothing good for me. He's clearly planning on...*exercising*.

I do my best to ignore his beauty, the way his golden skin contrasts so sharply with mine, the way the V at his hips getting lost beneath his pants makes him look like a Greek god. A statue of bronze crafted by the hands of a lover.

Fuck. Nothing good is coming my way.

Apparently, he ditched my suit jacket since I'm only wearing the delicate corset and pants. I look up, craning my neck so I can see my hands. It's not the leather cuffs that make my stomach drop, it's the wedding band that's been added to my engagement ring.

I think I'm going to be sick.

"Focus on me, little sunflower. Remember who your sun is."

My head drops, my gaze crossing his.

"I get it," I say calmly. "Not allowed to fight back. I'm fucking stuck with you."

"No. That was my warning before you pressed that trigger. Now that I know there's no making you listen, we're taking this up a notch."

I shake my head, keeping a semblance of dignity in a position that will leave me with none. "We're not taking it up a notch."

"Says the girl hanging from my ceiling. Until you learn there is no escaping me, you will be punished." He speaks in such a casual tone, it's eerie.

As he walks behind me, I sense him picking up something. There are already goosebumps rising on my skin when he reappears in my line of vision.

"Fuck no." It doesn't matter how much I try to keep my voice level, the reflex of pulling at the cuffs shows my despair. "You're not touching me with that."

"This?" He raises the crop he's holding. A fucking *crop*. "My little sunflower, you better get used to it. A masochist like you is bound to fall in love with it."

I pull harder at the cuffs. That's until I feel the leather tongue slap the side of my thigh. It doesn't hurt that much. I'm still dressed after all, and he didn't put that much strength into it, but the gasp comes from the shock that he dared use it. As if there was any doubt he would.

"You fucking—" He hits me again, harder this time.

"Listen to me closely, Kayla. You do not talk anymore unless I ask you a direct question or give you an order. I don't want to hear anything from your mouth apart from the cries of pain and begging. Is that clear?"

When all I give him is a deadly look, I get another hit in the exact same spot that stings noticeably more than the first two.

"I said, *is that clear*?"

"Yes," I hiss.

"Good. Open your mouth."

"Wh—" *Swoosh.* "Fuck!" Four times in the same spot is starting to burn like hell. And I'm pretty sure he hits harder every time.

"Open your mouth."

He's not happy with my first attempt at parting my lips, and he hits me again. "Wider."

When I do, he puts the handle of the crop in my mouth horizontally. "Bite."

And I do because there's absolutely nothing else I can do but obey.

"Mm, look at you. What an obedient little wife."

I cringe at the word *wife*, hating the sound of it as it comes out of his mouth with such ownership. It enhances my helplessness.

"Don't drop it, little sunflower, or I'll have to double your punishment."

Now that his hands are free, he traces the cups of my corset with his knuckles. I try not to tremble from his touch but fail miserably.

His eyes stay on me when he undoes the front clasps one at a time. I'm biting the crop so tight it should snap in two. Nate is keeping me prisoner in so many ways it's becoming overwhelming.

A wedding, a house I can't escape, cuffs around my wrists...and his eyes. His gorgeous eyes, dark like a summer night. Not black, not blue, a midnight color that promises nightmares and dreams. Monsters and heroes. Pain and pleasure.

My corset falls to the floor, my boobs lowering into place. He takes his time exploring them, rubbing his thumb over each nipple until they stand to attention.

"I'm going to punish these tits until you beg me to stop, little sunflower."

Struggling to breathe through my nose, a twisted fear flutters in my stomach. I squeeze my eyes shut when I feel myself getting wet.

"Look at me."

I do. Despite the shame, the fear, and the tension in me. Despite starting to feel my saliva gathering against the handle of the crop, I look up at him. The fucker won't understand what I'm feeling anyway. He's broken like that.

"This is going to hurt. You're going to take it. And when you've learned your lesson, you're going to thank me."

For lack of being able to answer, I simply keep

staring at him. To my surprise, he drops to his knees, and I only understand why when he unbuttons my pants. He takes his time rolling them down, sliding my legs out. His touch is delicate, his hands caressing my skin and promising me a kindness I know he can't express.

My thong is next, and just like that, I'm completely naked and bound before him.

He stands up again, takes the crop from my mouth, and observes me silently.

"Kayla," he says after a minute of silence. "There's something you must never forget. I am not doing this because I secretly like you. There are no feelings involved, no secret obsession. I'm doing this because you tried to ruin my life. Always remember there will be no mercy in this relationship. There will be no kindness, no love. You are my captive. You will obey or you will suffer. Today, you suffer."

I don't have even a second to digest what he's said.

The first time the tongue of the crop hits my right nipple, nothing happens for a second. Then I feel the fire spreading through the bud.

I gasp, surprised by a pain I should have expected. But it's so much worse than I thought. He doesn't even wait for me to get over the first hit. Before I know it, my other nipple is screaming in agony.

He alternatively hits both my nipples for what seems forever. All I can focus on is his beautiful body. The way his lean muscles tighten when he sends the crop flying through the air. The way his neck tenses when he makes contact with my body. He stays completely silent, focused on me while I focus on him. It's the only way to survive the pain.

He takes a step back at some point, and I use the break to dig my desperate gaze into his.

"S-stop," I rasp. I can barely take a breath.

He does leave my nipples alone, but instead, he taps my inner thigh. "Open."

I do so right away, incapable of fighting back in the slightest. Without him having to insist, I open my legs as wide as I can.

The next tap startles me. Because it's on my pussy. Because I'm spread open enough that the thick leather hits both my entrance and my clit. But mainly? Because of the very specific noise it makes.

Nate cocks an eyebrow at me. "You're incorrigible. What kind of little slut gets wet from getting her tits tortured with a crop?"

My eyes fall to the floor, earning me a stern order. "Look at me."

"Please..." I beg as my eyes meet his. "Don't..."

"It brings me immense joy to see you suffer in so many ways, little sunflower. The physical pain, the mental shame. It makes me feel alive."

As he taps my clit again, I bite my lower lip, desperate to hold back the noise threatening to creep out. A whimpered moan isn't the same as a painful whimper, and he knows that. I can't let him hear it.

"Show me you've learned your lesson. Tell me who you belong to, Kayla. Whose wife are you?"

I drag in a desperate breath when he slaps my clit harder. Fire burns up my body and lights me up.

"Please..." I moan, unable to hold back a shiver. "Don't... Don't make me say it."

The next hit is hard, painful, punishing.

"Whose. Wife. Are. You?" He punctuates every word

with a lick of the crop's tongue, bringing me despair and pleasure until I can't take it anymore.

"Yours!" I cry out.

"That's right. My precious little wife who is dripping from being hit with a crop. What a beautiful sight you are."

Another hit makes me lose it. I'm done fighting back; I just want to take any pleasure I can. So I moan. I let it out loud and clear, my head dropping back.

"Good," he purrs. "Give me more, little sunflower. Beg me to make you come with my crop."

Keeping the leather flat against my clit, he presses hard and makes tiny movements, rubbing it against me.

"Fuck...fuck." *Slap!* "Ow!"

"Watch your language when you beg your husband."

"Please," I whimper. "Please, Nate, let me come."

He slaps my clit again, turning my world upside down. I don't know what hurts and what feels good anymore. I'm not sure if the torture is the pain, or if there isn't enough of it. I just want to come more than anything. I just need the pleasure so I can think straight again.

"You're going to have to do better than that. Beg your husband to make you come with his crop, Kayla. Let me hear those words."

"Please." I gulp, knowing I'm completely losing myself. "Please, husband. Make me come with your crop. I need it... I need you to..."

Finally happy with my pleas, he starts tapping regularly, with a pressure that promises to take me to heaven. I can feel it building, a band twisting in my lower stomach. I'm close and my moaned *yes...yes...yes* are proof of it.

That's until he stops. There's nothing for a second, then a searing band on the underside of my right breast.

I don't scream from the pain, but rather from the loss of the orgasm I was about to have. When he takes a step back, I'm panting, looking at him with so much anguish in my eyes it makes him smile.

"Name it."

I shake my head before letting it drop.

"I want to know. Name it."

"Don't make me," I whimper pathetically.

His fingers grab my chin, making me look up at him. His eyes are dead. There's nothing in them but the satisfaction of owning me entirely.

"I will learn what every single emotion looks like on you, Kayla. Make it easier on yourself and tell me what you are feeling right now."

"Obedient." I can barely squeak the word past my throat. "I feel obedient."

He searches my eyes for the truth. I don't know if he finds it, but I know that's how I feel. I want him to take over me, to do anything he says and be rewarded in return. Anything to reach the high I'm desperate for.

"Then you've learned your lesson, wife."

Letting go of me, he presents the tongue of the crop, right in front of my mouth. "Say thank you to your husband for teaching you a lesson and kiss my crop."

"Nate, please. I need to come." God, I'm miserable.

He lightly taps my cheek with his crop. "No. See, only good wives get to come. Bad wives who try to kill me get left soaking wet and needy. Now say thank you."

"Th—" Fuck. I want to cry. "Thank you," I mumble. "For teaching me a lesson."

And to complete my utter humiliation, I kiss the end of the crop that was torturing me mere seconds ago. It's wet with my arousal.

"Good. Open your mouth for me, little sunflower."

I do, and he puts the crop back in the same way he did before he started the torture. This time, I bite without being told to.

"You're going to stay here until I know your little clit isn't swollen and needy anymore. That way, you won't touch yourself behind my back once I free you. You're going to keep that crop in your mouth as a reminder of what happens when you disobey. Drop it before I come back, and we'll start all over again."

He brings his hand to my cheek, caressing me like someone would to a person they love. "You wouldn't want that, would you, baby?"

I shake my head, my eyes wide.

"Good. Then stay still for me. And make sure all you think about is your husband, okay?" His patronizing tone kills something inside me. "I'll be back when I deem you've had enough time to reflect."

I'm helpless as I watch him walk away. He doesn't even look back to check on my reaction. He is completely uncaring of my state as he turns off the light and closes the door behind him.

He leaves me dying to come, for him to touch me. He leaves me with the object he tortured me with in my mouth, taunting me with it. I'm naked, bound, helpless, and I hate myself when I do exactly what he asked of me. I think of him.

18

NATHAN

Daddy Issues - The Neighbourhood

For heaven's sake. It takes all of my self-control not to let out the growl bubbling in my chest when I open the basement door again.

I always thought Kayla King was beautiful. Physically, she's gorgeous. The place where she grew up took a toll on her body, and yet it's hard for anyone to look at her and not notice she belongs on the cover of a magazine.

At first glance, there's nothing special about her. Average height, average weight, average boobs, black hair. A nice bubble ass, but that's not everything. Her porcelain skin isn't smooth, with scars and tattoos. It's her eyes. Her forest green eyes that could swallow a weaker soul. They grab onto you, dragging you in, refusing to let you go. And her lips, they're slightly pouted, and a perfect pink. It gives her an air of innocence that doesn't belong on her face, yet fits so perfectly.

I kind of want to kiss her. I never did, even when I played with her before prison. Back then, I didn't want her to think I had any emotional attachment toward her. I didn't.

Now... I'm dying to know what those pouty lips taste like. I also strongly believe it would weaken her even more. Maybe I'll time it better. She's too out of it right now.

Yes, Kayla King is beautiful, there's no denying it. Add her stubborn personality, her pride, her strength, and her loyalty to the people she loves. It makes her irresistible. It makes her such a perfect target for hunters like me, people who feed on secret weaknesses and taking apart someone strong but breakable.

I've had relationships in the past, but people who are easy to manipulate aren't fun down the line. People I use as a means to an end always end up boring me. Kayla is a perfect adversary. I can't grow bored with someone who wants to fight. And seeing her like this, bound and naked, hanging from my ceiling now that her legs have given up, it stirs something in me that I struggle to define. The kind of feeling that goes beyond ownership and beyond revenge. It's not the usual mellow *satisfaction* that I feel from getting what I want. It's stronger.

My heart palpitates, sending something warm and relaxing through my veins. My already hard dick becomes painful, and I blink a few times, struggling to understand what the fuck is going on inside my body. Something seems wrong physically, and yet there's nothing I would change to satisfy myself in this situation. In fact, I'm getting twice the fulfillment I expected to feel.

Tilting my head to the side, I focus my gaze since the only light comes from the door upstairs I didn't close. I still haven't crossed the second doorway I have downstairs. I'm just standing there, the door open, observing her with my hand on the handle, curious if she's awake or not.

Her head hangs, her chin to her chest, but she's still biting, meaning she's awake. I can't see her face, only her hair draping around her and the way her shoulders rise and fall ever-so slightly.

Shit. It feels really fucking good to see her like this. I can't compare it to anything else, can't find something else in my memory that's made me feel this way before, and because of that, I can't put an emotion to it.

"Little sunflower," I purr. She doesn't move, doesn't startle, but I hear the desperate whimper escaping her.

My cock hardens, and I'm forced to fist it through my pants. She's so exquisite like this. I'm going to fucking implode.

I take my time walking to her, purposely letting her hear my steps as I get closer. I want her to be dying for me to get there. I want her as desperate for my presence as I am to touch her.

When I finally stand in front of her, I pinch her chin with my thumb and forefinger, lifting her head. She hisses behind the crop, probably in an enormous amount of pain from her shoulders taking her weight.

I put my other hand below her mouth and speak as quietly as I can. I think if I speak louder, she'll crumble under me. Mainly, I'm worried it'll show how turned on I am.

"Release."

Saliva covers her chin, and her eyes are glassy. I don't think she has any idea what is happening anymore. All she hears is my voice, my order, and she executes.

The crop drops in my palm, and I throw it behind her. When I look at her again, she's stretching her jaw from side to side. I notice her swollen eyes and damp cheeks.

She cried.

An excitement like I've never felt before zaps through my body. She cried because of me. *For me.* Releasing her chin, I cup her cheek, rubbing my thumb under her eye. There's nothing anymore. I left her here all day so I'm not surprise she's not crying anymore. Eight hours alone, biting my crop and hanging from my ceiling. I know full-grown men who work for the Cosa Nostra and who begged to be killed in lesser situations.

My wife is as strong as they come.

My wife is the closest person to being my equal that I've ever known.

And I think she learned her lesson.

"Name it."

She doesn't hesitate.

"Defeated," she croaks.

She's lost all control over herself, and she needs me to guide her. I don't even think she's really present, most definitely not realizing what she just admitted.

But I need to know. I need her to tell me her emotion, and how she truly feels deep down, because then I can learn her tells. I can identify it in the future. I'll recognize her tone of voice and the features on her face. It'll make it simple to read her.

She names it, and I can study it. She names it, and I can remember what it looks like on her. I can't emphasize and feel bad or ever share her joy. I can only attempt to learn. Sometimes, I can link it to something I've been through, but that is a lot of work because I hardly ever feel much. But if I learn what everything looks like on her face, in her body, in her breathing. If I learn all her emotions by heart, there will be nothing she can hide from me.

Utter control.

What a fun game to play.

If I were a normal person, this would make me feel all sorts of ways. But with how I'm wired? My blood feels thicker, my body is so full of it, powerful. I smile, an unmatched happiness making me almost giddy. My head drops to the crook of her neck. She's sweating, trembling. Her muscles are tense and hard. I breathe her in, a need to be close to her so strong that I want to bite into her soft skin.

This feels good. Good. What is it? How else does it make me feel?

Ecstatic? Exhilarated?

"Well done, little sunflower. You've made me very happy. Now you get to leave this room."

Wrapping an arm around her waist, I quickly unbuckle the cuffs, and rejoice in her helplessness when she collapses into my arms.

"Do you know what you are right now, baby?"

She nuzzles against me when I hook my other arm under her legs and lift her up. Unable to talk, she shakes her head against my chest. She feels like dead weight in my arms, completely boneless.

"You're weak." I kiss the top of her head despite her little cry of despair.

She thinks it's a bad thing, but it's not. It's filling me with a sense of pride I can hardly describe.

I like her like this. I like her at my mercy. And she'll need to come to like it too, or she'll have a terrible time in my presence.

I don't bring her to the room I had her in. Instead, I walk all the way to mine with her in my arms. Her body is getting cold. She's shaking. Probably to do with being left thoroughly whipped and naked in my basement. Probably shock. Probably a need for reassurance that she doesn't realize she's exhibiting.

I lay her down on my bed on top of the covers. I'll warm her up in a minute. I just need to observe her first. Her nipples are not their usual dusty pink. They're red and swollen, still hardened from the beating.

Rubbing a hand across my face, I wonder how much harder I can get. I ditch my shirt, pants, and boxers, and I spread her legs, kneeling between them on the bed.

She startles, but she's too lifeless to do anything about it.

"Nate," she rasps, her eyes closed, her head resting to the side.

"Yes, little sunflower?"

"P-please." Her teeth chattering is another indicator of her defeated state, and I store it in my Kayla King file. "Please," she repeats weakly. Is she even awake? She doesn't sound awake. "Don't break me."

Oh fuck.

That is the hottest thing I've ever heard coming from her.

Insults? Threats? Miserable attempts at begging? Yes, she gave me that.

But a devastation so absolute that she can't help herself from begging for mercy? That's new.

My cock throbs, leaking precum down my length. I want her badly. I want all of her. I want my dick in her tight cunt and my mind to take over her soul. I want her every thought, her vulnerability. I want her fucking *grief.*

I spread her legs a little wider as my gaze drops to her pussy. "Oh, little sunflower. How can you still be so wet for me? You're a sucker for torture and you're taking me down with you."

I use my two thumbs to spread her lips and can hardly believe how swollen her clit still is. She's desperate for this.

Leaning over her, I put a hand on the mattress by her shoulder, holding myself above her while the other gathers wetness at her entrance. Circling her clit with my thumb, I relish the moan she doesn't bother suppressing.

"Can you hear me?" I whisper in her ear, unsure of how present she is.

Her nod is so subtle, I wouldn't have noticed it if I was not observing her so closely.

"Then hear this. I will undoubtedly break you. That's a promise. I will break you over and over again, and when you're nothing but a pile of *dust* from the woman you used to be, I will put you back together slowly, painfully, and exactly how I want you."

I push two fingers inside her, feeling the way she tightens around me. She's soaking wet, welcoming me home like she missed me all day long. Her mouth drops open, and while she doesn't have the strength to talk, I see the slight shake of her head.

"Take me, little sunflower. Let me show you how much you love this."

My fingers curl, rubbing against her G-spot, pressing and forcing her stomach to tighten. Her moan is long, almost pained. Her eyes flutter open, and our gazes cross for a millisecond. Fear, despair, *lust*. She's feeling all kinds of wrong and an infinite kind of great.

She's beautiful, desperate, on the edge of being a broken little thing.

"Stay aware," I growl as I rub harder against her inner walls. "Stay with me while I use you, Kayla."

She whimpers, her body curving to the rhythm of my

movements. I don't think she realizes her hips are moving with me, rolling to meet my thrusts.

"You're my dirty little masochist. *Mine*."

She gasps when I retreat. Instead of my fingers, I run my painfully hard dick through her wetness, and when I press myself at her entrance, she freezes.

How bad is one meant to feel when they're abusing someone while they're barely conscious?

I'm guessing at least *a little bit* bad. Or, surely, they shouldn't feel this good. I've always known that everything about me is wrong. I've hurt people for the pleasure of hurting them. I'm a sinner in the most literal sense of the term. I've manipulated, used, and killed even the sweetest souls. There is absolutely nothing redeemable about who I am.

At least I'm self-aware.

So why do I not care in the slightest?

I never thought it'd come to a point in my life where the person facing me would be so responsive to my destructive behavior. Kayla King *needs* to be ruined. The weight of her life is too heavy on her shoulders, or why would she be so ready for me to tear her apart? She's breaking at the seams with the need to be controlled, taken over, *owned.*

"N-nate." It's barely a whispered whimper, but I hear her. I hear her plea.

I grab her face roughly, my thumb gripping her left cheek, my other fingers digging into her right cheek.

She's shaking like a leaf, fear making her so wet she doesn't control the goosebumps on her skin.

"Tell me no," I growl, barely able to hold myself back at her entrance. "Beg me to stop. You know you love it."

Her glassy eyes don't even take me in. She's in her own

world. "Stop," she mumbles. "D-don't do it." She can't even articulate anymore, too far gone, but she gets wetter anyway. I can feel her dripping down my cock.

I don't want to know if it's the pleasure or the fear, the exhaustion or the need for me. I need to feel her. I need all of her like I've never needed anything else in my life.

I'm scaring myself, terrified of what I'm feeling at this moment. Of the fact that I've lost all sense of self-control.

I push another inch inside her. "Again." I don't recognize my animalistic voice. "Tell me how much you hate this. Tell me I'm *forcing you.*"

She doesn't. She moans instead, bucking her hips. But I don't want her to move. I don't want her consent. So I slide my hand to her neck, pressing against her windpipe.

"Don't," she chokes. "Stop...*s-stop.*" Something flares in her eyes, and that makes her come back to life.

"There you are, my pretty wife. Can you feel your cunt swallowing me? Can you feel how much you want me to own you?"

She nods despite her inability to breathe, let alone speak.

"You're my good little wife, aren't you? You're going to let me hurt you, huh?"

She nods again, rolling her hips.

"Don't move, baby. Let your husband own this desperate cunt."

I thrust harshly inside her, pushing past whatever tightness was trying to choke my cock. She gasps, coughing from the pressure on her throat.

I don't think anymore, letting the animal in me take over. I don't care what she feels. Fuck, I barely even care if she survives this.

Something wet makes my hand slip, and I realize the

cut from the knife I put to her throat yesterday is bleeding. It's a shallow cut, but my hand is pressing hard against it.

Releasing the pressure slightly, I let her breathe while I spread her blood to her chest. She cries out when I rub my thumb against the bleeding spot. I then take it to one of her nipples while still keeping a thrusting rhythm in and out of her. She cries out when I cover her tortured nub in her own blood.

My mouth waters, and I lean down, licking the thickness off her nipple. She screams. Maybe from her bruised skin, maybe from my relentless pounding.

It doesn't matter. I repeat the process with her other hardened bud, ignoring her whiny pleas. Her body is too exhausted to fight, and when she cries to stop, I push her harder.

And when I've used her for everything she has to give, I press my thumb against her clit. I rub her sensitive nub delicately, the opposite of the way I'm fucking her. My free hand collars her throat again, stopping her from breathing altogether.

"It's okay if you pass out," I rasp. "I'll still make you come."

But she doesn't pass out. My words tip her over, and the way she convulses around my dick while she orgasms brings me over the edge too.

I grunt, thrusting hard as I fill her up with my cum.

My hand tightening around her throat cuts off her cries of release. "Take all of me, all of my cum." Those words alone make her tighten around me again, ripples of her orgasm reverberating through me.

I pull out, my body exhausted, but I still kneel between her legs. I'm not myself when I push two fingers inside her.

"Don't you fucking dare waste a single drop of my cum,

wife." I did the same when I fucked her yesterday. Every time I pull out of her, something else takes over me. I want to leave my mark on her, *inside her.*

It's more than taunting or torturing her. I want her to feel all of me. Forever.

It's her pained grunt that makes me realize how deeply and roughly I'm pushing my fingers. I've overused her, and yet I can't stop myself from making sure she doesn't spill any part of me that's coating her cunt.

Even when I pull my fingers away and lie down beside her, even when I put the covers over our naked bodies and let her get space from me, I still slide a hand down her stomach and cup her pussy.

I made things clear with Kayla. I told her there were no secret feelings, no obsession. There is nothing that links her to me but the hate I have for her.

Maybe I lied.

Maybe there is a little bit of obsession. Maybe having her on my mind all day every day for the years I was stuck between four walls has turned me *slightly* obsessed.

But I have her now. I was fixated on revenge, and everything is going according to plan. Nothing to worry about.

I lie down in the dark on my side, my hand against her pussy, watching her chest rise and fall and her tormented nipples only lit by the light of the moon.

I should sleep now.

Stop watching her. Go to sleep.

I swallow, letting my gaze roam over her whole body and land on her delicate lips. Her mouth parts in the slightest, deep breaths coming in and out of her.

Right. Now, I'll sleep.

But ten minutes later, I'm still observing her.

There's something that stops me from looking away. I want to catch every single breath, all the ways her eyes shift beneath her lids. I want to make sure every micro movement she makes is a moment I can keep to myself.

One more minute and I'll sleep.

And I promise I'm about to roll over onto my back, when her body twitches violently. Her face twists, a gasp trembling up her throat.

I let go of her pussy, giving her some space, but it wasn't because of me since it happens again. It's sudden, her body twisting now, like something somewhere is hurting.

I feel my brow furrowing. What the fuck is that? I'm about to order her to name the emotion when I'm reminded that she's fucking asleep. But I can't read her if she can't tell me what she's feeling.

Is she scared? It's hard when I don't see the fear in her eyes. I run through the information I've learned from her.

Fear, despair, satisfaction, obedience, defeat.

I don't get it.

She startles again, her back curving. Then she tries to turn to the side, like she's avoiding something.

"Stop it," she groans. "Stop, let her go."

"Kayla." I don't even know what to say next. I've never dealt with whatever this is before.

She whimpers, her eyes scrunching, her face morphing. She's in pain, but she's asleep.

"No!" she cries out. "Don't break me... Don't break me. You're going to break me."

The words are barely articulated, like her jaw muscle can't function, but I still make them out. Is she having a nightmare about what just happened?

"Kayla," I snap, harsher this time. "You're dreaming."

"Dad, stop." A whimper escapes her again, and my body freezes. "You're going to break me!"

Dad?

Her hand lashes out in front of her. It's like she's trying to push someone away.

"Please, Dad..."

Ah. Fuck.

I wrap my fingers around her wrist, dragging her closer to me.

"Wake up." I don't fucking know what to say. I feel like I'm facing a puppy that has no idea how to listen to an order.

I shake her, and she starts to hyperventilate.

"I'll break..." She gasps, choking on air. "I'll break... No, *no.*"

What is this reaction?

I feel frustration rising within me. She's impossible to wake up. Is this some sort of sleepwalking?

"Name it, Kayla," I bark.

What the fuck am I doing? She can't hear me.

I pull her closer, lifting her slightly. She's so stiff I can barely move her, but she's as heavy as a dead body, completely asleep.

"Wake the fuck up."

I slide my hand behind her neck, attempting to sit her up, but she fights me out of nowhere, suddenly screaming her lungs out. I try to stop her from hitting me, and I lose the little balance I had to sit up.

I fall onto my back, and her head crashes against my chest.

Her hand comes to my arm and her small fingers wrap around my biceps. She squeezes hard, her nails digging into my skin. But suddenly, she's calm. The gesture seems to get her to rest again, and as quickly as it came, it disappears.

In a split second, she's fast asleep on my chest, her breathing even, her body relaxed. She's holding my arm loosely, and there's not a word coming out of her anymore.

I blink down, looking at the top of her head. This is fucking uncomfortable. I hate it.

She's heavy on my chest, my neck is at an awkward angle with the headboard, and her shoulder is digging into my ribs. But she whimpers when I try to move her, her body tightening against mine, leg wrapping around my hips.

"For heaven's sake, Kayla." I huff, sending a puff of air on her black hair.

But I don't move.

In fact, I barely breathe, not wanting to disrupt her sleep.

Fuck, I even put my hand in her hair to caress it.

"You're fine now," I whisper to her. Why? She can't even hear me. "No matter what he did, you're safe now." Would you listen to that hypocrite.

I don't sleep. I watch the summer sun rise early. I listen to the birds singing in the tree outside my window. But mainly? I listen to every single breath Kayla takes.

What is it?

Name it, Nate.

That warmth that spreads through your chest when she holds on to you.

Name it.

19

KAYLA

Something To Hide - grandson

A groan escapes me the second I feel my body wake up. My eyes aren't even open yet and my stiff neck lets me know I slept in a horrible position. It's one of those mornings where a pounding headache is my alarm clock. Fucking hate these mornings.

I'm on my side, practically on my front, really, my leg hooked around something hard, my cheek resting on a smooth and warm surface, and my hand holding...

Fuck.

In a split second, I'm attempting to pull away from Nate, but his hand resting at the back of my neck tightens, keeping me close to his chest.

"Let me go," I hiss.

"You weren't complaining last night when you hooked yourself onto me like a barnacle to a boat."

Last night is a fucking mess in my head. I don't even remember getting out of that torture room he calls a basement. All I know is the mix of pleasure and pain I felt.

I remember the soft sheets, the thrusts of his hard cock inside me that brought unmatched amounts of pleasure.

The clearest moment is when he asked me to tell him to stop. And that I did only because it turns us both on. I didn't want him to stop. I wanted it to last forever. Even when my body was sore, even when I couldn't breathe, even when I was in and out of consciousness. I wanted it all and more.

I said stop when I wanted to say harder. I moaned *no* when I wanted to beg him to hurt me more, to force me to take something so painful it would break me completely.

You're my dirty little masochist. Mine.

Yes. I really fucking am.

"I didn't hook onto you. Let me go, Nate."

I attempt to look up despite my awkward position, and he finally lets go, looking at me with his impassive face.

"Did your dad rape you?" His voice is so bland I don't even think I heard the question right.

I race into a sitting position, crawling away from him.

"What the—" Not realizing how far I've moved back, I fall off the bed, crashing onto the floor.

If that doesn't make my headache worse, I don't know what will. I put two hands on the mattress, helping myself into a standing position. Grabbing the pillow, I hide my naked body behind it as if he hasn't seen all of me. Fucking hell, he branded it.

"What the fuck, Nate? Who asks that?"

He shrugs. "You call your dad's name in your sleep, did you know? Asking him not to break you."

My mouth drops open, and I can only blink silently.

Throwing the covers to the side, he gets out of bed. While he walks around naked in his room, I can't help my eyes from dropping to his dick. It's half-hard, probably from morning wood, but I can't fucking stop staring at the silky skin. Who even has a dick that beautiful? It's ridiculous.

He goes to his suit pants, taking his phone out of them. He's not even focused on me, probably checking his messages and missed calls as he keeps talking. "You can tell me if he did. Maybe that's why you like being forced?"

"I—" Throat tightening and thoughts spiraling, I'm unable to respond.

This is not how these kinds of talks go. Not with a psychopath who couldn't care less about it. Not with someone who can't feel your pain.

He throws his phone on the bed before walking to me.

"Hey." Now standing inches away from me, he grabs my chin in his hand, forcing me to look up at him. "My foster dad raped me." He shrugs, and my stomach drops. "I was already fucked in the head way before, but I'm sure for someone who isn't, it must have a huge impact." He taps the side of my head with his index finger. "Did it fuck you up in the head?"

I can't even pick up my jaw off the floor. "Your foster dad? Oh my god, *Nate*." The empathy in my voice makes me want to die. This man is holding me captive; now isn't the time to feel bad for him.

But shit. That's...heavy. He can't talk about it like that. Like his foster dad once gave him a little slap or scolded him. He *raped* him.

"What?" he asks stupidly as his eyes flick around my face. "What are you thinking? Name it."

"I—I don't—"

"Name it, Kayla." His grip tightens, his frustration growing like all the times he can't read me.

"I-I'm sad." Fuck. That was a big mistake.

"Sad?" he asks, surprised. "Is that what you look like when sad?"

I shake my head. "I don't know! I feel bad for you."

"You're empathizing, then?"

"Oh my god." I try to shrug him away. "This is weird. Stop."

But he doesn't let me go. My arms tighten around the pillow I'm hugging against my body, and I look away.

"Look at me," he snaps. "I want to understand."

"Me too!" I bark desperately. "I want to fucking understand how you can talk about...about what happened to you without blinking. It clearly broke you."

"No, you don't get it. See, I was already like this. I was born like this. Nothing made me this way, Kayla. What Bianco did, it angered me. I was furious, so I decided to take over his empire. I stopped him from doing the same to my siblings. I played along, then I put him away and watched him suffer. Done and dusted."

"What? Bianco was your foster dad? I-I thought he was just your boss." My head is spinning. "So, you've always been part of the Cosa Nostra?"

"Ugh," he huffs. "This is a long story, Kayla. I have a lot of things to do today."

"Oh, yes, please, *excuse me.* I do forget you're busy. See, I'm stuck here with absolutely nothing to fucking do except wallow in despair, so I did have time for a little chat this morning."

The corner of his lips pinches into a small smile and, out of nowhere, he laughs. It's discreet, barely out of his chest when he adds, "That was funny."

"Nothing about this is funny." Maybe I'm starting to feel his constant exasperation.

He takes a step back, running his hand through his messy blond strands. "Okay. I get your frustration."

"Do you? I thought you couldn't understand what I feel."

He smiles, but it's cold. "Don't push me, I'm feeling kind now that I know about your dad."

I roll my eyes. He doesn't fucking know shit.

"See, my siblings and I were orphans. Then Mateo Bianco, yes, the same Bianco you've heard of, took us in. I was twelve, the twins were eight. Twelve was old enough for me to understand I had antisocial behavior issues, believe me. I already knew something was off, that's how I can tell you it wasn't him who made me this way. Turns out Bianco liked to take lots of kids to groom them into being his soldiers. My sister was the only unlucky one he wanted to keep to himself. So when I learned about it, I defended her. He raped me and threatened to do the same to her if we didn't start behaving or if we tried to leave. I got everyone in check. I forced my siblings to stay so I could protect them from him, and I spent ten years planning how to take him down."

His smile brightens. "And look. Now I own his empire, and he's dead. So who's the real winner here?"

Holy shit.

The man lives in complete denial.

When I don't respond for a few minutes, he waves a hand in front of my face. "Kayla?"

"You are so fucking broken." I don't mean it to come out as an insult, but this is as fucked as it comes.

He sighs, dismissing me. "Now you're being dramatic." Sliding a hand at the back of my neck, he steers me in the direction of the bathroom. "Come on, we need to shower before I leave."

I don't even have the strength to fight back. I follow along, watching him turn it on and walk in.

"You'd better drop the pillow if you want to join." My hands tighten around it, wondering if it's smart to shower with him. I could just wait.

"Kayla," he chuckles. "Remember when I chained you to my basement and hit you repeatedly with a crop?"

I narrow my eyes at him, pushing my words past my gritted teeth. "Yes, Nathan. I do."

"Well, you were naked for it. So drop that pillow and join me, will you?"

Choosing to save my energy for a fight after I take a headache tablet, I drop the pillow and join him under the hot water. The heat feels heavenly against my battered body, but I hate the way I startle when he settles behind me and cups my breasts. One hand is holding a loofah bubbling with shower gel that he presses against my right nipple.

"How are they feeling?"

"Guess, asshole."

He smiles against my neck as he skims my skin with his lips. "Where's the compliant wife I fucked yesterday?"

The feeling of his dick hardening against my lower back sends electricity up my spine. Did I not get enough of this yesterday? My pussy feels like it needs a break, not another round. So why am I already getting wet?

One hand slides to my lower stomach, and he plays with my scar there. I close my eyes, hoping with everything I have that he doesn't ask more questions about it.

"Tell me." He starts washing my breast, running gentle circles against it. I try to keep my breathing under control, but it stutters when he carries on talking. "What did your dad do to you?"

I squeeze my eyes shut. Of course, he wasn't going to let this go. I don't know why I thought talking about his past would make him retreat. If you can even call a proud speech about taking over your rapist's empire 'talking about your past.'

"I'll get it out of you, little sunflower. The question is..." His hand goes lower. "Are you going to drag the bad guy out of me and make me finger you while I make you talk? Or should we both play nice and share our stories?"

Two fingers slide between my nether lips, and I choke on a breath. The word squeaks past my tight throat when I speak. "*Stop.*"

"Talk."

"He didn't rape me," I blurt out. "Fuck...stop."

His hand retreats, going back to my stomach as the other calmly washes my collarbone.

"What did he do?"

"He beat me up. That's it. Nothing out of the ordinary for most kids on the North Shore."

He stops moving for a second, and I sense him turning my words over in his mind.

"No. That sleep talking, screaming, whatever the fuck that was you put me through last night is not from someone who got beat up as a kid. You were *terrified.*"

"I don't know what you're talking about." And I really don't. I dream about it sometimes, but Ivan never mentioned me screaming during the night. All I know is when I have dreamt about it, I wake up with a headache. "I don't remember anything."

"You don't remember dreaming about your dad? Screaming at him not to break you?"

I gulp. How the fuck does he know about that? Those

are the exact words I used to say to my asshole of a father when he lost it.

"I..."

"My, my." His free hand trails down my front, and he pinches my inner thigh. "You're a little liar, Kayla."

"I'm not. I don't remember."

"But you do know why you said those words."

My stuttered breath reverberates all the way down my back.

"He—" I lick my lips. They feel dry despite the mist in the shower. "He would beat me really hard if I tried to stop him from assaulting my mom. But her cries...it was horrible. Especially when he, when he..."

Dropping the loofah, he stops washing me. One hand comes around my wrist to press against my pulse, and the other lays flat on my chest. "When he what?"

I hate Nate's soft voice. I know it's only to coax the truth out to me. And yet I fall for it.

"When he raped her," I whisper. I squeeze my eyes, attempting to stop the onslaught of images. "When I was little, I wasn't sure what it was, but I knew it hurt her. And when I grew up, I understood it happened all the time. So I would try to get him off her, but when he moved on to me, the attack was brutal, and I was terrified he would completely *break me.*"

The grip on my wrist tightens, and I sense the frustration emanating from him. "He sexually assaulted you." His voice is a low, angry growl resonating in his chest.

"No. He didn't. I know what sexual assault looks like. I've witnessed it many times on my mom. He beat me. I'm not lying. It was unbearable and vicious, but he never sexually assaulted me, okay? Stop believing that. He only did it to my mom. That's how they had me, and that's how they had my brother. And Caden, he was too little to understand shit. So I'd just take him to his room and get him to focus on the only thing in my life that made sense. Numbers, math. Something simple like that."

I turn around in his hold and press a flat hand to his cheek, making him look down at me. My eyes cross with the storm unfurling in his gaze.

"What happened to you never happened to me, but I've seen the way it affected my brother. He doesn't remember, but he saw shit that changed him. He saw my mom crying and bleeding after being raped, and how I'd try to console her. Caden...now...he's just like you. He can't feel things, can't understand emotions. He doesn't relate to people's sadness or fear. Not even to their happiness. I know how you're wired, Nate. You can't understand me, but I understand you."

He stares at me for god knows how long, and I force myself to hold it. I don't care if I drown in him. I need to appeal to the human side of him if I ever want to get out of here. He thinks he doesn't care about what happened, but he shared a vulnerable event that affected him deeply. The almighty Nathan White wasn't always indestructible, and I need to hold on to that to survive.

He only breaks out of the hold when a chuckle escapes him. Tilting his head to the side, he bites his lower lip before smiling. Shit, he is way too fucking beautiful when he does that.

"Little sunflower, you're not trying to find something redeemable about me, are you?" His face falls, his entire demeanor darkening. His voice is a rough purr when he talks again. "Because that would not only be stupid." A split second later, my back crashes against the shower wall, his hand around my throat. "It would also be dangerous."

He's practically lifting me off the floor, my feet stretching so I can still stand on my own. My hands fly to his forearms. They're veiny, muscles tensing.

He is not playing anymore. He's over his little game of digging into each other's pasts and the way he presses against my windpipe makes me cough.

"Kayla," he says flatly. "Think again why you're here. Think real hard about why I would want to know what haunts your nightmares. It's not to cuddle you and make you feel better, and it's not so we can cry over our fucked-up pasts." He presses his forehead against mine, but I still notice the way he grits his teeth.

For the first time, Nate's impacted by what I said. He's angry, and he's trying to hide it.

"The only reason I want to know about your worst nightmares is to make sure I can replace them. There's only one thing you have to fear anymore, and that's me. Do you understand?"

My vision becomes dizzy, black dots covering the room.

He releases just enough for me to drag in air, but he keeps me immobile anyway.

"I said, *do you understand*, wife?"

"Y-yes," I croak.

"Atta girl. Now finish showering and meet me for breakfast."

I crash to the floor when he lets me go, unable to hold myself together, but I wait until he's out of the room to cry.

Because, fuck, this is too much. I feel like I've been here forever, even though I could probably still count the days on one hand.

I'm fucking married. I'm fucking stuck. I miss my family, and I miss my crew.

People must have been wrong when they called me

strong. I don't feel it. I'm not strong at all. I'm weakened and exhausted. There's always someone bigger and stronger than you. Scarier. Someone you shouldn't mess with. And I fucking messed with him.

The second I'm out of the shower and in a robe, I search the bathroom cabinets for band-aids. The cut at my neck keeps opening every time it starts to heal. Blame it on the man who's taking a liking to choking me.

Hands shaking, I open and close the drawers and cabinets.

I can't feel my extremities, and I can't stop sobbing like an idiot. It's because of him. Because he made me talk about my mom and the kind of shit I pushed to the back of my mind a long time ago. So long ago that I don't even think about them when I talk to my mother. I didn't even think about them when I lived with my dad as an adult. I hated him, period. I didn't need to remind myself why.

When my mom ran away, he'd still beat me and Caden up, but the second we both became too strong, he stopped like the fucking coward he is. Especially when Caden started hitting back. My brother sent my dad to the hospital when I got a simple slap out of nowhere. After that, he never touched us again.

"Fuck!" I snap when I realize I'm shaking so much I can't even stand still.

I hate feeling like this. I sacrificed my shell of strength to get into his head, and I'm still the one suffering.

A knock on the bathroom door startles me. I jump on a box of tissues on the side of the counter, running them under my eyes even as more tears fall.

"O-one second," I hiccup.

But the door opens anyway.

"Nate, for fuck's sake," I hiss as I turn toward the door.

But it's not Nate. It's a million times worse.

"What the fuck are you doing here?" My voice sounds harsh, but I can still feel tears streaming down my face, and my nose is blocked, making me sound weaker than I want to.

Emma holds a small metal box with *first aid* written on it. Her eyes widen when she sees my state, and she closes the door behind her.

"Shit, are you okay?" She extends her free hand toward my throat, but I swat it away.

"Don't fucking touch me."

I'm forced to wipe more tears, and I want nothing but the ground to open and swallow me when I notice her look of pity. I swallow them back, choking on every single one but refusing for Emma Scott to see me like this.

"Kayla..." She hesitates, taking a step closer as she observes the bruises on my neck. "Did he do this to you?"

"Oh my god," I snort. "What the fuck is this? You want to start a charity for abused women or something? What do you want?"

Her eyes drop to the box in her hand. "Nate said you'd need this. Look, this...this is fucked."

I shake my head, not believing what I'm hearing. "Are you alright? Do you know who I am? We're enemies, Emma, why do you care what happens to me? Are you forgetting you're the one who set me up for this?"

"I didn't set you up for *this*." She waves at my throat again. "Shit, I wanted the North Shore back, but I didn't want..."

I cock an eyebrow at her. "To see the consequences of your actions?"

"He's dangerous," she insists. She puts the box on the

counter and opens it. "This isn't about a North Shore feud anymore. Nate is pissing off the Wolves."

She takes out a couple of band-aids and some disinfectant.

I swallow thickly as she turns to me. "What do you mean, pissing off the Wolves?"

"I don't know exactly what he's doing, but people are being threatened, bodies are piling up, and it's coming from the Wolves. If he carries on, he'll start a full-on war between the Bratva and the Cosa Nostra. This is bigger than you and me, and it's fucking bigger than NSC and the Kings."

Nate mentioned they'd heard he's back, and that's why he's keeping a guard at the door.

A million thoughts still running through my mind, I ask, "Surely the Lucianos had something to say when you switched from them to the Bianco family. Do they know about the war Nate is starting? They won't let him."

"I don't know. I haven't been in touch with Vito Luciano in a long time."

I try to take the band-aids from her, but she pulls her hand away. "Sit on the counter."

I don't know what goes through my head, but I do it. I hoist myself on the marble counter in front of my lifelong enemy, and I let her spray my cut with antiseptic.

She dabs my skin with cotton, and her eyes cross with mine.

"You need to do something, Kay. He's planning some bullshit move and we're all at risk."

"Right. Because it's so easy to do something against Nate's will. You put me in here, now you figure it out without me."

When she sticks the band-aid, she presses hard, and I slap her hand away. "Bitch."

"I just needed to check the tough girl everyone knows as Kayla, *the ruthless* King is still in there somewhere. What, you're just going to let Nate turn you into a fucking housewife who's never even allowed to leave her house? Wake the fuck up."

I push her away, standing again. "Do you have any fucking idea the shit he has on me? Or what it would cost me to fight back? I'll get a one-way ticket to prison for lying under oath if I leave. A mansion in Stoneview is better than cement walls, don't you think?"

"With Nathan White?" she snorts. "I'm not sure."

Crossing her arms over her chest, she looks at me from top to bottom and back up.

"I thought I had an indestructible woman as my enemy. Had I known it would be that easy to take you down—"

"Shut the fuck up, Emma. You don't know anything that asshole is capable of."

She shrugs. "I saw him commit cold-blooded murder because Law tried to kill you the night of the Death Cage fight. I'm pretty sure I have an idea."

My mouth drops open. "What?"

"I just don't get how he stays so impassive when he kills."

"Because he's a fucking psychopath."

"A psychopath who cares about keeping you alive."

"To fucking *torture me*." It takes all of me not to scream in her face.

"I need to go back before he starts wondering why I'm taking so long. I don't even know why he asked me to come today, but I was told by some of my men that he asked them too. He's up to something."

I clench my jaw, different plans filtering through my thoughts until something finally comes to the forefront. It's crazy and will most certainly get me killed, but it's something.

"Give me your phone," I say in a hurry.

She doesn't hesitate, digging into her pocket. "What are you doing?"

"Better you don't know." I go into her contacts and look for the number I need, repeating it a few times in my head.

Numbers have always been easy for me. It's not a problem to remember a few digits. Giving her phone back to her, I point at the door. "Go back. I'm handling this."

She rolls her eyes. "You're fucking welcome."

"Fuck you. You're still the one who conspired against me with Nate."

PART II

OBSESSION

'Mad' is a term we use to describe a man who is obsessed with one idea and nothing else.

Ugo Betti

20

NATHAN

APHRODITE - Ethan Gander

The kitchen door closes, and I don't need to look up to know it's Sam. My friend's gigantic presence takes up a lot of space in a room. I keep scrolling on my phone, reading the article on my screen.

"They're waiting for you," he says seriously. "If you keep people from the Kings and NSC in a room for too long without supervision, you'll come back to a bloodbath."

"I haven't had breakfast yet."

I sense him looking around the room. "You haven't made any breakfast, Nate."

Finally looking up, I eye him standing on the other side of the kitchen island where I'm sitting. I take a sip of my coffee and put the mug back on the table.

"I was hoping my beautiful wife would make me breakfast."

Just as I say that, Emma is the next person to enter the kitchen.

"Your beautiful wife is still tending to the bruises you left around her neck." Her voice is a little snappy today. Who would've thought she would care if I hurt Kay or not?

I glance at her with new curiosity. "She likes it, don't you worry."

She slams her hand on the kitchen counter, now standing right beside Sam. "Never heard an abuser say *that* before."

Tilting my head to the side, I observe her small form. "I can assure you those things make her come. She practically begs for it." A small smile tips the corner of my lips. "You know what it's like when a woman comes, Emma. I don't need to spell it out to you."

It's no secret the head of NSC likes women.

She runs her tongue across her front teeth. "I sure know what it's like when your sister does."

Poor girl was trying to get to me. And she did. I can't stand anyone mentioning my sister in any way, shape, or form. Especially not to disrespect her.

But I bet she didn't expect two guns pointed at her head in a split second. Talking about fucking Rose in front of her brother and current boyfriend? Not exactly a smart move, is it?

"Holy shit." She takes a step back, palms facing us. "It was a long time ago. Everybody chill."

Sam's stare is deadly, but I bet his gun is deadlier. When I put mine down, he can't seem to do the same.

A laugh escapes me when Emma's strong stare turns defeated.

"Next time you think of mentioning fucking my girlfriend. Think twice."

I whistle, wiggling my eyebrows at Emma. "The boy's possessive."

She narrows her gaze at me. "I'll be in the meeting room. I'm sure you have wonderful news for all of us."

Don't I ever. She has no idea the Kings are also waiting with her crew in that room.

Even after she leaves the kitchen, Sam seems unable to lower his gun. I look at my phone again, scrolling.

"What do you know about night terrors?"

That finally brings him back. "Night terrors?" He puts his gun down. "A fair bit. Rose used to have them."

I crack my neck, hating that frustrating feeling.

"You'd know, wouldn't you," I say blankly, but he knows me. He knows my tells, when I'm annoyed.

"You asked. I answered. Stop being a shitty overprotective brother." He pours himself a cup of coffee, turning his back to me. What a brave man. "Why do you ask?"

I relax against my seat. I guess he has a point. "I think Kayla has them."

He sits down opposite me, taking a sip. "And you care because?"

"Because it keeps me up at night."

Something presses against my chest. A spike coming from inside me and attempting to pierce me from the inside out. A whisper of a threat calling me a *liar*.

"One night. It kept you up *one* night. You weren't sleeping with her before."

I shrug. "It kept me up last night. That's one too many nights."

He stays silent for a minute. A minute is long when your best friend is trying to read you.

"Trauma," he finally says. "That's all I know about it. She needs to heal." He relaxes against the back of the stool and takes another sip with his eyes on me. "I don't think

263

that's something you can provide her. So I'd say your solution is separate rooms."

A surge of anger rolls through me. My blood boils at the insult he throws my way. I'm capable of everything. Nothing can stop me. If Kayla needs to heal, then I'll fucking heal her.

Reading my mind, Sam shakes his head. "You need to be able to empathize with what someone is going through to help them heal. That's not something you can do."

"I can do anything." My cold tone surprises me.

I'm frustrated because he's underestimating me. Because he should know I can do anything I set my mind to.

I'm not frustrated because he thinks I can't take care of my wife. Right?

I crack my neck again. Something feels off inside, and I can't comprehend it. That's to be added to the list of things annoying me today.

The door opens, and Kayla walks in, in a pair of black jeans and a tight black tank top. Head held high, I can clearly see the band-aid covering the cut on her neck and the bruises from my fingers underneath.

My dick can see it too, according to the way it wakes up in my suit pants.

My wife crosses her arms over her chest, looking at me with that fierceness in her green eyes I enjoy so much. Nothing can take that woman down, not even forcing her to talk about the things that broke her.

"How's the neck?" I ask, extending my hand so she understands I want her to come to me. She sticks to her spot.

"Fine."

"I can call Marcie if you want."

She shrugs. "Sure, if you want a dead body in your house first thing in the morning."

Her hate for my doctor makes me chuckle. I turn to Sam. "Kayla doesn't like Marcie because she's into me." Putting a hand at the corner of my mouth, I point at her and whisper, "Jealous."

"I'm not jealous, Nate," she snaps.

"Sure thing, little sunflower." Putting my hand out again, I spell it out for her this time. "Come here."

She takes a deep breath and finally comes my way. Sam scratches his throat, and he leaves without saying a word. He's not one to waste his breath.

I take Kayla's hand and wrap an arm around her waist. Her hair is still damp from the shower, and she smells of my body wash. I'm not sure I like that.

"What's your usual body wash?"

"I don't know," she mutters, completely uninterested by my question.

"It smells like grapefruit. Do you know the brand?"

"Yeah, it's called supermarket. Ever heard of it?"

"Which supermarket?"

"The closest one to my house. You're being an annoying fuck."

I ignore her usual insult and drop a kiss on her pouty lips. It's not the way I want to. Really, I want to taste her like the finest meal. I want to devour her like the starved man I am. But it's the kiss she deserves. Something brief, that will leave her wondering what I truly mean by it. Something to drive her mad.

"My dear wife," I murmur against her mouth. "Will you cook me an omelet for breakfast? I've been craving one."

She stays still when I kiss her again, inhaling a trembling breath. How satisfying to keep her on the edge.

She doesn't answer, but she takes a step back and walks to the counter. Pointing at different cupboards, she asks, "Pans?"

I nod when she points at the right one, then go back to my phone. I could get used to this. My wife making me an omelet before I head to my first meeting of the day.

My eyes go to the article I've been reading.

How to support your partner if they have night terrors

The bullet list looks evident, and yet I realize I did none of those things last night.

1. Avoid waking them up.

According to the PhD in psychiatry who wrote the article, people can be violent during their night terrors, and they're unlikely to wake up.

Sounds about right. Kayla almost slapped me yesterday.

2. Talk to them calmly and try to soothe them.

Okay, so I guess no shouting at her to stop her shit. Maybe stroking her sweet cunt will soothe her.

No. She likes violence with her orgasms, that won't do. We'll stick to cuddles.

3. Make the bedroom safe.

What the fuck? There's more than thrashing around and screaming in my face? She could actually start walking around the room. That's interesting...and a little terrifying.

4. Wake them before the terror begins.

I lean closer to my phone. People who have night terrors suffer from PTSD. If they're not triggered by something specific in the environment, it's possible the terrors happen around the same time every night. Okay, let's start analyzing that.

"Nate?"

"Mhm?"

My thoughts still focused on how to help with night terrors, I turn toward her voice. I barely catch her shadow when the pan hits me right in the side of the face.

The sharp pain drags a grunt out of me as I fall to the floor. My hand flies to my temple, feeling the wound, and up to my hairline.

I'm bleeding.

My ears ring and my vision blurs as I notice her towering over me, pan in hand. She looks down at my lying form, a beautiful, sick smile spreading on her lips.

"How's your omelet, darling?"

That's when I realize there's cooked eggs all over the floor, and that the crazy woman hit me with a searing-hot pan she just used to make my breakfast.

I try to talk, but I'm still too dizzy. Taking a deep breath, I can smell the eggs on the floor next to me. I relish the sense of pride overwhelming me. Fuck, I'm so proud of her for still fighting back.

When I can finally look straight, I take in her determined eyes. I'm between her legs, each foot by my hips. She's standing like the super heroine of a comic book.

Super-pan woman.

Shit, I think I'm concussed.

"You look so beautiful like this," I rasp.

Her smile drops. "I'm leaving, Nate," she snarls.

I laugh, my eyes fluttering closed. "Don't. I'll miss you." I drag in a breath. "I'll miss you when you go to prison for lying in court."

There's a practical growl leaving her. A fury she couldn't hide if she tried. "I *know* I can't leave forever. I am leaving to see my crew and my family. We'll talk about your terms when I come back."

My little sunflower knows the situation she's in. She

can't run away. She just wants a little bit of freedom to see the people she loves. To take care of them.

That is absolutely out of the question.

No freedom for my wife.

No freedom for the person I want to possess so badly, I can barely have her out of my sight. For my new favorite obsession.

No freedom for the woman who is making me feel something I can't name.

Not until I understand what's going on in my body.

I murmur something, but she can't hear it.

"What?"

She leans down, lowering on her haunches and getting closer to me. I notice her fingers tightening around the handle of the pan, ready to hit me again if needed.

"I said." I grab the back of her neck, holding her face close to mine. Before she can defend herself, I've pulled out my gun from my holster, and I'm holding the muzzle against her stomach. "Your crew is already here."

Something dies in her gaze. Hope, I think.

"Fucking asshole," she grunts.

"Here's a lesson for you. Kill me or give up. Half-assed attempts at hurting me never work."

I can see she agrees with the way her jaw locks and her eyes blink a few times. She's got nothing to say to that. She knows I'm right.

"Now, drop the pan, darling wife."

The heavy pan hits the floor with a thud. I keep my gun pointed at Kay as we both stand up. Dragging the barrel to her chest, up her throat, I finally point it upward just under her chin.

"It turns me on like crazy when you do stupid shit like this."

I seize her hand, pressing it against my hard-on, and capture her lips. My possessive kiss surprises me, and according to her small gasp, it does her too. This doesn't feel as manipulative as the peck on her lips earlier. This is a first kiss if I've ever felt one.

This is...*fuck*...I can't control it. And I can't control the adrenaline kicking my heart into gear. The beat is so fast it pounds painfully against my chest.

It's ridiculous how badly I want her. It shows in the way I force my tongue past her lips and intensify the pressure of my gun against her.

With my other hand, I let her go for a millisecond just to unzip my pants. She hisses against me when I bite her tongue, but she doesn't pull away. No, if anything, she's now pressing herself against me, her back curving, her delicious boobs tight against my chest.

"Nate," she moans into my mouth when I guide her hand inside my boxers.

She wraps her soft fingers around my length, gripping tightly. When she doesn't need my guidance anymore, I release her to unbutton her jeans.

"Fuck," she hisses against my lips. But she can't say anything else. I'm swallowing her whole, needing to be as close as I can. Needing her lips, her warmth, *her.*

The possession becomes dangerous when she tries to pull away.

"No," I growl. I press my gun harder under her chin.

At the same time, I push her until her back hits the wall. She groans into my mouth and starts moving her hand, rubbing my cock into a painful hardness. I can feel myself leaking precum, and it turns me on even more knowing that it's going to touch her beautiful fingers.

I slide my hand into her jeans, below the waistband of her underwear.

A fire starts in me when I feel the wetness soaking her entrance.

"Why are you so wet for me?" She squeezes around my length, and I laugh against her lips.

There's nothing that can stop me from kissing her over and over again. Something burns, something tears me apart. It hurts desperately, and only her mouth can soothe it.

I push two fingers inside her, and flames lick my skin, burning all the way to my soul.

"Is your cunt desperate for your husband's touch?" I growl with need. "Will you come for me like a good little wife?"

Her body rolls against mine, answering for her. But that's not good enough. I want her to say it. I want to *hear the words.*

"I could kill you." I press the gun more harshly against her. "Or I could make you come."

That drags a whimper out of her, and it goes straight to my cock.

Her little fist accelerates, keeping my dick hostage and making it so delicious for me.

"What do you want, Kayla? A quick death, or to be my little fuck toy?"

Her moan is the only answer for another minute. She thrusts her hips, dragging me in deeper. She begs me with her movements, but no matter how good this is for me, I stay strong.

"Answer me, little sunflower." Another kiss, another hit of my new favorite drug.

"C-come," she breathes delicately against my lips. For someone so desperate, it's a discreet plea. "I want to come."

"You want to be my fuck toy," I snap, weirdly furious that she won't spell it out. "Say it." I press harder inside her, gritting my teeth when she retaliates with her grip on my dick.

"I want to, Nate. Please. I want to b-be your fuck toy."

I bite her lower lip to the point of breaking and lick her blood.

"Good wife," I purr as I curl my fingers inside her and watch her come undone. At the same time, I'm thrusting into her fist, exploding in her hand.

We're both out of breath, my forehead resting against hers, and I feel the blood from my torn eyebrow spreading on her skin. I don't care.

"Kayla," I whisper against her. She's still panting, her eyelids drooping. "Kayla, listen to me."

"Mhm," she mumbles on a whisper. "I am."

"I will never let you go."

Her body shudders, but for once, she doesn't fight back.

Maybe she can hear something she didn't hear in my previous threats.

I certainly do.

It sounds like the brush of an artist painting his muse. The notes of a musician writing his masterpiece. The tone of voice coming from a determined psychopath.

Utter obsession.

21

KAYLA

Scars - Boy Epic

He kissed me.

I will never let you go.

I don't think I heard that kind of determination from anyone before. Not even myself.

He barely gave me time to wipe his cum off my hand on a paper towel, barely gave me a chance to zip up my jeans, when he was already dragging me out of the kitchen by the hair.

"What did you mean?" I pant, barely holding back a grunt.

He kissed me.

How can someone go from so savagely loving to a pure monster again? He has too many faces for me to count or understand, manipulating anything and anyone he encounters, and I can't keep up anymore.

He kissed me and it felt *good*.

"What did you mean by my crew is here?"

"You just wait two more seconds, little sunflower."

He presses his hand on a door but turns to me before pushing it open.

"Just remember. The life of every single person in this room is in the palm of my hand. Their future too. Behave and no one gets hurt."

He kissed me and I don't think I will ever get over it.

He kissed me and I felt something I never had before.

But it disappears the moment we enter the room.

There's a buzz of violence hanging in the air. It's heavy, sticky, making it hard to breathe.

No need to wonder why.

In a large room, with a side purely made of floor-to-ceiling windows, dark green walls, and surrounded by guards...the biggest players of both NSC and the Kings are sitting around a mahogany table.

Who, in their right mind, would ever bring together our two gangs? Emma and I surely never did. If we ever had to meet, it would be just the two of us. Violence runs in our blood, and hatred for the opposite gang is vital to our survival. We've waged a deadly war for as long as any of us here can remember. Reasons have blurred over time, but pride is the most important thing anyway. The rest doesn't matter anymore.

So, no, no one in their right mind would call a meeting with NSC and the Kings.

But Nate would. Because everyone here knows he is anything but right in the head.

A chair scrapes against the floor as we enter, and a small gasp I know too well reaches my ears.

My eyes dart to Jade, her mouth hanging open and her fists tight on the table. She must have fought tooth and nail for her two boyfriends to let her come here, but she's one of the toughest girls I know. She had to be present.

She's not the one who stood up, though. She's not the six-foot-seven giant who is now standing with a deadly stare that won't leave the exact spot Nate is fisting my hair.

"Let her fucking go."

"I'm fine, Elliot," I grunt.

"Apologies for the delay, everyone," Nate says casually as he wipes some blood dripping from his eyebrow. "My wife and I had a slight disagreement."

He sits down at the end of the table, pulling me with him, and I land uncomfortably on his lap.

"I can take a fucking chair," I hiss in a whisper.

He's discreet when his answer caresses my ear. "I feel the best when your body is against mine."

My heart accelerates, skipping a few beats as it does so.

What the hell did he just say?

I don't even have time to process it.

"She said she was fine, Elliot," Nate insists when my friend and closest ally doesn't move. His eyes are stuck on the rings decorating my fingers. His brother, Ethan, is focused on the bruises around my neck.

"Really," I insist.

Both their gazes finally meet mine, and I nod, showing a strong face. It's not an easy task while sitting on the lap of a psychopath, but they trust me. They finally sit down, and I allow myself to scan the room. Five guards surround us. Four at each corner of the room, and one by the door that leads in.

Sam is sitting, his chair on the opposite side of the room to Nate and me, but he's not at the table. He's farther back, observing all of us.

And finally, on parallel sides of the long table, facing each other, are members of my crew, and my lifelong enemies.

To my left, the Kings.

Elliot sits in the middle of the Kings' row. He's my right-hand. I never do anything without running it past him. On his right is Jade, sandwiched between him and his dangerously impassive brother, Ethan. She's a tiny thing, but fuck if she can hold her own. Plus, she's one hell of a driver. And Ethan, no one in this room but us knows, he's a serial killer who has gotten away with more than one should in a lifetime. When I need him to, his job is to torture people for me. The real hardship is to get him to keep them alive.

On Elliot's left is Cuts. He manages all my drug dealers. Once the man gets our products, he and his team cut our keys of pure cocaine into bags, split our methamphetamines into manageable custom-size packets, and distribute them in all the areas that belong to the Kings. Sometimes even in gray territories we're fighting over. On Cuts' left is Ana Sofia. People tried to get the nickname Colombian Strap going for her because she is my arms girlie. But most of them ended up dead so they stopped. With such a pretty name, it really would have been a shame to reduce her to her job and nationality. Since the Wolves let us go and they're not our providers anymore, Ana Sofia has been pretty much out of a job, especially since I can't find someone new to work with.

And the last of my crew here today is Cole. Cole, the collector, aka the man who collects our debts. At first sight, he's your typical blond, All-American-Jock with the attitude of a golden retriever. He's got such bright white teeth and a killer smile. Don't owe us money and you'll never have to meet his dark side. We're loan sharks; if you can't pay back your debts, Cole will gladly go from golden retriever to hunter in no time.

Elliot, Jade, Ethan, Cuts, Ana Sofia, Cole. These people are the essence of the Kings' crew. They're a team I put together to make us the most effective gang on the North Shore. Well, before Emma pulled the rug from under our feet.

On my right, Nate has called upon the equivalent of my team, but from NSC. The North Shore Crew have their own smartly put-together squad.

Emma, of course, sits on my right, the closest to Nate and me. And she brought all her besties with her. Logan, her right-hand man. Racer, who pretty much does anything she asks. Nino, her arms guy. Her collector is missing, Law, but I now know he didn't last long after Nate laid down his own rules. And her IT girl is here, Tamar. No one ever sees her because she prefers to hide behind her computer.

To my surprise, on their side of the room but not sitting with them, is Xi. He's leaning against the floor-to-ceiling windows, arms crossed, wearing his usual scowl.

Xi is equivalent to Cuts for NSC. Or at least used to be. He's meant to have left this life behind since his girlfriend begged him to. But see, this is where the ties on the North Shore become complex, and this is where Emma gets her advantage. She might not be the smartest, but she sure as fuck can pull a good scheme.

Emma is Xi's stepsister. He would never let her down if she ever needed him. Doesn't matter if he's in or out, family is family in their eyes. But hold on, it gets better. Emma's other stepbrother, or Xi's blood brother, if you prefer, is Lik.

And guess who Lik's boyfriend of many years is?

None other than Sam, aka, Nate's right-hand man.

And that's why the Kings were never at an advantage in this situation. Emma, in one way or another, has ties with

Nate. Emma has family dinner with Sam every single week. She's had something on me I managed to keep under control while Nate was in prison, but that power is all hers now. NSC is in with the biggest fucking threat there is. Nathan White.

And me? Well, I'm completely fucked, and I know this meeting is going to end up making my people suffer.

Unless I keep Nate under control. And for that, I have to play nice. I have to be his very, *very* docile little wife. And maybe then I can protect the people I love.

"Wanna tell us why we've been waiting here for fucking hours while you and your girlfriend beat each other up?" Xi's unimpressed tone is the same as I've always heard.

"Wife," Nate corrects instead of answering.

My eyes dart to Elliot, his already on me. I need him to stay calm. He can be volatile when his patience wears thin. Lucky for me, Jade is already wrapping a hand around his tense biceps, keeping him collected.

"I don't care," Xi answers. "Some of us have other shit to do."

"Pretty little Stoneview girls to see," I taunt him.

He straightens up in a split second, pointing a threatening finger at me as his face shuts down completely. "Mention her one more time and see what happens."

"Kayla," Nate chuckles behind me. "Play nice."

Releasing my hair, his hand caresses my back, and I understand he's the one playing. Playing every single person in this room. Because while his voice defends Xi, his reassuring touch tells me he likes that I riled him up. A silent *well done*.

And because Nate thrives in the chaos he causes, he adds, "No need to mention Alexandra. We all know she's his weakness."

Xi's jaw settles in a tight lock, and his gaze digs into Nate's. They stay silent for a few seconds where everyone watches while at the same time probably wondering if Nate knows the weaknesses of every criminal around the table.

I would say the answer is yes.

"But anyway," Nate continues casually. "We're here to discuss the future of the North Shore because the most important topic is business. And I intend on keeping everyone employed."

"What do you mean, keeping everyone employed?" Emma jumps in. "NSC won the North Shore, fair and square."

My snort cuts her off. "Fair and square, my ass, you scheming little bitch."

She narrows her eyes at me, but keeps going. "Point is, we split territories, we applied the rules we all set in our town. I'm not giving the Kings a fucking *job*. They can go find it themselves."

"Well, here's something interesting," Nate chuckles. "You control the North Shore, and I control you. So, I think it's safe to say if I decide something, we go with my plan. And my plan is to unite the North Shore."

My mouth drops open, but I'm not the only one in shock. Every single person in this room has gone mute, jaws hanging, eyes wide.

In my twenty-five years of life, I have never heard of such a stupid proposal. Not only do we all hate each other, not only has it been like this for decades, but there isn't enough work on the North Shore, criminal or not, to keep everyone busy, and certainly not to get them all paid. We struggle enough as it is.

Emma stares at me, her eyes round as saucers. "Did you know about this?" she hisses.

I wish I could control my reaction, and maybe hide what I do or don't know from her, but my shock is too great. I'm shaking my head before I even realize.

"We're not *uniting* the North Shore. I am not working with anyone from the Kings," Emma says, in what I'm sure she attempts to be a steady voice. It's not.

"Then you won't be working at all. I'm your supplier, and you have no one else to provide for you." He shrugs. "It's no headache, really."

Elliot's voice rises from my side of the table. "You're going to supply both crews."

"Forget about your useless crews. If you all work for me, there's no Kings or NSC, only my business. That's all that matters. Currently, both sides have what I need. Drug dealers, collectors, enforcers." His eyes go to Racer on Emma's side, and Jade on mine. "Drivers who can move my money quickly and discreetly. You all have great assets that are perfect to extend a criminal organization in Silver Falls, Stoneview, and all the areas around. I have more supplies than one crew can handle and, lucky for me, I can have twice the people if I use both crews. This is a perfect business move. Not that any of you would understand that."

His voice lowers, and I know he does it on purpose. He could keep this conversation going in the same bored tone forever. Emotionless is his reset setting. But he wants to threaten them tastefully.

"But do you know what isn't good for business? For any empire in the building?" Looking around the room, his hand lazily circles my lower back. "Civil war."

Tension suffocates the room, everyone processing the news in their own way.

"So..." Jade's hesitant, and I'm surprised she even talks. It's usually better for the firecracker to stay quiet if we don't want an explosion. "Are we, like, all part of the Cosa Nostra now?"

Nate waves his hand next to his head. "Forget the Cosa Nostra. You're part of my team, and we don't belong to anyone anymore."

And the surprises keep on coming.

Nate has always been affiliated with the Bianco family. In fact, until this morning, he was telling me he took over his empire. And now he wants to separate himself from the Italian criminal organization? That means, he's having issues with the other families. The Lucianos and the Rossis, no doubt.

What the fuck is he doing?

Jade looks at me, her eyes full of questions, but I nod slightly at her.

Just go with it.

Because this is better for the Kings. And if it means we're working under Nate, then so be it. I'm stuck with him one way or another.

Emma keeps rolling and unrolling her hair around her index fingers, staring at Nate, but it's Xi that speaks up.

"So you're saying you'll only supply the North Shore crews if we work together."

When Nate answers, he's looking at Emma, knowing ultimately, she'll be the one making the decision for her crew.

"Feel free to find other suppliers to keep your people working, but the Wolves won't work with North Shore gangs anymore, and I think you lost all value to the

Lucianos. I've got shipments coming from Canada, Georgia, and Mexico in two weeks. Warehouses will be full. All I need is enough people to do the work."

"This is bullshit," Emma hisses. "That's not what we had agreed to, Nate."

"Deals change all the time. Welcome to the big boys' playground."

Her angry eyes shoot to mine, and her accusing stare means everything. She thinks I was in on it.

"As I said, shipments are coming in two weeks. Emma and Elliot, you have until then to report to me on your decisions. You're dismissed."

His movement of getting up forces me to stand too. He guides me out of the room with that same hand on my lower back, and I follow like an idiot.

His last words stay with me, though.

Emma and Elliot.

He's waiting for a decision from Emma and *Elliot*.

"See..." He talks discreetly to me as we cross the entrance hall and walk to a different hallway together. We're going to a more private place, where the ones he deems below him can't hear us. "I told you when you traded territories with Emma to just go with it. She thought she'd have it all, that she'd take your house and your street. Now she has nothing."

He knew from the beginning that he was going to unite the North Shore. He used Emma and her greed, promised her things he knew he was never going to give her, and now he has every single one of us in the palm of his hand.

But I can't discuss anything with him other than the two names he mentioned as he dismissed everyone. The second we enter his living room, and he closes the door behind us, I spin around, pinning him with a stare.

"Emma and *Elliot*," I hiss. "Elliot is not the head of the Kings, Nathan. *I* am. Here's a little tip to help you next time. *My* last name. *My* crew."

He laughs gently, pushing me to the side as he steps to his sofa. There's a glass coffee table in front of the giant L-shaped furniture, and a manila folder is waiting on it.

"Your name is White now."

"No," I push through gritted teeth. I will never take his fucking name. I don't care what our marriage certificate says. "I make the decisions for the Kings. Elliot doesn't lead my crew, do you understand?"

"He's someone you trust, and I agree, he's a good soldier."

"He is not the *boss*!" I shout.

My blood is boiling. He might be keeping me captive here, but he will not take away everything I've worked so hard for.

"If the Kings are going to work with NSC under your rule, then I get to lead my crew again."

"Please," he snorts.

"Look at me." Now sitting on the sofa, he looks up at me from the folder he's opening.

"Yes, little sunflower?" His taunting voice could drive a priest to murder.

"I'm the leader of the Kings. I will be the one telling you if we accept your deal or not."

He slowly stands, rounding the coffee table to reach me. I keep my head high. Seeing the people who work for me, *count* on me, has given me a new strength. It fed my fire.

"Kayla," he purrs, his hand coming to caress my cheek. I keep my arms crossed over my chest, not bothering to push him away. That isn't the point.

The forced marriage, the kidnapping, I could fucking live with it if it means I can still work with my people, direct them. I will do anything for the Kings to know they can still count on me. Working for my crew means I can get out. It means I can see my girls. It's all that counts.

"You are not part of the Kings' Crew anymore, please stick that inside your stubborn mind."

I am ready to pounce like a lioness.

"You will not take this away from me, Nathan."

"I already have. You're not their leader, you're my wife."

I open my mouth, but his eyes narrow, his head tilting to the side. Suddenly, he appears taller, stronger. His hand on my cheek turns into a handful of my jaw, his grip holding me still as he walks me backward and slams me against the wall.

Air freezes in my lungs, and I squeeze my eyes shut to swallow the pain.

"My *wife* isn't part of a petty gang, do you understand? My *wife* deserves more than to work under the tough ruling of a criminal organization just so she can survive."

"I don't want more," I squeak. "This is who I am, what I've always done. It's my *life*."

"Kayla, you are so incredibly unaware of your worth." His eyes bounce between mine, unable to grasp how I feel about this. But there's more, a plea for *me* to understand his point. "The way you handle the art of war deserves better than for you to focus on Kings' and NSC's pathetic issues. That would be a lack of esteem to your intelligence. I won't let you do that to yourself. You're owed respect, from everyone, but firstly from yourself."

A ball tightens in my throat. This...this is hitting too close to my heart.

"I know my worth," I grit out. "I built it every single

time my father knocked me down. I chose what it would be when my mother decided she didn't love me enough to take me with her. I *chose* to become the thing she hated the most. I *chose* to take my father's place just to prove a point that I was as tough as him. He's not the one they call the ruthless King. *I am.*"

He shakes his head, almost disappointed with my behavior.

"This is tragic." His lips press into a thin line before he crushes everything I ever believed. "Those are the goals and hopes of a little girl so she can grow beyond the abuse. Why did you stop there? Joining your gang because your mom didn't love you? Taking your dad's place because you wanted to prove a point? *That's it*?"

"I'm not like you!" I yell as my eyes sear into his. "I'm not a fucking psychopathic megalomaniac. I know when to stop! Look at you...building your own army because being at the head of a Cosa Nostra family wasn't enough for you. You're turning your back on the Lucianos, on the Rossis. Nothing is ever enough for you. Not destroying the man who raped you, not taking his organization. It wasn't enough to just kill me for what I did, you have to drag it out. To take me from everything I've ever known, to force me to *marry* you. You're insane."

"See. That's your problem. Your narrow-minded, weak brain thinks I'm insane when I'm *unstoppable*. I want this pitiful, short-sighted image of the world out of your head. I want you to understand everything you're capable of. You and I, Kayla, we could rule the world. I will worship every fucking thing you touch. I will burn down your enemies, I will bury anyone who ever made you feel like you weren't enough, like all you could do was stay in your shitty town and rule your shitty gang.

You were made for the greatest things that ever existed. You were made to build your own path, and I want you to be with me when that happens. I want to see you sit on your throne and watch everyone else bow to the goddess you are."

It's eternally frustrating that his tone stays so balanced when mine grows angrier every time it's my turn to talk.

"You suddenly got those big ideas of me in your head because I've been fighting you back. Because I'm still standing after you tried to crush me, and you think if I can survive the dangerous Nathan White, then I can do anything. But you're wrong. I am strong, but my place is among my crew," I rasp. "If you won't let me go back to them, at least let me lead them from afar. Let me make the decisions I know are the best for them, their safety, and their future."

Clearly frustrated I'm not accepting his point, his upper lip curls. He wants me to pretend to be someone I'm not. Someone who has more ambitions than I do. I don't want a husband I can advise on how to rule his empire. I don't need to go above and beyond my *petty gang*.

His tone takes a strange, possessive tone. "Your place is here with me." He presses his lips on my forehead. Hard. Obsessively. "You will be the queen by my side, Kayla. You are worth nothing less than that."

When he releases me, I'm forced to acknowledge the speed at which my heartbeat races. I'm surprised he can't see my shirt moving, my chest trembling.

He's already facing away from me, walking back to the sofa, but I'm not done.

"And if I don't want that?" I call out, my hands tightening into fists.

The sick smile he shows me as he glances back brings a

chill down my spine. "Then you can be the slave at my feet."

"I hate you." My trembling voice threatens to break. "So, what? Elliot is the head of the Kings now?"

"Elliot is nicely doing what he's told. The man cares about you. All I had to do was pay him a visit to tell him your life is at risk if he doesn't follow orders. Why do you think he didn't try anything today?"

"But you won't kill me." I narrow my gaze at him. "You prefer to see me suffer, don't you?" I don't know why I sound so petty. Maybe because his little manipulating schemes are getting to my head.

"He doesn't need to know that. What he needs to do is take hold of your crew, accept the deal—which he will because it brings him closer to me and so closer to you— and just keep on living his little life as a gangster. Really, I'm being fair to everyone here. I don't know why you're making such a big deal out of it."

"Because you took my freedom!" My scream bounces against the walls, resonating in the room for a few seconds. My throat hurts from everything it took out of me.

He's doing it again, making the walls close in on me by forcing me to acknowledge my situation.

He leans back in his seat, relaxing against the cushions of the sofa. He wipes dry blood off his cheek from earlier, looking at it with a sick satisfaction I don't even think he realizes himself.

Tilting his head to the side, his gaze burns bright with embers of satisfaction. "Well, so did you, my darling wife. I thought we had an understanding about that."

"Nate," I rasp. "I can't do this. Let me go."

The veil of irritation falls over him again. He's unimpressed. "I think seeing your crew today has given you the wrong idea. You are still here. You are still mine. There's no changing that."

"Please," I whisper desperately. "You *have* to let me go."

"Ah, despair." Pride shines in his eyes at figuring out how I feel.

And instead of fighting him with violence, I give up. Maybe he's right, maybe seeing Ethan and Elliot did something to me. Maybe seeing Jade and the way she looks up to me brought out the distress from this situation.

He's taking everything from me. The thought of being able to handle him if I could still lead my crew has been crushed by him refusing that for me. Because that's the real problem. He has the power to refuse me anything.

I need to leave. In any way I can.

"What do you want? I'll beg. Is that what you want?" I step away from the wall and toward him. "I'll beg on my knees."

He freezes for a second, surprised by my deplorable state. "Well, I can't say I don't love that idea."

That's all it takes for me to drop to my knees. "Please, Nate. I am *sorry* for what I did to you. I took your freedom away out of fear and greed. I wanted my town and to own it, and I sent you to prison to strike a deal with your enemies." I take a deep breath. "I learned my lesson. I will stay out of your way. I'll work for you. I'll have the Kings work for you. I'll unite the North Shore; we'll be the best soldiers you ever had, but please, *please* let me go. Let me go back to them."

He'll never understand who I mean by *them*. I'm happy for him to believe it's my crew when I truly mean the two pieces of my heart I can't live without. And I will beg on my knees a million times for *them* if I need to.

Sitting up slightly, his night-blue eyes focus on me. They're sparkling with excitement at my debasing act.

His eyes are so special.

During summer nights, when the ocean meets the sky, the horizon line mixes two blues to give the most exceptional color there ever was. Nathan's blue eyes make that color laughable in comparison. There's nothing more extraordinary than this man's eyes. Nothing can enthrall, manipulate, and betray like they do. Nothing can give you the same hope.

They don't belong to such a heartless man. It's dangerous. Deadly.

"Why don't you try crawling to me?" he purrs.

I lick my lips, but I'm set on doing anything I can. So I press my palms to the floor and take one humiliating step at a time, crawling toward him. When I'm by his spread legs, I notice the outline of his hard cock through his pants.

I can't take my eyes off it, pretending it's to avoid his stare, not because I know the magical ways he can make my body feel.

"Please," I try again. "I don't want the power you have. I don't want the respect of what you think I'm worth. I want my town. I want my home, my crew, my family. I want to be with them."

A wave of emotions gets to me, and I barely swallow back the tears. He can see them shining in my eyes when I look up because when I try to wipe the one threatening to fall, he snatches my wrist violently, stopping me from reaching my face.

"Let me see how desperate you are to escape me."

He observes me for what feels like forever, and all I can think about is that maybe I've got him. Maybe that's what he wanted all along. For me to apologize, debase myself, and beg. Maybe he'll really let me go.

"You would do anything right now, wouldn't you?" The satisfaction in his voice feels like acid eroding my veins, but I don't care. I'm close, so close.

I nod. "Anything."

"I could slam you on this table. I could fuck every single one of your holes, use you like a dirty little slut, and you'd let me. I could torture your body, leave my mark on you anywhere I wish, and you'd let me. Wouldn't you, little sunflower?"

"Yes." This time, my voice is a pathetic rasp. Not the kind that comes from the fear of being close to him and the need to escape. It's the lustful kind I can't control.

"Good." He nods. "Very good. Because in private, that will be your place as my wife, do you understand? My little cum slut who will do anything for me."

Every ounce of hope I've clung onto evaporates.

"W-what?" Panic surges inside me, and I try to pull my arm away.

He tightens his grip, looking at me like he doesn't understand what it is I can't grasp. So, he explains again. The wrong thing, of course. As if I asked *what* because I couldn't hear.

"I will do all of those things I mentioned," he says slowly. "And you will do anything for me. My little whore, who will take me in every single one of her needy holes. I'll do it all to you, baby. Not right now, of course. I have all the time in the world for that."

"But..." I try to pull my arm away again, my knees now aching from putting all my weight on them. "B-but I *begged*." I can't even believe it myself. I fucking begged. "I got on my knees. I crawled to you. You have to let me go!"

His brow furrows, showing his confusion. "No. I don't have to. But the begging was beautiful. You're breathtaking on your knees, Kayla."

The room descends into darkness around me. I feel like I'm free falling.

"Are you okay? You look pale."

"I…" Lungs freezing, I can't find my breaths anymore. "I c-can't…"

"Do you want to cry? I think it'll help."

A whimper escapes me, but I shake my head. "*I hate you*," I croak. My head falls on his lap, terror and exhaustion catching up to me.

I've been on edge for days, and not only is my body giving up, but my mind too.

"Shh." He caresses my hair with such a soft gesture a sob catches in my throat. "Name it."

I try to talk, but I choke instead. My eyes squeeze shut, forbidding tears from falling, but I realize he's let go of me, and I still haven't moved from the floor. I'm still on my knees between his legs, my head resting on his lap like a desperate sixties housewife.

"Name it and you can rest."

"Hopeless." I release a sob. It's a dry, painful sob that doesn't allow tears to fall.

I feel him pensive above me as I wait.

"I understand. Remember, it's only been a few days," he explains in a soothing voice. "You're still adapting. It was too early to let you see your friends. That's my bad. It won't happen again until you've accepted your situation."

The knot in my stomach tightens, and before I know it, the only thing that can soothe me is his hand repeatedly caressing my hair, his smell that makes me feel so safe, the feeling of his suit against my skin that is so familiar.

"I like you close to me, little sunflower." I can barely make out his words in my haze. "I like...the way you make me feel."

I don't know when my arms come to wrap just below his knees, and I don't know how long I stay like a supplicant at his feet, but all I know is that when there's a commotion somewhere in the house that startles him, it's barely enough to bring me back to life.

I think he did it.

He made me give up on myself.

And all I can do now is to exist through him.

22

NATHAN

Golden Boy - Bryce Fox

There's a bang somewhere in the house. A door slamming, someone stomping.

For a split second, I think we're under attack. But I added more guards in and out of the property this morning. The Wolves are angry I'm back, taking over Stoneview and its surroundings. Fuck, I'm about to operate on the whole East Coast. It's only a matter of time before they try to kill me. I would too if I were them. Adding more security to this house is not only to protect me. I don't want them to get their hands on Kay.

But then a seething voice resonates, and my eyes automatically roll.

"Five months?" The shouting comes from the main entrance. "Five months, Nate?"

I'm in for a long conversation.

"Kayla, baby."

I hear doors opening and slamming shut. I hear a *please, calm down,* from Sam.

Kayla stirs between my legs, and I wonder if she's fallen asleep. I don't want to move in the same way one wouldn't when a cat settles on their lap. She's finally calm, and I don't want to disturb her peace.

"Kayla," I insist.

"Mhm?"

"You're going to want to sit on the sofa for this. It will be long and painful."

Her head snaps up. "What?"

"Not for you. For me."

She's barely up, rubbing her eyes and attempting to tame her black mane when the door to the living room is flung open.

"You've been out of prison for five months, you fucking asshole?"

I look back at the door, giving my younger sister a bright smile.

"Hello, Ozy. I missed you too."

"Didn't think it was worth telling me? Fuck, Jake is going to lose his shit." Her deadly glare has killed weaker men in the past.

It's the exact same as mine, a blue that always reminds people of dangerous nights.

But while my hair is a dark blond, hers is inky black.

Someone comes running in, only to stop when they bump into Rose's back.

"Fucking hell. I tried to stop her. I promise." Her boyfriend, Lik, tries to wrap a hand around her waist, but she slaps him away.

Good, I wouldn't want to have to cut it.

"Don't you fucking dare touch me, you little liar."

"You were meant to be at home with Rachel and her,"

Sam appears behind both of them, and they're almost complete. "And how the hell does she know?"

"She bullied me into telling her!" Lik snaps. "I told you she knew something was up. I told you not to leave me alone with her."

"If you guys hadn't lied to us, maybe this wouldn't be such a mess."

I try to look behind Rose, Lik, and Sam to see where the last voice comes from, but she's too small, hidden by all of them, but mainly my best friend's gigantic body.

"Lovebug, I'm *so* sorry. You have to understand."

"I'm sorry too," Lik jumps in.

They both look pathetic, apologizing to her like pouty children about to lose the right to their favorite console.

"This is a mess," the fourth voice repeats in a huff.

"I can't believe you hid from me." Her eyebrows pinch together. "Why?"

I finally stand. "Because I had a lot to deal with. I never want you in the middle of dangerous things, and your desperate boyfriends were meant to keep you away from this."

She looks at me, completely unimpressed, but her gaze softens when the fourth member of their group finally makes it past the two men behind Rose. A small, blonde woman looks up at me, then Kayla, to finally land her gaze on Rose. I only ever saw her from afar, but I know she's the best thing that ever happened to my sister.

"Are you okay?" she asks Rose.

Finally relaxing, she wraps an arm around her waist. "No. My asshole of a brother has been out of prison for five months and our two boyfriends have been hiding it from me."

I smile because there's no one like my blunt sister, and

extend my hand toward the blonde. "You must be Rachel. I'm Nate."

My sister slaps my hand away, narrowing her eyes at me. "Don't even try to touch her with your filthy hands."

I chuckle to myself, straightening again, and putting my hand on Kay's lower back. "Rose, this is Kay, my wife. Kay, my sister, Rose. I'm sure you've heard of her before."

"Who hasn't?" Lik scoffs.

Barely present, Kay nods to herself. "Yeah. We met before."

"Your *what*?"

I catch Sam running a hand from his forehead to his chin, annoyed by my surprise announcement.

"Wife. My wife. It's a long story." But that's not what bothers me. I turn to Kay, bringing her closer. "Did you say you met before?"

"Uh-huh. Met them all."

I can't keep the surprise off my face. "*You* met my sister. And her boyfriend. And her fiancée. And her other boyfriend." I spin my finger in the air at the other group. "All of them."

Kay nods again. "Yes, Nate. I did." She narrows her eyes at them, tilting her head to the side. "I got her"—she points at Rachel—"fixed by my on-call doctor when she was disfigured."

And that's when I notice the scars running from the corner of Rachel's left eye and down her cheek.

"Ah, fuck," Lik mutters. "I forgot about that."

"The four of them were begging at his door because they didn't have anyone to turn to and they didn't want to go to the hospital. We didn't ask any questions, but I did ask for a favor." She pauses, and her gaze shifts, going from Rachel to Sam. "Remember?"

His jaw tightens, and Lik automatically wraps a hand around his biceps, as if to stop him from jumping Kay.

"Yes," he clips. "I remember."

"And what was the deal?" I ask slowly.

Kay chuckles sarcastically. "He was meant to keep you away from me if you ever got out of prison."

I can't help the genuine laugh that escapes me. "That's not the kind of promise he could have kept, believe me."

"No, I see that now. I guess you two always act almighty because you're part of *bigger, better* criminal organizations. You're not like our ridiculous petty gangs, are you? But see, between the Kings and NSC, when we owe a favor, we stick to it. We might not have much, but we still have our word."

I don't stop her when she walks away from me and shoulders Sam to get out of the room.

A lot happened today, and it's barely lunch time. She needs her space.

I will give it to her for the rest of the day, while I catch up with my sister, but she better not push me away when I find her later.

Because she's been gone for a few seconds, and I already feel the pull in my gut, wanting to bring her back right next to me.

Rose watches her leave. "Did you kidnap Kayla King?"

A warmth spreads inside me. I missed my genius of a sister. She always catches the smallest details and comes to the right conclusions.

"How did you know?" I ask, excitement buzzing in my chest. Yeah, I did kidnap Kayla King, and I made her all fucking *mine*.

"You call her your wife, but she obviously disagrees with that. If not that, she's sporting bruises around her neck and the face of someone whose freedom is now out of reach. Plus"—she shakes her head in the same way I do when I'm unimpressed with someone—"the ruthless King isn't one to let a man shackle her."

"Shackle," I snort. "As you can see, she's free to roam around however she wants."

"Inside your house."

"Details, Ozy." I wave a hand dismissively and step up to her, putting a hand on her shoulder. "Let me take you out to lunch."

"With Jake," she mentions her twin right away. I guess he should know too.

"Jake won't want to see me." My brother and I have had strong disagreements in the past, the main one being him stealing the girlfriend I was manipulating and using to get information on the twins.

"Stop making decisions for others, Nate. We give him the information, and he decides what he wants to do with it."

I huff. "When did you become so wise?"

"Healing. You should try it."

"I have nothing to heal from," I say bluntly.

"Sure thing, brother. Let's go." She turns to Rachel. "Are you coming, Sunshine?"

Rachel nods excitedly. "Sure." She takes the hand Rose is extending, and the three of us walk out of the living room, Lik and Sam on our heels.

That's until Rose freezes and turns around. "What do you think you're doing?"

"Um, going for lunch?" Lik says tentatively.

Dropping Rachel's hand, she crosses her arms over her chest, narrowing her eyes at the two men. She says nothing until Sam cracks.

"We'll give you time."

"Enjoy your lunch, princess," Lik adds.

"Again. I'm sorry," Sam says, sounding pathetic.

"We both are."

"I love you." Sam's eyes shine with truth.

"We both do," Lik repeats.

"Fuck off."

She turns back around, snatches Rachel's hand, and we all head out without her boyfriends.

"You've got those two wrapped around your finger so tightly it makes me a little sad for them."

Rachel giggles next to Rose. "You have no idea."

"I love this place," Rose says as we leave Silver's. It's a simple diner halfway between Stoneview and Silver Falls.

"How did you know to get the nachos?" Rachel asks me.

The more we talked during lunch, the more I realized that she is so good for my sister, but she deserves so much better than someone like her. Rachel is as pure as they come, and Rose...well, she's a White. We all come with little feelings and a god complex. Rose might have Lik and Sam wrapped around her finger, but love truly made Rachel blind.

"Jamie, of course. She's always said they have the best in town. I only come here for the nachos."

"Same," Rachel laughs. "She says the same thing to everyone. She's right, though. How do you know Jamie?"

"Ah," I chuckle. "I'm sure you've always known Jamie with Jake."

She nods, and I can already see Rose rolling her eyes. "Here we fucking go."

"She was mine first," I say simply.

"What?" Rachel chokes. "But Jake and her are so... perfect?"

We all get in my car, Rachel at the back and Rose next to me. I drive out of the parking lot and make my way to Silver Falls rather than back to Stoneview.

"Nate was only using her to spy on me and Jake," Rose tells her fiancée. "Don't feel bad for him."

"I was in love," I lie.

"Shut the fuck up. You wouldn't know love if it hit you right in the face."

That gets a laugh out of me. I cared about Jamie, in a possessive way. But mainly, I cared the same way I do about everything that is useful to me. As long as they serve a purpose, I like to have them around. I used her all the way till the end. Shit, when she found out I even used my story with Bianco to squeeze some more out of her. She was so fucking clueless it could have broken my heart. It didn't, though.

I used to have a favorite coffee shop when I was younger and lived in D.C. I would go every day without fail. I liked many of their drinks, the staff was nice, and it was within walking distance of where I lived. It was perfect.

That place was special to me.

Then one day they turned it into a restaurant, and it lost its purpose to me. It became useless for my coffee needs.

So I stopped going.

I *adored* Jamie when she was useful. She was my favorite. I was loyal to her. She was special to me. Then she fell in love with Jake, and she became useless. So I let my brother have her.

Suddenly, she meant nothing. But it's hilarious to taunt

my brother about my past with her. Probably why he refused to see me today.

"Well, you have a wife now," Rachel says politely. "I'm sure you're well over Jamie."

She must have spent a lot of time with Lik, Sam, and Rose, to not even mention the fact that I admitted I kidnapped Kay. She seems used to that kind of shit.

"Love will do that to you, I guess," she keeps going. I see her looking out of the back window, chewing on her thoughts.

She doesn't even realize what she's just done. She doesn't understand the way my stomach tightens, the way my lungs harden.

Because suddenly, I see a difference between Jamie and Kay.

Kay isn't *useful* to me. I do have uses for her—and she will find out about those soon—but I could have chosen anyone. I chose Jamie because she was lonely, because I saw that Jake had set his eyes on her. I did my homework and picked the best victim.

Kay... Kay is just revenge. I could kill Kay.

Except I couldn't.

What the fuck? I've only had her for a week. *A week.* Maybe if I hadn't spent so long obsessing about her in prison, I wouldn't feel like this. Maybe if I hadn't focused my every thought on her, it would be different. I should have gotten a job in the kitchen or the library. I should have played chess with the other inmates. Instead, I spent every single hour of every single day consumed with Kayla King, and now my body thinks it got the reward of its life by having her. I hate her. She took everything from me. But I spent so long thinking about how much I hate her that when I finally saw her again, it was like seeing your idol for the first time. Her being mine feels like the ultimate win.

Rose is speaking next to me. Something about if I hate her so much for putting me in prison, she doesn't understand why I keep her so close to me.

But all I can focus on is the cold sweat dampening my back and the sickness in my stomach.

Name it, Nate.

I shake my head, slowing down the car.

I meant the things I said to her today. Kayla is a goddess, and she needs to understand that. But she was right too. Her strength and the way she is surviving me is what impresses me. It's what's keeping me addicted.

Addicted?

Try obsessed.

Kayla is becoming a passion. Something I want to see everywhere. I want her to be the subject of every conversation I have with everyone. I want to go to rallies in her name. I want to find someone who understands me so we can discuss her for hours like fangirls do about their favorite band.

Oh, it's bad.

It's bad, but it's not love. Because love feels like...like...

"What does love feel like?" I blurt out.

My sister stops her rant, her eyebrows reaching her hairline as she turns to me. I'm crossing the bridge that leads to the North Shore.

"Do you want to answer my question before I answer yours?"

I look at her pointedly. "What was your question, Ozy?" I say impatiently.

"Why are we going to the North Shore?" she repeats.

"Don't worry about that. Now answer mine."

A cold smile tugs at her lips. "Don't worry about what love feels like."

I hold back a frustrated growl as I speed down the streets and all the way to Kayla's house. I forgot that when I talk to my sister, I'm basically dealing with myself. And fuck if we have the most unbearable personalities.

I park, slamming my door behind me as I make my way to Kayla's front door. I open it with my copy of her keys. She doesn't even know I had that done the moment I walked out of prison.

I stride to her bathroom, the burnt smell annoying me. She's been living in this shithole with walls that barely hold the roof above her head, and she dares demand to be sent back here.

She needs to be by my side. She needs to understand everything I can give her.

Wrenching the shower curtain open, I finally put my hands on what I've been looking for. I snatch her grapefruit body wash, but it's awfully light. I push the cap open with my thumb, turn it upside down, and shake.

It's fucking empty.

"For fuck's sake," I growl.

I take it with me anyway and make my way out. Just as I'm about to reach the door, I notice a few framed pictures on the shelves by the door. One of them is a family picture.

I grab it, tilting my head to the side. And against everything, I take the frame with me.

Because I fucking know she'll be happy to have a family picture with her.

I jog back to the car, feeling anxious, unwell.

There's an itch inside me. I want to be close to Kayla. I'm having withdrawal symptoms, and I want to feel her skin against mine.

I throw my findings on Rose's lap and start the car. Opening the map on my phone, I search for the closest supermarket. It's a small convenience store not far from here. Again, I'm speeding through the streets, in a horrible hurry to get back to my wife.

My sister watches me with wide eyes as I take the bottle of body wash and exit my car again.

I burst into the store like a madman. Going straight to the toiletries section, I finally find what I need. The cashier's mouth falls open when I drop ten bottles of body wash on the counter.

"Um..." She hesitates. "Would you like a bag?"

I cock an eyebrow at her.

"Yes," she answers herself, nodding repeatedly.

I walk out with two full bags that I toss on my sister's lap again as soon as I sit down in the car.

"What the fuck is all this?" she asks stupidly as I drive away from the convenience store.

"Are you blind?" I snap. "It's body wash. Kay uses that one."

"Why the hell did you buy this many?"

"Because I like her scent, and she hasn't been smelling like herself since being at my house. It's annoying."

"Annoying," she repeats slowly. "And what, Kay needs ten bottles?"

"I don't want her to find an excuse to come back and buy it here. They don't sell that shit in Stoneview. They're too snobby for supermarket brands."

"You bought ten bottles of supermarket body wash so Kayla doesn't have an excuse to come and buy it here."

"Yes."

"Yes," she repeats.

"Oh my god, Ozy." I rub my temple. The girl is giving me a headache. "What are you? A fucking parrot?"

"Oh, Nate," she laughs, her head hitting the headrest from how hilarious she thinks she is. "I think you're starting to know exactly what love feels like."

In the back, Rachel giggles too. The two women are having the best time making fun of me.

I accelerate down the streets of the North Shore and quickly join the highway. I can't answer my sister, no matter how much I want to. No matter how annoying she is and how much I want to shut her up.

Instead, I turn to my thoughts, to everything I feel inside. It's a fucking mess, and I can't focus. No matter how much I try to make sense of everything, I keep coming back to the same need.

I want to touch my little sunflower and feel her soft petals between my fingers.

I want to make her mine over and over again, so she has no doubt in her mind who she belongs to.

I want something as simple as feeling my wife close to me.

23

KAYLA

Dangerous Game - Klergy, BEGINNERS

A hand wakes me up. It's pulling at my shoulder, forcing me to go from sleeping on my side to my back. It's still sunny outside. The curtains are drawn and there isn't much light in the room, but I can see it's not night yet. All I had to do was sleep, so I did.

"You came back to my room." Nate's voice is thick with so much pride it's almost missing a *good girl* at the end of it. He sounds like a master who's happy with the way he trained his pet.

But then his touch goes from my shoulder to my waist, my hips, and it feels more like a lover who missed his mistress. And when he reaches the waistband of my thong, a sigh of relief escapes him. Like a soldier who finally came home to the safety of his life, to the embrace of his woman.

The delicate way he rids me of my underwear feels dangerous. I'm only wearing that and a t-shirt, and he removes that too.

I finally decide to open my eyes. To my surprise, he's

only wearing a pair of boxers. He's standing by the side of the bed, and he spreads my legs with both hands.

"You're so beautiful when you sleep," he whispers, as if I was still in the exact state he described.

He moves me around so my ass is by the edge of the bed, then drops to his knees.

"Kayla," he murmurs, his head now between my legs. "I missed you today."

I shake my head, forcing myself to ignore him. But how long can you ignore someone when they hook your legs on their shoulders and start kissing your inner thighs? When they spread you open and give you a long, erotic lick all the way to your clit?

I have no weapon against basic instincts, especially when they're forced upon me by Nate. So I let the pleasure overwhelm me when he eats me languidly. He's patient, attentive. He listens for every sound, watches out for every twitch.

He spends time coaxing me into a comfortable pleasure. So long, that I forget my own body and anything that can make a woman feel uncomfortable when a man has his mouth between her legs.

I forget about everything that makes me *me* and only focus on the slow strokes of his tongue.

I let my moans loudly resonate in the room. He doesn't say anything, doesn't taunt me. He doesn't make it hurt. He focuses on me, my bliss. He engages in a sensuality I didn't even know had a place between us.

"Oh," I pant. "Nate..." I choke on my own breath, feeling my orgasm just on the brink.

"Come for me, beautiful wife."

I tear apart at the seams. My body breaks and bends to

his will, and everything in my world shifts in a way I can't control.

When I come back down, desperately trying to catch my breath, he puts a hand on my lower belly.

And he licks me again.

"Whoa, Nate," I murmur softly. "That was more than enough."

But he doesn't hear me, back at it. Same pace, same patience. My legs close around his head, unsure how it feels anymore.

He makes sure to show me. He keeps going until it feels good again, amazing even. He licks my wetness, my orgasm. He plays with my clit, making me forget why I tried to stop him, and before I can truly grasp what's happening, I'm exploding against his skillful tongue again.

My mouth opens, but the sounds of hedonism barely make it out before he's back to devouring me.

"Holy shit," I squeak. I grab the sheets with one hand, his hair with the other, and instead of fighting the current, this time, I let the waves swallow me.

I push myself against his mouth, needing more pressure, and he notices that. He's completely attuned to my body, and his tongue presses harder against my clit. Soon, my needs are met a split second after my body expresses them. His teeth nibble, two fingers press inside me, and he pushes from the inside.

I'm shaking when I orgasm again, my entire body drowned in the carnal sensation.

When I finally relax, and my back hits the bed again, my lips part to say something.

But I'm cut off by his unrelenting mouth.

"Oh my god!" I scream as my body convulses beneath him. "Nate..."

I lose count.

All I know is that at some point, my sweaty body stops twisting and bucking and writhing, taken by an exhaustion I can't fight anymore.

And finally, he stops. He stands up silently, leans over my shattered body, and takes hold of my mouth.

His kiss tastes of me. It's strange.

"You're delicious," he growls against my skin. "Addictive."

I don't agree. I taste sweet and bitter, nothing terrible but nothing nice.

I have never experienced this in my life before. It feels like it's been an eternity, and I almost expect the sun to be up. So, when he separates from me, I croak, "How long?"

I lift my head from the mattress to catch his eyes darting to the watch on his wrist, and he smiles up at me. "One hour and twenty-one minutes."

My head falls back. "You are completely insane."

"And you're completely mine."

He heads for the bathroom, but I'm asleep before I even hear the shower turn on.

When he comes to bed, he shakes me awake again. He's got something in his hand. A frame.

"I went to your house today. I got this for you."

A spike of adrenaline wakes me up, and I grab the frame as I sit.

My heart freefalls to my stomach. I can't even breathe for a few seconds.

"Why?" I rasp.

I feel him shrug as my vision narrows on the picture.

"I was looking for your body wash, but I thought you'd like to have this."

My hands feel sweaty around the frame.

It's a simple family picture of me, Caden, and my dad. Caden is holding a toddler, and I'm holding another one. We can't even see their faces properly. It was impossible to keep them still and get them to look at the camera. The picture isn't very clear. It's bad quality printed on normal paper that we framed rather than photo paper. It's stupid, and I love it.

"Who are they?" He points at the photograph. At the two toddlers.

"My dad's kids."

That came out too fast, without a split second of hesitation.

I eye him next to me, waiting for his answer.

He blinks at the picture, perplexed.

Alarm bells ring in my head, my entire body on high alert.

He knows, he knows, he knows.

But then he nods, his voice as flat as ever. "I didn't know you had other siblings."

"If you can call them that." I force my voice to stay steady.

I have people to protect, and they mean the world to me. I will not put them in danger because I failed to stay cool in a dangerous situation.

"He had them really late with a woman who didn't give a shit about him. He saw them once a month, and I personally probably saw them, like, twice. One of those times we took a family picture and that's it. Haven't seen them since he died."

I shrug, putting the picture on the bedside table that's on my side of the bed.

"Thanks, though," I murmur.

With my back to him, my eyes linger on the two

toddlers. This picture was taken around a year and a half ago. They were just two. They're going to be four in December.

And I need to be out of here by then. I must. A ball of pain grows in my throat, and when I swallow, it falls to the pit of my stomach. *I miss them.* Nothing hurts like the way I miss them. I will not be whole until we're reunited. No matter what, I will do anything to go back to them.

Barely able to see my future as far as tomorrow, I lie down and look at the ceiling, refusing to look at Nate.

"Are you still mad at me?"

His question surprises me. It sounds so genuine, like the answer matters to him.

"You're asking me if I'm still mad that you forced me to marry you and won't let me leave this house? Or if I'm still mad that I can't run my gang anymore and you're just giving it away to someone else?"

He's still sitting up, and his hand comes to my cheek, nudging me to look at him. "All of it?"

"Nate," I snort. "Can you hear yourself?"

"Just answer." He licks his lips. "Please?"

"My mood shouldn't matter to you."

"What if it does?" He shifts to face me completely.

"If it does, let me go."

His eyes close, and he looks like he's searching for patience deep within himself. "I can't do that."

"You *can*." I sit up beside him, putting a hand on his chest. "Let me go."

When his eyes open again, for the first time, he looks at me with a *sorry* emanating from his body. "I can't, because I need you by my side, little sunflower. At least until I can make sense of this."

"Make sense of what?"

He grabs my hand on his chest, drags it to where his heart is, and looks deep into my eyes.

His heartbeat is uneven, racing one second, skipping beats the next. For a minute, I wonder if he's having a heart attack.

"This," he explains again.

My mouth drops open, but no words come out.

"I..." *Know what you mean.*

It doesn't come. I try to say it. I try to be vulnerable.

But my tongue won't. At least it's on my side. Unlike my heart.

24

KAYLA

madhouse - Nessa Barrett

The next day, I wake up clinging to his body again. And all the days in the following two weeks too. Every morning, I'm holding on to him, a headache beating in my skull.

Every morning, he's ready for me with a tablet and a glass of water.

"At least you didn't slap me this time," he tells me softly before heading for a shower. But I don't even know what he's talking about.

My days are interminable. All I do is wait, talk to the guards, plan an escape, and fail to put my plan into action. And when I'm sure it's safe, I call my mum. I ask for news of my family while avoiding questions I can't answer. The pain of not being free to join them never goes away.

Weirdly, I look forward to every night. To the heat he brings to my body, the pleasure he makes me feel, the hours he spends on me.

I might not be free, but fuck, I'm a sexually satisfied captive.

Every time Nate tries to put me into the role of a housewife, I make him regret it. Two days ago, he texted me asking for dinner to be ready when he came home.

He chewed on two forkfuls of Bolognese before he realized he was eating glass.

My ass had a meeting with his crop, but I still don't regret it.

Yesterday afternoon, he *required* I join him in his office after dinner. He said a good wife does what she's told.

I walked in with a bottle of vodka, a rag inside it, and a lighter. I threw my Molotov cocktail at his desk and walked out.

It smells burnt down there now. Just like home.

So when he comes out of the shower, looks at my naked form still in bed, and casually says, "I'll be at meetings this morning, but I'm taking you shopping this afternoon."

I reply just as casually. "I will cut every single thing you buy me to pieces."

"I have dinner with an important partner tonight. He's bringing his wife, and I need someone to keep her company."

"Ooh," I say as I sit up, pretending to be excited. "What do you think I should talk to her about? Our favorite meals to cook? Which school I'm going to send my future children to? Oh, I know, how well our maids make our beds?"

He dries his beautiful hair with a towel before throwing the damp material at my face. "What will it take to make you behave, little sunflower?"

"Freedom," I snap back.

He shrugs. "I guess I'll just have a misbehaved wife, then. It's okay, I like punishing you." Pausing for a second, he thinks to himself. "But then again, so do you."

He walks into the closet, and he's already half-dressed when he comes back out. Pants on, belt hanging, he's sliding his arms into a black dress shirt.

He buttons it as he keeps talking. "I'll be back by lunch. Be ready to go."

"You're my worst nightmare," I say bluntly. "Everything you say makes me want to jump out of the window."

"Give it a try, it might save me some headaches." Finally, he slides a tie around the collar of his shirt. "Come, do my tie like a good housewife."

My legs are moving before I can control them. Naked, I stand up and walk to him. I grab the two ends of the tie as he keeps talking.

"You know, it's an occasion for you to go out. I could always just pick a dress from your closet and be done with it."

Gritting my teeth, I look into his eyes. "Fine. I'll fucking go. But I get to choose the dress."

He's as passive as ever when he replies with a simple, "No."

Finishing the knot at his chest, I push it all the way to his throat, and then some more, choking him.

He coughs, grabbing my wrists with both hands and pushing me away. I smile brightly at him as he loosens the noose.

"You'll pay for that later." He scratches his throat. "And stop turning me on before I have to leave for work."

One step, a tight arm around my waist, and he's dropping a kiss on my forehead. "There's something for you on the kitchen table. Sign it before lunch. With your maiden name."

"What? A contract?"

"Yes. Sign it Kayla *King*."

"Surely, that won't be valid now that I have your last name?" I can't help the bitterness in my voice.

"We're going to antedate it to before the wedding."

"Ante-what?" I hate when he uses words he knows I won't understand, just to mess with my head.

"Backdate it."

I cross my arms over my chest. "What the fuck is that document?"

"It's on the kitchen table. Why don't you go check for yourself. I'll see you at lunch."

That document is a deed of ownership, apparently. It's twenty pages long and looks like my worst nightmare in terms of combinations of words.

But I can't fucking sign something and not read it. Especially when it comes from Nate. So I pour myself a glass of water, sit down at the kitchen island in nothing but a robe, and get to work.

I've not finished the first sentence when the headache comes back.

Fuck. I hate words.

It says something about a hotel.

"Cascade Hotels?" I murmur to myself.

Isn't that some fancy chain of hotels? There's one in Silver Falls, on the South Bank.

I look at the name of the current owner. Campbell?

I read the next line, murmuring to myself. "...*Cascade Hotels*...ugh, fuck." That's the same line. I go back to the name, reading the line three times before I realize I haven't moved forward.

"*Fuck*," I snap.

Putting my index finger on the page, I bend closer and follow as I read.

I startle when the door to the kitchen opens.

"Kay, what the fuck? I told you to be ready to leave by lunchtime."

"Huh?" I snap my head up, my neck screaming from the stiffness.

"Did you sign?"

"What time is it?"

He stalks toward me, slapping a hand on the contract and sliding it toward himself. Going to the last page, he notices it's lacking my signature.

"You're a stubborn brat, you know that?"

My head feels like it's full of cotton, and my headache is back tenfold. I shake my head. "I just wanted to read it."

"So? Did you?"

He looks back to the page I was on, then back at me, and cocks an eyebrow. "The small battles you fight are not going to be worth it in the long run, little sunflower."

Gripping my upper arm, he forces me up. In a split second, I'm bent over the kitchen island.

"Why are you stalling?" he growls in my ear at the same time as he shoves my robe to my waist. "You know you're going to lose, and you'll end up doing what you're told in the end."

"I wasn't stalling!" Frustration claws at my chest. "I was reading it."

"Oh, really? I was gone for *five hours*, Kayla." A harsh slap lands on my ass cheeks, making me push on my toes.

"Feet flat. Right now."

I fall back, grunting when he slaps me again. "Five hours and you're on page *three*? What the fuck are you playing at?"

Smack!

I hiss, attempting to reach back. He grabs both my wrists and holds them in one hand at the small of my back.

"I'm a slow reader." *Smack!* "Fuck! Nate, it hurts. I promise you I wasn't fighting back. Words are complicated... I... They're very hard for me."

The slaps stop, but my breathing is out of control. Fire spreads across my ass cheeks.

"What?"

"I-I'm just stupid, I don't know. It's fucking hard, okay?"

Smack!

"Take that back right now."

"I can't fucking read!" I shout. "You want me to say that doesn't make me stupid?"

"You can read." *Slap!* "You're perfectly intelligent." *Slap!*

"Stop!" I shriek.

"Take it back."

"Okay, fuck, I'm not stupid!"

His grip on my wrists disappears. I stay bent over the island, but I prop myself on my forearms. I feel him shift before his lips meet one cheek in a soft kiss, then the other.

"Good girl. Grab the pen."

My trembling hand goes for the pen, and I hold the contract under me.

He caresses my lower back, his hand under the robe, while the other comes between my legs. "My beautiful wife, always letting pain turn you on."

"Shut up," I moan as he pushes a finger inside me.

"It's a transfer of ownership," he explains calmly. "The Cascade Hotels belonged to Mr. Campbell. Now, they will belong to you."

Another finger enters me. "Wh-why?"

"Sign, Kayla. I'll be a major silent investor in the hotel, and you'll be the owner. That's it."

My eyes flutter shut, and I struggle to hold myself on my two forearms. "You...you," I pant. "You're going to wash your money with the hotels." Feeling myself getting wetter by the second, I release a moan. "And you're putting them in my name, so they're not directly yours."

He chuckles behind me, his fingers accelerating. He adds a third one, and I scream in pleasure at the same time as he pinches my burning cheek.

My grip tightens on the pen. "You want me to sign Kayla King and backdate it." And it hits me. "Nate, you're an asshole."

He slows his fingers. "I won't get caught."

"But if you do, if the feds learn there's money being washed with those hotels, you're going to put it on me. *They're in her name. She had the hotels before we got married. I had no idea what she used them for.* That's what you'll say in court, isn't it? You'll put the blame on me."

I bite my lower lip as anger and pleasure mix like a poisonous cocktail.

"Lie in court to protect myself? To get you in trouble?" He curls his fingers, making me moan even louder. "Who could have inspired me to do that?"

His words leave me speechless.

Revenge. It's always about revenge.

"Sign the contract, little sunflower. Because whether you want it or not, this is happening. So put your pretty name on there before I make you."

I need to find a way to turn this around. I need to find some semblance of a silver lining.

I'm going to be the owner of hotels for his criminal organizations. They will belong to *me*. I'm fucking covered.

I could leave him and have something that is mine. Excitement rushes alongside the arousal through my veins until something hits me right in the face.

"The prenup," I groan.

Fucking bastard. He chooses to finger me harder over saying anything.

"You made me sign the prenup because you knew there would be value attached to my name down the line. If I leave, if I die, the hotels will go back to...to you."

Sweat pearls down my back, my orgasm so close I could cry.

"See? You're very smart. Your reading pace doesn't define your intelligence. Now sign so I can make my wife come on my kitchen island. This is your last warning."

I lick my lips, panting, as I press the ball of the pen to the document.

His fingers pump faster, and my hand traces my signature on the paper before crashing flat on the counter as I'm overtaken by euphoria.

I roll my hips, riding his hand and taking anything I can from him. Every day, he takes a little more of my sanity. At least I get some pleasure in return.

My arms give up, and I let my chest fall onto the marble. He kisses my shoulder, my neck, the back of my head.

"Don't worry, baby, you're never leaving. And I'd kill myself a hundred times over before I let anything happen to you. Those hotels are yours, and any profits will be yours. Separate account and all."

"For real?" I whisper, hardly believing anything he says.

"For real. You're taking all the risk, after all. I told you, if I die, my siblings can have everything that's mine. But those hotels are yours. If anything happens to me, I want you to be able to live a comfortable life."

My heart squeezes painfully in my chest, making me realize two things that I completely refuse to accept.

One, Nate can be caring when he wants to be, and that's utterly terrifying.

Two? I don't want anything to happen to him.

I push him off me so I can stand and look at him.

Fuck. The man forced me to sign another contract that could send me to prison, and all I can think about is the business opportunity he just threw my way. All I can think about is that I would have done exactly the same because it's smart as fuck.

And all I can think about is that it feels really good to be given a chance to rule by his side.

"Those hotels." I lick my lips, wondering if I'm making a huge mistake helping him, but I go for it anyway. "That's where the Wolves sell their women. Some of the rooms are reserved all year long for trafficking and...and for the buyers to *enjoy* themselves."

He stays passive for a few seconds, swallowing the information.

"So, now that they don't own the hotels through Campbell anymore, I not only took away where they were laundering money, but also the places that helped their sex ring function?"

I nod slowly. "Two birds, one stone."

A smile spreads on his face.

"Oh, baby. I love when you play the gangster game with me." Grabbing me by my hips, he lifts me on the counter, and spreads my legs. "Let's destroy the fucking world."

His hard cock is out in less time than it takes me to drag him closer.

Maybe Nate was right. Maybe I want to play a bigger game than owning the North Shore. Maybe ruling a criminal empire by his side is more tempting than I cared to admit.

When he pushes inside me, I don't need pain to feel pleasure. As he thrusts in and out, exhilaration is what makes me tremble. Being held by him, owned by him, and protected by him brings me to highs I hadn't reached before. Being his equal is what takes me to my orgasm.

He fucks me hard with a need to possess me.

He makes me come with an obsession that defies reason.

And he kisses me with something that resembles love so closely...I could be fooled into believing it.

25

KAYLA

Joke's On you - Charlotte Lawrence

"What the fuck is this place?"

We're standing in front of a shop that screams *only rich people allowed* from even before you get in.

His & Hers, that's what it's called. We didn't leave Stoneview, instead drove to the main street so Nate could accomplish his dream of dressing me up like a rich cunt.

"I don't want to go in there," I groan. "I'm going to fight with someone, I just know it."

"I had them close the whole thing. There will be no other customers."

My heart skips a beat, and I want to crush it with my own hands.

"You closed the entire shop so you could find me a dress?"

"Yes, for three hours. Now we're late, thanks to you."

"Shut up." Oh...I really meant for that to sound less playful. "I don't even want to go to your stupid dinner."

He takes my hand in his, looking down at me from

where he's standing next to me. "I take you out of the house and this is how you thank me?"

"What the fuck am I? Your pet? You take me on a walk, and I should suck your dick in the fitting room?"

His lips pinch, clearly stopping himself from laughing. "I would never ask my cat to suck my dick, but to each their own, I guess."

"You have a cat?"

His eyebrows rise to his hairline. "You haven't seen my cat?"

"Okay, there's no cat, is there? Where would you even have kept it when you were away?"

"I took him in when I got out. I didn't have one before."

I narrow my eyes at him, and he looks at me with his signature blank face.

"There's no cat," I huff.

"What the hell do you do all day? Don't you walk around the house? Don't you play with my cat?"

"There's no cat!" I almost shout. Why does he have to play mind games for even the most insignificant things?

He shrugs. "Okay, well, if you don't want to believe me."

"There's no cat."

"Sure, Kayla. Can we go in now?"

He has to ring a bell. This is the kind of shop where they sell *clothes,* but it's locked, and you have to ring a bell. It's just...dresses.

A petite woman hurries to the door, opening it wide for us and stepping to the side so we can walk in.

It's a small boutique shop, with the first floor and what looks like a mezzanine. On one side, a black sign says *His* and on the opposite end of the room a gold sign says *Hers.* It has twenty or so dresses hanging far enough from each other, a whole person could stand between two hangers.

Sure different from the thrift shop clothes all bunched together, where you grab one piece on a hanger and ten will come with it.

"Mr. White, hello. I'm Suzanna, we..." She looks up at him, her mouth hanging open as she takes him in, and I know I've already found the person I'm going to fight with in this shop.

Holy shit, she might as well drool at this point. Her gaze drags all the way from his brushed-back blond hair and black glasses, down to his suit hugging his shoulders and chest perfectly, all the way to his shoes.

Breathe, Kayla. If you punch a bitch the first time you're allowed out of his house, it'll never happen again.

"We?" Nate wakes her up with a single, unimpressed syllable.

She giggles like a fourteen-year-old. "We spoke on the phone. I'll be your shopping assistant today. It's just us in the shop, so please make yourself at home."

Walking to a counter, she comes back with a tray holding two flutes of champagne. Nate pulls his wallet out of his pocket, drops a black credit card on the tray, and takes the flutes, offering me one.

"You like champagne, right, little sunflower?"

That stupid nickname being uttered in front of Suzanna makes my face heat.

I flatten my lips, nodding, even though the truth is written all over me. I've never had champagne in my life. And when I take a sip, I'm ready to spit it back out right away.

This shit tastes disgusting.

Nate notices my pinched face, and a smile tips the corner of his lips. He takes a sip of his, his mouth twisting, and puts the flute back on the tray.

"Terrible," he says casually. He takes the flute from my hands and puts it back too. "Don't drink this, baby. It's not nice."

Suzanna flushes. "I am so sorry, Mr. White. It's the same one I always serve. Can I get you anything else?"

"Dresses."

She turns away, hurrying to the counter to rid herself of the tray, and Nate uses the occasion to wink at me. Just like that, I know the champagne was fine, certainly to his tastes. He just didn't want me to feel uncomfortable not liking it.

The woman comes back to me, a newfound fake smile plastered on her face.

"You must be Mrs. White." So she knew all along that the man is married, and she still didn't stop herself from ogling him.

Instead of letting the last name raise my hackles as usual, I simply nod.

"Please, follow me. We have two collections at the front. Those are all next year's spring/summer, so you'll look perfect wearing them at the end of this summer. I've got Met Gala, and the latest summer/spring Paris Fashion Week from June. I know temperatures are starting to drop at night, so just to let you know we have some winter collections at the back." Her mouth twists. "They're this year's collection, of course. So, they're a bit old, but please, don't be embarrassed to ask. I sold plenty of January fall/winter Copenhagen just last week."

Embarrassed to ask? I don't even know what the fuck she's talking about. Does the collection's year really matter?

I can hear Nate behind me picking up a call, and my anxiety rises. I have survived being shot, beaten up, and almost murdered many times in my life, but I'm near a panic attack in a boutique shop next to a woman who talks *fashion*.

She caresses the dresses as she goes, and I walk alongside her, internally begging for a translator.

"Here we've got Vivienne Westwood, Prada, Carolina Herrera. I sold the Versace from the Met yesterday, but between you and me," she giggles to herself, "it was the worst one. Anything catching your eye?"

The fact that she's now directly asking me a question makes me sweat. "Erm..."

I eye the dresses. They look like gowns. I thought we were only going to a business dinner.

"Do you have something a little more"—I look at my own jeans and plain white t-shirt—"casual?"

Even her work outfit is more dressed up than my everyday clothes.

She gives me a sorry smile, her eyes blinking rapidly. "Oh, sweetie, once you choose, I'll have Melania cut it to any occasion you want. What is it for?"

Who the fuck is Melania? "Just a..." I lick my lips, my eyes darting to Nate again. He's facing away, looking at the street while he talks with a hand in his pocket. "Just a country club dinner."

"Sure thing." Rolling her lips and tasting her red matte lipstick in the process, she nods. "I'm assuming it's Stoneview Country Club. Is it at Lakeview restaurant, The Moonlight bistro, or The Small Star?"

My eyes widen. How many fucking restaurants do they have?

"The...uh—I..."

"That one," a deep voice says behind me. I turn to look at Nate pointing at one of the dresses. "The one on the right of it too. And the Chanel minidress over there." He points at a white dress with a huge white flower pinned to the front.

My upper lip curls. I don't think I'm into fashion. Those dresses look like I'm about to wave at a crowd of voters while holding the president's hand.

"We're going to Lakeview. Bring her some shoes too."

"Of course, Sir." Suzanna picks the three dresses and heads for the stairs.

He puts a hand on the small of my back. "Go try them on with Suzanna. I just need to make another call, and then I'm coming up for a show."

His hand goes up, rubbing around the middle of my back. Eyebrows pinched, his eyes bounce between mine. "Your heart is beating insanely fast. Are you okay?"

I nod, biting my bottom lip, but somehow my gaze can't quite meet his.

"Hey." He grabs my upper arms and turns me until I'm facing him properly. One hand comes to rest on my cheek, his thumb grazing my lips. "Do you want to name it?"

I jerk in his hold, my instinct telling me to step away, but his other hand is still wrapped around my biceps.

"If you don't name it"—his eyes capture mine, and I'm drowning in the stormy waves—"I won't understand it. And if I don't understand, I can't help."

Did he just admit to needing to hear how I feel so he could...*help*?

I blink up at him. I want more than anything to find something. The truth, honesty. But life with a psychopath wouldn't be so complicated if I could just read him.

No, with Nate, I have to take risks. I have to jump. I'll either crash miserably or be caught by the devil himself.

"I'm anxious," I whisper.

He smiles. "And I thought they called you the ruthless King."

"Give me a gun and I'll show you why. But fuck...I'm way out of my depths here."

He brings me closer to him, his hand sliding to the back of my head, forcing me to crane my neck and for him to become the only thing I see in this room.

"Try something for me, little sunflower. Let go. Be a good little wife, try on some dresses, and let me handle everything."

A violent *no* is already at the tip of my tongue, so he cuts me off.

"I promise you, no one will ever know you put down your arms and let me take control." He leaves a peck on my cheek, whispering close to my ear. "We'll tell everyone you fought me till the very end. It will be our little secret."

His phone rings, and he takes a step back. "Are you alright if I take this?"

I nod numbly, and his reassuring hand squeezes my arm one last time before he picks up and walks away.

Upstairs, I try on the three different dresses. One of them is the white one, and she gives me white heels with it. They're open, with a bow at the back that makes me look like I'm a gift for a sweet sixteen birthday party.

The dress reaches just above my knees, and the flower at the front is so huge it's less than an inch away from tickling my chin.

"This is a bit...much."

"Oh no. No, no, no." Approaching me, she stands behind me while we both look at each other in the mirror. "No, this is great for Lakeview. If you feel uncomfortable, I can take off the flower, but the dress suits you perfectly." She reaches for some pins on the small cushion attached to her wrist and puts them around the flower. "It'll be gorgeous without it. Make sure to wear red lipstick."

She pulls at the waist, and I'm forced to suck my stomach in.

"If I get Melania to pinch it a little more, it'll hold whatever's left of your postpartum belly."

I jerk out of her hold, spinning to face her. "What did you just say?" I hiss.

Her eyes widen. "Oh dear, I'm so sorry. I didn't mean this in an insulting way at all. We all have it, no matter how many years it's been. I have it too, it's nothing to be ashamed about. I just thought you'd want to look perfect in the dress."

The room tilts, and I have to put a hand on the mirror. "I don't—I'm not—" I scratch my throat. "I don't know what the fuck you're talking about, but watch your mouth."

It hurts to even think about it. But until I'm free, I can't take any risks.

"I'm so sorry. I saw your C-section scar, and I assumed... I'm *so* sorry."

"That's not it. And if I hear those fucking words from your mouth again, I'm throwing you over your fucking mezzanine. Clear?"

She nods in a panic, taking a few steps away from me as she grabs the next dress. While she does, I look around to make sure Nate still hasn't come up.

She does her best to regain composure while I put on the second dress, and so do I. I have to pretend everything is fine. I don't have a choice if I want to get out of this shop alive. If I ever want to go back to my true loves.

The dress is a green the same color of my eyes, bustier, and the skirt flows all the way to my ankles. Suzanna silently kneels by my side, working on the length and pinning the dress some more. I'm wearing red heels now, and I keep them on while I try on the last dress.

It's a black satin dress. At first glance, it's simple. The back is open, sleeveless, and a fake-diamond necklace attached to it ties around my neck to hold it. Suzanna steps away, grabbing something else while I observe my throat closely. The necklace is tight, more like a choker, and the way it clicked when she put it on makes me feel claustrophobic.

I run my thumb against it, and my heart stops.

"Wait...are these real diamonds?"

"Of course," she giggles, seemingly over my outburst. "What else?"

She approaches me from behind and slides a belt of diamonds through two discreet hoops at the sides of the dress. It doesn't come to attach at the front, she simply clips it at my back and it pulls the dress tighter around my waist, embracing my shape perfectly.

"H-how much is this dress?"

"Seventy-five thousand dollars." She nods, as if this is the most normal thing in the world.

"*What?*" I choke. I bring both my hands to my neck again and pull at the necklace.

"Oh, please don't," she panics.

"Can you... Can you take it off?" I'm starting to hyperventilate.

"It needs a key," she explains, as her hands hover over mine. "Please, don't pull. I'll get it."

Now this really doesn't fucking help.

"Why does it need a *key*?" I panic.

"They're real diamonds," she explains calmly. "It's just so no one can unclasp it from your neck and steal them."

I point at the green dress hanging not far from me. "How much is that one?"

"Twenty-two thousand dollars."

"Holy shit." I point at the white one for tonight.

"That one is only nine thousand dollars."

"*Only?*" I squeak. "Oh my god, get this shit *off* me." I can't fucking breathe with this much money on my body. Does she have any idea how many kids I could help on the North Shore with one of these dresses?

"Please, calm down. I—" She looks down the stairs, checking if Nate is coming. When she deems us safe, her attitude changes for the worse. "Okay, that's enough. I'm so done with all you trash girls coming in with your sugar daddies and causing a scene in my shop."

My mouth drops at the sudden fury in her voice.

"You're lucky enough that your pussy is buying you dresses that cost a small fortune. How about a simple thank you to the man who's getting it for you? I would *kill* for a man like Mr. White. I have done everything right. I went to an Ivy League, for fuck's sake. And you..." She looks me up and down, her upper lip curling back. "With your trashy face tattoo, and your hands that have never seen a manicurist in your entire life, you somehow got a ring around your finger. So stop trying to destroy my dress, and be grateful."

My hands fall by my sides, my jaw still hanging. I feel my fist curling, the letters tattooed on my knuckles stretching. I'm taking an angry step toward her, ready to punch her lights out, when Nate appears right behind her, a warning look on his face.

He chuckles, startling her as he puts a hand on her shoulder. "Be careful how you talk to my wife, she packs a mean punch."

Letting her go, he juts his chin toward the stairs. "Put it all on the card."

"No," I interject. "I don't want these dresses."

"Little sunflower, we talked about this."

"I'm not letting you buy me a hundred and six thousand dollars' worth of fucking *clothes*. You—"

"Suzanna." His stern voice makes her jump on the spot. "I said put it on the card. The two pairs of shoes too."

She doesn't wait any longer, running down two stairs at a time.

"This is bullshit," I rage. "These prices are outrageous. This shopping trip is the price of a house on the North Shore! A nice one too."

"Remember one important detail when I take you shopping, Kayla." He takes a threatening step toward me, and I wobble on my heels as I take one back. "You don't have a choice."

My fingers ache with how tightly I'm clenching them, and I'm surprised I'm not drawing blood from my nails digging into my skin.

"You don't have a choice on when I allow you out of the house. You don't have a choice on what you wear or how much I decide to spend on my wife." His hand goes to his belt, slowly unbuckling it.

"What are you doing?" Taking another step back, my eyes dart to the rest of the room. If he tries something, Suzanna will hear everything.

"I'm teaching you a lesson on being grateful."

"Nate..." My back hits the wall. I didn't realize I was that close already.

I put my hands in front of me. "Don't." Shaking my head, I think of how to get out of yet another insane situation he's put me in. "I'm not ungrateful. I'm just discovering a side of money I didn't even know was possible. I just..."

"Why don't you save yourself further embarrassment and just take it? Turn around and lift your dress."

I shake my head, panic overwhelming my senses. "Don't."

"Every second you make me wait is an extra lash to your pretty ass."

"I can't believe you," I hiss. Still, I turn around. "I can't believe for one second I thought you cared about anything I fucking feel."

"I do care about what you feel, Kayla. But I don't care for you refusing me anything."

I lift my dress to my waist, and goosebumps raise across my skin when his knuckles trace my spine. "The diamonds against your pale skin make you look irresistible."

"Get this shit over with," I grit out.

"Are you going to scream for Suzanna?"

"I hate you."

He tuts, mocking my dire situation. "Do you know what's funny? I hate you too, and yet something is starting to feel different, isn't it? See, I think the more you say those words, the less you believe them."

Swoosh!

The first lash against my skin takes me by surprise. I cry out, biting my lower lip too late.

"I bet our lovely shopping assistant won't be so jealous of you now that she knows what it really takes to satisfy me."

The next strike makes me grit my teeth harder. I'm trembling by the one after, sweat coating my lower back.

"Push your ass out. I'm not going to let you hide from something you love so much."

I count them in my head. Eight in total. Eight painful flames licking my skin and creating a tornado of confusing feelings within me.

I can barely breathe when he stops. "Turn around."

My knees buckle when I do. I can't look at him. I can't see the look of satisfaction on his face.

"Now, why don't you get on your knees and thank your husband for spoiling you?"

I don't hear anything downstairs, but I know she's there.

"Please…"

"Do I have to buckle this belt around your neck and drag you down there myself, Kayla?"

"You're a fucking bastard," I rasp, falling to my knees.

"And name it while you're down there."

"Fury," I spit at him. "For being stuck with someone who can't feel shit. Who can't realize when they're humiliating someone else past what they can take."

"Oh, I do realize it, baby. And I know you can take it. Open wide."

He pulls out his hard cock. It's already leaking precum, desperate for my touch.

His hand gripping the top of my head makes me whimper. My scalp stings as he pulls at my hair.

"Open, Kayla."

I've barely parted my lips when he pushes harshly into my mouth. Forget about giving him a blowjob, he's already fucking my face so violently there's nothing stopping the gagging sounds coming out of me.

"Don't ever refuse me spoiling you ever again," he growls above me. "I own you. I buy you whatever the fuck I want."

His thrust is so hard it almost makes me fall back, but his grip on my hair holds me in place.

"If I decide to cover you in diamonds, and take you out on a date in nothing but jewels, you will fucking do it, do you understand?" *Thrust.* My eyes water. "You take what I give you." *Thrust.* I choke. "You kneel at my feet." *Thrust.* My knees burn against the floor as I try to hold myself up. "And you thank me for it." He releases in my mouth, much quicker than I would have expected him to.

Nathan can spend hours fucking me and making me feel all kinds of bliss. But this wasn't for me. This was a lesson, and it's over the moment he makes his point.

His hand pinches my jaw, forcing me to open my mouth. "Show me."

I open, showing him his thick cum coating my tongue.

"Say thank you."

My confused stare meets his stern one, and he nods pointedly. So, I say it. I attempt to thank him the best I can with a mouth full of him.

Some spills down my chin, and he catches it with his thumb, pushing it back into my mouth.

"Now listen to me. You are not allowed to swallow until we get back in the car, understood? Maybe that'll save you from saying stupid things in front of others."

Panicked, I blink up at him, shaking my head like a crazy woman.

"Keep it in your mouth until we get in the car and your lesson is over. Swallow a second before your ass touches the passenger seat and all you'll be eating for days is my cum." He pauses, giving me time to acknowledge his words. "Are we clear, Kayla?"

Pressure builds at the backs of my eyes, but I silently

order myself to hold back every single tear. This is not how he breaks me. Not here, not because I can't take it.

He helps me up, and before we go down, he slides a hand beneath my dress.

"So. Fucking. Wet."

I squeeze my eyes shut.

"You're my perfect slut, baby. I could not have asked for a better wife."

I keep silent when Suzanna comes and finally lets me out of this stupid dress. I keep silent when she rings everything up and when Nate pays a total of one hundred and seventeen thousand dollars.

I keep silent all the way until we're back in the car because I don't have a fucking choice.

And when he asks me to show him his cum again when we sit down, I obey.

When he orders me to swallow, I gag around the thickness and force myself to.

And when he pushes his hand inside my jeans to check if I'm still wet, I force myself not to beg for an orgasm.

26

NATHAN

Obsessed - Royal Deluxe

The dress is beautiful. Suzanna had the huge flower taken off and now it's a simple white silk dress, perfectly fitted to Kayla's body, with a black silk belt around her waist.

She's standing in front of the mirror in my bedroom, dabbing foundation on her face. I told her to hide her hands, neck, and face tattoos, or people will be wondering what she's doing at Lakeview Restaurant, and as much as I don't care what people think, I don't need any attention on us.

Jerome Wynne needs to sign a nice import deal with me, and we'll be good for the night.

I walk to Kayla, standing behind her as I observe her in the mirror. Ignoring me, she puts more foundation on her face, dabbing and repeating the process again. I had someone come do her nails, and they're painted a beautiful blood red. The same color as the lipstick she's now grabbing.

I let her finish. I let her ignore me, until she has nothing else to do but to stand there and acknowledge me.

"I have something for you," I tell her. I know she doesn't like the way I talk. Emotionless, plain, but by now she must know that it's better than when I'm angry or taunting her.

She cocks an eyebrow at me. It's strange to see her like this. Dressed to perfection, her long black hair curled, her tattoos hidden. She's beautiful, of course, but it doesn't feel like *her*.

I show her the gold choker I'm holding. It's a simple, sturdy gold band with a diamond hanging from the front.

"Pull up your hair." She's annoyed, but she does it anyway.

She's been silent since I told her to swallow in the car. I think I can understand. She said she was furious, so I guess it comes with the silent treatment.

I settle the choker in place, close it, and let go. She releases her hair, and it flows down her back.

"A million-dollar collar," she deadpans. "Wonderful."

She drags a laugh out of me, but she doesn't reciprocate.

"It's just a necklace and it looks beautiful on you. I'm not the kind of man who puts a collar around your neck. I don't need anything to show people who owns you."

She raises her left hand, showing me her ring finger decorated with my rings.

"And what the fuck is this, asshole?"

I give her a bright smile. "A proof of love?"

"And your initials on my ass?"

"You deserved that."

She rolls her eyes, pushing me to the side so she can continue getting ready.

"I can't walk in heels," she tells me, opening the box. "I hope you're ready for me to embarrass you."

I take the box from her and put it on the bed. "You could never embarrass me."

Pinching the pants of my suit, I lift them slightly and fall to my haunches in front of her. Her eyebrows rise to her hairline. She doesn't say anything, though.

"So you're telling me your little show at the shop wasn't because I'd hurt your male ego and embarrassed you in front of Suzanna by not wanting your gifts?"

Taking her hands, I place them both on my shoulders. Next, I take the shoe out of the box.

"You did not hurt my ego." I wrap my hand around her right ankle, lifting it, and I feel her hands tighten around my shoulders. "I want to spoil you, Kay." I slide the shoe on her foot and pull it to rest on my thigh. "I want you to wear something that's deserving of you. I want you to walk into a room and have everyone look at you and wonder how they could ever be you."

I clasp the shoe and let my hand wander up her calf. "They could never be you, but I'd like to see them try and fail miserably."

Looking down at me, I notice the confusion on her face. I put her foot back down and grab the other shoe, repeating the process.

"I didn't like that you wouldn't let me take care of you."

"You want to treat me like a doll. Keep me in your house, leave me alone all day, come back at night to play with me. Parade me around, dress me up, choose everything for me."

She pauses when I clasp the other shoe.

"I am not a doll, Nathan. I have feelings and dreams. I have a style of my own. I have my favorite clothes, my favorite foods. I have places I like to go to, plenty of things that make me feel *good* inside. Warm, satisfied. Don't you have those?"

It hits me that since having her here, I haven't had time to think of anything else but her, and yet, I feel the exact same way when she described her favorite things.

It's her. She does all that to me.

My hand slides along her calf again, tighter this time. "I can be those things." I look up at her from my position. "Let me be those things for you."

"I lived an entire life before you. You can't replace everything."

I drop a kiss on the side of her knee. "Then how did you do it?" I whisper against her skin.

She matches my tone of voice. "Do what?"

"Become everything that makes me feel warm." I kiss her again. "Satisfied." And again. "Good."

Her gulp is so loud it makes me look up at her.

"You..." she hesitates. "You're just repeating my words. You don't know what it really feels like."

"I do. You make me feel it."

She shakes her head in a panic. Her ankle wobbles in the heel on the floor, and I wrap my hand around it.

I don't understand why she doesn't want to believe me. It took me weeks to make sense of them because I had never *felt* them. But surely she has? Those are feelings she should understand.

"Do you want me to describe it?"

"No," she hisses, face flushing beneath her makeup. "There's nothing to describe."

And yet I can't help myself. I'm overflowing with the need to share the impact she has on me. There's that stupid, warm thing in my chest. Hope.

Hope that she feels the same way.

"The moment I see you when I wake up, I feel like I'm entering a dream. I haven't had nightmares in forever, but it's that exact same feeling of waking up from one and realizing you're safe."

"Stop it, Nate."

"When you have your night terrors and you cling onto me, my entire being wants to protect you."

She tries to pull away from me, and she ends up falling on her ass, so I crawl on top of her, keeping her between my arms. "When you say my name, I feel like I'm having a heart attack, and my entire focus goes to you. It's very strange."

"You're just... You're..." She licks her lips.

"Have you ever been so cold you could barely feel your hands? And you're outside, freezing, maybe walking to your house, and you just want to *be there*, you know?"

Her eyes keep bouncing between mine.

"Have you?" I insist.

"Y-yes."

"And then you get home," I keep explaining. "And it's warm, and you get to put your cold hands against a radiator."

She's still blinking up at me, completely lost, when I know...I just *know* this makes sense.

"And slowly you can feel your hands again. It starts at the tips of your fingers." I graze her forehead, her cheek, her lips with the tips of my fingers. "Then it's your knuckles." I use the knuckle of my index finger to trace her chin. "And finally, your palm."

I press my palm against her cheek.

"You feel it all again," I rasp, observing her entire face,

her pouty lips, her harsh lines, her beautiful forest eyes. "And it's all better."

Her mouth parts, as a small breath leaves her.

"I know it makes sense. I might not feel much, but I feel *that* like I never have anything else before."

I wait for a reaction, and I wonder if that's how she feels about me. If every time I understand her feelings, she expects me to react to them.

For the first time, I understand what it's like to be on the receiving end of my antisocial behavior.

"We should go," she whispers. "It's a business dinner."

Something threatens to turn me violent. To keep her here, force her to take me, and make her hate herself for enjoying it. I want to imprint my soul on hers and make it hurt so badly she will never forgive me. That way, she'll *feel* something toward me.

But I don't.

I pull away from her, stand up, and offer her my hand.

And I let her punish me with silence.

I take the menu from the waiter and turn back to our table. I specifically booked a round table to make it more intimate, friendly. I want Wynne to feel like we're friends, even though I'm going to use his business to smuggle cocaine across the country and all the way to my hotels.

Lakeview is packed as usual, but we have a table far enough from everyone to speak freely. As long as we don't shout about drugs, we should be fine.

"Francine." I pull out my most ravishing smile as I look at her. "The face of W. Beauty. I can see why your husband is using you to sell his products."

As I say that, I bring my hand to Kayla's thigh. She's

sitting on my left, her social anxiety pouring from her like steam out of a kettle. She feels at odds with the people here, and I can't blame her. I grew up in Cosa Nostra money, with flashy rich people who loved to show they were made men, but nothing prepares for Stoneview. The one percent is a truly different breed.

Jerome is twenty years older than Francine, but I guess when you have that much fuck-you money, you can afford to marry an old model.

Francine laughs politely. She's sitting next to Kayla, and her husband is between me and her. Still, she finds a way to put her hand on mine resting on the table, and all I can feel is Kayla tensing next to me.

"So," she says with fake excitement, tapping my hand before pulling hers back. "This wedding. We didn't even know you were dating anyone, Nathan."

It's funny how among rich criminals who pretend to live a normal life, no one even bats an eye when you come back from four years in prison.

"It was very intimate," I explain. "All we wanted was to tie the knot as quickly as possible. Right, darling?"

I squeeze her thigh under the table, and she nods. "Right," she rasps.

"And where are you from, Kayla? I've not seen you in Stoneview before, have I?" Francine continues. It's her role, after all. Her husband brings her so he can play up the façade of a casual dinner, and her boring conversations are a front while we sort out the details of our contract.

"Erm," Kayla hesitates. "I'm from Silver Falls."

"Oh, how lovely. The South Bank is so beautiful. It feels so...normal next to Stoneview, right? It's good from time to time to step out of here and into the real world. How cute."

Kayla's jaw tightens, and her eyes dart down to her

menu in front of her. "Yes," she says stiffly. "Very cute." And she doesn't add that she isn't even from the South Bank. Poor Francine would faint if she knew Kayla was from the North Shore of the falls.

"Oh, Jerome," Francine squeaks excitedly, tapping her husband's shoulder. "The oysters are back on the menu. Let's order some for the whole table. Do you like oysters, Kayla?"

"Sure." She nods, and I recognize the lie in her tone because it sounds exactly the same as her pretending she liked champagne.

It's crazy how much you can learn about a person when you truly listen. When Kayla lies, her voice dips, her words shorten, and she meets your eyes with no shame whatsoever. The exact same way she's meeting Francine's right now.

"Let's order two dozen for the table. How many is that each?" she asks her husband.

Jerome takes a second to think, but Kay's voice cuts through his thoughts.

"Six," she answers right away without a hint of a second thought.

"Right," Jerome chuckles, confirming the number to his wife.

They talk among themselves, and I look at my pretty wife with a calculator inside her brain.

Her eyes squint as she looks at the menu, and I can't seem to stop observing her. Jerome is saying something to me, but all I can focus on is her beautiful red lips mumbling to herself as she reads one item after the other, but what surprises me the most is when she repeats the same line three times before realizing she hasn't moved on.

It's all in the way her eyes move, in her frustrated huff,

and how she then presses her index finger to the paper so she can keep going.

"What's ercasgot?" she whispers, wide eyes looking up at me.

"Oh, sweetie." Francine explodes in a haughty laugh, a hand held to her chest. "It's *escargot* not ercasgot." She laughs some more, finding herself hilarious.

Jerome heartedly joins in. "So you can count, but you can't read, it seems." His eyes shine with mockery as he gets his petty revenge because Kayla hurt his ego by calculating quicker than him.

Kayla's eyes snap up, and I expect her to jump over the table and strangle Francine and Jerome one by one. I steady myself to stop her, but instead, I feel her leg trembling and notice the way her shoulders deflect. Her gaze falls over the words again, her brow furrowing in confusion.

Something in my heart fissures. I think I want her to lose it. I want her to grab Francine's face and smash it against the table because this isn't like her. I hate seeing her like this. Out of her element, unable to defend herself because she knows it's not appropriate to punch a woman right now and that's how she's used to imposing herself.

"If you'll excuse me. I need the bathroom." Jerome stands up, still chuckling as he shakes his head. "Ercasgot. That's a good one."

I watch him leave, my hand caressing Kayla's thigh and my eyes annihilating him from behind.

"They're snails," I tell her softly, still unable to take my eyes off Wynne. "The French have it wrong, if you ask me. It's chewy and tasteless if not for the sauce." My eyes go to Francine. "One could so easily choke on it." I narrow my gaze at her, a silent threat.

Kayla catches the way I look at Francine, a small smile spreading on her face. "Would be a pity," she adds. Feeling more secure, she shrugs. "We don't really have snails in our diners on the North Shore."

It's her turn to look at Francine, gauging her reaction.

"The...the North Shore?" she repeats. Fear now tames her earlier loud voice.

"Oh yeah." Kay nods, smiling from ear to ear. "Sorry, I thought I told you I was from Silver Falls?"

"I'll be back," I say as I stand up. I drop a kiss on the top of Kayla's head as I arrange my suit jacket and follow Wynne.

I find him right as he exits the men's bathroom.

"Whoa," he chuckles. "Nathan."

I smile at him, but I know the one I'm using. The kind that reminds him I'm not someone to be messed with, and that he just landed on my bad side.

"Everything alright, my friend?"

Of course, he feels the need to call me his friend out loud, to put a name on our relationship, as if asking me to treat him as an equal.

He isn't my equal.

He is a fucking insect I can crush under my foot. He is someone who works under me because at any point I can stop huge cash flows from entering his company. Mainly? He is an insignificant little man who thinks himself better than Kayla because he can pronounce a French word no one gives a shit about and can't stand for a woman to do math quicker than him.

"Come here. Listen."

I casually put my hands in my pockets. We can see our table from here, where his wife is awkwardly shifting her chair away from Kayla.

"I appreciate the business we do together. I really do." He must notice death slowly clouding my eyes because he takes a step back, plastering himself against the wall. "But if you ever make fun of Kayla again, I'm afraid our next conversation will involve my gun, your head, and a nice hole between your eyes."

I pull my hand out of my pocket, grab his tie softly, and slap his mouth with it in a playful yet demeaning gesture.

"There should be nothing but respect in your tone when you speak to my wife." I think my calmness scares him more than anything else. "Now get back out there and try again. Who knows? You might live until tomorrow."

Wynne is strangely polite until the end of dinner. We focus on our contract, how he'll receive the powder at his factory in Texas, the routes I want him to take, and how many keys I expect delivered every week. The powder will be in the same parcels as the bath bombs his beauty and self-care brand will deliver to the Cascade hotels, so some people at his factory need to cut the coke when they receive it and package it in luxurious bath bomb bundles. I have people I trust for that. People he's going to hire as factory workers.

The man gets a deal with a chain of hotels, all his products will be used in our rooms, and he'll receive extra *shut-the-fuck-up* money.

I get fifty keys of cocaine delivered every single week. And with the North Shore gangs working for me, that shit is going to sell all over the area.

Ka-ching, motherfucker.

Francine has really been forcing herself to talk to Kayla all night, and my beautiful sunflower has made absolutely no effort. It also turns out she doesn't like oysters, doesn't like lobster, and doesn't like lamb. So she hasn't eaten anything and is now attacking her chocolate fondant eagerly. But Jerome is in a rush to get things over with.

"Shall we retreat to the cigar room, my friend?" He smiles, dollar signs decorating his pupils. "The wives can have one last cocktail at the bar, I guess."

I shake my head. "Kayla stays by my side," I answer casually. "She can be trusted with anything." Except not punching Francine in the face once they're on their own.

He makes a low, disappointed sound in his throat and turns to his wife. "Why don't you get Sanders to take you home? I'll be here a while."

Signing won't take long, but I'm sure he's eager to invite his mistress to one of the private rooms afterward to celebrate.

Relief crosses Francine's face now that she won't have to spend any more time with Kay, and she nods eagerly. "Of course. I'll see you at home." She's already up, saying bye to us and leaving.

Jerome follows, and I nudge Kayla. "Come on. We're almost done with this shit," I murmur once they're far enough.

"But my dessert," she groans as I grab her hand and force her to get up. "I'm starving."

"I'll get you some food as soon as we get home."

She stretches her free hand toward the table, managing to get one last bite as I drag her away. "The chocolate is so good."

"I'm going to spank your ass. This is almost over, and I managed to not kill him. Who knows how much longer I'll hold."

"Kill him, for all I care." She still follows me, and I drop her at the entrance of the cigar room.

"Not until he signs that contract. Take a seat in there.

It's booked for us. I'm going to get the contract from the car. Can you behave for five more minutes?"

She narrows her eyes. "I've done nothing but behave. Can *you* behave?"

I ignore her, hurrying toward the exit. I can't see Wynne by the valet service, and he's not in the parking lot either. I somehow missed him coming back in. He must already be in the cigar room.

Alone with Kayla.

And I don't like that one bit.

27

KAYLA

you should see me in a crown - Billie Eilish

Jerome Wynne is already sitting in a leather armchair by a fireplace.

Why would they light up the fireplace in summer?

There's another chair near him, only separated by a small, wooden coffee table.

His legs spread before him, and he's grabbing a cigar from a box. He smells it, hums to himself, and puts it back.

Ignoring him, I walk around the room. It's an old money kind of room, the whole building is. There are some ugly-ass rugs on the floor and shelves full of books. Not many colors except every single shade of brown and red that's ever existed. And wood. Lots of wood and old leather.

I bite the nail of my index finger as I look at the shelves, pretending to read book titles. It's even harder to walk around in these heels now that they're being swallowed by the giant rug at every step I take.

I hear him shift in his seat behind me, the leather creaking under him, and I take a book in my hands, opening it and dragging my eyes along the lines. It takes me forever to read the dedication, and I've already got a headache from all the wine I drank at dinner. The food was nothing like what I've tasted before, and I didn't eat much of it, so the alcohol is getting to my head. No chance of reading now, but I can still pretend.

A hand lands on the book from behind me, and I startle, dropping it to the floor.

"What the f—"

His hand at the back of my neck cuts me off, and the next second, I'm plastered face first against the shelves.

My first instinct is to fight back. I raise my leg, attempting to crush his foot as I slam my heel to the floor, but I miss and instead hurt my ankle when I lose my footing from the heel's instability.

"Fuck," I hiss. "These fucking shoes." The pain tearing through my ankle drags a whimper out of me. I wouldn't be surprised if it's sprained. That was a very unnatural movement.

Wynne presses me harder against the shelves, and I throw my elbow back, but my strength is not much use now that I have a weakened leg and no footing. Without balance, it's hard to throw a punch, especially to someone behind you who you can't really see.

"How much does he pay you?" His free hand comes to the hem of my dress, and he's already pulling it up.

"What are you doing?" I heave, my lungs suddenly freezing. "I—He's not paying me."

Wynne isn't exactly a young man, probably in his late fifties, but his strength is surprising, to say the least. With my cheek against the spines of the books, he easily brings a hand to my face and wipes the foundation I put on my tattoo with his thumb.

"I've been seeing this shit under your makeup all night. North Shore trash suddenly married to a Stoneview resident? What are you if not a whore?"

I press my palms against the shelves, attempting to force my body back and get him off me, but my ankle screams painfully, and he easily slams me back. My head hits the edge of the shelf just above me, tearing a grunt from my chest.

"Get off me," I bark. "I swear to god, you don't want to fucking mess with me."

I wish I could accompany this with a bullet to his head, or at least a knife in his chest, but I'm slightly limited in self-defense right now.

"Give me a price to fuck him over and send him straight back to prison."

My heart stops for a second.

"You..." I try to catch my breath. "You don't want to do business with him?"

He cackles behind me, slapping my ass in the process and making me want to vomit the wine I drank.

"Want? No. You can't survive doing business with an unpredictable psycho. But if you want to work on the East Coast, you have to pick some mobster to work with, and when Nathan White offers you a contract, you don't refuse. We were all safer when he was away. So tell me. How much?"

He pinches my hips and drags my underwear to my knees.

"S-stop." Panic overtakes me, making my ears ring. "I won't tell you any fucking price if you *touch me.*"

I won't tell him shit, but I need to delay this until Nate comes back.

"Or...you could make it a very, *very* nice price, and I won't hurt you." I hear some disgusting, wet sound behind me, and I understand he licked his hand when he presses two fingers between my legs.

A broken gasp cracks through my throat. My eyes squeeze shut, and my entire body stiffens.

Fight back, Kayla!

This is the first time in my life that my fight-or-flight response dysfunctions. The first experience of not being able to grab fury from deep inside me and throw it into someone's face to hurt them. I just *freeze.*

He presses against my entrance, making me feel like he's ripping through my dry skin.

"Please..." I whimper. I fucking hate that whimper.

"How much to have you set him up and sent back to prison? Answer, trashy whore!"

"Oh, she already tried that, Jerome. It didn't work quite like she expected."

Nate's completely dull voice is the most beautiful sound I've ever heard. My muscles relax instantly.

"Now why don't you step away from my wife?"

Wynne's hands are off me in a split second.

"Nathan," he blurts out, suddenly so far away from me I don't even know how he moved that quickly.

Strengthless, I drop to my knees the second Wynne isn't holding me up anymore. Two hands catch me at the waist, and Nate is already bringing me back up.

He observes the thong around my knees clinically. His eyebrows pinch in the slightest way possible, barely a line showing between them, but I notice it.

Softly, he helps me lean against the shelves. He releases me, his hands hovering around my waist until he makes sure I can stand on my own, and then he drops to his haunches.

"Nathan." Wynne's terrified, and it brings me happiness. I'm dizzy, unsure what is really going on, but the terror is clear, and I like that.

Nate raises a hand, cutting him off with a simple gesture. "The contract is on the table. Sign it."

He doesn't even turn around to check if Wynne is listening. He knows he will, and I can testify to that as he grabs a pen from his breast pocket and takes the contract with trembling hands.

Maybe he thinks if Nate still wants to do business with him, he's not that angry.

But I can feel it in the way he delicately drags the thong back up my legs, the way he caresses my hips as he settles it there... I can sense in the way he looks up at me, his gaze empty, his face completely blank... I *know* it in the way he slowly stands back up, puts a hand on my cheek and observes my face...

That this is complete, barely restrained, *fury.*

"Go sit down over there, little sunflower." He points to a sofa in the corner of the room. "I'll be just a minute."

He walks to where Wynne is sitting in his armchair, his legs trembling, his foot anxiously tapping the rug.

"It's all okay, my friend," he tells Nathan. "This...was just a misunderstanding, alright? I was fucking with her, okay?"

"Did you sign?"

"Yes. Yes, of course." He points to the contract with a shaky finger.

Nate nods as he takes the contract, folds it in half, and puts it in the inside pocket of his jacket. "Very good."

"Misunderstandings happen when you bring North Shore girls here, Nathan." Wynne laughs to himself, the sound low in his throat and disgusting. "I thought she was a whore."

I try to keep listening and stay in touch with the situation, but my head is pounding, and a raging pain hammers in my ankle. It keeps bringing my attention back to my own body.

Everything sounds like I'm underwater, and my heart beats unsteadily. I keep having to take shallow breaths, unsure if I'm breathing at all.

I blink at what's in front of me, trying to focus on the room. Nate stands right next to Wynne, his hand creeping up.

"You thought she was a whore, huh?" He suddenly grabs him by the hair at the back of his head.

The room tilts slightly. Or maybe it's me. I try to focus again, but everything feels so far and quiet.

Another blink, and Wynne's head is being smashed against the table.

"She is not a *whore*," Nate hisses, punctuating the last word by smashing the man's head against the table again.

I hear cries and apologies, but I can't quite make them out.

"She." *Smash!* "Is." *Smash!* "My." *Smash!* "Wife." He drops the bloody man, who falls off his seat to his front, and he grabs the cushion that serves as the back of the armchair.

Kneeling next to him, he presses the cushion to the back of his head, reaches inside his jacket, and pulls out a gun.

"Nate," I call out weakly. I try to stand up, but fall right back onto the sofa, too lightheaded to even move. "Don't."

My husband presses the gun against the cushion.

"Nate," I try again.

And shoots.

He looks up at me across the room, a dazzling smile brightening his face. "Yes, little sunflower?"

Breathing through my mouth, I attempt to stay conscious as the vertigo worsens.

He stands up, puts the gun back in his holster, and strides all the way to me. Kneeling on the floor in front of me, he takes hold of my jaw with a gentle hand, forcing me to look straight at him.

"Breathe for me, baby."

"I wasn't gonna do it," I croak. "Put you back in prison."

He nods. "I know."

"Y-you defended me at dinner tonight. I know you had a talk with him." I gulp a breath.

He doesn't say anything, so I keep whispering hushed words I want him to hear. I feel like I'm dying, and I want him to hear them before I do.

"I wasn't going to betray you...I swear. I th—think." My eyes flutter shut, and for a second, I feel myself falling, but I snap them open again. "I think I'm starting to like your crazy ass."

He smirks. It's beautiful, devilish.

"I know, baby. That Stockholm syndrome is doing wonders for you."

I laugh. Truly, wholeheartedly laugh.

"Bastard."

And then my soul leaves my body.

I gasp when a slap cracks against my cheek, my eyes flying open.

"What the fuck do you think you're doing, Kayla?" His harsh voice startles me. "Wake the hell up."

"I'm dying," I say, all too seriously, as he wraps an arm under my legs, one at my waist, and lifts me up.

"You're not dying. Your body is going into shock. A man just sexually assaulted you. It'll do that to you."

He stands up easily and strides across the room. The second we're out, he calls a member of the staff. "Mr. Wynne is having a private moment with a friend of ours, if you know what I mean. Make sure his privacy is respected."

The man looks at the way he's holding me, not daring to ask a single question, and nods. Before I know it, we're in the car, and while the dizziness is gone, I'm shaking and feel sick to my stomach.

I huff as he starts the car, pulling out of Stoneview Country Club.

"Don't drive so fast. I feel sick."

"You drank tonight and barely ate anything. I didn't see you sip on water once. No wonder you're feeling sick. And someone attacked you, too."

I hold on to the door, not liking how quickly he's driving. "Your logic is undeniable," I bite out bitterly.

"There she is," he chuckles. "I thought we lost you for a second."

"I thought I was dying," I snap back. I press a hand to my forehead, hating the shivers running through my body. "I feel like shit."

"Seriously, with all the adrenaline you must have gone through in your life being part of the Kings, you don't know what it's like to be in shock?"

"*That* kind of shit never happened to me on the North

Shore." There. He did it. He pissed me off. "Being thought of as a whore, being attacked because some rich fuck thought he could just take what he wanted, having his fingers..." I shake my head, forcing the thought out of my mind. I can still feel them. "That never happened to me on my shitty side of town! Only since you took me. Only because of *you*."

He accelerates, his grip tightening on the steering wheel. "Don't, Kayla. He paid for it, and anyone who hurts you will pay for it with their lives. He was dead the second he made fun of you anyway. I was just waiting for him to sign the contract."

"Anyone who saw me tonight at that restaurant had a reason to make fun of me and it's your fault! You're the one who took me out of my life and forced me into your fancy one, with your rich cunts, your contracts, and your pretty restaurants with fucking ercasgots!"

"*Escargots!*"

"It's not my fucking fault I can't read!" I yell. Steam is starting to cover the windows, and I press on the demist button. "Now fucking slow down!"

"Stop talking shit about yourself. You *can* read," he growls. "You're dyslexic."

"No, I'm not."

"You are, and I swear to god, you're going to end up in my basement again if you talk disrespectfully about yourself one more time."

Where the fuck is this argument going? I thought I was screaming at him for changing my entire life for the worst. Now *he* is mad at *me* for talking bad about myself?

"So now not only are you keeping me captive, but you've found yourself a new hobby of giving me a diagnosis about shit you know nothing about."

"It's pretty fucking obvious, but I'll make you see a speech therapist just to prove you wrong."

"Stop *making me* do anything! And fucking slow dow —"

Whatever it is, it hits us at a violent speed.

Violent and deadly.

28

NATHAN

Babylon - 5 Seconds of Summer

"Kay," I rasp. I want to hear her voice.

Despite the ringing in my ears, I can hear the metal groaning around me.

Everything and nothing hurts all at once. My body keeps going from excruciating pain to numbness in split seconds.

"Kayla," I call again despite it making my lungs burn. I can't fucking breathe with the airbag so tight against my chest.

Something is dripping on me. It takes me a few seconds to realize I'm upside down, and it's blood from a wound in my leg.

"Baby, talk to me."

My neck screams in agony as I try to turn my head to the side, but nothing hurts like the panic that seizes my heart.

She's not here.

She was ejected from the car.

Reality hits me in the face. The road, the speed.

But I didn't do anything wrong. It was dark, but no one was there. We were driving the country roads that lead from the lake, through the woods, and back to the residential areas of Stoneview. There was absolutely no one there. I remember a crossroads, but we were on the main road.

No, that car came out of nowhere. It didn't even have its lights on.

This was planned.

"Kayla!" I roar, adrenaline finally kicking in. "Run!"

I don't even know if she can hear me. Fuck, I don't even know if she's conscious. But on the small chance that she is, she needs to get out of here.

Steps come my way, crushing glass and stopping right by my broken window. The position I'm in stops me from moving entirely. I'm upside down, my seatbelt practically strangling me, the airbag crushing me against the seat.

Someone kneels by me. "Kayla is taking a rest by the side of the road."

A Russian accent.

Superb.

"I see the puppies are out to play," I groan painfully.

I knew the Bratva Wolves were after me. I should have taken a page out of their books and had my meeting at home.

I see the flash of a blade, and the airbag starts deflating. My seatbelt is cut and before I can do anything, I'm being dragged out of the car by my shoulders.

I grunt when he drops me on the grass. Closing my eyes, I lick my bloody lips before opening them again and looking around. We're off the road. It looks like the car tumbled down until it hit the line of the trees. Farther back, I can see a body lying by the road next to a huge pick-up truck with a custom bullbar attached to the front.

"That's some fucked-up vehicle you have."

Standing above me, I watch him put his knife away.

"Is that my wife lying over there?"

He nods slowly, looking down at me with hard black orbs. "She was thrown out right away. Quick death."

I chuckle to myself, feeling a fury like never before boiling in my veins and taking over my senses. And to think I had the exact same thought not long ago when Wynne touched her. People are really testing my patience tonight.

"I'm afraid I can't say the same about your death," I say.

I reach inside my jacket but come back empty handed. I try the other side. Same.

My guns must have fallen out during the tumbling.

"That's seriously unlucky," I huff.

He pulls out his own gun, taking his time. "Viktor Volkov sends his regards." As he points it at my head, my eyes focus on his finger on the trigger.

That's how I know the sudden *bang!* doesn't come from him. Because he hasn't pressed his trigger yet.

But my wife has.

And she looks absolutely gorgeous standing next to the Wolf's dead body, her nine-thousand-dollar dress covered in blood, mud, and grass stains. Her hair is disheveled, a long line of thick red liquid running down her face from her hairline.

I smile. "I could fuck you right now."

"I fucking hate you, Nate." Her croaky voice gives me the strength I need to stand up.

My hands hover over her body, not daring to touch, until she snaps at me again. "The Wolves. You decided to go to war with the *fucking Wolves*. What kind of idiot does that?"

She sounds perfectly fine to me, and I can't keep the joy to myself.

I grab her by the back of the head and slam my lips to hers. Her small gasp allows me to slip my tongue inside her mouth and stroke hers. I deepen the kiss by dragging her closer to my battered body and wrapping my other arm around her waist.

"For a second, I thought you were dead," she murmurs when I pull away.

"How did that feel?"

"So fucking good."

Short sentence. Low voice. And she looks right into my eyes. I know what that means.

I smile. "Liar."

I press my lips to her cheek, the side of her head, her forehead. I can't fucking stop until she tries to push me away.

"I never thought for one second you were dead."

"Oh, really?" she snorts.

"You're invincible, baby. We both are. The world can't take us down. I promise." I drop another kiss to her lips. I can't get enough of her.

"You're lucky one of your guns was right next to me." She shows me something else in her other hand. "And this."

My phone.

"What would I do without you, little sunflower?"

I take the phone and dial Sam's number right away. Kay helps me hobble to the side of the road, and we sit on the ground.

"Your leg," she points out, just as my friend picks up. "You need a doctor."

"*I'm on a date, Nate. This better be urgent.*" He already sounds done with me, and his night just started.

"Not with my sister, I hope."

"Nate," Kay hisses next to me. "Now? Really?"

"*I'm with Lik, actually. And I would have loved to spend time with my boyfriend without you pestering us.*"

"Who do you use to hide tricky bodies?"

He huffs loudly, making sure I'm aware I'm ruining his night. "*It used to be Xi, but he doesn't do that shit anymore, so it'll have to be me.*"

"Call Xi. He's back in business. Offer him whatever amount he wants."

"*His girlfriend's family are billionaires. He doesn't need your money.*"

"Then threaten the girlfriend. I need him to move someone at Stoneview Country Club, and I need you to come get me and Kayla. The Wolves tried to take us out with a crazy pick-up truck."

"*Fuck. Send me your location, I'm on my way.*" I hear him talk away from the phone. "*Lik, call your brother.*" Then back at me, he asks, "*Are you alright?*"

I sigh lovingly. "Thankfully, my wife saved my life because she can't live without me." I smile at her rolling her eyes. "But I am bleeding pretty badly, and she probably needs stitches on her face. Call Marcie and have her waiting for us at the house."

"No," Kayla interjects. "That bitch is not touching me."

I pull the phone away from my face and press my finger against her wound, making her hiss in pain. "Do you want to die? No. Marcie is coming, and that's final."

"Fucking hate Marcie," I hear her mumble as I talk to Sam again.

"And call Garcia-Diaz, too. Ask her if my contract with W. Beauty is still valid if Wynne...disappears."

"*Nate...why? Why did you kill him?*" he asks, his voice so annoyed I almost feel bad.

"He touched Kayla, so he died. As simple as that."

My friend stays quiet for a few seconds. "*Alright, I get that.*" And for once I don't want to kill him for dating my sister. He knows what happens to men who hurt our women. Women and man in his case.

"Oh, and Sam? Get some chocolate cake for Kay, please. She hasn't eaten anything tonight."

I hang up and look ahead, wondering if we could use that guy's truck to get back home quicker, but the destroyed windshield is not exactly giving me *discreet* vibes.

"Your contract." Kayla's voice is like beautiful music in the dead of the night.

I turn to her, noticing the shock on her face.

"What about it?"

She looks away to the other side of the road. "You...you didn't even know if it was still going to be valid and you killed Wynne anyway."

"Little sunflower." I press a hand to her cheek, forcing her to focus on me. "What did he do?"

I watch her throat tightening as she struggles to swallow. "He assaulted me."

"Then he dies." I lose myself in her incredible eyes as I repeat, "It's as simple as that."

"But that contract was so important to you. What if it's void because he's dead?"

I shrug. "Then I'll need to find another company to transport my cocaine." I notice my gun still in her hand

and softly take it back. "I'll take that if you don't mind. I know you sometimes have slightly murder-y thoughts toward me."

She explodes in a genuine laugh, her head falling onto my shoulder as she calms down. "I hate you."

"I know, little sunflower. I know."

"Mr. White, come to your office," Marcie calls out the second I pass my front door. Kayla helps me onto the leather sofa in there, and my doctor kneels on the floor next to me.

"Do her first," I order her without thinking.

"*No,*" Kay says categorically. "He's been bleeding for ages. It's urgent."

Marcie nods.

"Kay, will you get me a whiskey? And pour yourself one too. You're still shaking."

She walks to the wet bar next to my desk, her back to us as she pours two glasses of whiskey from the decanter.

When she turns back around, she notices Marcie got me out of my pants, and her eyes narrow in on her.

"Kayla," I say, tone stern. I don't need a dead doctor on my hands right now. "Play nice."

She hands me a tumbler that I down right away. She fills it again, and I repeat.

"Mr. White, I really wouldn't advise drinking right now. It will thin your blood and slow down the healing process."

I shrug, downing the third glass Kay passes me. "Stitch tighter, maybe?" It makes my beautiful wife laugh, and that's all I needed to heal.

Marcie shakes her head, disappointed, continuing her job.

"Hurry, Marcie." I can't help the impatience in my voice. "I can see she's bleeding. From the head too."

Kay presses a finger to her forehead and looks at the blood. "I feel fine."

"You don't look fine."

"I'm almost done," Marcie cuts us off. "I had to pull out some shards of glass and it slowed me down, but you'll be fine. It didn't touch any arteries."

"No shit, Doc?" Kay snorts. "He'd be long dead if it had."

As Marcie finishes, she puts her hand on my thigh, caressing me as if to soothe me. "I know you, Mr. White. I've taken care of a lot of your wounds. This is nothing for you."

Kayla's mouth twists, the daggers coming from her eyes metaphorically landing directly in Marcie's back.

"Do you want to die?" The hiss in her voice could make a soldier run back to his mother.

My doctor looks up, cocking an eyebrow at Kay. "I'm sorry?"

"Get your fucking hands off him."

My mouth drops open at her blatant display of jealousy, cock twitching like it heard its name.

"I'm helping him, are you blind?"

"By stroking him close to his dick every time you dab off some blood? I'm not blind, but you will be in a second if you don't take your hands off him."

Oh. She's drunk.

"I'm just cleaning up the rest of the blood."

"Bitch, the stitches are done. He can take a shower to clean the rest. And he'll have that shower with me. Now *take. Your hands. Off. Him.*"

Marcie lifts her hands, putting her palms in front of her as if to ask my crazy wife to relax.

"Okay, do me now. Then you can fuck off."

Kay pours herself another glass and drops into my office chair.

Just as she gets settled, Sam knocks on the door, quickly asking if he can talk to me in private. I stand up, putting my pants back on.

"I'll be a minute," I tell the two women.

"Mr. White, please, don't leave," Marcie calls out desperately as she approaches Kayla.

"You'll be okay. She's just a little drunk, but she's inoffensive. Right, Kay?"

She raises her hands, acting innocent. "As harmless as an ercasgot."

I pinch my lips to stop myself from laughing. "Escargot, darling." And I step out.

"Update me," I tell Sam, as we walk toward my kitchen.

"Wynne is all set, and Xi is moving on to whoever that Wolf was. Lik is getting rid of his car and taking care of yours."

I wave a hand. "Junk it. I'll get another one. So, how did you get Xi on it in the end?"

He pins me with a stare. "You know how."

I laugh to myself, drinking more whiskey from my tumbler. My leg hurts like a bitch.

"You threatened your boyfriend's brother's girlfriend. That's low, my friend."

He snatches the glass out of my hand and puts it on the counter. "You're buzzed like a college sorority girl. Stop drinking. Look, I didn't want to mention her to him, but it's not like I had much of a choice. I blamed it all on your crazy arse anyway."

"As you should. I would have killed her if he hadn't listened."

He runs a hand across his face. "Anyway. Garcia-Diaz said it should be fine, but she'll get back to me in the morning when she's looked at everything. Paperwork is at her office."

I huff, taking back my tumbler from the table and sipping on it. "What the fuck do I pay her all that money for if she doesn't keep all my files on hand."

"Might surprise you, but people have lives. Like my date with Lik that you ruined, for example."

I notice the chocolate cake on the kitchen island and slap his shoulder. I think he's right. I'm a little buzzed. "Thank you for tonight. Please, go back to your boyfriend."

He nods as he stands. "I'll be here first thing tomorrow. It's the deadline for the Kings and NSC to tell you if they'll both work for you."

I raise my glass. "See you tomorrow."

I take him to the door and head back to my office.

Nothing could have prepared me for what I see when I open the door.

29

NATHAN

Kiss Bang - grandson

Kay still sits at my desk, her feet propped up, sipping on her whiskey. She has a huge white band-aid awkwardly taped to her forehead, and I already know she put that on herself.

I look for Marcie and find her quicker than I thought. On her front, lying on the floor, with a letter opener stabbed into the back of her neck.

"Little sunflower," I say carefully as I step in. "Care to tell me what happened?"

She spreads her arms wide, the whiskey sloshing in the glass. "She said you deserved better than me."

I wipe my mouth with my hand, making sure to hide my smile.

"You killed my doctor."

"She wanted to fuck you. She wanted me out, so she could be in."

"Marcie was very useful to me."

"And now she's dead." With a shrug, she drinks some

more whiskey and points at her forehead. "And look," she slurs. "I fixed myself. I can be the doctor now."

I huff, slowly making my way to her.

"That's very bad." I step over Marcie's dead body. "And another body to add on our list for tonight."

I take a second to think to myself, before admitting, "We have issues."

"We do." But that little smile at the corner of her mouth shows me she doesn't give a shit about my half-assed telling off.

"We went out of the house together *once* and killed for each other."

She imitates my low, stern voice and scowls dramatically. "We did."

"It's problematic."

"Is it?" She shrugs carelessly.

There's something more problematic than tonight's murder. The fact that despite trying to scold her, I can't stay mad at her. Not with the pretty face looking up at me. I brush away some strands of wild hair on her forehead. Some of it is stuck under the band-aid.

"It's safe to say you're no doctor."

I pull it off, making her wince, and drop a soft kiss on her wound. "You're drunk. You haven't eaten anything, and you hit your head. I'm not happy, Kayla."

She looks up at me, her drunk ass pouting like a four-year-old, and her eyes innocently wide. "I'm doing my best. It's not my fault I don't belong in this town. It's not my fault I'm a fucking mess."

I pinch her chin and pull her closer as I lower my head. Can someone become addicted to kissing? It's the same two lips I've been kissing for weeks, and I still seem to want more.

"You're perfect," I murmur as I pull away.

We observe each other for a minute, keeping silent in the light of tonight's event. Things feel different, and I'm not sure I can pinpoint how.

Maybe it's her letting her guard down. Maybe it's because I killed someone for her and her for me. I guess that means something, right?

I want to ask her to name it, and yet I hesitate. Something stops me.

Before dinner, she refused to acknowledge what I was trying to express, and it created a dangerous fear inside me.

What if Kayla doesn't feel the same way? What if I can't make her? What if the way she's acting, the sweet words, the jealous behavior... What if that's just her trying to get on my good side so she can leave? She could be playing me.

What an utterly terrifying possibility.

I'm scared she truly doesn't reciprocate how I feel toward her, and that grips my gut like a parasite. It makes me sick to my stomach. It makes my chest so tight I can hardly breathe.

I take a deep breath, deciding to give up. If I don't ask her to name it... If I don't know how she feels... I can live in my own fairy tale. I can pretend Kayla is by my side because she wants to be, not because she's forced to be.

"So," I say blankly. "You like chocolate cake."

Her eyes light up, and she nods eagerly, looking much too innocent. "I love chocolate cake."

I grab her waist, hauling her out of her seat, and she wraps her legs around me, her arms circling my neck.

"We've just been in a car accident." She nuzzles her nose against my cheek. "Why do you still smell so good?"

I chuckle, cut off by the pain in my thigh when I start walking, holding both our weights.

"Do you know how many times I thought of killing you?" She keeps blabbering as I make my way to the kitchen.

"Do I *want* to know?"

"So many. Fuck, so, *so* many." I drop her on the kitchen island, standing between her legs as I grab a spoon out of the drawer and drag the cake from across the island.

"So why did I not just let him shoot you?" she wonders out loud.

"You're drunk, Kayla." I think I'm a little drunk too, and I don't really want her to stop talking. I just know she'll regret it tomorrow morning.

"Chocolate cake tastes so good when you're drunk."

"Does it?"

She nods excitedly, stars in her beautiful green eyes when I open the box. As she licks her lips, I cut a spoonful straight out of the round cake.

"Say 'ah.'"

For someone who can barely ever feel happiness, I want to understand what the fuck is going through my body when she opens her mouth and closes her tempting lips greedily around the spoon.

She talks as she chews, sending crumbs of chocolate on me. "Take your shirt off."

"What? Why?"

"I think this cake will taste better if I can eat it while staring at your abs."

For the second time tonight, I wipe my mouth with my hand to hide my dumb smile. I put the spoon down, then slowly take off my suit jacket, and unbutton my shirt. I fold it in two and put it on the kitchen counter.

"Happy?"

She gives me the spoon back and opens her mouth for more. My cock isn't going to survive this. I cut another piece and push the spoon into her mouth.

"So happy," she giggles.

She points at one of my tattoos. I have so many, they're hard to distinguish, but the bleeding rose covering the scar near my heart is unmissable.

With a gulp, she licks her lips. "That's a bullet wound."

"Like the one on your arm," I say. I noticed it years ago before going to prison, and she had told me about NSC coming all guns blazing into a Kings meeting.

I push my glasses up my nose. "Rose. She shot me."

Her eyes widen. "Your sister shot you?"

I feed her a bigger bite. "It was a different time. We were young. Hell, she was too young to even know how to shoot and yet she had a perfect aim. I was the horrible brother keeping the twins from escaping Bianco's house. So she took a gun and shot me. Aimed to kill. To this day, I'm not sure if she missed or didn't really want to kill me."

Kay blinks up at me.

"I *was* dead for one minute and twenty-five seconds. In the end, they managed to leave. I never told them I was forcing them to stay in that nightmare of a house because Bianco had showed me what he'd do to them if they tried to leave. I...." I run my tongue against my teeth. "I really didn't want them to suffer the way I did. But they suffered in other ways. There was no winning, really."

"There's no winning with an abuser," she murmurs. "Only once you escape, or once they're gone. Even then. It always stays with you."

We stare at each other in silence before I ask, "More cake?"

She nods, smiling. "More cake."

I want to bask in the feeling I get when she opens her mouth again, and again, and again, until she shakes her head, her eyelids becoming heavy. My fingers tingle when I press my thumb against the corner of her lips to wipe crumbs away.

"Do you remember the last time you were here? In this exact position?"

She looks away, sober for a split second, before nodding with a heavy head.

"You took whatever you wanted out of me. You still do."

"Did you hate it?"

Her eyes are back on me. I drop the spoon to the side, putting my hands on her thighs instead. We're both dirty from the accident, the skirt of her silk dress completely ripped.

"No."

"Did you love it?"

She shakes her head. "No." Bringing a hand to my chest, she presses her fingers against the tattoos there. "I didn't love it because I was terrified of how good you made me feel that night."

I feel a smirk spreading on my lips. Kay hates those smirks, calls them devilish.

"I made you feel good when I fucked your beautiful cunt while you were bent over this very counter?"

Her eyes flutter shut, her hand fisting on my chest. "Yeah."

"And I made you feel good when I took your tight ass in my bed?"

She shudders. "Yes." Her eyes open again, but she stays focused on the ink on my body. "Why did you do it? Why did you make me come back one night every week?"

I pause, hesitating to tell her the truth. In the end, I don't want to lie to her. I don't need to. She's not going anywhere.

"It was to my advantage to have someone from the Kings at my mercy, Kayla. Back then, I didn't have the power to unite the North Shore, but I needed peace anyway. I could keep control of NSC because they worked for me. I needed to keep you scared to have a hold on the Kings. It was just…"

"Business," she adds when I trail off.

"I know you can understand that. You would do anything for your business."

She licks her lips, looking uncertain.

"I was scared," she admits. "Every time I got a text from you saying to come over, I was fucking terrified." She swallows roughly. "But you didn't care. You knew you could keep me afraid and make it nice in the process, make me doubt everything I felt, so you did it."

"Yes. I did."

She throws her head back, both her hands slapping my chest once and staying there, and I suddenly feel the need to explain myself. She's the only person who makes me feel that way, like I'll feel better if she understands me.

"Control by chaos and manipulation is how I thrive. I don't need to worry about not understanding what people feel when they're unsure themselves. Make it hurt, but make it good. Don't give them a choice, but give them a purpose. That's the only way I can function."

"How do you *live* like this?" Her voice is desperate, and I'm struggling to get it. She was fine, so why did she go into this conversation?

"It's how I'm wired." What is it she doesn't understand? "I don't feel remorse, Kay. I only live with the consequences of my actions. When those consequences fit my goals, then that's good enough for me."

"What about me?"

My eyebrows raise in surprise. I hate when that happens with her, when I can't grasp the sentiment behind the tone of her voice or the expression on her face. I'm desperate to comprehend it. I just know I'm incapable. "I don't get it."

"Of course you don't," she snorts. "What am I, Nate? A consequence of your actions? Collateral damage? Revenge? Your way of functioning works for *one*. Do you truly not care how any of it impacts me?"

"You'll adapt."

"You keep saying that, but I'm *not adapting*."

"You were until you brought up the past."

She slaps my chest harder, as if to wake me up. "Tell me you feel something, *anything* that could bring us close, that could make us understand each other."

"I feel plenty of things," I retort, frustration growing inside me. "I just can't relate to what *you* feel."

It's not entirely true. I mainly feel frustration or satisfaction, but I hate when someone points it out. My feelings are very black and white, which makes the situation with her even more complicated. It's confusing.

"But—"

"Name it."

"Right now?" she hisses. "I'm pretty fucking angry—"

"Not now. I can read your anger easily. But with me, in general. Name it. How do you feel? Because I told you many times. I explained. I said—" I show my hands, and she pushes me back.

"Yes, your fucking hands were cold and now they're not."

"It's a way to explain," I say to her back as she walks away and out of the kitchen. I follow her, unable to comprehend how quickly our conversation turned. "You do it if you're so fucking good at it. Name it."

She spins around at the bottom of the stairs. "*Safe.*"

I stop in my tracks, an inch short of bumping into her. "Safe?"

"Yes. As fucking insane as it sounds, when I'm around the man who kidnapped me and forced me to marry him, who leaves bruises on my skin, who forces me to take pleasure in a way I fucking hate, who *hurts* me...I feel safe."

A small laugh bubbles out of me, doubling her anger.

"You're a bastard," she fumes, turning around to go up the stairs.

"Stockholm syndrome, little sunflower!" I shout as I go after her. "I told you it would happen."

She closes my bedroom door in my face, but I'm quick to follow her in.

"Kayla," I call after her as she storms into the bathroom. The door slams, and the lock clicks. I rasp my knuckles against it, pinching back a smile. "Kayla, baby, I'm *joking.*"

"Fuck you, Nate!"

"Please, open the door. I was just surprised. I...I don't even know what safe feels like. Maybe that's how it works?"

"I'm going to *kill you!*" she shouts, and I can hear her emotions seeping through. How much this has upset her.

"But you just saved me. That would be such a waste."

"I should have let him shoot you. I would have been free."

"Please," I groan, pressing my forehead against the wood.

"Go fuck yourself."

I try the door again, knowing perfectly well it won't open. "Don't make me break this door. Let's talk."

"I'm done talking to you."

But I'm not even close to done. My chest tightens as I let out another groan.

"Kayla I... Look, 'safe' took me by surprise. But who am I to judge how you feel next to me when I'm the first one to admit I feel all kinds of fucked up next to you."

There's a silence that stretches for long enough, I wonder if she somehow managed to escape.

"You're the first person in my life I want to keep safe besides my siblings." My heart threatens to escape through my throat as the words tumble out. "Maybe... the reasons I'm keeping you here are shifting. Maybe I forgot over the last few weeks why I took you in the first place. I didn't plan to have an annoying, bratty hell of a woman by my side. The plan was to make you feel the way I did locked behind bars. Fuck, Kayla, I don't want you to feel even remotely close to how I did there. I want you to feel *safe*. So maybe if that was the first answer that came to your mind, then for the first time in my life, I'm doing something right?"

I huff, pressing my palm against the door. I hate to say these things out loud, but it's easier with something separating us.

"I know I did a lot of bad things. I know that while I justify them to myself, they can't always be justified. I am not a good man, and you've experienced that firsthand."

I swallow thickly. "I'll never be a good man, but I don't need to be if *you* feel safe. I've had to learn to live with my demons, Kay. I keep them close, embrace them, or I'd never keep on living. What if that's what I am to you? Your

384

demon? What if you just...embraced it and kept me close? You could try."

I take in a shuddered breath, terrified by the lack of response. "Please?"

When she doesn't say anything for a whole other minute, my fist slams on the door. This woman is driving me past the point of crazy. I'm hot and cold at the same time, feeling like I'm losing my mind because she holds all the cards. I hate that. I hate to love it.

"See, *this* is why you're a captive here, Kayla," I hiss. "Because you don't want to fucking understand—"

The door is wrenched open. "You were doing so well." She shakes her head, wiping the blood that's started to spill from the wound again. "Why did you have to ruin it?"

"You weren't saying anything." Why am I panting like I ran a marathon? Is this what she's turning me into? Someone whose heart kicks into palpitations when he waits for her to give him the time of day? Is she turning me into some sort of lovesick puppy?

I don't agree with that.

Wait...I don't have a fucking choice, do I?

"I was processing the fact that this is the most fucked-up thing that's ever happened to me. Do you mind?"

I lick my lips, failing to stop the smile spreading on my face. "Take your time."

"Thank you. I'm going to shower now."

"I'll come with—"

"No. I'm going to shower alone. I'm going to scrub off that accident and get the feeling of Wynne off me. You can go shower somewhere else."

"I can wash you."

"Nathan," she sing-songs. She blinks up at me with that rare sweet-face weapon she hides so well and twists a strand of hair around her finger. "I thought you wanted me to feel safe. Showering alone makes me feel safe."

"Oh, you..." I run my tongue across my teeth, shaking my head. "You're fucking good, you know that? You manipulative little vixen." I pull the same strand of hair she's playing with.

"There are countless bathrooms in this place. Go shower somewhere else," she snaps, then slams the door back in my face again. But this time, I can breathe.

"You better use your grapefruit body wash!"

I'm clean, lying naked on my bed, and overthinking when she finally comes out of the bathroom. When she closed the door in my face, I ran to the nearest guest room, washed in less than five minutes, and ran back here to make sure she wouldn't be waiting for me.

And when I say I ran, I mean, I sped through the hallway like a good dog fetching his ball.

Turns out, she spent almost an hour in there. I know. I've been watching the clock.

She's naked when she walks out, and I sit up in bed, immediately at attention like the infatuated man I am.

"Are you alrigh—"

She presses a finger to her mouth as she makes her way to me. The lights are off, the room only lit up by the gray light of the full moon. Her porcelain skin is radiant as she sashays to me.

Like an angel coming down from heaven to greet the devil on earth's neutral grounds.

She straddles me, her hot core pressing against my already hard cock. Fucking dick with a mind of its own. It poisoned my brain with its obsession for Kayla's body. How am I meant to function when I'm hard ninety-eight percent of the time she's around? And she's my captive. She's always around. I played myself.

She leans down, her lips meeting my neck. She smells of grapefruit and I think I'm becoming high as I breathe her in.

She doesn't kiss me, just grazes my skin, bringing painful goosebumps as she moves up and down my neck.

I groan when she finally licks the vein popping along my skin. She bites, her teeth threatening to puncture my artery. Sucking and licking me better with her tongue, she drags a moan out of me.

It's not just that. I can feel her pussy getting wetter against me. My hands come to her ass, the tips of fingers skimming over the mark I left there.

"Mm, you're mine," I groan as she bites me again. "I can feel it on your skin."

She bites harder, probably drawing blood. Then she licks again. "Stop talking."

I nod, panting as she starts moving her wetness against me.

"I know what you want the most, Nate," she rasps. Lust coats her voice in the most beautiful way I've ever heard.

Talking against the heartbeat in my neck, her breath on my skin is the hottest sensation I've ever felt. That's until she squeezes her legs against me, her knees digging into my hips, and presses her weight into my dick.

"F-fuck," I choke. "Kay..."

Her hand slides up my chest and curls around my throat.

"You want to be mine." Has her voice always been this enchanting? It must have been if I ended up in this situation. "You want to have all of me and give me all of you. You want your entire being to belong to me."

She thrusts, pressing hard against my dick, coating me in her wetness.

"Fuck, yes," I groan.

"Who owns you, Nate?"

My eyes close, my teeth gritting. "You do."

"What's my name?" She susurrates along my skin like a witch cursing me to love her until the end of my days.

"Mrs. White."

She rolls her hips. "*Shit*," I hiss.

"What's my fucking name? Tell me who owns you."

"K-Kayla," I moan. "Kayla King owns me."

"That's right."

Lifting her hips, she releases my throat so she can grab my dick and put me at her entrance. "Be a good boy and stay still."

She pushes me against her, barely enough for my dick to stay in place as she releases me.

"Do you want to be inside me?"

"Yes," I bite out.

Fuck, I would do anything to be inside her right now. I will take the spot that is reserved for me in hell anytime she wants, just let me be inside her first. Then I can die.

"But you're going to wait, aren't you? You're going to wait until I give you the permission to fuck me."

She lowers herself the tiniest bit, and electricity shoots up my spine, leading right to where she's speaking against my neck. My dick twitches.

"I could keep you like this all night, Nate," she chuckles.

"No." I swallow thickly. "Fuck. Please, baby. Let me be inside you."

"Mm, you're even hotter when you beg."

"Please. Kayla, baby..." I'm mindless for her, rambling. I don't even recognize my voice.

"Fuck me. Fuck me like a good husband fucks his wife."

That's all I need. My hands fly to her waist, and I hold her as I thrust all the way inside her. I could scream from how good it feels, but I'm cut off by her beautiful moan she uses as a melody to captivate me.

She keeps her body tightly against mine as I thrust up, meeting her pussy and hitting as deep inside as she can take.

"*Fuck!*" she screams, as a shudder runs through her. "Nate..."

Her pants keep me eager. I aim to please, to keep her moaning in my ear.

And fuck if I do.

I keep thrusting, thoroughly, taking care of both our pleasure.

"Give me all of you," I ask—scratch that. I sound like I'm begging. "Please, Kay. Let me have you."

"You have me," she moans against my ear and presses a kiss to my neck.

"No." My jaw clenches, my teeth gritting as I shake my head. "Give me *all of you*. I want the happiness and the anger. I want the line that forms between your eyebrows when you're thinking deeply about ways to kill me. I want the way your jaw locks when you want to scream at me. The way your lower lip trembles when you're desperate for me." I breathe her in, relishing our sweaty bodies meeting and becoming one. "I want you from morning to evening. I want you all night long and until you wake again."

I press her flush against me, moving slowly and sensually. "You c-can have that."

"And your smiles?" I rasp. "Can I have your smiles? And that pout you make when something upsets you?" A whimper escapes her lips when I hit the perfect spot. "Can I get those puppy eyes pointed at me when you want something badly?"

She grinds her hips into me. "Yes..."

"And your orgasms?" I growl in her ear. "Can I have those?"

Her pussy tightens around my length, and I feel the exact moment the orgasm ripples through her entire body. "Yes!" she screams so loudly against my ear it starts ringing.

"Thank you," I groan.

I wrap my arms around her back and shoot up into a sitting position, forcing her up too before I roll us to switch positions.

"I'll take it all," I whisper before thrusting inside her again. "Over and over again, little sunflower. Give it all to me."

I pull out until my tip is just past her entrance and roll my hips so my dick hits her G-spot. At the same time, I press my palm against her clit, covering the small bud.

"Nate." The way she elongates the *a* in my name when she moans makes me shiver all over. I hit her harder, with more purpose.

The purpose of making her fall apart on my dick.

And she does it so beautifully, I can't help but try again and again...*and again.*

I rub her hard nipples with the tips of my thumbs, massaging her breasts with my palms. She arches into my hands, throwing her head to the side as she fists the sheets.

"I can't... Fuck..."

"You said you'd give it all to me. Do this for me. Come one more time."

She gasps a deep breath, the small of her back lifting from the bed as she writhes under me.

"Be mine," I rasp. "All mine."

"I'm yours! Fuck...fuck...*fuck!*" Her eyes squeeze shut with another release, nails digging into my shoulders as she tenses. A soundless scream escapes her wide-open mouth, and I'm sure it'll be the end of me.

But then, she thrusts her hips up, and it gets me going again.

"Big mistake," I growl. "Now I'm going to fuck you until your soul leaves your body, Kay. I'm going to trap that pretty soul and keep it to myself."

I pull out, dragging a whimper out of her. Grabbing her hips, I flip her around and pull until she's on her hands and knees.

"Fuck me, you're a goddess."

I slap her ass, and revel in the way her porcelain skin turns pink in the shape of my hand.

"Do you want your husband to fuck you, baby? Do you want to take my dick until you pass out?"

She presses her ass back into me. "You promised to make me yours. Now fucking *do it.*"

A low noise resonates in my chest. I spread her ass cheeks and push in. "I'm going to take your ass after this beautiful pussy. I'll watch my cum drip from your tight hole."

She moans as I thrust harder, encouraging me to go along with my promises.

I pull out, replacing my dick with my finger as I gather her wetness. "Are you going to come with my dick in your ass, little sunflower?"

"Oh, god," she moans, her head dropping between her hands.

"Sunflowers worship no god, only the sun. One of us brings you life, the other empty promises."

I press my wet thumb against her tight hole, pushing my throbbing cock back inside her pussy at the same time.

"Who's your sun, baby?"

The moans escaping her bring me to the brink of sanity.

"Y-you...are."

"That's right." I push inside her ass, slowly, bringing more wetness with my other hand as she contracts around me. "I'm going to fuck you with my fingers, and then I'm going to push my dick inside your ass and make you scream."

She trembles under me when I pull out my thumb and push in my middle finger instead. I go in and out, taking my time to prep her before I add another one.

Panting under me, she swears with all she has before she starts pushing back.

"Naughty girl is in a hurry to get her ass filled."

"*More*," she orders sternly, as she throws her head back, hair flipping. "I need more."

I caress her ass with my free hand, moving slowly inside her with my fingers and my dick.

"Answer me honestly, baby. Do you want me to make it hurt?"

She whimpers, her eyes squeezing shut.

And she nods.

"Say it."

"Please, make it hurt."

Electricity courses through my body, making me bite my lower lip so I don't cry out in pleasure. "Again." I can barely let out the growl.

"Fuck me. Fuck my ass and make it hurt."

"Your wish is my command."

I pull out of her pussy and line myself with her tight entrance. I press the tip there, pushing in slowly. I'll give her her wish, but I don't want to hurt her beyond repair.

"Relax. Push out as I push in."

I watch her take a deep breath, and she finally relaxes her muscles as I press inside her. The tightness chokes my dick, making me groan.

"Oh, Kay..."

Her head falls forward on a gasp the deeper I go, and I grab her by her hair, wrapping the length around my fist. I pull back, making sure I can hear her beautiful cries. "Scream for me, baby."

I drag everything out of her. Her pleasure, her sanity. I pound inside her, pulling her hair and slapping her ass. I hurt her because I know she needs it. I hurt her because I want to feel everything with her.

This time, to make her come, I force her legs farther apart with my knees, spread her wide open, reach around with my hand, and slap her clit harshly.

"I thought you promised screams, beautiful wife? Take my dick and come until you can't *fucking breathe.*"

I slap her again. I'm brutal, and she swallows it all like liquid gold from the gods.

"Nate..." Her voice raises higher every time she repeats my name. "Nate...Nate..." She keeps screaming it as she reaches nirvana, but the consonants are barely formed.

I can't take it anymore. I let the light blind me, accelerating as I explode inside her.

Her arms give up, and I fall onto her body as she crashes against the mattress, my dick still in her ass.

"Kayla," I rasp, a hand coming to caress her hair away from her face. "What are you doing to me?"

30

KAYLA

I Wanna Be Yours - Arctic Monkeys

One of his hands comes to caress my nipple as he hugs me from behind. We're back in bed after showering, and no matter how spent I am from the way he fucked me, I find myself letting out a needy sigh.

He does it again, and I squirm in his hold.

"Could it be that you are insatiable?" he chuckles behind me, his head resting at the top of mine.

"Sex with you is like chocolate cake. I can never get enough of it."

"I'll make sure to remember that." He holds me tighter, and his warmth brings a new sense of safety.

Since his little speech while I was in the bathroom, I feel like I've tamed the most dangerous beast there is out there. It's strange to have a feared man at your feet, to turn a raging lion into a cub.

I notice the way he's acutely attuned to every single one of my movements, attentive to the slightest changes in my voice.

Nathan White is addicted to me. Obsessed.

And that's an advantage I never thought I'd have.

"You should sleep," he says calmly. "I'll be waking you up at four-fifteen."

"Sorry, what?" I roll over in his hold, but he doesn't look like he's joking. His face is blank, his eyes impassive.

"That's fifteen minutes before your night terrors. I read we can avoid them if I wake you up fifteen minutes before."

I feel my eyes widen, and I sit up, forcing him to let me go. "I-I'm confused. How do you know what time my night terrors are? How do you even know I actually have night terrors? I don't know if I do."

"Because you don't remember them."

He sits up, yawning as he twists to open the drawer of his bedside table. Then he turns on the small lamp. "I know because they wake me up." Opening the small notebook he just pulled out of his drawer, he shows me what he's written in there. "Look."

There are lines and lines of days of the weeks and times.

"Monday, four twenty-seven," he reads. "Tuesday, four thirty-one. Wednesday, four thirty, Thursday—"

"Whoa, wait, wait, wait." I snatch the notebook out of his hands. "You...you've been keeping track of when those things happen?"

"How am I meant to help if I don't keep track? That's what the article said," he explains as impassively as ever.

My heart swells, and I press a hand against my stomach when something blossoms in there. It unfurls so strongly it tingles all the way to my toes.

"Nate..."

The notebook disappears from my hand as he grabs it

back. "Anyway. I think four-fifteen is a good choice. What do you think?"

He looks up at me, gaze focused. As he observes me, he doesn't notice my awed expression, or if he does, he doesn't understand it.

"So you should really sleep now. It's late."

I can barely talk through the ball in my throat. "I... erm..." I shake my head, pressing my hand harder against my stomach. "Can I name it?"

His eyebrows pull up, and he tilts his head to the side. "Always, little sunflower."

"I'm grateful," I rasp. "That you did this for me. It—it makes me feel taken care of."

He nods slowly. "I didn't realize that. It's just paper and ink, you know? But that's good, I guess."

"Yes," I chuckle. He is so oblivious to how caring what he did is. "It's good."

I startle when he wakes me up, my body sweaty and my hands aching from being curled into tight fists.

"What the hell?" I croak. "My fingers hurt."

"Yeah, because that's how they always start. You get cold, you sweat, and you tighten all over." He huffs. "And then the screaming and kicking and slapping starts. I'm glad we're avoiding that tonight."

In the dark, I can barely see him, but I notice his messy blond hair and the way he runs his hand through it. He's not wearing his glasses, and it gives him a less serious look than usual. He seems more relaxed like this, more approachable.

"Sorry for the kicking and slapping," I murmur.

"Don't worry, we'll put a stop to these. I'll have you see a therapist or something. The article said—"

"Holy hell, that article is your bible."

He laughs softly, lying down by my side again. "Maybe we should just start with a doctor."

"Maybe." It's weird talking about the future like a real married couple. And yet I can't stop. "And if I see a therapist, maybe you could see one for...you know."

"What?"

God, he's completely clueless.

"What your foster dad did."

He snorts and shakes his head. "I don't give a shit about that."

"I do."

He turns onto his side, facing me. Putting a hand on my cheek, he caresses just under my eye with his thumb. "You do?"

"Yes. I think it would do you good to try to heal from it."

"You know it won't change the way I am."

"And that's okay. I can live with who you are, with the essence of your psychopathic soul because the pieces of that are whole. But how can we deny the parts that he crushed? I can't live knowing I didn't try to help you heal from something so traumatic."

"You have broken pieces too."

I nod, not wanting to ignore that. "We'll heal each other."

He blinks blankly at me. "That's a thing? A thing people do?"

I lick my lips, thinking hard about how to explain that two people in love can help each other, even though I can't even name what we both feel. "I think...it's a thing they try to do, and that's what counts. Trying."

"Okay. I want to try to help you with your night terrors and your dyslexia."

"*Possible* dyslexia," I correct.

"Sure," he chuckles.

"I..." I bring my hand to his cheek too, mirroring him. "I want to try to help you move on from the lifelong revenge you want against Bianco. I want to try to help you do things for yourself, not because you want to hurt him for hurting you."

His sudden gulp surprises me. "Fuck," he scoffs. "You really got that right."

"I know. I see you."

Kissing me, he whispers against my lips. "Let's sleep. I've got important meetings tomorrow."

He falls back asleep with a smile on his face. It's incredibly satisfying knowing it's a genuine feeling inside him. I know because, with Nate, it has to come from within him. He can't empathize with others, so whatever he feels has to be dug out of his own emotions.

Guilt pinches inside of me.

I have done everything in my power to end this man, and I'm starting to think maybe...just maybe, he isn't as bad as I thought he was. At least not toward me.

When I'm sure he's fast asleep, I discreetly slide out of bed and go to the bathroom. I keep the phone he gave me in there. He texts and calls me on it sometimes, but I always think that if he doesn't see it physically, then he won't take it back.

I take the cell and walk through the room again to get out. I need to make a call. Fuck, I need to call off everything I've put into motion. I can't do it anymore. We're building trust, and the smartest way to get back to my family is to talk to Nate, to find a compromise. I won't live without them, but maybe it doesn't have to be the end of him.

There are no guards in our hallway. They're everywhere in the house, night and day, but not near our bedroom. Nate likes to make me scream when we fuck, and he doesn't want anyone to hear me. I agree.

In just a silk gown, I walk to the room as far away from ours, and that still won't get me too close to the guards. I slip inside and close the door softly behind me.

But nothing prepared me for the fear that rages through me as I turn around. A terrified gasp escapes my lips, my heart bouncing painfully as I see a tall shadow holding a knife right in front of me.

Wolf!

After the night we had, that's the first thing my brain goes to.

I'm about to scream, taking in a huge gulp of air when I recognize the pitch-black hair, the lean body.

Mainly? The crown tattooed on his neck. The exact same one as me.

"Oh my fucking god, Caden," I snarl. "What the fuck are you doing here?"

My younger brother switches on the light, his cool gaze reminding me of Nathan's. His is the same color as my green eyes, but they share something common in theirs: emptiness.

"I'm coming to take you home, what else?" he asks blankly. The similarities with Nate are starting to pile up, and I'm not sure I like it.

I blink up at him, a million things running through my mind, but only one comes out.

"Elliot is a little fucking snitch," I huff.

"Elliot did the right thing. I'm rescuing you from a kidnapping, Kay," he explains slowly.

"Stop talking to me like I'm a fucking idiot. I'll punch you."

He snorts, tilting his head to the side. He observes me from head to toe. "Is that from him?"

I know he's talking about the wound on my head. Was it because of Nate? Yes. He's the megalomaniac who is going to war with the Wolves. But was it *from* him? I shake my head. "Car accident."

Next, his eyes dart down to my ring finger. "Take off the rings."

My hand automatically closes into a fist. "Cade..." I hesitate, unsure how to go about this. "Listen—"

"I don't want to fucking hear it. Take off the rings. I can't look at my sister knowing those two rings were forced on her hand."

"It's more complicated than that."

"Kay." He smiles at me. It's dangerously cold and would send anyone else running for the hills, but that grown man used to braid my hair as kids as a way to calm his dark urges. He doesn't scare me. Not even the cold monster inside him can make me shake. "I thought I was on a rescue mission here, want to explain what kind of Stockholm syndrome bullshit I'm facing?"

"If I hear that term one more time, I'm going to shoot someone. It would be really fucking unfortunate for that someone to be you. I don't need rescuing, Cade. I know what I'm doing."

"Where's his room?"

Just to piss him off, I say, "You mean, *our* room."

He chuckles and takes a small step back. "I'll make him suffer just because you fell for him."

It's my turn to laugh. "Fell for him? What am I? A fifteen-year-old getting attention for the first time in her life?"

"Fucking seems like it."

He takes a sidestep, going for the door, but I plaster myself against it. "Don't."

"Kay," he grits out.

"I *know* what I'm doing." I give him a pointed glare. "You're forgetting who I am."

"*You're* forgetting who you are. You're Kayla motherfucking *King*. Or have you been brainwashed into thinking you're just Nathan White's wife now?"

"You're not my rescuer. You're my little brother. You're the boy I saved from Dad as kids. You're the psycho *I* had to raise when I was just a little girl. Step the fuck back."

He narrows his gaze on me and does as I say. "Fine. What's your plan?"

"Not sending my brother to slice his throat in the middle of the night, that's for sure. When I kill Nate, he won't have a chance to stop me."

He cocks an eyebrow at me. "How?"

"I am not telling you. This plan is in my head and with whoever is helping me execute it. That's not you."

I don't add that I was coming into this room to cancel said plan, that seeing him is messing with my head yet again.

Nate opened up to me like no one ever has before. But seeing Caden makes me doubt my change of heart.

"Kay." He looks away, then back at me. "I know what it's like to manipulate someone into falling in love with them. That's exactly what I did to Billie. And do you know what's around her finger now? *My* ring." He puts a hand on my shoulder. "Whatever plan you have. Do it. Whatever he does, whatever you feel, just do it." A smirk spreads on his lips. "Look at Billie now, she's stuck with me forever, and the poor girl thinks it's out of her own free will."

I bite my lower lip, barely stopping myself from hurling insults at him. "Congratulations, you're yet another narcissist who locked the girl he wanted by manipulating her. What can I get you? A medal, maybe?"

"I'll tell you what you can do. Don't become that girl."

I shrug him off. "I'm smarter than Billie Scott, thank you very much."

"Sure," he snorts. "You're smarter than everyone else, except you're the one locked in a house with no way out, your name on a marriage license you never wanted in the first place."

"Tell you what," I snarl. "If I'm not out of this shit by the girls' birthday, you can get me out."

"Another four months, then? Are you joking?"

"I'll be out way before then. Do you think I could spend that long without seeing them? I know what I'm doing."

He observes me, deep in his thoughts, and I feel the trust coming back. He knows I would never leave behind the two reasons that keep me alive. They're my everything.

"Fine."

"How the fuck did you get in?" I ask seriously, looking at the shut window.

He snorts. "I'll have to keep my secret because, when I come back in four months, I don't want your Stockholm syndrome ass to have an advantage over me and stop me from coming in."

I roll my eyes. "You're ridiculous."

"Goodnight, big sis. I'll see you soon."

He heads toward the window, but I call to him one last time. "Cade."

A hand on the glass, he twists around to face me.

"Elliot." I scratch my throat. "Did he tell you about his decision regarding the North Shore?"

He shakes his head. "Fucking hell, what have you become? Waiting for Elliot to make a decision for the Kings."

"Just answer the fucking question," I grit out.

He shrugs. "I don't know. I'm here for you, Kay. I don't give a shit about the fate of the North Shore. It hasn't been my problem for years."

He hushes me away with his hand. "Now go back to your husband."

"Shut up," I bite back. Siblings are truly infuriating.

I look down at the phone. I'll think about the plan again tomorrow.

I have Nate's fate in the palm of my hand. I just need to decide what I want to do with it.

PART III

RETALIATION

No friend ever served me, and no enemy ever wronged me, whom I have not repaid in full.
    Sulla

31

NATHAN

how will i rest in peace if i'm buried by a highway -
KennyHoopla

I silence Sam's call as soon as it comes in. Kay didn't have any night terrors after I woke her up last night, but she's still clinging to me like she can't sleep any other way. And I somehow can't get myself to push her sleeping form away from my body.

I send my best friend a text instead of calling him back.

> Nate: I'm in my room. Come have our meeting here.

He doesn't reply, but a minute later, he's pushing the door open. He looks at the scene, mouth slightly agape.

"What the—"

I put my finger in front of my mouth, shushing him. Then I send him another text.

> Nate: Can't you see Kayla is sleeping? Text me.

He glares at me with the most hateful stare I've ever seen from him.

> Sam: This is the most ridiculous thing I've ever witnessed in my life. Just get out of bed and come talk downstairs. You have a fucking office you can use for business.

It's my turn to pin him with a glare. I look down at my phone and type frustratingly.

> Nate: I don't want to wake her up. Update me.

He huffs loudly, his jaw tightening, and his thumbs type aggressively on his screen.

> Sam: It's done. The Kings and NSC have agreed to work together. We can have them distribute the next shipment.

A smile spreads widely on my face.

> Nate: I'll contact the Canadians today. They'll have the shipment here tomorrow. And Garcia-Diaz messaged earlier to say the contract was still valid. M. Beauty will be delivering to my hotel as early as next week.

> Sam: Can you get out of fucking bed now?

I send back a gun emoji with a question mark, and he rolls his eyes so hard they disappear to the back of his head.

> Sam: You've got a trip to Baltimore coming up, remember?

> Nate: My question is, who can we trust here for that?

> Sam: Well, you have NSC's contact who sells in bulk all over the tri-state area. Racer can map out some routes. Jade is your best driver. You just need to get Elliot's and Ethan's approval to get her working. They're protective.

I'm about to answer, when he messages again.

> Sam: If the cops ever get hold of either of our phones, we're fucked. Will you stop being a fourteen-year-old driven by his dick and get downstairs so we can talk?

I huff. He's not wrong. My heart is heavy when I slide a hand in Kay's hair and slowly wake her up.

"It's late, little sunflower. I need to get to work."

She groans a complaint, tightening her arms around me, and my eyes go to Sam. "How am I meant to get out of bed?" I ask him, dead serious. "Have you no heart?"

Kay looks up with pinched eyebrows. The second she notices Sam, she jumps away from me, bringing the covers all the way to her neck despite wearing a nightie.

"What the fuck?" she spits. "What are you two doing?"

"We were having a meeting," I answer obviously. "But I really need to get out of bed now."

"Just get out of bed and have your meeting somewhere else!" she barks, ever the gentle wife.

"I told you," Sam backs her up like the fake friend he is.

"*Leave*," she orders him sternly.

"There's a body in your office," he says as he leaves.

Ah yes, I guess we need to take care of that too.

I capture Kay's mouth with a kiss before she can throw any insults, and when I pull away, I relish the pink tinting her cheeks and neck.

"Name it," I murmur.

"Annoyed," she grumbles.

I smile, giving her another kiss. "Liar."

It's a long day, and it gets longer every minute that passes without seeing Kay. We waste time cleaning Kay's mess in my office. Our call with the Canadians lasts forever, and until we find something to blackmail them with, we'll be paying a shit ton of money to stop them from working with the Lucianos. They're used to providing weed to all the Cosa Nostra families on the East Coast. No more.

The rest of the day is spent going to places all over the North Shore, meeting my new dealers, assigning areas to everyone. I stopped three fights and one stabbing attempt between NSC and the Kings. Sam and Emma are with me all day, and I desperately wish Kay was here too, but I can't take that risk. Not yet. If she comes back to the North Shore, she'll want to stay, to be away from me. I can't have that.

I can't risk losing her.

The whole week is intense. Separating from what I've always known to build my empire is just as much work as I expected. Infinite.

There's always a fire to put out, a mole to kill for spying, a finger to cut for asking too many questions. People make mistakes, I can understand that. Once, though, not twice.

But fuck, there's always someone unhappy to take care of, and I didn't sign up to be anyone's dad. The North

Shore gangs have lived too long by their own law, and they're struggling to adapt to mine.

Today, Emma is the one breaking my balls. In the afternoon, she shows up at my house, barging into my office with a picture that she slams on my desk. The girl has been feeling way too comfortable since she's the only person I let Kay see. I can't have anyone from the Kings speaking with Kay, but Emma is safe enough.

I look up from a contract Garcia-Diaz just drafted for me, hoping my unimpressed glare takes her down a notch. It doesn't.

She stabs the picture with her index finger.

"This bitch broke into my house in the middle of the *fucking day*. She shot my dad!"

I look down at the grainy picture of a redhead in a navy suit. She's tall, her eyes lacking any emotion. The picture is taken on Emma's front porch, from the point of view of her door. Probably one of those doorbells with a camera.

"Is your dad okay?" That wasn't me. I couldn't care less how her dad is. No, that was the voice of my sweet wife, caring for things that shouldn't matter to her.

"He'll live. I don't think she wanted him dead."

The two better not be becoming friends. I'll kill her. *Her* being Emma, of course.

I tilt my head to the side, looking behind Emma. Kay is passing my office doorway, advancing toward us with a focused look on her face.

I know what's happening. She's bored to death, and she wants to work. Her business is being a criminal. It's a high like no other to work on the wrong side of the law, and Kay is in need of her fix.

"Who's this?" Kay asks, looking down at the picture.

There's something I don't understand in her eyes, and when she catches me staring, she changes it right away.

"Lucky," Emma snarls.

"Lucky?" my wife repeats.

I lean back in my chair. Okay, I guess I can give her that. It has nothing to do with my business, after all. If Lucky was after me, she'd have found me. No, she's after Emma.

"Her real name is Lana Anderson. But the Cosa Nostra calls her Lana, *Lucky Strike,* Anderson. Lucky for short. She's Vito Luciano's enforcer."

I know what surprise looks like on Kay, and there's none on her face right now. Something feels off; I just don't know what.

"Do you know her?" I ask her stupidly.

She snorts, crossing her arms over the dress I had her wear today. She hates it. It looks too Stoneview, but I can't get enough of the way it hugs her body.

"Why would I ask if I knew?" She digs her gaze into mine, and I simply nod. I don't have the capability to understand this further.

"Emma," I huff. "The Lucianos are clearly after you for begging them for a deal, pulling out of it, and coming to me instead. Lucky came to kill you. Good thing you weren't home."

"I know why she came for me," Emma snaps. "You're meant to protect me from this shit."

A chuckle escapes my lips. "Why does Lucky know where you live?"

She takes a short step back, avoiding my gaze, but the answer is on her reddening cheeks.

"Ah. Well, you're the girl stupid enough to invite a lethal woman into your bed. Not my problem, is it?"

"You could at least pretend to fucking care."

"Nate," Kay backs her up. Oh, they're definitely becoming friends. "We can't just let the Lucianos kill her for helping you."

"Helping me kidnap you, baby. Remember that before becoming best friends with her."

Kay pins me with a stare. "Nate."

I flatten my lips, showing my wife I'm not happy with her participation. "To be clear," I tell Emma. "I don't care, and I won't pretend to. But I'll protect you."

"Good. How? Are you gonna kill Lucky? Send Sam?"

"Kill—" I bark out a laugh. "Are you fucking crazy? There are some people in this business you know to stay away from. Just because you didn't, doesn't mean I'm going to risk my very useful enforcer. Lucky is fucking insane, and that's coming from *me*."

When she doesn't get it, I add, "No, Emma. I am not sending anyone to kill Lucky."

"You can stay here," Kay adds. "In this house. There are guards everywhere."

"Uh, no," I correct right away. "You can't."

"Nate, her life is at risk."

"I don't *care*. What is it you two don't understand?"

"I do." And all it takes is her begging pout to break my will.

"Oh, for fuck's sake, Kayla," I grumble. "*Fine*," I tell Emma. "You'll take the farthest fucking room from me in the house."

Emma's shoulders drop in relief. "Thank you." She turns to Kay, and they smile at each other like two kids who convinced their moms to have a sleepover.

"Now get the fuck out of my office."

They both turn around, walking away before I cut them off. "Not you, Kayla. I'm taking you to see Dr. Karls in fifteen minutes. And come give me a kiss for keeping your new bestie alive."

The second Emma is out, she huffs. "I don't want to see Dr. Karls."

"Tough."

Last week, she got her dyslexia diagnosis, and apart from the fact that I was right, the speech therapist I hired to help her said she could work with her even though there's only so much she could do. It would have helped even better if she had been diagnosed as a child, but I guess that wasn't really her main worry growing up on the North Shore.

"Dr. Karls looks at you like she wants to fuck you. She asked a thousand questions about you during my first session. The bitch would die for you to come in with me. She hated that you waited outside."

I smile at her mockingly. "Maybe I should, then. Would that make you behave?"

"I'll stab her in the neck. Would that make *you* behave?"

The laugh bursting out of me takes us both by surprise. It keeps happening around her, and I have no idea how to control it anymore. She walks to my chair, not hesitating one second before straddling me. The red Prada dress she's wearing hikes up her thighs, and she wraps her arms around my neck.

"Please." Giving me those sweet eyes, she takes off my glasses and puts them on the desk behind her. "I don't want to go." She kisses my mouth, my cheeks, my forehead. "I really, *really* don't want to go."

I shake my head. "You've already used your spoiled princess card on Emma today." I reach around her to grab my glasses, putting them back on. "I can't concede to two tantrums in one day."

"Why not?"

"Because then you'll get used to it." I slide my hands up her thighs until my fingers reach her ass. "And I can't have that."

She narrows her eyes at me. "I'll kill Dr. Karls."

"No, Kayla," I huff. "You're not killing her."

"I will if you make me go."

"Okay, then to make sure you don't, I'll stay for the whole session. That way, I can stop you."

I can't stay, I have too much to do. But she doesn't need to know that right now.

She rolls her eyes, knowing she doesn't have a choice anymore. "*Fine*. I'm going and I won't kill her. Happy?"

"Good girl."

"I hate you."

"Kiss me like you do," I rasp.

She doesn't kiss me like she hates me at all. In fact, she kisses me like she's feeling quite the opposite.

32

KAYLA

Coming Down - Halsey

"Mrs. White?"

"King," I correct the second Dr. Karls's secretary advances toward me.

She nods, smiling politely. "I apologize, but Dr. Karls just had a health emergency and had to leave the office."

I hope she's dying. But then I'd have to explain to Nate that I had nothing to do with it.

"Oh." I've been waiting here for fifteen minutes, and Nate won't be back until the hour-long session is supposed to be over. "So...I can leave?"

Her brow furrows. Fuck, that sentence sounded weird. When the hell did I start asking permission? Nate has been ruining me.

"I mean, I'll just leave, then." I stand up, holding the bag Nate gifted me. It only has my phone and the credit card he's given me. It's stupid, too big for just those, but I need it since the dresses he buys me have no pockets. Ridiculous shit.

My heels click as I exit the waiting room. I can't believe I can walk in these now. They're not very high, small-heeled, pointed white slingbacks that go perfectly with the red dress I'm wearing. If it was up to me, they'd be in the trash, but my *husband* likes me in them.

I catch myself in the mirror of the practice's entrance hall as I leave. The last time I was in this building, I was with Nate, and I didn't even notice that mirror was here.

My stomach twists.

Who the fuck is this woman?

My hair is shiny and curled, because I'm still not allowed out of the house unless he lets me. I try to call my mom every morning before preschool, but it's not always possible. I sneak to a different part of the house with my phone so I can talk to my girls. But once that's done...that's it. I slip back into bed and wake up later. And then...then I have time. I have *time* to do my hair in the morning. That had never happened before.

My dress looks perfect on me because Nate sends someone to the house to get my clothes fitted. My shoes look expensive, my handbag too.

My features have softened. I sleep more. I don't have the stress of people relying on me any longer. My face looks more relaxed. Being taken care of all day, every day, instead of taking care of others, does something for you. I feel it in the way I hold myself straighter.

The only thing that still looks like me is the tattoos. The one along my hairline tells everyone that I don't really belong in expensive clothes. Rich people don't have tattoos on their faces. Not on their necks either, especially one that tells the locals I belong to a North Shore gang. And not on their hands. Stopping in front of the mirror, I bring my palm to my lips. The skeleton mouth tattooed on the back of my hand makes the bottom of my head look like a skull. It breaks the perfect image that was reflecting a minute ago, makes me look like a part of myself is still there.

But the real part of myself that I need, I don't have. The two parts that are a necessity to my happiness are not with me, too far for me to feel, too precious for me to call whenever I want. I can't risk anyone finding their way to them. I can't risk *Nate* finding out about them.

An emptiness takes hold of my heart, digging all the way to my stomach, and before I know it, a tear is falling down my face, all the way to the skull on the back of my hand.

I miss them. I miss them like nothing I've ever missed before. And the worst thing is, I've spent the last week not arguing with Nate, without fighting back. I didn't try to leave. I didn't try to kill him. All I tried to do is negotiate being let outside alone. Apart from today, it didn't work.

Stockholm syndrome is a wonderfully complicated thing.

My hand falls from my face, and I press it against the mirror. His words from weeks ago are eating at me from the inside.

You won't realize it. All you'll feel is happy and in love, and you won't believe anyone who tells you otherwise.

Like I didn't believe Caden. I wanted to build trust. I spent this week playing along because I thought...what if I can make this work? What if I could have them—always my priority—and him. Both?

Fuck that. He is never going to let me go. He is going to dress me up, play with me, make me a good little housewife. And to think I almost let him.

I take a step back, looking at the woman in the mirror with widening eyes. Terror grips me, and I run out of the practice, the uncomfortable shoes digging into the heels of my feet.

Before I know it, I'm jumping into a cab, asking the driver to take me to the North Shore. I tell him to wait for me in the parking lot while I run to an ATM. I take out all the money I can.

Three thousand dollars.

Fuck it. I'll do it again.

The driver takes me all over the North Shore. I go from ATM to ATM, and when he finally drops me home, I've got twenty-one thousand dollars with me.

I'm panting as I burst into my house. I didn't even fucking know you could take out that kind of money. Probably only on the kind of card Nate has. And he has many of them.

The burnt smell feels familiar, and when I look around at the tiny place, barely bigger than Nate's bedroom, I feel myself relax.

I'm home.

The first thing I do is get rid of the painful heels.

And then the rings.

I throw them somewhere in the living room, feeling like I've lost fifty pounds. Fifty pounds of fucking trauma. Smiling to myself, I look around the space, and I scream.

Once, twice, until I can't feel my vocal cords anymore.

Fuck, this feels good. No matter how temporary it is.

I drop the bag and run to my bedroom, stripping off the dress and grabbing a tight pair of black jeans and a large t-shirt I had cut to a crop-top. It has a sexy she-devil drawn on it in all red. Throwing clothes into a duffel bag, I walk around my house. I add family pictures and other shit that I'm stupidly sentimental about, and I zip up the bag.

"Fuck," I huff. "This feels good," I say out loud this time.

The next thing I do is take ten thousand dollars out of the pile of money in my purse before throwing it to the side again. I split them into four piles of two-thousand five hundreds, and I tie each pile with hair ties that are just lying around.

And then I'm on my way. My car is still here from before Nate took me, and I'm surprised it hasn't been stolen yet.

I'm going to drop half of the money to Nyx because I know she needs it, and I'll drive with the other half to West Virginia. And then...then, I'll be *free*. Free and reunited with my family.

It takes me about fifteen minutes to drive to Nyx's mobile home. She lives in the trailer park with her dad. It's a Sunday, so she'll be here.

Her eyes grow as wide as saucers when she answers the door.

"Kay," she sighs as she jumps into my arms.

My eyes flutter shut, hugging her close to me. She feels skinnier than usual.

"I thought I was never going to see you again," she mumbles against my shoulder.

"Yeah, that crossed my mind too," I chuckle. "Let me in."

She steps back, and I climb the two steps to get in.

"Your dad here?" I ask as I look at the place.

She shakes her head. It's a shitshow in here, as usual. Empty bottles of cheap beer are scattered everywhere. It smells of cold cigarettes and stale alcohol.

I put my hands on my hips. "How is he?"

She shrugs and looks away. "Same as usual. I've been

using all my savings to repay some debts he owed, and anything I earn from the shop, I give him to play with."

"Nyx." I take a deep breath, trying to stay nice. It's not her fault her dad is ill. "Don't give him too much. Just enough."

She nods. "I know. Not enough for him to get out of control, but enough so he won't steal from me if he wants to play. I give the same amount you usually give me."

Nyx's dad is not just an alcoholic. He's also a gambling addict. The illness runs in their family, and her mom left to find herself a rich man when she started owing too much money to loan sharks. One of them was me. When I met Nyx, I cleared her debt, paid the other collectors, and took her under my wing. Every month, I give her enough money to keep her dad out of trouble, and then enough to eat. There's not much else I can do to help. I can't do shit for her dad, and I couldn't take her into my home either.

"You've lost weight," I tell her. "Have you been eating?"

She shrugs again. "Whatever I can buy."

Being with Nate meant that Nyx has had no one to support her. And the worst thing is, I know where her mom is. In Stoneview with her new husband, enjoying the billionaire life while her daughter deals with an addicted dad. She doesn't care about her. She has a new family now.

"Here." I pull two stacks out of my duffel bag and give it to her. "This is for your dad. Anyone coming to collect, you give them anything they want, okay?" I snatch a pen from the table, and grab her wrist, writing my number on her forearm. "This is my new number. If they ask for more than you can give, call me. If you need more time, tell them I'll take care of it. Always mention my name if you're in trouble."

She nods, taking in all the info. I finish writing the

number and throw the pen back on the table. I don't know when exactly I'll be able to come back to help her. Nate will be looking for me, but I'm hoping this will help for now. Pulling out another two stacks, I give them to her.

"This is for you. To feed yourself, get yourself to school, anything you need." Glancing around the room, I search for her instrument. "How's violin going?"

Her gaze darts to the side.

"What? What happened?"

"The last guys who came to collect..." She hesitates, unable to meet my eyes. "They took it, said they could resell it. I told them it was a worthless one, but they didn't listen."

I bite my inner cheek, feeling my lips twist. Fuck.

Then I dig into my bag, pulling out another five hundred dollars. "Is that enough to get a new one?"

Her eyebrows just about reach her hairline. "Uh...y-yeah."

I add the bills to the ones in her hands. "I can't stay. But promise me you'll contact me if you need anything."

She nods, eyes watering. "Are you... Are you going to be gone for long? Where were you? People in high school are saying you got, like, kidnapped?"

I shake my head and smile to reassure her. "I was with someone who's even more trouble than me."

She laughs softly, sniffling as she tries to stop the tears from falling. "No one is more trouble than you. You're Kayla King. You're the baddest bitch around."

How I fucking wish I was.

"I'll be back soon," I lie, wiping a tear making its way down her cheek. "You're not alone, Nyx. I'll always take care of you, even if sometimes it takes me longer to come to you."

She nods as a sob escapes her. When she jumps in my arms again, I hug her tightly. "It's been lonely without you."

"I know, baby." I caress her back. "It's been lonely without you too. I miss everyone."

There's a knot in my throat as I drive away from the trailer park. In my mirror, I can see Nyx standing at the entrance, still holding over ten thousand dollars of cash in her hand.

Stupid kid.

I drive to the other side of the North Shore before needing my phone. I have to put in the directions to my mother's town. I used to go once a month, more, if possible. I would visit them as often as I could, but I can never remember the directions for the entire five-hour drive.

They've already started wondering why I didn't visit this month, and I don't need to lie to them about being too busy for a second time because I'm *free*.

I dig into my duffle bag on the passenger seat while I'm at a traffic light. And then my heart stops. My phone is in the purse Nate had given me.

And so is the rest of the fucking money.

Shit.

Doing an extreme U-turn, my tires screech as I speed down the road. I need to get that purse from my house and get on my way. It's not like that doctor's appointment can buy me an entire day.

I run into my house, my eyes scanning the living room for the purse. I grab it, ready to sprint back out, when the door bursts open.

"You are in trouble, wife." My stomach sinks.

I know it's not the fun kind of trouble.

Nate is absolutely fuming, and I barely have time to drop the purse. He's already right in front of me, his eyes darting to my hand. I'm too late to put it behind my back. It would be an obvious move anyway.

"Your rings."

"I-I can explain." But the second I put my hands in front of me to keep him away, his one shoots to my hair, making me wince as he wraps the length around his fist.

"I was clear, Kayla," he hisses, dragging me with him as he walks the short length of my living room. "From the beginning, I told you, the rings stay on. You were aware of that, weren't you?"

"Y-yes," I stutter, barely capable of keeping up with him. Pain shoots through my scalp, and I slap his arm. "Let go!"

He takes me all the way to the kitchen, looking through drawers and making me stumble as he moves.

"So you agree that you knew. That you were fully aware you were disobeying me. I want you to remember that when I punish you. And it's going to fucking hurt."

When he finds a kitchen knife, my eyes widen. "What are you doing?" I shout, as nerves ricochet throughout my body. "Nate, please wait. Let me explain."

"You will be punished for taking the rings off. Explanation or not. Better get it over with."

He bends me over the small table. It can barely hold my weight from how old and used it is.

Letting go of my hair, he grips my left wrist, slamming it next to my head.

"What are you doing?" Panic seizes me fully, freezing my muscles. Fuck...is he going to cut my fucking finger?

"Where were you running to?"

"Please, don't. Please..."

"*Where were you running to?*" he repeats with a purpose that makes my entire being tighten.

"I-I—"

"I trusted you to go out on your own. I made the mistake of thinking you were adapting. Imagine my surprise when the bank called me asking why I was withdrawing enormous amounts on the North Shore."

"I am adapting!" I yell so forcefully I hurt my throat. "I am, that's why I panicked. I-I was going to come back. I just needed a moment to myself. I needed to breathe."

"You can't. Don't you understand that? I will *never* allow you to breathe without me." His grip tightens on my wrist, and I look back at this face, my own twisting from pain. Even with his blank expression and empty eyes, I can *feel* the betrayal like we're directly connected through a wire. "Do you think I'm stupid? Taking all that money? You were going to run."

"Please, don't hurt me."

"You can't even tell me I'm wrong." Something breaks in his voice, and it fissures my heart. "Can you?"

My silence is a death sentence, but I can't get myself to lie to him again. And I sure as hell am not telling him where I was going. He can torture me, kill me. He'll never know.

"You're lucky I'm not doing it on your fucking face," he growls, palpable anger making his voice tremble.

"Do what?" I cry out. "What are you—"

A fire sears my finger, and I turn to face the hand he's forcing flat on the table.

It takes me a few seconds to comprehend what is going on.

The knife, it's tearing through my skin. He's marking me in the same way he did on my ass, carving into my flesh. Except this time, it's on my ring finger. Not even where the rings should have been—no, he wouldn't want them to hide it. It's below my nail, between the middle and top knuckle.

"No! No, please!" I wriggle, but he lets go for a second, bringing the knife to my neck. "Stay still and I won't do it to every single one of your fingers. The longer you make this last, the longer I make it hurt, do you understand?"

"Nate," I whimper. The realization sets in that every single step we have taken forward together has been erased. We're back to square one, fear consuming me, fury blinding him.

There is nothing connecting us, only possession and terror.

The N is the most painful, and it takes everything in my power to not cry and beg for mercy.

I swallow the tears like I've always done, and I close my eyes.

I'm numb by the time he gets to the W. Physically, I am, but inside, I mourn the freedom I almost had. I was so close to seeing my girls again. Worse, I mourn the man I got to meet, the one who made me feel safe and worshiped. He's gone, and everything inside me hurts, dying to get him back.

"Ah, despair," he spits. "It's back on your face. How fucking lovely."

And from those sarcastic words only, I understand he's mourning that man too, blaming me for making him disappear.

"For a split second—" he chuckles as he keeps carving into me—"I thought something happened to you when the bank called. I thought, *what if someone robbed her? What if she's in trouble?*"

Blood covers my hand, creating a small puddle on the

table, and I know he's going deep so it'll scar. He said it the first time he did it.

"But then I remembered you're Kayla *King*." He emphasizes my last name, taking his back and breaking my heart in the process. I thought I hated his last name, so why don't I now? "No one would fucking dare rob you. No one would dare go against you."

"I'm sorry," I rasp. And I think I truly am, because I already miss *us* and what we'd made of our crazy situation. "I am, Nate. I'm sorry."

"I know you are, little sunflower." He's finished, throwing the knife to the side and pushing the hair away from my face. "You really are."

I squeeze my eyes shut and nod against the table.

"Because you can't live without me," he snarls dangerously, fisting my hair again. "A sunflower can't live without its sun, can it?"

"No." The truth bubbles out of my mouth. "I can't."

"I *know*. And you will keep on being sorry, believe me."

He pulls me off the table, dragging me with him as I hold my bloody hand to my chest, and he walks us back to the living room.

"Where are they?" he says in my ear. "The rings."

I shake my head. "In-in here. I'm not sure where."

"Not sure?"

This will only get worse, but I have to say it. "I threw them, didn't look. But they're here somewhere! They are."

He pushes me hard enough to make me stumble and fall face first to the floor. "Find them. *Now*."

I go on all fours, ready to get up, but his foot lands on my back, forcing me down again. He presses so hard I can barely breathe.

"I'm g-going to look for them," I stutter, confused.

"Didn't I tell you, wife? Didn't I say if you didn't want to be the queen by my side, you'd be the slave at my feet?"

No. This can't get worse. Please, let it not get worse.

"Answer me!" he barks, making my muscles lock.

"Yes! You did," I answer shakily.

"Right. So here we are. Find your rings. On all fours, like my little bitch. Because that's what you are, baby, isn't it? That's where your place is now." He presses harder against my back. "At." And harder. "My." And harder, cutting off my breath altogether. "Feet."

Releasing me, he snaps his fingers. "Now crawl."

And when I don't, too shocked to even move, too terrified to accept the situation, I hear the click of his gun, and feel pressure behind my head. "I said *crawl*, little sunflower."

So I do. I get back on my hands and knees, and I crawl around the room, ignoring my bleeding hand and the pain, desperately looking for the two gold rings I carelessly threw earlier.

The degrading act feels like it takes forever. My vision is limited at this height, my body is trembling in pain, and it makes it harder to move. I'm slow, humiliated, and terrified of his gun that keeps pointing at me wherever I go.

This is worse than it ever was. And the location makes it worse too. It's one thing to be stuck in Stoneview with him, at his mercy. But this is my house. This is the North Shore. This is my territory. And here I am, *still* stuck doing whatever he orders.

He's sitting on my shitty sofa, but Nate looks like a king on a throne wherever he is. Worse, a god on the highest summit, ready to send his wrath down on us mere humans.

Except he's a god without rules.

He doesn't listen to the prayers we send his way. He doesn't care for the worshipers at his feet.

Nathan White.

Ruthless leader.

Cold-blooded killer.

Brutal, merciless, lawless god.

My husband for however long he wishes.

A sigh leaves me when I finally find the engagement ring behind the foot of a chair and thank fuck the wedding band isn't far.

"Found them?" His voice is a rasp. Contrary to what I thought, I don't think he's enjoying this. Maybe he likes humiliating me, but he hates the betrayal.

"Y-yes," I whisper.

"Bring them to me."

I close the fist of my good hand around them, and awkwardly crawl back to him, stopping right between his legs. Sitting back on my feet, I look up at him and deposit the rings in his open palms.

"Give me your hand."

My bloody hand shakes when I lay it flat on his black suit. He looks beautiful in all black. Everything matches. His suit, his glasses, his heart, his soul. Perfect.

"You will never"—he slides the engagement ring around my finger, making me whimper from the pain— "ever"—the wedding band is next, and I bite my lower lip when it grazes against the cut—"take these off again. Have I made myself clear?"

"Yes," I croak, swallowing roughly.

"Do you understand what will happen if you do it again?" He's asking like an adult scolding a child gently, but it's happening *after* he butchered my finger. The gentleness won't fix anything now.

"Y-yes."

"Look at me." And I realize my eyes are stuck on my hand. I look up, trembling under his dead eyes. "Apologize."

"I'm sorry." I don't even recognize my own voice, it's so hoarse I can barely make out the words.

"What for?"

"F-for running away and—and taking the rings off."

He nods, and I'm dying to hear that he forgives me. I want to be in his arms, to hug the man who made me feel so cherished in the last week.

"Can I be in your arms, please?"

I hate myself for asking, for being vulnerable, but I can't help it. He *made me* this way.

And I hate him even more when he says, "No. I'm not done with your punishment. You'll get to touch me when I decide so."

My shoulders drop, my breath catching in my throat.

"For now, you stay on your knees and don't move an inch."

He takes something out of his pocket, and my eyes almost bulge out of my head when I see a syringe. Just like when he sedated me that first time in my bathroom. And right after the wedding.

"No," I whimper, shaking my head. "Please. I'm coming back with you. D-don't put me to sleep."

He wraps a mighty hand around my jaw. "I said don't move, Kayla."

"Sorry," I whisper, hopeless. "Sorry. But please, you don't have to do this."

"I can't trust you," he says. And I hear it again, that noise that makes it sound like something has broken inside him. It makes me wish I could go back in time to just a few hours ago. I should have told him the truth. The man he was then might have let me go see them. Maybe he would have understood. "Wives who can't be trusted get sedated. You'll get some rights back when you can behave."

He takes the cap off with his teeth, turning his head to the side and spitting it away from us. His hand stays on my jaw, keeping me still. I don't even *dare* to try to stop him anyway.

When he pushes the needle in my neck, the liquid burns. It's weird. It's like I can taste its bitterness at the back of my throat as it works through my body.

My eyes grow heavy, my body heavier.

"Please," I hear myself whisper, even though I don't mean to say the words. "Don't hurt me. Don't—don't break me."

He shakes his head. I sway to the side, and he catches me, bringing his hands under my armpits and dragging me onto his lap.

"I won't break you, little sunflower. But it will hurt."

I try to shake my head once more, but instead, it drops to the side completely, my muscles becoming useless.

"Please," I plead. It feels like I'm talking in slow motion.

"Only good little captives get rewarded, baby. I thought you understood that." He sighs, like he hates this situation, even though he's the one putting me in it. "It seems you didn't."

33

KAYLA

Love Into a Weapon - Madalen Duke

Yet another time I wake up at Nate's house with a pounding headache. I remember everything instantly, and I wish I'd stayed asleep forever.

I'm not in his basement this time, but I can already feel the restraints on me. I squint down at my body.

A chair.

Handcuffs.

And my red dress. He put me back in that fucking red dress.

"Nate," I rasp, dehydration forcing my voice into a whisper. My wrists are bound to the arms of the chair, and the sturdy handcuffs dig into my skin.

I'm in our—*his* bedroom—and everything feels familiar. Too familiar. I shouldn't feel at home when I'm bound to a chair in my captor's house.

"Nate..."

I let my head fall forward until I hear keys in the door.

The bastard locked me in!

"Hello, little sunflower."

His voice sends a chill down my spine. I don't know this man anymore. Cold, calculated Nate disappeared last week. I'm not ready to face him again.

Leaning against the doorframe, he slowly pushes his glasses up his nose before putting his hands in the pockets of his suit.

He's such a calm man for the chaos he causes. My body trembles, anticipating whatever he's got in mind. Subconsciously, I'm already submitting to him, no matter how much I want to fight it.

But that's not something he only does with me. Everyone knows Nathan White gets what he wants, one way or another. After all, when a force of nature walks into a room, everything bends to its will.

"Nate, please. Undo these." I pull at the cuffs, making sure he knows what I mean.

He shakes his head, his face impassive. I should be used to it by now, but it never gets any less terrifying. What goes on in his mind?

I'm sure he feels angry, deceived, but how am I meant to know for sure?

"What do I have to do, Kayla?"

I lick my lips as I try to make sense of what he's asking. "What you have to do?"

He nods slowly, but refuses to give me any other clue.

My body is hot, cold sweat gathering at the base of my back. "I don't—I don't understand."

Tilting his head to the side, he takes one step toward me, his body relaxed. "No?"

My god, he scares me. How can someone look so shockingly beautiful and chilling at the same time?

His hair is messy, like he ran his hands through it over

and over again. Strands are falling over his glasses, but he doesn't bother to push them away. And that's when I notice the other details. His jacket is gone, his sleeves are down, cuffed around his wrists, but they're wrinkled. He's been pulling them up, like he does when he gets agitated, when he doesn't find a solution to an issue. And the first few buttons of his shirt are undone, like someone who's been suffocating in it.

"Tell me." His voice is thick, his steps heavy as he approaches. "What do I have to do?"

The question is clearer now that I've observed him closely, so clear I don't understand how I did not get it before.

"To keep me, you mean?"

"So you did understand the question."

My head shake is painful from the throbbing in my neck. "Not the first time. But I know how to read you now."

Pride shines brightly in his eyes, and instead of answering his initial question, I take a risk, and jump.

"Name it, Nate."

His eyes roam over me, and I expected the shadow of a smile, for him to want to play, but there's nothing.

"If you can read me, why don't you give it a go?" He stops right in front of me.

I swallow thickly, but I go for it. What do I have to lose at this point?

"Just now, you felt pride." He cocks an eyebrow at me, so I explain myself. "You love it when we're on the same page. When you feel understood."

I take a staggered breath, licking my lips as I hesitate to point out the rest. "That's why... That's why my betrayal hurt you so much. Because you thought we understood each other, and my actions took you by surprise."

His face is blank, but it's his lack of response that tells me I'm on the right path.

"I *do* understand you, Nate. You might not be capable of expressing yourself easily, but it shouldn't stop others from listening. You're not inhuman, you're not impassive, you simply don't speak the same language as everyone else. But I promise you, I've come to understand what you struggle to articulate, and I know. I *know* how betrayed you feel from what I did, but if you hurt me more, if you go too far, there will be no going back from this. We'll never find the closeness we felt."

He puts both his hands on my thighs, leaning down to face me. His lips are inches away from mine.

"Answer the question."

I close my eyes. We're at a standstill here, and one of us has to surrender.

Just as I open my eyes again, he falls to his knees. "What do I have to do, Kayla?"

Looking up at me, his hands spread my legs apart. "To keep you? To make you mine?"

He pushes my dress up my thighs and all the way to my hips.

"You don't understand the things I'm capable of." Nuzzling against my inner thigh, he lowers my underwear at the same time, until they're completely gone. "You can't even fathom what I'll do if you try to leave again."

"I wasn't—"

"*Lies* have no place in this relationship, do you understand? Call me whatever you want, point out all the horrible things I do, but I would never lie to you."

He pulls at my hips, putting me in an awkward position with my ass on the edge of the seat, and my wrists still tied to the arms. Grabbing one ankle, he forces a foot flat on the edge, and then the other, so that I'm completely exposed to him.

"Nate," I gasp. "This...is not a fair conversation. I need us to be on equal footing to discuss. Not...not—"

I'm cut off when he buries his head between my legs. My body heat rises a hundred degrees, my knees suddenly shaking as his tongue explores my entrance.

He doesn't listen. He doesn't care. He doesn't want to know what I have to say.

He pushes inside me, sending a wave of pleasure crashing through my body and a rush of wetness to my pussy. He licks me, bringing my arousal to my clit, and swirls his tongue around it.

"*Oh.*" The sound escapes me, followed by a long moan I can't control. He grazes his teeth, taking a breath, and licks my nub over and over again to a rhythm I can't keep up with.

He does that thing where everything disappears, where all I can do is focus on the pleasure. I throw my head back, incapable of doing anything else anyway.

My chest is rising and falling to a senseless rhythm, barely dragging any air in, but pushing moans out I can't control. Noises I didn't even know I could make.

He pulls his mouth away but talks so close to my pussy his breath makes me squirm. "This is what you want, isn't it? Me, on my knees, begging you to reciprocate my feelings. Me, at your feet, desperate for crumbs of attention."

His flat tongue licks me all the way from my entrance to my clit, and I'm seconds away from coming when he stands up. Pressing my jaw tightly, he forces me to part my lips, and his tongue comes to caress mine, making me taste just how much of an effect he has on me.

"I have nothing more to give you, Kayla. If you don't want me now, you'll never want me. I can't have that. I can't have you not feeling the same obsession I feel for you."

And I hear the words that frighten me the most.

"I'm sorry."

My eyes widen, chest tightening, my body still buzzing from the need to come. "Sorry for what?" He takes a step back, turning around and walking toward the door. "Nate... sorry for *what*?"

With his hand on the handle, and his back to me, he barely twists his head to the side, not meeting my eyes. "I'm sorry I'm going to hurt you. But I want to make you mine. Your body is mine, and I'm going to hurt it. Your soul is mine, and I'm going to taint it. I've already broken your mind, and I'll do more, little sunflower. I'm going to crush your heart in the palm of my hand and order it to beat for me."

He opens the door, and a woman is standing behind it.

"What—Who? What are you doing?" My feet fall from the chair, crossing my legs in the hope of hiding my nakedness.

I pull at the cuffs, the pain around my wrists enhancing the tingling sensation Nate left after licking me. What is wrong with me? I'm terrified, turned on, and so scared of what's about to happen I can't focus anymore.

"This is Mimi."

The woman waves, smiling awkwardly. Her short bleached hair has bright pink tips, and her nose and ears are pierced. She walks in with a black bag, her eyes stuck on my bound wrists.

"Not gonna lie," she says in a stressed squeak. "This isn't my usual at-home job."

"I didn't pay your gambling debts for you to comment

on the situation," Nate answers casually, standing behind her as she drops her bag next to me. "I paid for you to pierce and shut the fuck up."

"Pierce?" I gasp. "Pierce what?"

My dear husband comes to stand behind me, pushing the thick straps of the dress to my shoulders.

"I want to do something we'll both like in the long run."

"Nate." My panicked, wavering voice comes from somewhere deep inside. I don't think I've ever sounded like this in my life.

"Name it for me, little sunflower."

I can barely take my next breath as he lowers the neck of my dress below my breasts. I'm not wearing a bra, as the dress is tight, fitted perfectly, I didn't really need to. How I wish I did.

"I c-can't," I stammer. "Nate, please."

"I can put numbing cream," Mimi suggests softly.

"Mimi. Be kind and keep quiet. I would hate to have to kill you for not upholding your end of our deal."

She nods quickly before meeting my eyes.

"No cream," he continues. "My wife loves pain. It turns her on."

"Fuck!" I scream, knowing what's coming. "Don't fucking do this to me."

Nate pinches one nipple after the other, hurting me on purpose, and instead of fighting back, a sigh of pleasure leaves me, reminding me of how turned on I was a minute ago.

"S-stop..."

"I'm just making them hard. Why are you fighting something you love?" He lets go and kisses the side of my head. "Think of all the fun we're going to have with these."

The size of the needle makes my eyes bulge out of my head. "Shit."

"Name it, baby."

"I-I—" A gasp freezes my lungs. "Panic," I exhale. "Terror. Please, don't do this. Nate, I swear... I swear I'll never forgive you."

His hand wraps around my throat, just below my chin. He pulls, sending my head back and forcing me to look up at him.

"See, that's your problem. Because it doesn't matter if you forgive me, if you want me, if you love me. Either way, you'll be here, by my side, and I'll take it all, Kay. I'll take the anger, the tears, the terror. I'll take it, and I'll turn it against you, and I'll make you so fucking desperate you'll have no choice but to want me back."

He's right...that's *exactly* what my problem is. I did want him back, and that's why I ran. That's what got me in this situation. This is an endless, torturous cycle.

"Y-you're insane."

"Insane?" he asks passively, as if only now thinking about it. "Probably. Infatuated? Passionate? *Obsessed?* They work too."

His empty eyes fixate on mine, and he murmurs, "It's happening. Don't move."

The pain is like nothing I've felt before. My eyes squeeze shut, a desperate whimper escaping me.

I bite my lip, but the curse comes out anyway. "Fuck!"

"Shh, just focus on me."

And I do. I open my eyes to focus on the midnight blue staring back at me. There's nothing there. Not even the obsession and passion he talks about. But his hold, his breathing, I feel them. They want to possess me, to keep me. I can't help but want that too.

His other hand comes to my cheek, caressing my skin. "She's going to do the second one now."

The pain is even worse. How is that even possible? I'm whining wordlessly, squirming on the spot from the wetness I can feel leaking out of me.

It's a good thing he doesn't ever plan on letting me go. Who else could understand me but the monster who created me? Who else could love me but the devil who helped me discover my darkest desires and chose to want me despite them all?

"You're doing so good," he growls in my ear. "I'm going to let you orgasm the second we're finished. It'll be your reward for being such a good wife."

A sob clogs my throat. Everything in me is telling me to fight, but I'm too taken by his power to do anything anymore.

When it's finally over, Nate lets me go, and Mimi is quick to pack up. I don't want to look at her and see her real thoughts about the situation. I don't want the judgmental outside world to show me that this is fucked up.

I already know.

I already can't fight it.

I look down at my reddened nipples. They're hard, swollen, and they are now decorated with gold barbels, each with diamonds on the ends.

Nate stands in front of me. One hand lands on the back of the chair, the other snaking down my body.

"They match your engagement ring." He pushes two fingers inside me, pointing out that I'm dripping wet.

I just let go. I let him coax a soul-shattering orgasm out of me, drinking up my reward for suffering at the hands of my beautiful demon.

And just like he did with his, I embrace him and the darkness he creates inside me.

Later that night, I'm sitting on his bed, wearing a black silk sleep dress. I'm still locked in his bedroom, my nipples throbbing despite wearing only a thin layer. He's left me here for hours. I've heard him walking around the house, heard something that sounded like drilling, and I was so worried I ended up grabbing a book in the drawer of his bedside table. All he keeps in there is the notebook he uses to track my night terrors and the book *Frankenstein*. And now I'm attempting to read the first page. *That's* how much I need to escape. I'm willing to open a book.

I startle when he comes in. He's discarded his suit jacket, rolled up his sleeves, and his hair is a mess of blond strands framing his sharp face. He wipes his forehead with his forearm, and that shows me he's holding a drill. My eyes automatically go to his other hand.

A chain.

The chain.

"No." I throw the covers to the side, ready to get out of bed and run the fuck away from him, but the second my feet touch the floor, his sharp tone freezes my movement.

"Don't make me hurt you."

"Nate, this is insane."

"I don't care." He advances toward me.

"You can't keep me chained here. I know you're angry, but–"

"Angry? No. Angry is when you don't listen. Angry is when you're being a brat and I have to put you back in your place. This...ah, you know I'm not good with feelings, little sunflower, but I think I can safely say this is *wrath*."

I jolt at the sound of his voice, knees weakening as he kneels by my feet, opening the leather cuff attached to the chain.

"No!" It's not as self-assured this time. More of a plea. "Nate, please."

"I don't want to hear you. Choose whether you want to shut it or be gagged, but I don't want one more sound. I might end up doing something stupid."

I gnaw at my lower lip, trying to decide if I want to fight harder or give up. That would have never happened before. He's weakened me so badly it affects more than my ego. It affects my survival.

My thinking takes too long anyway. He's already drilling the chain to the floor of his bedroom by the time I come back to reality.

I rub a hand over my face. "You knew I was going to try to run away," I murmur. "That's what happens when you steal someone's freedom."

"Yes." He stands up and stretches his neck. "And now we know it's not happening again. I even put new locks on the windows. Just for you."

I grit my teeth, choosing silence over anything else that could spill out of my mouth.

His eyes go the book on the bed, and he tilts his head to the side. "Enjoying Frankenstein?"

"Yes. As you know, reading is my favorite pastime."

With an unexpected snort, he rounds the bed and comes to his side. As he gets rid of his shoes and shirt, I avert my eyes to not look at his tempting body. I wish his tattoos would hide his hard muscles. All they do is enhance his beautiful strength, the way everything moves in harmony every time he makes a movement.

I shift, bringing my feet back on the bed and hating the feeling and sound of the chain.

He grabs the book, caressing my thigh with his other hand. His entire body relaxes now. His face softens, his breathing evens out. It's like now that he knows I really can't go anywhere, he's reassured.

"Where did you get to?" he asks softly.

I sigh, looking away. "I think I just read that first page about ten times. It's a letter."

He nods. "Yes, the first four chapters are an epistolary novel."

I dig my gaze into his while I rub my thumb against my lower lip. "Right."

He chuckles, grabbing my hand and stopping my movement. "It means it's a story in the form of letters. Technically, they're not the first four chapters, just four letters."

I feel my cheeks heat. I hate that he's learned to read me so well he knows when I don't understand something, but am too ashamed to admit it.

"You could have just said letters."

A laugh bursts out of him. "Yes, I guess you're right. Did you like that first page?"

I shrug, my eyes going to the leather around my ankle. "I want to know more, but I'll never be able to read it all. I read about three books in my life. Takes me months to go through one, and Frankenstein sounds complicated as hell."

His hand leaves my thigh, and he taps his lap. "Come. Put your head here."

I hesitate, my eyes bouncing between his lap and his face.

"Let's both escape for the night, Kay."

My heart skips a beat, my eyes fluttering shut.

And I rest my head on his lap.

He puts his hand in my hair, caressing from the top to my ear, repeating the movement until I relax.

"*Frankenstein* is my favorite book."

Fuck. I know how hard it is to hate him when he opens up.

"Why?" I whisper, as if not asking too loudly means I didn't ask at all.

"I'm not too sure," he says pensively. "But I like to assume I can relate to being a monster of a creation, so much so that the creator regrets it entirely. I would assume that's why my parents abandoned me, right? They created a monster they couldn't bear to keep. This book is all about the consequences of your actions. It's important to keep in mind."

I take a shaky breath.

"I'd like to think I won't ever make the mistakes Victor Frankenstein made. Anything that comes from me, I'll cherish with all I have, no matter what."

I swallow thickly as my heart beats harshly in my chest. "Like kids? You want to be different from your parents?"

He takes a deep breath, but his is completely even compared to mine. "Sure. Like kids."

There's a moment of silence while I feel the truth at the tip of my tongue. It almost slips...

"If you're interested in reading, but it's too hard, I'll read it to you." And now it's too late.

"You will?"

I'm speaking toward his knee, my cheek on his lap rather than looking up at him. He can't see the conflicted longing in my gaze.

"It's not fair for you to miss such a good story because of something you can't control."

He readjusts himself on the bed. "*Letter One*," he reads.

For what feels like hours, I listen to his soothing voice reading *Frankenstein*. I don't know to what chapter we get to before I feel my eyes grow heavy, but it's getting hard to reconcile the man who chained me to his bed with the man who reads to me because I'm dyslexic.

I don't even feel the cuff around my ankle when I finally fall asleep on his lap.

34

KAYLA

RUNNING - NF

Sitting in front of the vanity mirror in the far corner of our bedroom, I look down at the phone in my lap.

I have plenty of messages from last week. Messages I have ignored. Not only that, but I also forgot to delete them. Nate could have found out anytime.

> Unknown: North Shore girls can't be trusted.

I take a deep breath, throwing my head back. The curve in my back makes my nipples press against the silk robe I'm wearing, and I wince at the contact. It was yesterday, and the pain is getting worse every hour. I wonder when they're meant to stop hurting.

The worst is the way Nate is using them against me. He's fucked me five times since yesterday, and every single time it started with him playing with the barbel, forcing pain upon my body and knowing perfectly well how much it turns me on.

I sigh to myself, looking at the message sent this morning.

Unknown: In or out.

There are many reasons for me to escape Nate, but the main one is currently wrapped around my ankle.

I'm chained. Again.

The little trust we'd managed to build is completely gone. I'm back to square one. And if he can't trust me, if I never get a chance to leave on my own, then I won't be able to get back to the people I love the most. Ever.

That's not an option.

I lick my lips, feeling my throat tighten.

But among a hundred reasons to want to escape him, there's one powerful one not to.

I have fallen in love with my captor.

I squeeze my eyes shut, stopping the tears that threaten to fall. How? How could I have let this happen? But I know that's it. I know because I have never felt this way before. There're no words to describe it. It's a feeling too strong to comprehend, to explain. I wonder if that's what Nate was trying to portray when he talked about cold hands on a winter day. Is it? But then, why didn't he just say it? Why didn't he say he's in love with me, and then we could have worked from there?

His language is incomprehensible. So much effort to try to communicate that I'm exhausted, confused... completely lost.

In or out?

Did I lose the need for independence? The powerful link I have to the North Shore?

In or out?

Stockholm syndrome is a wonderfully complicated thing.

But he doesn't understand. He doesn't know what waits for me outside. Who. They need me. Our love is unconditional. No one can get between us.

In or out? You're the one who put this plan into action. Remember why.

In or out, Kayla?

You're in love with him.

I grab the phone, text my response, and delete everything.

Then I look up at the mirror, swallow the tears shining in my eyes, and apply makeup on my face.

We have to go to a charity ball at Stoneview town hall. Well, Nate has to, but he doesn't want to leave me alone, so I'm forced to come along. He has to be present, mingle with local politicians, company owners. So much he has to do to keep people blackmailed and in his pocket.

The dress he got me from that shop is hanging on the closet door. The black satin, the diamonds...I gulp. Seventy-five thousand dollars.

I startle when the door opens.

"My beautiful wife, there she is."

The glare I send him through the mirror should have killed him. Why is he still standing?

"Where else would I be, Nate? You've chained me to the floor."

He smiles and kisses my cheek from behind. "We need to leave in thirty minutes. Will you be ready?"

As he places a velvet box on the vanity, I ignore it. I won't ask what it is. Something to torture me, surely.

His lips press against my neck, and a shiver ripples across my entire body.

"Aren't you at least a little bit happy that now I keep

you because I can't live without you? This is not about revenge anymore, little sunflower."

"Wonderful," I deadpan.

"Now the only reasons you'll suffer are when you try to leave, or don't give me what I want. There are no more grudges, I promise."

Tightening my jaw, I look up and through the mirror. "I hate you."

He shrugs. "What are you going to do about it? Run away?" His eyes go to the point where the chain is locked to the floor. "Good luck with that," he chuckles playfully.

I finish my makeup in silence, choosing to ignore him. It's a little harder to do that when he's the one helping me into the dress.

No underwear. That's what he chose for the night.

I lift my hair, giving him access to my neck, as he locks the diamonds attached to the collar of the dress.

I let my hair fall down my bare back, and he pulls at the chain of diamonds attaching the dress to my waist.

"*Bastard,*" I squeak, the feeling of the dress tightening around my sore breasts cutting off my voice.

"I'm just getting you wet," he murmurs behind me, focused on his actions.

"I don't want to get wet," I grunt back.

"But you'll still do it for me, won't you?"

It's not like I have much control over my body.

Walking around me, he kneels on the floor between me and the mirror. He grabs a satin heel and helps me slide my foot inside. It's an ankle strap pump, and the chain is made of diamonds. Please, let those ones be fake. I'm going to have to be insured for the night if he keeps dressing me in expensive shit. To do the other one, he finally unlocks the cuff around my ankle, and a sense of relief crashes over me. That thing makes me feel claustrophobic.

When he stands back up, he puts a hand on my cheek. "You look beautiful."

I look away, not wanting to participate in anything that would make my heart betray me more than it already has.

Before I know it, he's back behind me, lifting my dress all the way to my waist.

"I just spent hours getting ready. Do you really want to ruin it all?"

"I like the *my-husband-can't-stop-touching-me* look on you. You'll wear something for me tonight."

"I'm already wearing your stupid dress."

He spreads my legs with a tap of his foot, and that's when I notice something in his other hand.

"What—"

"Put your foot on the stool."

I eye the small cushioned stool next to us.

He drags what looks like thin metal down to my stomach and to my mound. It's about as thick as a hairpin, and it's already warm from being against my skin.

"This can be pleasurable, Kayla, baby. Just be a good girl and it won't hurt."

"What is it?" I panic, but at the same time, I lift my foot, letting the heel rest on the stool.

"Have you ever heard of a clit clamp?"

My heart stutters. I haven't, but it's pretty self-explanatory.

"Why are you doing this?" My voice is dead, my body giving up as he kisses my neck.

"Because I know how wet you'll be when I finally push my cock into you later tonight, and I'm doing us both a favor by doing this."

I watch him rub my clit, making it swell from his skillful touch, and he then softly pinches it with dexterous fingers.

"Fuck," I pant.

"That's good, baby. Now, this thing is adjustable."

He finally shows me what he's holding. I was right, it looks exactly like a gold hairpin, except it's not as tight as one, and it has a small bar you can slide along to adjust how tightly it pinches your clit.

"So," he explains as he puts it in place at the base of my clit, "if you're good, it doesn't have to be so tight, right? Just enough to hold. And if you misbehave tonight..." He adjusts the clamp, tightening it.

"Oh my god!" I shriek. "Stop, stop!"

He releases it again, keeping it just tight enough for me to feel its presence and keep me turned on, but not enough to hurt.

"Pretty clear, isn't it?"

I nod, panting, as I watch him play with me some more. There's a small diamond dangling from the clamp, and I can't believe this is actually happening.

He is batshit crazy.

He lets the dress fall, but I'm still shaking from the feeling of the clamp.

"We really have to go." He turns to the vanity, opens the velvet box, and grabs two bracelets inside.

"Am I a fucking Christmas tree, Nate? Are you done decorating me yet?"

He pinches his lips, clearly wanting to laugh at my predicament. "The last time you were allowed outside, you tried to run. I'm not taking any risks, baby. Show me your wrists."

I narrow my eyes at him as I present my wrists. He

secures one bracelet, then the other. There's something weird on them, like an extra clasp just dangling on the side.

"Oh...*fuck off*," I hiss with fury.

"Turn around."

"You can't be serious."

Grabbing both my wrists, I feel him attach the two bracelets together at my back. "I'll undo them the second we arrive at the town hall."

"These are just fancy handcuffs!"

"Indeed, they are. And they look beautiful on you."

"This is too much," I say, my voice dropping. "It can't carry on like this, Nate."

"Only until I feel I can trust you again."

I clench my jaw, grit my teeth, and stay quiet. There's nothing to say anyway. No way to win.

The ride is uncomfortable with my hands cuffed behind my back, but nothing beats the fact that there's a clamp pinching my clit. This is going to be a long night.

True to his word, Nate undoes the delicate cuffs the second we park in front of the town hall. They're just two normal diamond bracelets now, and by the time we're going up the stairs, what I feel the most is the soft satin against my aching nipples.

Someone is waiting at the top of the infinite stairs, right by the entrance, and while I recognize the long bleached blonde hair, I can't process the outfit.

"Emma?"

She's wearing a long, white gown that hugs her petite body perfectly, and the delicate threads of blue sewn into it make her eyes pop.

She turns to us, looking at the time on her phone. "You guys are late. I left the house twenty minutes ago."

"Why are you talking about my house like you have any right to stay there?" Nate asks bluntly.

She rolls her eyes. "You're the one who asked me to come here. I'm here."

"Why?" I ask, understanding there's something I'm not aware of.

"Someone has to keep an eye on you while I talk with people. I might get distracted, and who knows what you'll do then."

"I am *not* trying to escape," I grit out. "I don't need a fucking babysitter."

He smiles down at me, holding my hand as we start walking it. "No? Consider it a girls' night out, then."

I'm already fuming as we enter, and the heat of the place makes it so much worse. My skin is feeling oversensitive in so many places in my body that I can't focus on anything.

At least I don't have to. All I have to do is be a trophy wife, smile when he introduces me, and hold on to his arm while he speaks with people I can't stand.

Emma stands next to me the whole night, like a fucking bodyguard. It's only when Nate walks to the bar with some man that I turn to her.

"You don't have to stand right here all night. I'm not going anywhere."

She shrugs and looks around. "Yeah, I know. You wouldn't dare. But it's not like I have anything else to do anyway. Plus, the bastard pays really good."

I swallow my insult at her words. I wouldn't dare? I barely even tried to and ended up with initials carved on my fingers, pierced nipples, and chained in his fucking bedroom. What does she know about daring or not?

When I don't answer, her eyes dart to my bandaged finger. She juts her chin toward it. "You alright?"

"I don't know, Emma. My *husband* has carved his initials on my finger because I took my rings off. You tell me if I'm fucking *alright*."

There's a heavy silence between us before she whistles low. "That man has serious issues."

"He does."

"But I guess you have even bigger issues since you fell for him."

"I do—Wait, what?"

She chuckles, and that's when I realize I was not even looking at her until now. No, I was looking at Nate and the woman next to him at the bar who keeps laughing like he's fucking hilarious.

"You might as well take a gun to the girl," she says. "It'll be more efficient than the daggers you're throwing with your stare."

I shake my head, but my eyes keep going back to her. She's a real Stoneview girl. Rich, elegant, with long blonde hair and a bright smile that lights up the room. I bet she's sweet as a fucking peach.

"So you love the man."

"I don't love the man." My nostrils flare with a breath. "And why are you so interested in my love life suddenly?"

She stands right in front of me, blocking my view of my husband and the bitch clinging to him. I'm forced to take a step back, and everything touching my skin heightens. The clamp, the piercings. I feel my face flush, but I guess Emma assumes it's because of the conversation.

"If you consider your captor/captive relationship with

Nathan White your *love life*, then I can promise you, you have bigger issues than he does."

I narrow my eyes at her, jutting my chin. "Nate was right. I should have remembered your participation in said relationship before letting you stay at the house."

The hint of a smile spreads on her lips, and she nods. "I respect you for everything you've been through, Kay. I don't know what sort of brainwashing you went through to come to a point where you consider *me* your friend, but thank you for letting me stay while I settle my issues with the Lucianos."

"*Friend* is pushing it. Let's say you're my most convenient ally."

"Sure," she snorts. "If that's what you want to call it."

I grab two flutes of champagne from a passing waiter and give her one.

"Do you ever think that...we wouldn't even have hated each other if it weren't for our families? If my last name hadn't been King and yours Scott, we could have ended up in either crew."

She nods slowly. "We'd have met at school and probably just joined whichever crew. We were even in the same math class at North Shore High."

"That's because you were stupid, and I was smart. I'm a year younger than you, remember?"

She laughs into her glass of champagne. "Your brain works weirdly when it comes to numbers. No one can fucking keep up with that. I bet you know stupid shit like 2200 times 345."

I smile at her, take a sip, and say, "759,000."

"Fuck off," she snorts. She takes her phone out from the pocket of her dress—lucky bitch has pockets—and types the numbers in the calculator app.

Unsurprisingly, I was right.

She looks up at me with wide eyes. "How the hell do you do that?"

"I don't know. I love numbers. They're easy compared to words." My face twists, and she laughs some more.

"We would have been the best of friends in that math class if you'd had just given me the answers." Her eyes lower, her face falling. "But then again, you and your girls beat up Billie."

I roll my lips, remembering when some other Kings' girls and I left Emma's little sister for dead.

"I..." I hesitate, but the pain on her face is evident. "I'm sorry about that. I was trying to prove myself to my crew. I was surrounded by violence at home and had no idea how to control myself. I know it seemed like it was because you were trying to steal fucking Georgio from me, but I promise it was deeper than that in my teenage mind."

"Georgio." She looks at me, eyes sparkling with mockery. "First of all, you have issues with how possessive you are of your boyfriends." Her eyes dart to Nate and that woman. "Or husbands. Secondly, I wasn't trying to steal Georgio from you. I was trying to keep him away because I had a stupid crush on a straight girl who was my enemy."

I choke on my champagne, and some of it comes up my nose. I'm coughing loudly, bringing some attention to us as she taps my back. People roll their eyes, huffing at how unladylike we both look, but we ignore them.

I look at her with watering eyes and my jaw falling. "A crush?"

She nods.

"On me?"

She grins at me. "Talk about impossible love, huh? You were part of the Kings *and* not interested in girls."

"You're fucking with me."

But her cheeks flush, her eyes shiny.

"Oh, fuck." I laugh some more. "I'm that irresistible, then?"

"Shut up," she cackles. "I can promise you it was gone as fast as it came."

"Are you sure?" I taunt her, batting my eyelashes.

"You're fucking unbearable."

I pout at her, then smile brightly.

"I don't know how Nate does it."

I puff out a loud breath. "Believe me, he's fine."

We drink in comfortable silence, with me watching the blonde girl with all my focus. She looks young. Too young for Nate.

I hate her.

"Look," Emma cuts off my staring. "As your most convenient ally, I think I should let you know. That girl is Alexandra Delacroix. She's Xi's girlfriend, and I highly doubt Nate is hitting on her. My guess is he's manipulating her, and probably politely threatening her, because he wants Xi back in the game."

"*That's* Xi's girlfriend? And what, she finds threats hilarious?"

"Well, he probably hasn't gotten to the threat part yet. Point is, she is not interested in Nate, believe me. She attends these balls because of her mom." She looks around us. "Who I'm sure is around here somewhere. And Alex is probably just playing the nice Stoneview girl until she gets to go back to Xi."

"Why does Nate want Xi back in the game so desperately?"

"He's the best dealer around. He's smart, committed. He's got a lot of soldiers who respect him and who are used to listening to him. He knows the clients, especially in Stoneview. They trust him and they're huge consumers. He's discreet too. Nate knows all of that. Plus, he's not scared of the Wolves, and Nate has started a war by stealing their territories."

I huff to myself. I've been left out of everything. All I'm used for is signing contracts so Nate's name isn't on them. A mob wife, that's what I've fucking become.

"Nate had huge amounts coming in," I explain. "Powder is being stored at his hotels. He has people cutting in the basements, behind the storage rooms. Weed in his Baltimore warehouses while it's being packaged, and he stores the pills in Stoneview. Got a whole-ass mansion for them. He has a family living there and all. As discreet as it comes."

"How do you know all that?"

"Turns out, he's so used to having me around, he doesn't notice when I'm right there while he talks business. Plus, I looked at his books while he was in Baltimore last week. We're talking huge amounts. That's probably why he needs Xi."

"Huge like?"

"Fifty keys of powder every week, for example."

"What?" Her mouth drops open. "NSC does not have the manpower to move fifty keys a week. When Bianco was alive, we could barely move fifty keys a *month*."

"We're a team now, remember?" I say bitterly. "He's got both our crews to run everything. The Kings were already taking care of ninety percent of Silver Falls, and now he'll get us to do the surrounding areas. Other close cities. And the bastard has access to plenty of contacts all the way to D.C. He grew up there when he was with Bianco."

Emma runs her tongue across her teeth. "I guess we'll be making a lot of money, then?"

"Sure. We're also part of a huge criminal organization now. Bigger risks with the law, bigger enemies. His shit works as long as he has the upper hand, but our crews are inexperienced soldiers when it comes to organized crime."

My eyes cross with her questioning, worried gaze.

"The Lucianos and the Rossis have huge hierarchies in place." I continue. "People who are trained to be part of big organizations. They will catch up, and when they do, it's our soldiers who are going to die. And don't forget he's taking over the local arm dealers who used to work with the Wolves. And their hotels. When those wild dogs come out of their cave, they'll hit. And they'll hit hard."

"Three crime families. That's a lot of enemies."

"A lot," I confirm. "Nate is a megalomaniac. He can never get enough." My eyes narrow as I see him put a hand on the small of Alexandra's back and lead her toward the stairs. "And that will be his downfall."

I'm already taking a step forward.

"Kay," Emma calls out as she follows me. "I told you, you have nothing to worry about."

When I get to the security guard at the bottom of the stairs, I stride past him without a second look, and I hear him telling Emma that she's not allowed upstairs.

And yet I am. Is that what being Nate's wife grants you? Access wherever you want?

Too blinded by jealousy and murderous thoughts, I keep going. The double staircase leads to a balcony landing that has a view of the main room. The music can't be heard as loudly, and downstairs conversations become a low background noise.

There's one hallway, and it leads to different meeting rooms.

I push open the door to the first one, but no one is here. Just a long table and multiple chairs, a screen where one could display a presentation.

I hear voices in the room next to it and slam the door open. "Bitch, I will *end you*."

Alexandra Delacroix sits at a meeting table, wide hazel eyes on me, and Nate is standing at the other end, arms crossed and gun on the table.

"What the fuck is going on?" I grit out.

"I think my jealous wife is barging into a business meeting, that's what I think is going on."

"A *business* meeting?" I eye the girl, then him again. "Do you want to die, Nate?"

"Should I...leave?" Alexandra asks, her voice barely a squeak.

"Yes," I snap, just at the same time as Nate casually says, "You're fine."

"You're not fine," I insist. "I *will* kill you."

"She won't," he adds.

"I have for less than this."

There's a long pause. I watch Nate, gaze narrowed on him.

His tongue pokes at his cheek, and his fingers come to rub just below his ear.

His thinking finally coming to a conclusion, he turns to Alexandra. "No, it's true. She has."

Alexandra jumps up from her seat. "I'm leaving."

"No, no, wait," Nate insists as he goes after her. "You're fucking unbearable," he tells me as he walks past.

He catches Alexandra by the wrist, and I'm about to fucking lose my shit.

Why?

My main mission is to escape the man I hate. I need to stop letting rage engulf me when I see him with other women.

"I'm unbearable? You're the one flirting with women in front of my eyes!"

Alexandra whirls around, shrugging out of Nate's hold. "We were *not* flirting. I'm not interested in him. He's completely insane! Only a psycho would flirt with him."

Nate pinches his lips, clearly wanting to laugh at her backhanded insult thrown my way.

Regaining composure, he tells her, "Think about my offer. Let your mother know. And tell Xi to call me."

She cocks an eyebrow at him and crosses her arms over her chest. "I already told you. I've had people threaten me to get to Xi before. It didn't change anything."

"And yet you came up here with me."

"You said you'd hurt my mom!"

"And I absolutely would have," he answers calmly. "The people who threatened you before weren't me. They didn't have the power I do, and they didn't mention taking away everything Xi worked so hard for."

Her chest rises and falls rapidly as she takes a step back. "He'll call. That's *it*."

"That's all I need. Now, if you don't mind, my wife is desperate for attention."

Alexandra shakes her head, her long blonde waves bobbing as she does so. "Goodbye."

She closes the door behind her, and Nate turns to me, but I talk before he does.

"Her fucking *mom,* Nate? You threatened her mom?"

He shrugs. "Business."

"That's fucked up. What do you even want with her mom?"

"She has connections, and mainly information about the Lucianos. She could be a great help."

He takes a step toward me, but I take one back.

"And Xi? What did you say?"

He shrugs, as if his threats were nothing. "I know the people who can cut all the funding that goes to her mom's art gallery. They are so deep in my pockets they've not seen the light of day in a long time. She's the one who supports Xi's painting career. If he doesn't start working for me, I'll cut it all off, and he'll have nothing and no choice anymore."

He stops right in front of me. "Aren't they, like, billionaires or something?"

"Alex's mom is, yes. But Xi won't take a cent from them." He shakes his head. "Pride, am I right?"

Standing right in front of me, he looks down into my eyes as I plaster my ass against the table. "Now." He softly takes my hand, bringing it to his lips. "Let's punish you for barging into my meeting. You're very possessive, my little sunflower."

My heart accelerates, my body suddenly aware of the toy he attached to me.

"Do I need to remind you that you stabbed a man's hand for barely even flirting with me? And I don't even think that was his intention."

"Do I need to remind you who makes the rules?"

I grit my teeth, hating that we still have no equal footing in this relationship, and yet I'm completely aware that my body is loving it.

"Come," he purrs as he drags me out of the room and back to the hallway. I wobble on the heels as he stops on the balcony, looking down at the people drinking and chatting. Leading me in front of him, he lets go of my hand as he keeps me between his hard body and the barrier.

He takes my purse, the short chain falling off my shoulder easily. "Bend over, baby."

My heart stops.

"W-what?"

His free hand presses between my shoulder blades. "I said bend over," he murmurs in my ear. "Look down at everyone downstairs to see who looks up while I fuck you."

"You can't be serious." But the excitement is already bubbling through my veins.

I'm hot, my body heat rising at an incredible pace. Before I bend over, he brings the chain of my handbag to my mouth.

"Open."

A haze takes over me, my ears ringing from the raucous downstairs, eyes heavy from the lust suddenly overtaking me.

And I open my mouth. I let him put the chain between my teeth, and close when he tells me to close. He bends over with a soft touch, and the second my upper body hangs over the barrier, I have to clench my teeth to not let the bag fall all the way to the guests downstairs.

"If I were you," he says as he nudges my legs apart with his foot, settling himself between them. "I would keep that beautiful, smart mouth closed." He brings the hem of my dress to my hips, and plays with the clit clamp, pulling it ever-so slightly and letting go. "What if your purse falls? It'll make everyone look up. And then they'll see you being fucked by your husband against the railing."

My breathing accelerates, and I panic when he thrusts his fingers into my pussy. Not only because it's insanely wet, but because it pushes a moan up my throat, and my jaw is desperate to fall slack.

I can't talk back, can't say anything, and instead of fighting him, I push my ass against him.

"What an eager little slut you are. I'm so proud of you."

He keeps teasing me with his fingers, pushing in and out, slapping my pussy to make sure I hear how wet I am.

And when I feel the crown of his dick at my entrance, I'm forced to clench my teeth harder. He pushes in so slowly I'm bound to faint from the teasing. I want to beg with all I have, and I have no way to do so with my mouth. So I push against him and squirm when he holds me back with two hands on my hips.

He takes his time pushing inside me, and I squeeze my eyes shut when I become full of him. Nate is long and thick, but I'm desperate tonight, and I clench around his length.

Oh god.

When he starts moving, following his own pleasurable pace, I'm forced to stay still and take it. He takes it slowly, rolling his hips sensually, as if we have time for this, when there are hundreds of people downstairs.

And despite all my attempts, he keeps it that way. He takes his time, and my hands on the railing tighten to a white-knuckled grip. I breathe through my nose as his pace slightly increases, my head falling farther down as my muscles give up.

With painful precision, he harshly thrusts inside me, slow but forceful. And with intent to kill, he slides a hand in front of me, flicks the clit clamp, once, twice...and three times before I'm broken at the seams by a powerful orgasm.

He keeps going, fucking me into the railing until he

tightens the clamp and sends me into a second high. The blood rushing to my nub is painful and electrifying, making my clit throb in the best way possible. The release is overwhelming, enhanced when I feel him come inside me. In a blink of carelessness, I open my mouth to take in much-needed air, and gasp when I feel the bag slipping past my lips.

My eyes widen in panic, just as Nate's hand catches it. I hear him laughing behind me, and I'm ready to fight through the orgasm haze and tell him to go fuck himself, when I feel his hand pressing against my pussy.

"Squeeze, baby. Keep me inside you." He pushes his fingers inside. "Someone is going to feel my cum leaking down her legs for the rest of the night." Straightening me up, he turns me around and pinches the clamp.

"You can't keep this on you too long, no matter how greedy you are."

He pulls it off, and my mouth falls open, a scream stuck in my throat as I feel the pain from the blood rushing back to my nub.

His phone vibrates in his pocket, and he pulls it out. As he looks down at the screen, his face tenses. "Well, that's annoying."

"What?"

"It seems someone just tried to set fire to my Baltimore warehouse." He looks up at me, grabbing me by the elbow. "He got caught and the fire was controlled, but we need to go."

"Why do we need to go so quickly if the damage has been avoided?" I blurt out as he drags me with him down the stairs.

"Because he's going to get tortured, and we'll know who sent him very soon. I need to be able to act by the time I know. And we need to reinforce security everywhere else."

Fuck. This is bad.

He takes me all the way to the foyer and leaves me there. "I'll get our jackets."

He doesn't look panicked or even in a rush, but I notice the tension in his shoulders as he turns into another hallway.

I huff, searching for my phone in my purse. The second I find it, I walk outside, ready to make a quick call with the little privacy I'm finding. There's a small area at the top of the stairs that's empty, the noise from inside completely cut off.

I turn my back to the stairs, keeping an eye on the entrance to check for Nate.

I'm fumbling through the numbers I want to type, when I feel a gun at the back of my head. I've had enough to know. That heavy, cold pressure of a muzzle cannot be mistaken for anything else.

I keep my calm as I swallow thickly. I don't even know who it is, but it's never a good thing when they have a gun.

"Give me the phone, Kayla." A woman.

Raising my hands by my head, I show the phone, and she takes it out of my hand.

"I promise you this can go smoothly. You get in the car with me, we go on a little road trip, and I get to teach your husband not to fuck with us. But if you like acting brave, I can make this very, *very* painful. And I can make it last hours too. It's a little trick of mine."

I lick my lips, keeping my hands high. "The gun really isn't needed—"

"Kayla!" The second I hear Emma's voice and her clicking heels, the woman behind me wraps her forearm around my throat, dragging me to her chest as the gun comes to my temple. Fuck, she feels really tall, and I'm in heels too. And *fuck*, she's strong.

All I see is Emma stopping in her tracks, her eyes widening as they look above my head.

Her voice trembles when she finally says her name. "Lucky."

Oh.

Fuck.

They sent *Lucky* for this?

"Little Emma Scott." Her voice resonates against my back as she talks. "How's your dad?"

Emma's hands tremble by her sides as they curl into fists.

"If you take her...you'll have Nathan White after you. You won't survive that, I promise you."

Lucky laughs. "Oh, sweetheart, why do you think we're taking her? He's not after us. We're after him. But hey, since you're here."

I feel the gun leave me, and the only thing I see is Lucky's arm extending toward Emma.

She puts her hands in front of herself. "Lucky, don't..."

"Don't!" I gasp, barely able to breathe in her hold. "Don't kill her. I'm coming." I take a breath. "I'm coming with you."

"One doesn't cancel the other one out," she says calmly.

"Nate is going to be out in a minute," I babble. "And he's armed. Armed and really fucking angry already."

"Ah." I feel Lucky nod above my head. "The Baltimore warehouse."

The door opens, sounds of the party flooding out, and Nate is there.

He pauses, analyzing the situation for a split second before his hand shoots inside his jacket.

"Lucky, you fuckin b—"

But her gun is already back against my head. "Nate, come on," she chuckles. "Let's not hurt your pretty wife."

"Get your fucking hands off her," he growls.

He's already striding toward her, but Emma holds him back. "Stop," she orders him. "She'll fucking shoot her. You know she will."

And when I hear the click of the safety, I'm starting to think she doesn't give a shit about taking me with her, as long as Nate learns to not mess with the Luciano family.

With that knowledge in mind, when she presses her gun harder against my temple, a whimper escapes me.

It's one of the rare times in my life I believe I might die.

"Let her take me," I rasp, my voice trembling.

His jaw is so tight, his teeth are bound to break.

"Kayla." His tone is stern, but there's nothing I can do to obey him.

"Just let her."

His nostrils flare as he takes a shaky breath, and I can safely say I've never seen him like this. For a man who is always ten moves ahead, in control, seeing him so helpless is one of the most difficult things I've ever had to witness.

"I'll find you." His words are barely formed, teeth grating.

"I know," I whisper, as my throat tightens.

"Cute. Let's go." Lucky drags me by the hair as she goes down the stairs, her gun still trained on me.

She takes me to a blacked-out SUV waiting at the bottom of the stairs and forces me inside, following right after me.

I can finally see her properly. She's wearing a dark gray

suit, long red hair falling all the way to her waist. When her green eyes snap to me, I startle back.

There is nothing but death raging in them, and my heart races. She's got a scar almost shaped like a tear at the corner of her right eye, and it somehow makes her look even more terrifying.

I thought I was a tough girl, but I don't think I ever imposed this much terror on anyone.

"Make yourself comfortable," she says as she taps the front seat. The car starts and she turns to me again, her smile chilling. "New York City is a five-hour drive."

35

NATHAN

Rain - grandson, Jessie Reyez

"I don't give a shit about your warning, Sam. I'm almost there anyway."

"We're going to fucking die," Emma grunts next to me.

I'm not sure if she's talking about the speed at which I'm driving, or the fact that she knows we're about to enter New York City and go straight to the Luciano's compound.

Probably both.

I waited one entire hour before following Lucky to New York City. I knew if she saw me following her, I would risk Kay being killed. But there was nothing stopping me once I knew I couldn't catch up with their car.

"*Nathan,*" Sam snaps over the car speaker. "*Vito is well aware that you know where to find him. He either isn't keeping Kayla at his compound, or he is waiting for you to do exactly the stupid shit you're doing right now. He will kill you on sight.*"

"He wants to talk, or he would have killed her by now and sent a message. If he's keeping her alive, he's waiting

471

for me. I'll talk to him." Taking a staggered breath, I grit my teeth. "Check my messages again," I tell Emma.

She opens my app and shakes her head. "Nothing new."

All they did was send a picture of Kayla in a basement, sitting on a chair with her hands tied behind her back. She didn't look hurt, but I don't know how long that'll last.

"*He will kill you.*"

"He will talk. I've worked with that man for as long as I can remember. He doesn't feel threatened by competition. He knows there's enough work for everyone. But I should have told him my plans."

"*He's probably pissed that you took his suppliers and that you're angering the Wolves. Especially knowing the Bratva still associates you with him. It's not like you sent a memo to tell everyone you weren't associating with the Cosa Nostra anymore. Your actions have repercussions on his family.*"

Fuck, fuck. I hate when he's right.

"I'm almost there," I repeat. "I just don't fucking understand why he didn't just...*call.*"

"*Because you're not an associate anymore.*"

I huff. The look in Kayla's eyes when she asked me to let her leave with Lucky broke something inside me. I think it was the remnant of my sanity. I need to see her, and I need to see her *alive.* The second she's out of the Lucianos' hold, I'll be able to talk with them.

"You stay in the car," I tell Emma the second I stop outside their compound. There's a guard waiting in front of their gates, and I open my window.

"Tell Vito Nathan White is here."

He kisses his teeth, arranging the machine gun on his shoulder and eyeing whatever is inside the car.

"Before I gouge your eyes out would be a good idea," I add.

He presses a walkie talkie clipped on his jacket and announces my name. A few seconds later, the gates open.

"Fuck," Emma huffs next to me. "Fuck, we're so going to die."

"Emma," I say, my voice dropping from anger. "I have very little patience right now. Do yourself a favor and don't make this worse."

"What if they kill her? Shit, two months ago, I hated the girl, and then your psycho ass made me feel bad for her and like her and now I don't want her to die."

I stop my car in front of a gothic mansion that makes it look like we've traveled all the way to the English countryside. In this remote part of the city, the Lucianos have enough money to keep building and expanding their compound.

I've been here before. I've had meetings with Vito and Emiliano, his dad, many times when I worked for Bianco. Hell, we've known each other since we were kids. But since being out of prison, I haven't contacted Vito to tell him my plans, and that's been a big fucking mistake. Especially since I took over the Canadian suppliers.

I groan to myself. I've been so focused on Kayla and my obsession with her, that I've not been running my business how I should have. And now her life is in danger. And theirs too, since I'm going to kill everyone in my way if they don't let me get to her.

Two guards approach our car, and I turn to Emma. "I'm going to say this one more time. You stay in here, do nothing, say nothing, and don't fucking look at anyone. I'll be back soon."

She hits her head against the headrest. "Starting to work for you was the biggest fucking mistake ever."

"I'm sure your bank account disagrees."

I open my door, nodding at the two guards as they walk me to the entrance. The outside lights are on, basking the dark porch in a yellow glow. It might have been the beginning of the night when they took Kay, but it's two a.m. now that we've had to drive five hours.

I dust off the tuxedo I'm wearing as I enter the marbled entrance and do my best to act fresh and collected, even though inside I'm already murdering everyone.

When a third person approaches, I'm already taking out my two guns from their holsters. I don't need to be told anything. I've danced this dance many times before.

I hand him my guns and stand still as he pats me down. When he nods at the others, they walk with me again. I already know where I'm going. Straight to Emiliano's office.

There are two more guards posted there as we approach, and one of them opens the door for me. I straighten my shoulders and walk inside the warm room.

Mahogany is the main theme here, and the yellow lights give it a comfortable appearance. The bookshelves all around the room remind me of my foster dad's office. Bianco kept tons of books on his shelves too. I remember staring at them when he forced himself on me.

Shrugging the thought away, I advance inside the office as the door closes behind me. I ignore Lucky sitting on a dark green leather sofa on the side of the room, and instead go toward the desk, even though I know her eyes are on me like a hawk on its prey.

"Nathan," Emiliano greets me, standing up as if seeing an old friend. He comes around his desk to shake my hand and clap my shoulder gently.

His son is next. Vito straightens from where he was leaning against his father's desk, his dark eyes digging into me, and shakes my hand briefly.

"Please, please, take a seat," Emiliano says, pointing at one of the burgundy leather armchairs in front of his desk.

I unbutton my tux and take a seat, folding an ankle over my knee, and look over my shoulder. "Watch and learn, Lucky, it's called politeness. Maybe next time, try to talk before threatening to kill everyone."

She cocks an eyebrow at me, but only gives me a smug smile as a response.

I turn back to Emiliano, and he waves a hand dismissively. "Ah, you know how Lucky is. We love her because she has her own methods."

I dig my gaze into his, pausing for a second so I don't reach for the paper holder on his desk and smash it against his skull.

"I want to see my wife, Emiliano. It's a low blow to go for a man's family, and you know I never would have."

He nods, but Vito takes over quickly. "Oh, please. Your psycho ass would kill a blind man's guide dog and not feel a thing. Don't talk to us about a low blow."

Would I, really? No, I'm sure I wouldn't do that. Who knows.

"Nathan," Emiliano says slowly, picking his words carefully, even though the ball is in his court. That man must never be underestimated. He'll tell you he's about to kill you with a reassuring voice and a sorry stare. He's been in this business long enough to not need useless violence. "Your dad—"

"Foster dad."

He nods. "Mateo Bianco was pointlessly ruthless and look where it led him. You don't want to be like him."

475

"I'm not like him."

"You took our suppliers. The Canadians work for us. You separated yourself from the Cosa Nostra, cutting all ties with us and the Rossis. That's a move he would have done. Hungry for world domination, drunk on power."

I roll my eyes, not needing a life lesson from someone barely older than Bianco was.

"Have the Canadians, then. I don't care. But I want to see Kayla. Right now."

"You'll see her," Vito continues. "You just have to switch places with her."

"Fine." I don't even hesitate one second.

"Fine?" Vito repeats.

"Fine. Tie me up in your basement. Torture me, cut all my fingers, be a brave Cosa Nostra boy. I don't fucking care, Vito. Let her go."

There's a low, mocking whistle behind me, and Lucky laughs to herself. "The boy is in love, gentlemen."

My head snaps toward hers, and I offer her a chilling smile. "You should be worried about what I'm willing to do for her. Who I'm willing to kill."

"I'm shaking, Nate," she says with a voice as flat as mine.

There's always that funny thing that happens between two psychopaths. Not only do we recognize each other, but we also weirdly fucking hate each other. We can see through the masks we've spent years practicing, and the effort we've put into making others believe we're emotionally functioning falls to the wayside all of a sudden.

That's how Lucky and I interact. Because we're exactly the same, and I can't fucking stand her. It's like looking in a mirror. Fuck, I must be exhausting to other people.

"We're about to spend a lot of time together, Lucky," I tell her. "You should be a little nicer to me if you don't want me to drive you insane."

"The time we spend together depends on how long I keep you alive."

"Lucky," Vito huffs, already done with our interaction. "Let's move."

I stand, doing the button of my tux, and give Emiliano a nod as I follow the other two out. The Lucianos won't kill me.

Or at least, I don't think they will.

It wouldn't be my first go at spending a bit of time in a mafia family's basement. Not even theirs. There'll be a bit of pain. They'll get the Canadians back, probably a lot of my business, and we'll agree to stay out of each other's way. Or at least me out of theirs. My business will hurt, but I won't die. Mainly, Kayla will be free, and that's all that counts.

We go down the cement stairs that lead to their basement of tortures, and the coppery smell of blood hits my nostrils, setting my nerves on fire.

She better not be hurt.

My breath catches in my throat when I see her. She's sitting in the exact same position from the picture. Nothing has changed at all. She's tied up but unharmed, fine, *alive*.

"Nate," she sighs, but her face falls, and her eyes don't shine like I expected them too.

She's not happy.

"Why did you come?" She shakes her head.

Is she disappointed I'm here?

"Why did I come?" I repeat. "Why did I come to rescue you from kidnapping? Because you're my wife, Kayla. And no one gets to hurt you."

Her head falls forward as Vito undoes the cuffs behind her. She brings her wrists to her front, massaging them.

"Get up."

His order pisses me off, and I let him know right away. "Watch your tone with her."

Looking at me, he presses his lips together. "Don't you think you're in enough trouble as it is with us?"

Instead of answering, I talk to Kayla, who's still sitting. "Get up, Kay. Now."

"Nate—"

"Get up!" I bark harshly. I need her out of here. I need her safe.

"Let's just go," she tells me weakly as she finally stands. She's still wearing her satin dress, the expensive heels, her diamond bracelets I can use to cuff her.

She's beautiful, breathtaking despite looking exhausted from being held here.

She falls into my arms, breathing me in, and I wrap my arms around her waist. My heartbeat settles with her against me. "You're fine. Everything's fine."

She shakes her head in the crook of my neck. "It's not..."

I don't let her get into her emotions. I step away from her, pushing her to the side, and sit in her place.

"You're going to go home with Emma, little sunflower. And you're going to wait there until I come back."

"Which won't be any time soon," Lucky adds brusquely.

I narrow my gaze at her, letting Vito cuff my hands behind my back, making me nothing more than a harmless victim.

But I'm not scared. As I watch Kayla take a step back,

knowing she's safe and free to go, I know this was the best decision I ever made in my life.

Until Lucky pulls out her gun.

And gives it to Kayla.

When my wife points the gun at me, my heart stops.

36

KAYLA

Godless - BANKS

He chuckles to himself. That's what he does first.

My heart is already breaking, and the bastard is practically laughing like the psycho he is.

"Oh, little sunflower," he finally says as he calms down. "It doesn't matter how many times I was warned, I still underestimated you."

"I know," I rasp, barely any power in my voice.

This does not feel good. Not at all. It was meant to be the moment I find my freedom, my happiness. Where is it?

"Tell me," he says. "Tell me how you did this. I want to see the extent of your scheming little mind."

"You don't need to know." I shake my head. I feel like I might be sick.

"Amuse me. When did you start planning?"

"The... The day you sent Emma to check on me in the bathroom. I took Lucky's number from her phone."

"Huh. What else?"

"I contacted her on the phone you gave me. Told her to

pass on messages to Vito for me. That you were building your own army. That you were going to start wars." My gaze drops, unable to hold his enchanting eyes. "That you needed to be stopped."

As usual, I'm sacrificing something for survival. Except this time, it feels horrible. Disgusting.

"Look at me, baby. It's okay. That was smart. But I checked your phone regularly. I didn't see anything there."

Oh, god. I can't listen to this. The way he calls me *baby*, the way he's the one trying to reassure me... His praise should be reserved for the love we share. Not for this situation.

"I always deleted everything."

"And remembered Lucky's phone number every time you needed to text her?"

I nod, looking up at him again.

He's smiling. "Of course. Numbers are easy for you. And when did you plan this?" He looks around, obviously talking about his current predicament.

"A few weeks ago... Fuck, Nate. I wasn't going to go ahead with it. I wasn't. And then yesterday...you could have fucking saved yourself had you not been such a possessive asshole."

That drags a soft laugh out of him. "I wasn't going to let you go. This is your only solution. But you made me worry. I thought your life was at risk."

"I know." It takes all of me not to say *sorry* for making him worry.

He sighs. "I'm glad you're okay. Was the kidnapping from the town hall planned too?"

"I didn't realize they were going to send Lucky to actually kidnap me." Her hard gaze darts to the redhead.

"There really was no need, was there? The plan was for me to just get in the car and..."

"And you knew I was going to come for you."

"You've got a soft spot for me, Nate. And let's say you hadn't come for me. Then I would have been free, and you wouldn't have been hurt. But you did and...well, the Lucianos wanted you here."

"I will always find you." He smiles dumbly, like this is not a life-or-death situation.

"Stop." Distress threatens to strangle me. "Please, stop."

His eyes flick to the gun and back to my face. "Sam warned me. He said you earned your reputation for a reason." He nods to himself, like remembering the conversation. "He said I should kill you before I become one of the people who wish they had."

I lick my lips, but they still tremble when I breathe in. "Do you wish you had?"

The hint of another genuine smile breaks his flat lips. "No."

"Even though I'm about to kill you."

He nods slowly. "Even though you're about to kill me, baby. I don't regret one single moment with you."

What?

No, Kayla. He's manipulating you. Again.

I shake my head, chasing the thoughts away. "I told you, Nate. I *told you* to give me back my freedom. I *told you* to let me go, that I wouldn't adapt." I pause for a split second, losing my voice. "I told you yesterday that I wouldn't forgive you."

"You did. And I didn't listen."

"Why?" I croak. "Why didn't you listen? Why didn't you just give me what I needed?"

"Because." He shrugs and shakes his head. "I don't

know. It wasn't an option for me, little sunflower. I have no way of explaining it."

"Kayla." Vito's voice brings me out of the conversation. "You need to do this. The longer you wait, the harder it will be."

"Just... give me a fucking minute."

I swallow thickly as my hand trembles. I have killed countless men before. My hand has never shaken. I crack my neck, looking deep into his eyes.

"Name it," I push out with a wobbling voice.

His eyebrows shoot up to his forehead, surprise clear on his face. It's one of the only emotions that is so clear on him. It breaks through the mask, softens his features.

"I don't know."

"Nate," I plead. I'm holding the gun, he's bound to a chair, and yet I'm still the one begging. "You know your weakness. It's me. You let me get under your skin. You got addicted to me. You wanted to keep me safe, to protect me. You know what that is. Like warming up your hands on the coldest winter day. You bit more than you could chew. You did."

"I did," he admits, his eyes never once leaving mine. "All you're saying is true. But it's your choice to get your freedom, not something I will give you. Put the gun down, we'll go home, and everything will go back as it was."

"*I can't do that*," I hiss between clenched teeth. My pulse thunders in my ears, my hand holding the gun now sweating. "I can't go back to your house as your captive. Tell me how you feel. Name it, and maybe...maybe we can move forward."

"Kayla—"

"Name it!" I yell. "I did it for you. Every day, every time

you asked, I named it. For once, please. *Just this one time.* Name it."

"Love."

His voice is flat, his eyes empty, his face relaxed.

But the way he swallows, his Adam's apple bobbing up and down roughly, speaks to me. The way he shifts in his seat is telling. He cracks his neck, and his shoulders twitch with the need to move. Maybe his hand wants to rub just below his ear.

"I am in love with you, Kayla."

Weirdly, not much changes within me at his admission. I already knew.

Because Nathan White has his own language, one I understand, even if I didn't think I could. When he doesn't speak, I hear him, and when he can't express himself, I listen.

I knew because there is a connection between us that feelings cannot express, not even if we name it over and over again. It simply exists without a name, so strongly that it's indescribable.

No one else but us can comprehend it.

Despite my burning shoulder and my entire body begging me to drop the weapon, I straighten my arm. "Say it, Nate." My throat is so tight I can hardly speak, and the tears that threaten to fall are becoming painfully unbearable as they burn my eyes.

I don't want to do this.

But I will if he doesn't give me a choice.

"Say you'll give me some freedom. All I need to know is that I'll be free to come and go as I please. We can give this a chance if we just start from the beginning. If I'm free to choose."

He smiles at me, and as rare as it is, I see the apology in

it. "I can't, little sunflower. You're mine. If I give you freedom, I give you a chance to leave me. If not today, tomorrow. If not tomorrow, maybe in a year, two, ten. No. I can't have that. I'd rather you kill me than live with a chance of you deciding you don't want me and walking away."

"I won't!" I cry out.

"You might. Shoot. I don't care. Life isn't worth living with a risk of you finding out my demons are too much for you to handle. My heart can't beat without you around... isn't that the same as dying anyway? I won't give you what you want to hear. Shoot."

"Please, Nate," I whisper.

It's when his brow furrows that I realize my cheeks are wet.

"You're crying. I've never seen you cry."

"I'm crying because I'm going to kill you. Because you're breaking my heart."

"I don't want to break your heart. But I won't set you free. I am your sun, little sunflower. Now and forever."

A sob wrecks me, tearing through my chest. "Nate..."

The look of absolute resolution in his eyes wrenches another sob out of me. Tears are streaming infinitely down my cheeks, my stomach twisting.

If I don't have my freedom, I don't have my family. And I can't do that. Not to them.

We're at an impasse with only one solution to move forward, and he clearly knows it too.

"Is there anything you want to tell me?" He digs his eyes into mine. "Anything, Kayla."

I deny him any additional information with a stiff headshake.

"I'm sorry, little sunflower. That we won't get to live through it all."

"Please..."

"That it wasn't for better or worse. That we're not making it. I..." He swallows thickly. "I really wanted us to make it. I wanted to see you happy. I love you."

I wince, my chest shaking as I try to breathe. I aim the gun at his chest. Everything hurts from the inside out. A sickness engulfs me, my muscles aching.

"I love you too, my sun." And without looking away from him, I shoot.

Blood splashes against my face, and the smell of gunpowder chokes me.

His white shirt soaks in the ugly, thick, red liquid, and his eyes stay on mine.

He smiles as he takes his last breath.

He smiles at me like I did him a favor.

Like he really didn't want to live if it was without me.

37

KAYLA

I Found - Amber Run

I drop to the floor, my knees unable to carry me.

"Oh my god!" I scream, head shaking rapidly. "No, no, no..."

"It's okay." Vito is on me suddenly. I forgot he was here. Him and his psycho of an enforcer. "You did the right thing."

He takes the gun away from me, at the same time as Lucky advances toward Nate.

"No, don't touch him!"

"For fuck's sake, Vito. Get her out of here." She huffs, like I'm a bother to her.

Vito grips me by the shoulders, lifting me back up. He holds me tightly as he walks me out. I watch Lucky put a white sheet over Nate's body. His head has fallen forward.

"He's dead," I sob as Vito drags me upstairs.

"He's dead," he confirms sternly. "It's okay, Kayla. We'll take care of it from now on."

"He's dead," I repeat like a crazy woman.

He brings me all the way to the door. "Listen. It's fine. Our family will take over the North Shore, over the whole Silver Falls and Stoneview area. We'll take care of you, okay?" He squeezes me harder. "You earned our respect, Kayla. We'd already heard about you, but now we know why you're the ruthless King. Well done."

I couldn't care less about the North Shore right now. I would rather die than live up to my reputation. I can't fucking breathe.

I killed Nathan White.

I killed my husband.

I killed the only person who made me feel every single emotion on the spectrum. But the one he made me feel the strongest was too much for either of us to handle in a healthy way.

The toxicity killed us.

I killed him, and his death killed me.

Vito opens the door to a car. Emma is already in the passenger's seat. Her eyes widen, and she jumps out. Maybe it's my state, maybe it's the blood on my face.

"What happened? Kayla, are you okay?"

I look at her, swaying on the spot. "I killed him."

"*What?*" It's not only the shock that makes it worse, it's the genuine pain that floods her features. "Kayla..."

"Go," Vito says as he pushes me into the passenger seat. He puts my seatbelt on, I think. I can't register anything anymore, only the smell of Nate in the car. His car.

When Emma starts the engine, I look at Vito's mansion with a desperate cry. As if it isn't already too late. If I just look a little bit longer, maybe he'll run out. Maybe I missed. Maybe...

He doesn't come out.

He doesn't because he's dead. The feeling of his blood

on my face will forever haunt me. Just like his rare smiles, the flat tone of his voice, or the way he could hug me so tightly.

We're on the highway when Emma finally speaks.

"Why?" she rasps.

I can't talk about it. All I can do is ask for her phone. She doesn't have Caden's number in it, but I find Billie, his fiancée. Of course, she's Emma's sister.

When Billie picks up, her voice is heavy with sleep.

"Put Caden on the phone."

Something scratches, then there's movement. A door opens, voices, and more scratching the mic. She was probably sleeping and Caden is somewhere else in the house like the insomniac he is.

"*Kay? Are you alright?*"

"I killed him."

There's a long pause. I know he can hear the tears in my voice, and he's probably wondering if he was right or not when he mentioned Stockholm syndrome.

"*Good,*" he finally says. "*I'm still in town. I will see you soon.*"

"A few hours," I answer.

My emotions are leaving me, and I'm starting to feel number and number as I keep going.

"*Okay. Come to Elliot's house.*"

I nod, even though he can't see me.

"*Kayla.*" He scratches his throat. "*Mom is here. She hadn't heard from you in two weeks, and she didn't know what to do, so she drove all the way here.*"

A sense of relief finally envelops me. I did the right thing.

I'm free, and I'm going to see the two pieces of my soul that have kept me surviving for the last month.

Something knocks against my chest. My heart. It's weak, broken, reminding me that I'll never truly be free without the man I love.

For now, I have to force myself to ignore it. I must.

"At Elliot's too?"

"Yeah. We're all here."

I nod. "I hope they're awake by the time I get there."

"I'll make sure they are."

"Thank you," I whisper.

Emma doesn't try to ask about Nate again. She spares me the torture. All she does is put a hand on my thigh and squeezes tightly.

"It'll be okay," she tells me softly.

I let my head fall against the headrest and look at the dark of the night through the window. "I don't know."

It's eight a.m. when Emma parks in front of Elliot's house. I haven't said another word the whole ride and neither has she. Not even when she saw me wipe Nate's blood off my face. I'm cold, my muscles so tense they ache like I ran a marathon. But I push myself to walk to the door. I can already hear voices and giggles, and my heart swells with joy.

I open the door without knocking, practically running inside. Elliot and Ethan are on their living room sofa. In between them, Jade is playing with a little girl on her lap. And at their small table in a corner, Caden and my mom are sitting with another girl, trying to get her to eat some breakfast.

Everyone's heads turn to Emma and me, and a sudden shriek of joy resonates in the room.

"Mommy!!"

My little one on Jade's lap jumps off, tripping on her own two feet as she runs toward me.

I drop to my knees, the weight of the last month taking me down.

But when I open my arms and Lia jumps into them, everything else disappears.

"Mommy, I missed you. I missed you. I missed you, Mommy."

I smile into her black hair, inhaling her like a drug. She always does that thing of repeating the same sentence in different variations and hearing her do that makes me feel like I'm home.

I instinctively wrap her into one arm, keeping the other one wide open as I hear small steps coming our way. Livie might not show excitement the same way her twin does, but she still runs toward me, falling into my arms in silence. All I need is her sigh of relief to feel whole.

Finally. Finally, I'm reunited with my family.

Finally, my heart is fixed.

Except for that one tiny, fissured spot with Nate's name on it.

38

KAYLA

Lost - Ollie

I spend the whole day with my daughters. The whole day and then the rest of the week. But then that week turns into two, into four, and into a month.

And then a month turns into six weeks.

The whole time I refuse to participate in any conversation other than ones that include the wellbeing of Lia and Livie. Caden took care of having the bedrooms in our old house redone. When I walk in today, with Livie on my hip and holding Lia by the hand as she walks next to me, I can't even smell the burn anymore.

"Mommy, it's so pretty! Do you see, Mommy? It's so pretty. So pretty."

I laugh and let her hand go as she runs around the house.

"Cade, you didn't have to have the floors and everything redone. I thought we agreed on just making the house safe and livable."

He cocks an eyebrow at me and pulls at my ponytail. "That carpet was not livable, believe me."

I huff. I try to put Livie down, but she holds on tighter, so I shift her to my other hip. "I don't know how I'll pay you back," I admit. "I have nothing."

That's not true. I have the ten thousand I stole from Nate, but I'm saving that for whatever I need for the girls over the next few months while I get back on my feet. And I have the hotels Nate put in my name. I have fifty fucking keys of cocaine coming to them every week. For now, Emma is working with all that. She's collecting the money, handling the dealers. Sam is letting her because she told him I was out of the game, but behind his back, she promised to give me shares of everything.

I'm surprised he's letting me live at all, but I can't focus on that. I have to focus on anything else but the things that remind me of Nate.

Either way, I can't touch that money. It doesn't feel right. It doesn't belong to me. It belongs to my dead husband.

I swallow thickly, running a hand over my forehead.

"Kay, it's fine. Billie and I can afford it, okay? She's a UFC fighter, for fuck's sake."

"Great," I bite out. "The kid I beat up and left for dead when I was a teenager just paid for my house to be redone. I've officially reached rock bottom."

He rolls his eyes, but I don't want to talk anymore. I walk into the living room, nudging Livie's cheek with my nose. "Do you like it, sweetie? We can live in our old home again."

"She doesn't talk, Kayla. Give up." My mom's cigarette-broken voice makes my spine stiffen.

She's still here "helping," she says. Apparently, she

doesn't trust me with the girls. Not after I had to leave them with her. I think the truth is, she has nothing, especially no money, and she was surviving on me sending her money to take care of the twins. So now she's here.

"I know that, Mom." I try to keep my voice light in front of Livie. "But we won't stop trying, right, my lovely girl? No, we won't."

In the back rooms, I hear Lia gasping and cooing at how pretty the house is now. Livie has never said a word. She makes noises sometimes, especially when she cries, but even those are rare. She's quiet. I tried not to worry at first, but when Lia started becoming a chatterbox and spilling a hundred words per second, I knew something was wrong. I hate to think of it that way. There's nothing *wrong* with my daughter because we understand each other perfectly. She just doesn't want the rest of the world to understand her.

"Mom, go back to West Virginia." Caden's voice is void of any emotion, not caring for even a split second what she thinks of him.

"And leave my granddaughters with a criminal? I don't think so."

I spin around, gritting my teeth, and yet it doesn't stop the words from spilling. "You never minded leaving your children with a criminal *and* an abuser. I don't see the problem now."

She shakes her head, uncaring of what I have to say as she grabs a cigarette from the pack that is constantly glued to her hand.

"I did what I had to do to survive. Sacrifices had to be made. You wouldn't understand."

"I wouldn't–I *shot*"—I mouth this word so Livie doesn't hear—"the man I love to get back to my daughters. To protect them. What the *fuck*"—I forget to mouth that one —"do you know about sacrifices? You ran away, you stupid b–"

"Alright. Let's go take a breather outside." Caden gets between us, and I realize how close I had gotten to her. Threateningly close. I'm only realizing now my hand is fisted around her pack of cigarettes, my fingertips grazing her skin.

"You're a coward," I hiss low as Caden separates me from her. He walks me to the kitchen, and to the door that leads to the small porch on the side of the house.

My back is killing me. The girls are so heavy now that it's not as easy as it used to be to carry them for as long as Livie likes to be carried. I take a step toward Caden, nudging her his way, and she lets go of me to go into his arms.

"Here we go," he tells her. "Hey, pretty."

She cuddles against his neck and puts her little thumb in her mouth. I stay quiet as I watch her midnight eyes close slowly. She doesn't even try to fight it, sleeping comfortably in her uncle's arms.

"The man you love, huh?"

I run my palms against my face and press my tear ducts with my middle fingers. "Please, Cade. Don't."

"He k—" He stops himself, holding himself back in front of his niece. Instead, he mouths the words "*kidnapped you.*"

"I know, thank you," I answer, deadpan. "I was there."

"Then act like it. I told you this was some sort of Stockholm syndrome shit."

"Okay." I shrug.

"Okay, what?"

"Okay. It's Stockholm syndrome. There."

"What?" he hisses. "Are you stupid? Take that shit back."

"Why does it matter?" I rasp. "He's d—" My own grief cuts me off, heavy in my chest, tight in my throat. "He's dead."

As my lower lip trembles, even the October cold wind can't cool the waves of dread burning through my body. "I love him, and he's dead."

A tear rolls down my cheek, and I wipe it. I wipe the next one too, but I can't wipe all of them. There are too many.

My brother looks at me like I've grown a second head. "You are Kayla King," he says sternly. He pulls his head back, tilting it to the side to check if Livie is really sleeping. She is, so he continues without filters. "You're independent, you're a single mother who kills grown men who try to take her down. You owned the North Shore for years, led the Kings' crew. This..." He points at my trembling form. "This isn't you."

"Or maybe it's exactly me, Caden," I cry. "Maybe I'm tired of being a leader and strong, and everything you all want me to be. Maybe I am this way because I was never given a choice. I was barely four when I had to grab a newborn, *you*, from my mother's arms and go hide in a closet. Before ten, I had to take Dad's hits to save you. When Mom left, I became responsible for you, and if I didn't want to have other men besides my father hurt me, I had to show them I was just as strong as they were."

The wind could freeze my tears if they weren't falling so fast. I feel so depleted I can hardly take a breath without feeling pain.

"By day, I helped you with homework, and by night, I had to prove myself to Dad. And even that wasn't enough. I killed to show that man I belonged in his crew. So I wouldn't become one of the women he sent to the streets. And even *that* wasn't enough. Nothing was enough. Not my strength, not my brains, *nothing.*"

Bile rises up my throat. "Do you know about the first time I spent a night with Nathan White? Because Dad sent me to *broker a deal* with NSC when he was in deep shit after refusing Nate's offer. That same offer he took to NSC. *I* fixed his mistakes with my body and my sanity."

I can barely push out words with how tightly the ball of sadness knots in my throat. It's a serpent of emotions that is uncoiling, and I feel the need to puke it out.

"Do you know what being Nate's captive was?" I inhale a shaky breath. "A *fucking vacation.*"

"Your daughter is right here," he hisses back.

"Not from them!" I step back, taking my head in my hands. I've got a headache from all this. "From all of you! From responsibilities. The whole time I was there, I wanted nothing but to come back, but now I'm back, and I want nothing but to hold my girls and be taken care of. Do you know who took care of me? Nate."

I throw my head back, looking at the gray sky threatening to spill an apocalypse onto us. The storm weighs heavy in the air, like my heart in my chest. Is that what my life is going to look like? Every day without my sun will be gray.

Loving Nate when you can't get that love back is a burden to carry. It's going to rot inside me, kill me, reduce me to dust.

A sob bursts out of me as I look back at my brother.

"I can't do this. I won't go back to that life. You can tell Elliot to meet with Emma and let her know the North Shore is theirs to handle."

He looks at me with a blank face, holding Livie closer. He nods. "I'll tell them, Kay. You take all the time you need."

I open my mouth when I hear a scream in the house.

"Lia," I gasp.

I run back inside, followed closely by my brother. Another shriek, and she's sprinting out of the hallway leading to the bedrooms.

"Thank you, Uncle Caden!" She runs to him, hugging his legs tightly. I use the distraction to wipe my tears. I can't let her see me like this. She'll worry. "I love it, Uncle Caden. So pretty. So pretty, I love it. Look, Mommy!"

She shows me a small blue teddy bear with *Celia* embroidered on its belly. "I saw yellow one for Livie!"

Livie stirs in Caden's arms, woken up by her excited sister, and when Lia screams again, she pushes away to be put on the floor.

Caden squats to let her go and Lia grabs her hand, dragging her sister to the bedrooms.

"Look," I rasp. "Thank you. For everything. For trying to save me from Nate, for fixing the house, for being here for me and the girls whenever I need you."

"You kept the both of us alive growing up," he answers simply. "It's the least I can do."

I shake my head, not wanting his thanks. "You don't need to repay me." I roll my lips to gather myself. "But I need a bit of time to grieve."

"You'll get all the time you need. I'll be staying here."

If only that was Caden talking.

"Just go back to your house already," Cade snaps.

"Look," I huff. "I'm grateful for your help with the girls. Stay as long as you want, but know I don't need you anymore."

I turn away from her, leaving the living room to join my daughters in their new bedroom. I can only focus on one thing at a time, or the void Nate left behind starts grabbing me by the throat. So I focus on my daughters playing with their new teddy bears. A blue one for Lia and a yellow one with *Olivia* embroidered on it for Livie. Lia is running around the room because, apparently, her bear can fly. Livie is lifting it up and down in front of her as she sits on the floor.

"What's your bear's name, Lia?" I ask.

"Mr. Superbear," she giggles as she keeps hopping around the room.

I squat next to Livie and push strands of pitch-black hair away from her face. "And you, baby. What's the name of yours?"

She blinks up at me, but doesn't answer. I don't care. I will never give up on talking to her.

"Livie bear has a name, Mommy," Lia exclaims, jumping onto her bed.

"Lia, I told you not to put words in your sister's mouth. You can't make up a name for her bear. Just because she didn't share it with us doesn't mean she didn't pick one."

"But she told me, Mommy. Livie told me."

I straighten up and come to sit beside her on the bed. "Did she *say* it?" I ask calmy.

Lia shakes her head. "No, Mommy. Livie no talk."

"How do you know, then, honey?"

She shrugs, toying with the bear some more. "I understand Livie."

I smile to myself, feeling a wave of emotions crashing into me. "Of course, you do. She's your sister."

"Her teddy has a name. A name. The name is *Mommy*."

I turn to my other daughter. "Livie, is your teddy bear's name *Mommy*? Like Mommy?" I point at myself.

She looks at me, silent, and hugs the bear closer to her. Then she stands up and pushes it against me, and tight to her again. She repeats the gesture a few times.

"See!" Lia screams. She kicks her feet on the bed and lies down. "I love my bed. It's my bed. I love it."

I laugh, taking Livie in my arms when she pushes her head against my stomach.

"Mommy," Lia wonders out loud. "I sleep in your bed tonight?"

A laugh bursts out of me. "Of course, honey. You can sleep with Mommy any time you want."

39

KAYLA

lovely - Billie Eilish, Khalid

I hear a vague scream through the haze of my sleep. A headache is pounding inside me, probably because the girls wanted me to read a story last night. It's always painful for me to read, and especially out loud. Even children's stories.

"*Uncle Caden!*"

Lia.

I wake in a split second, sitting up in a gasp. My hand shoots under my pillow until I remember I don't sleep with my gun when the girls sleep in my bed.

"Calm down, Kay."

Caden's even voice helps me regulate my breathing.

"W-what's wrong?" I croak.

My brother turns on the light, and I put a hand in front of my eyes. He's holding a crying Lia, and Livie is hugging his leg like her life depends on it.

"What happened?" I jump out of bed, taking Livie in

my arms. They both fell asleep in my arms. I should have felt the second they left me.

"You happened," he says. "Lia ran to my room saying you were dying. You've got really bad night terrors, Kay. Did you know?"

I rub my eyes, kissing Livie's head as I hold her close to my chest. I'm unconsciously bouncing, soothing her.

Lia extends her arms to me too, and I'm forced to take her despite already struggling to hold one of them.

I fall onto my bed, sitting so I can hold them close.

"You two left the room without telling Mommy?"

"You were screaming and slapping around. You scared them to death."

"I...yeah. Nate told me I had them. I never remember. He was trying to help me with them, so it's been a while."

Caden huffs, running a hand through his messy hair. He looks like he has a hundred things to ask, but instead he just says, "Go back to bed."

I head out for groceries early in the morning. When I drop Caden off at Billie's house, I don't bother going in. He said he was staying there for the rest of the week. After that, I make my way to my local supermarket. I don't like leaving my mom with the girls anymore. I realized by her being here for almost two months that I hate her. Plain and simple. There is so much resentment between us that we'll never be able to love each other.

She left me with my dad, knowing full well what he was capable of.

And I remind her of him. She said it to me while she was drunk.

Your stupid hair and your stupid eyes. You both got

everything from him and nothing from me. Even the way you look. Tough. With that don't-fuck-with-me face. It's disgusting.

I huff for the hundredth time today as I put my keys in the door with a paper bag propped on my waist. I need to tell her to leave, and she needs to leave *today*.

I find the girls at their little table in the living room. It's a bright blue plastic table with chairs that can only fit toddlers. Lia is giggling, finding it hilarious that she's coloring everything outside of the lines, and Livie is hyper focused on coloring the flower in all yellow. Only yellow. Every single petal, *yellow*. She's going extremely slow, biting her tongue with her nose practically touching the paper. And she's pressing so hard that the marker is making a screeching sound as she moves it. I'm surprised she hasn't ripped the paper yet.

"Mommy!" Lia exclaims. Instead of running to me, she tries to stand up on her chair, but I stop her with a pointed look.

"What did I say about standing on the chair?"

"No!" She imitates my stern voice. "No, Celia! No!" With a giggle, she sits back down.

I give them both a kiss on the head and pull out two small boxes of apple juice I got for them.

"Here. Because you've been such good, patient girls for Mommy."

Coming back here has meant being pulled out of preschool in West Virginia. I'm going to put them back to school here after the Christmas break. I just wanted some time for them to adapt to being back in this house.

"Thank you, Mommy," Lia mumbles, already back to coloring like a maniac.

Livie calmly takes hers and hugs my leg before showing me the straw. I put it in the bottle for her while I talk to Lia.

"Where's Nanna?"

"In the kitchen with the mister."

My spine straightens, muscles freezing. "What mister, Celia?"

"The mister with the drawings." She draws nonsense on her sheets and points at it. "Like this! On his arms."

Who the fuck did my mother bring to the house? For a second, I imagine Sam. Nate's enforcer came to kill us all.

"You stay here with your sister. Do not move from here, got it?"

"Got it!"

I try not to run to the kitchen, so I don't alarm them, but I'm quick on my feet, my body vibrating from the inside out.

When I push the kitchen door open, I stop dead in my tracks.

The bag of groceries drops to the floor.

And my heart explodes into a mix of anxiety and relief, sending butterflies and shards of ice to my stomach.

"There she is. My little sunflower."

40

KAYLA

Bodies - Bryce Fox

"Nate."

No matter what people think of me and the reputation I've always upheld, I am not ashamed to say I have never been so terrified in my life.

And it's not because Nathan White is sitting at my kitchen table, a gun right in front of him and two arms crossed over his chest. It's not because the gun is placed in a precise way, so that he could quickly pick it up and point it at my mother if she moved from her position opposite him.

It's not even because I shot him, aimed to kill, and that he is now back very much alive. I'm not worried for myself.

I'm worried for my two daughters coloring in the room next to us. About what he's capable of doing to them.

"Nate," I repeat, swallowing thickly. "We can talk."

"We will," he replies with ease as he pushes his glasses up his nose.

He's wearing a simple white t-shirt and some blue

jeans, and it's somehow scarier to see him like that. The elegant man I know isn't really here, like he's given up on him. This is Nate in his purest form.

"We will," I agree. "But not with my mother here. Let's... Let's go somewhere else."

"Not with my daughters in the other room, you mean."

It's not even a question. My heart hardens, my deadly gaze going to my mother.

"You told him?" I hiss at her like a snake ready to bite.

She doesn't get to answer anything. Nate is already talking again.

"She didn't have to." He turns to my mom. "You can go now. Leave the house."

"Mom, take the girls."

"Take them and you'll have your brain covering that brand-new carpet before you take a second step."

His threat doesn't do anything to me, and it shouldn't do anything to my mom. The most important thing is protecting the twins.

"Take them, Mom!" I step to follow her into the living room, but he's on me in a split second.

Grabbing me by the hair, he pulls me back toward his chest, and before I know it, I've got a gun pointing at my temple.

"You stay here, my darling wife. And don't scream, you're going to scare the girls."

My mother looks at me with barely the semblance of a sorry in her eyes. "I'm sorry, Kay."

"No. No, no, no. Coward." Fury is a weak word for how I feel. "I hate you. Fuck!"

I hear the front door too quickly. I know she didn't take them with her. She abandoned me. Again.

"Nate, please." I'm a trembling mess in his hold, and

when he flips me around and slams me against the wall, his gun to the side of my head, I can't stop myself. "Please, don't hurt them. Hurt me. Don't—"

"Are you out of your mind, Kayla?" His question is collected, but the tightness of his jaw shows me how he's really feeling. He's angry. "Do you think I would hurt my own daughters?"

I shake my head. "I don't—I don't kn—" I cut myself off. He wouldn't. I know he wouldn't.

"Kayla." He kisses my temple, my cheek, the corner of my mouth. I can't help but melt into each one. "You lied to me. The whole time I had you, I waited. I waited for you to admit I had gotten you pregnant, and that you decided to have my children. I waited for you to admit that you had twin girls who you sent to your mother so they would be protected from the North Shore. I waited for you to admit that the reason you wanted to be freed so badly was because you wanted to go back to them."

He sucks on my lower lip and presses the gun harder against my head.

"And you never did." He kisses my lips. "You would rather kill me than tell me about my children."

"I'm sorry," I whimper. "I'm sorry. Th-that I shot you. How did you? I watched you... You were dead."

He chuckles against my lips. "Not all wounds to the chest are deadly. I am invincible, baby. You should ask my sister. You know she tried the same shit you did."

"But the Lucianos..."

"Why don't you worry about yourself. Why don't you worry about your *lies*. I'm not a good man, but I was honest with you. I gave you my truths as I discovered them. Every single thing I started understanding about myself, about us, I told you. And in return, what? You plan my murder behind my back so you can go back to *my* daughters?"

"Stop calling them yours. They're mine. You didn't carry them. You didn't bring them into this world. You weren't there to watch them grow."

"Because *you* put me in prison!" His roar startles me.

"Shh," I panic, bringing my palms to his mouth. "Please, please, don't scream. Don't bring them in here."

There's almost a look of disgust on his face as he pushes my hands away. "Is that why you put me away? So I wouldn't see them?"

"I sent you to prison because that's the deal I had with the Wolves. I had no choice. They had already started helping us. You know that. It's the rules of our business."

"That's the lies you told everyone."

I shake my head. "I didn't know. I promise you. I didn't know. I was in denial. I learned about it when I was five months pregnant."

His eyes round. "Five months?"

I nod, licking my lips. "You were already gone, and I'm the one who put my daughters' father in prison. You were a criminal, dangerous. I couldn't tell you. I was scared."

"Kayla," he growls. Something else is angering him. Something new. It's like there's nothing I can do to stop the onslaught of emotions overtaking him. "Were you with Ivan when you found out?"

I bite my lower lip to stop it from trembling. And I nod.

"You let another man raise my girls."

"No. Yes. It's complicated," I babble.

The frustration in his eyes seems to burn more recklessly than a wildfire.

"I should have made him suffer more. His death was too quick."

"Ivan was a good man, Nate. He helped me because we were dating but he wasn't too involved with them. They were little when I sent them to my mom anyway. The North Shore was too dangerous for them."

"All I'm hearing is excuses as to why another man was close to them while I was rotting away in prison. You could have told me about them the second you knew I was out."

"You *kidnapped me*," I whisper-yell.

"I had you for weeks. Why didn't you say anything?"

There's despair in his voice I'm not used to. It's a whisper of betrayal, thin and cold, like the bony fingers of death gripping your throat.

"I gave you chances. I asked you why you wanted your freedom back. I told you I wanted to keep you safe. I brought you that picture, knowing perfectly well who they were, and I watched you lie to my face. Fuck, Kayla, that very first day I pointed at your scar and asked what it was. Do you think I'm so stupid I don't know what a C-section scar looks like? Even before you shot me, I said, *is there anything you want to tell me?* Because I knew why you were doing it. I was pushing you. I was not giving you what you wanted because I wanted the truth. It never came. You shot me instead."

I am well aware of the way I'm putting my life at risk as I think over my answer, but I decide to go for it. Because if he wants the truth, I'll give him the truth.

"You are a psychopath, Nathan."

His eyes narrow at me, his teeth gritting. He truly hates that word, and I can see it.

"You are a psychopath, and your reactions are unpredictable. There's bad, but you're worse. There's mad, but you're the maddest. I will never, *ever* take that kind of risk when it comes to my daughters."

"*Our* daughters." His anger whistles in my ears, bringing fire to my chest.

"How did you find out?"

"Do you think you being pregnant and giving birth wouldn't be known to my people on the North Shore? Sam told me right away."

"But you didn't say anything to me."

"I was in prison. I had no way of being sure. And then I took you, and revenge was leading me, obsession. Every time I secretly nudged you and you still kept the truth to yourself, it was a reminder of why I should hate you. Sometimes I even thought, maybe they really aren't mine. Maybe they have a dad. A dad who's not me. But then I saw them today. Those eyes, baby? They're mine. They're my family's eyes."

And don't I know it. That blue exists nowhere else, not even nature can produce it. No, only the Whites have it.

"And with your black hair." He snorts. "They look exactly like Rose as a kid."

My eyes drop. We're at an impasse.

Again.

Except this time, he's the one with the gun.

"Kayla. Those little girls could have your eyes and your hair. Your features, your personality, your everything, I would still know they're mine. I walked into your house today, and I *knew*. There's no taking that away from me."

"I'm scared," I admit, unable to slow my pounding heart. "I'm scared you're going to hurt them. Hurt me. I'm scared even if you don't, it's going to change them forever."

His gun is still at my temple, and I wrap my hand around the barrel. "I'm scared about your revenge, for trying to kill you."

He shakes his head. "I knew what I was getting myself

into when I decided to take you. I knew I was facing the ruthless King. Your reputation precedes you, and that was my choice to make. You shot me to go back to our kids? Good. Would I have preferred for you to just tell me about it so we could discuss it? Yes. Do I regret you shooting me? I don't think so. It was kind of hot, and I know you're the type of woman who would never let anything get in her way. Not even the man she loves."

His utter insanity brings a small smile to my lips. How did I fall in love with this guy?

"You're suicidal." He really is.

After he let me kill him, I understood one thing clearly. Nate isn't a megalomaniac like I always thought. He is suicidal. I should have known from the night I met him. The first thing he did was ask me to try to kill him. He thinks himself immortal, and that makes him a danger to his own life.

I'm hoping a bullet to the chest for the second time in his life has taught him a good lesson.

His arm falls, the gun finally away from my head. "You said you loved me, little sunflower. You can't take it back now."

"I said that because I knew you were about to die." Stomach flipping, I swallow past the lump in my throat.

"That's not true."

My lips pinch, a sense of relief engulfing me. "No. It's not true."

"So be a good girl and tell me you love me."

I have never done anything Nate has asked me out of my own free will. Fighting him became second nature the second he took my freedom away. Everything he's ever wanted out of me, he had to pull it out by force. Especially when it came to my feelings.

Name it.

Expressing what I feel so strongly within myself that I could never have the shadow of a doubt as to what it is? I can do that.

I dig my eyes into his, hoping with all my might that he can see the truth in them.

"I love you, Nathan."

There's a growl low in his chest, and it reverberates through my entire body. Something animalistic that links us, that makes my toes curl. "I love you too, little sunflower."

And then his lips are on mine in a flash. He kisses me, long and hard. This is not a kiss from a psychopath. This is a kiss from a dying man who has found his ultimate reason to live. And he's bringing life back to me too. His tongue strokes mine with feelings he can't express and, for a minute, I forget about everything around us.

When he pulls away from my mouth, he presses his lips to my ear. "You will be thoroughly punished for the shit you put me through. But not now. Right now, I want to meet my daughters."

I nod, tucking strands of hair behind my ears. "Okay. I just—" I take a deep breath as he steps back. "Put the gun away first. No firearms."

He opens a cupboard and puts it high enough that the girls wouldn't be able to reach.

"And, um. Wait." I can't stop shaking as my mind races.

"Baby, calm down."

My accelerated breath slows for a second, but my vision narrows.

He presses a soft hand to my cheek, and I look up at his unbelievable eyes. "I need to understand you. Name it."

"Panic. I'm panicking," I squeak.

"I won't do anything. I just want to meet them."

"Just, be gentle, okay? Don't, don't mention you're their dad yet. They never asked about it. They don't get it. I don't think so."

"Okay." He nods, waiting for any other information he needs.

"Livie—that's the one with the tiny scar just below her nose. She doesn't talk. She's...she's taking it slowly. And Lia gets easily excited, so no shocking news or she'll lose it."

"Noted." With a nod, he takes a step toward the door.

"No, wait!" I run my palm over my forehead. "Let me talk to them first. I need... I need to prepare them. Introduce you."

"Kayla, calm down."

"Please," I say on a breath.

I see him hesitate, and to my surprise, he takes me in his arms. He smells exactly the same as usual. God, I love his reassuring scent. He strokes my hair, my back, and puts pressure between my shoulders, helping me regulate my breathing.

"We're going to do this together, okay?"

"Okay," I say against his chest.

"Now, please, can I meet my daughters?"

"Okay." I can't believe this is happening.

I pull away and take his hand, guiding him to the living room.

"Girls," I call out as we join them.

Livie is still completely focused on her flower, but she's barely halfway through. Lia has made a mess of the table and chair. She's standing up behind her sister and trying to color Livie's hair with the pens.

"Mommy! Look!"

She shows her arms, where she scribbled over and over

again with a black marker. "Like the mister. See? The mister?" She points at Nate, and a huff leaves me.

"This is Celia." There is no better introduction than the state she is currently in. "Yes, I see, honey. But your arms are not for drawing. We use paper for that. And stop trying to draw on Livie's hair now."

I swallow through the dryness in my throat. "And this is Olivia," I say, pointing at my other daughter. "Girls, this is my friend, Nate. He wants to meet you."

"Hello," Lia says as she sprints toward us. She bumps against my legs, hiding her face and pretending to be shy for a second before she pulls away.

"Hi, Celia." I want to facepalm when I hear the lack of *anything* in his voice, but that's just who he is, isn't it?

It doesn't bother her. She takes his hand and drags him to the table. "My name is Celia!"

She can say that like a grown girl. She doesn't sound so little when she speaks those words compared to her other barely articulated sentences.

She pushes Nate and forces him to sit on the chair she was in. The tiny plastic chair. It bends under his weight, his knees coming up to his chest, and I have to pinch my lips not to laugh.

"Olivia." She points at her. "Livie is my sister! My sister," she repeats.

"Hi, Livie."

She doesn't even look up from her drawing. Lia runs around the table and stands behind her sister. She puts her hands on Livie's shoulders in a protective gesture and observes Nate.

"Livie is *my* sister," she insists.

I stay back, watching apprehensively as Nate tilts his

head to the side, observing the two girls I've been hiding from him for almost four years.

His gaze narrows slightly as he thinks, then he brings his index to his ear, rubbing behind it. He pushes his glasses up his nose, and my breath stops, waiting for his reaction.

"I'm your dad."

My heart drops, my hands coming to my face in shock. "Fuck. Nate!"

Lia looks at me and repeats, "Fuck!"

"No, Lia. Don't say that, honey." I run to her, and all Livie does is look up from her coloring book. She blinks at Nate and looks back down, pressing the yellow pen against the paper again.

"Mommy, what is fuck?" Lia asks innocently, completely ignoring the truth bomb Nate just dropped. "What is it?"

"A bad word. Nate, why?"

"I panicked," he admits as calmly as ever. I might laugh if I wasn't so overwhelmed.

"You don't look like you're panicking."

"I have Daddy?" Lia changes the topic as quickly as her thoughts run through her head. She doesn't articulate the question well, but her little voice pierces through my heart.

"Honey..." Her question leaves me speechless, and I turn to Nate, completely out of my depths. He nods, nudging me with a single look. "Yes, Nate is your dad. He's been away for a while, and now he's back, and he'd like to meet you and Livie, to get to know you."

"Uncle Caden," she replies simply, referring to the only other male figure she knows well.

"Well, it's different. Uncle Caden is Mommy's brother.

Nate is..." My eyes dart down to the rings I still haven't taken off, and then to Nate, silently screaming for help.

He stands up from the tiny chair and comes to squat next to the girls. "Your mommy and I once loved each other so hard that you two were born. See, that makes Kayla your mommy, and that makes me your daddy."

Lia looks at me, a hundred more questions in her eyes that I can't answer. For once, nothing comes out of her mouth.

"Hey." I take her hand in mine and kiss her knuckles. "It doesn't have to change anything. You, me, and Livie are a team. And then if you want, *only if you want*, Nate—"

"Daddy," he corrects me right away. I'm going to have to explain to him that I won't force my daughters to call him Dad or Daddy until he's earned it or if they want to do so.

I roll my eyes. "He can join the team too. But that's your girls' choice. Okay?"

Livie looks up again, and she pushes her hand toward me. I take it too, kissing her knuckles like I did her sister. She brings her hand back to herself, and reaches out again, touching Nate's knee.

"Hey," he says simply.

She looks at me and brings her hand to my knee this time.

"Well," Lia drawls. "If Livie says yes, I say yes too."

She says that in a way that explains Livie has somehow already said yes, and I smile at her. "Okay. We can take it a little bit at a time, yeah? And if you don't like something, you can say no whenever you want. Do you understand? Both of you?"

Lia nods repeatedly and dramatically. "I understand!"

"Do you girls have any questions?"

Lia pinches her lips dramatically, rolling her eyes and

pressing her index finger against her mouth. "Ummm... Yes."

"Go on."

"Can I color the mister drawing, Mommy?"

Livie's eyes widen, sparkling with eagerness too.

"That's up to him. And you can call him by his name, honey."

"Daddy?"

"Or Nate," I explain slowly. "Whatever you want."

She nods, trying to figure out something even us adults can't. "Mister Nate, I color the drawings." She smiles brightly. "Please?"

"Sure," Nate says, already offering his arms as a smile spreads on his face.

She shrieks with happiness, stomping her feet as she gathers markers and runs to the sofa. Livie follows languidly, holding her yellow pen tightly, and Nate joins them. Sitting between the two.

There's a mix of anticipation and fear swirling inside me. It's like I've waited for this my whole life...but that also meant waiting for the most lethal man to complete this picture.

An hour later, Nate's arms, hands, and even fingers are completely covered in colors. Every single minute he's spent with them, my body relaxed a little more. This is coming naturally to him, like there is nothing else in this world he's meant to be but a father to Olivia and Celia King.

"More!" Lia exclaims. She pulls at his t-shirt, trying to get under it.

"Lia, calm down." I try to stop her.

"It's alright," he says. He's been completely quiet, observing the girls and every single movement they make.

He's learning them by heart. Absorbing their every reaction and trying to understand them. He did the same thing with me because he loved me. The effort he's putting into this goes straight to my heart. There is no complicated history with them like he has with me. No, everything he's doing is purely because he wants their happiness. It's a selfless act because they're a part of him, a result of us.

Big, bad Nathan White, tamed by two littles girls.

But hasn't told me anything about how he feels, or what he expects moving forward. This is something I'll have to dig out myself.

Nate takes off his t-shirt, leaning back in his seat.

Livie silently climbs on top of him and points just under his chest, near his abdomen, with her yellow pen. She turns to me, and my mouth drops open.

"Nate." My gulp can be heard even through Lia's random noises.

He looks down at what Livie is pointing out. She's about to color, but I stand up, striding to her and taking the pen from her. "Sweetie, you're going to hurt him."

How it doesn't already hurt like a bitch is a question as good as any.

My fist tightens around the pen, and tears gather in my eyes.

"Why?" I rasp.

He shrugs. "Because you're with me, all day, every day. You're in my head, in my every thought, in my lungs with every breath I take. You're in my heart, every beat pumping you into my veins. So I tattooed you on my skin."

"Around the scar I gave you," I say numbly, even as my chest warms.

"Yes. To remind myself my little sunflower is lethal. You're under my skin, baby. It's only normal for it to show on the surface. The effect you have on me runs much deeper than the scar. You're mine. I keep you with me. It's not a big deal."

Livie wanted to color his tattoo yellow because it's a sunflower. The center isn't shaded with ink because it's a raised, pink scar from the bullet that tore his flesh when I shot him. It's clearly new, ugly. I can almost feel it throbbing. Around it are the petals of a sunflower. It's not perfect. It looks like it's been crushed, stomped on. Some petals are falling, showing lower on his abdomen. They cover some of his other tattoos.

"It's a broken flower."

"It's a flower that's surviving despite everything it's been through."

"Thanks to its sun?" I ask with a tipped smile.

He chuckles. "Of course, thanks to its sun."

Not far from my scar is the one his sister left him when *she* shot him.

"You're going to have to stop angering the women around you," I tease.

"Absolutely. I'm running out of skin to tattoo."

Livie starts whining. She shakes her head, unhappy with something I can't quite comprehend. Nate's hand shoots toward me and takes back the pen I'm fisting tightly.

He gives it to Livie, stopping the beginning of her tantrum. But instead of coloring him again, she falls against his chest and wraps her arms around his neck, hugging him tightly.

He bites back a grunt, her body on his scar clearly painful. But before I can get her back, Lia jumps on him.

"I want to hug Mister Nate!" She wraps herself around him in any way she can, and he looks up at me as he wraps his arms around both of them.

"How does it feel?" I ask. And I know he hates that question, but he's going to have to try.

"Like something unbelievably powerful belongs to me."

"They're just two little girls," I laugh, even though he's right. I feel it too when I'm with them.

"They're *my* two little girls."

"You're already sounding possessive."

He smiles. "Try to take them away from me and see what happens."

Why am I feeling so proud that he's already attached to them?

"It's a lot of responsibility. Very little time to yourself. It's worrying too."

"I'll take it all."

I cock an eyebrow at him, putting a hand on my hip.

"They're expensive."

His answer comes without hesitation.

"I'm a very rich man."

"You can kiss goodbye to your privacy. And your personal life."

"My personal life is you, Kayla. It's you, and them. I need nothing else."

I lick my lips, nodding. Shit, that feels really good to hear. "Okay. We'll give it a go. But only because being a dad looks so hot on you."

He tilts his head to the side, his eyebrows pinching. "I didn't realize you thought you had an option. This was not an interview process. I was only showing you what it'll be like from now on."

Of course. How silly of me to think I had a choice in this.

. . .

He spends the rest of the day with the girls. I wonder if he even remembers I'm here. When they get bored with coloring, they all watch videos on how to fold origami. When they get bored with that, Lia shows him over and over again how she can count to eleven. Specifically, eleven. Well, sixteen, according to her, but she also insists that sixteen comes after eleven. Then they each show him how they can spell their own name now, or whatever the weird shapes are meant to be.

I make them dinner, and he helps both of them eat. He clears the table, washes the dishes, runs around the living room with them until they finally tire out. For the whole day, he looks like a completely normal person. And even I forget there's something with him that's different from us.

But as Lia starts to cry her heart out when I tell them to go to bed because she can't find Mr. Superbear, I watch Nate's face go blank.

"Sleep without it," he says calmly.

"Doesn't work like that, Nate," I huff as I look under the girls' beds. "Lia, when did you last see it?"

"It's an inanimate object," Nate insists to me.

"Mommy!" she cries out. Panic rips through her voice.

Nate is holding Livie, and when Lia starts pulling at my jeans to get me from under the bed, sobbing like someone just died, I hear him shift.

"What is happening?"

"Mommy! Mommy, no! Come back!"

"Celia, it's fine!" I call back as I push some toys around under the bed.

"The monsters!"

"Lia, why are you screaming?" Nate asks, as if he's talking to an adult.

"She's scared," I send back, my voice barely audible over Lia's scream.

"Mommy!" She pulls so hard on my jeans I hit my head under the bed. I reverse back out and turn to her.

"Lia, I'm fine," I sigh. She jumps into my arms, holding me so tightly I can barely breathe. I stay on the floor while she hugs me, catching my breath.

"I don't want Mr. Superbear," she cries against my neck. "I want Mommy."

"Okay, honey. I'm here."

Livie looks down at us, putting her thumb in her mouth, and turns back to hugging Nate.

"Welcome to parenthood," I huff.

"I'm confused," he admits blankly.

"Okay. Awesome, I will just have to run you past my emotions, and theirs too. I'm really looking forward to it."

"Can you name it?" The way he asks, it's impossible to feel irritated. He's trying so hard to understand us.

"She was panicking, Nate. Because she thinks there are monsters under the bed, and she thought I was going to get hurt. She was scared for me."

He nods, and I watch his jaw tighten, his eyes focused like he's taking a mental note. "Okay. I can remember that."

"This is going to be hard," I admit, renewed nerves swirling in my stomach.

The second Lia calms down, she gets off me and runs to grab a book. "Mommy, story."

My head falls back against the mattress. This is the worst part of my day. I love spending time with my girls, but reading to them is a task I don't think I'll ever enjoy.

"You make Mommy read every night?" Nate asks Lia as he takes the book from her. He puts Livie to bed, and I use the occasion to stand up and do the same with Lia while she nods purposefully at Nate.

"But it's so hard for her," he explains with a tilt of his head.

"No, is not." Lia defends me with a fierceness that makes me laugh.

He goes to sit on the floor, but Livie pulls at his t-shirt, and she keeps going until he's lying down with her in her twin bed, so I lie down with Lia in hers.

"I'll read the story tonight. We'll give Mommy a break."

"But Mommy," Lia whines. I caress her hair and drop a kiss on her head.

"Just tonight," I whisper to her. "Let's try."

She huffs. "Mmkay."

Lia quickly changes her mind. The way Nate reads is much different from how I do. Like someone who doesn't feel like it's a chore. Even I feel sleepy by the time he finishes. And I could have the best dreams if I fall asleep every night watching him, his strong arm wrapped around Livie and his tattooed fingers holding a book.

We slide out of their beds and walk back to the living room. I quietly close the hallway door and turn to him.

"We need to talk."

His voice is a cold, deadly hand digging into my chest, and fear grips me so tightly I wonder if this entire day was a mistake.

I did try to kill him, after all.

41

KAYLA

505 - Arctic Monkeys

He sits down on the sofa, waiting for me, and I pad toward him, unsure what I should do.

"What is it?" I ask, standing in front of him, but he taps the seat next to his.

"Sit down, little sunflower. We need to talk about you attempting to kill me."

My gaze darts around the room, avoiding his, and I sit down. He twists so he can face me, an arm on the back of the sofa as the other comes to my knee. His blue eyes, the exact same as our daughters, search my face. He has no idea what it's been like to see him in them for four years. A piece of him never left me.

Instead of waiting for him to take control of the conversation, I start talking.

"How did you survive?"

"You missed."

"I didn't miss. You have a pretty scar to prove it."

I think he's amused by the way his fingers start tapping

lightly on my knee, but there's nothing else that shows in his voice or facial expression.

"You were in a terrible state. You missed any vital organ."

My pride takes a hit, and it's difficult to swallow that. "But the Lucianos were there, and they wanted you dead too. Lucky should have finished the job."

He cocks an eyebrow at me. "Is that right?"

I retreat slightly, my voice weakening. "I-I mean because they wanted to kill you too."

"You're mistaken. You wanted me dead and went to the Lucianos for help. But you forgot I grew up with those people. Vito and I have known each other since we were kids. The Lucianos don't care whether I'm alive or not; they care that we don't impede on each other's business. When Lucky told him I wasn't dead, he nursed me back to life so we could negotiate a truce between us. He's better off with me alive and sharing suppliers and routes with him than dead and not knowing what to do with the army I built."

I lick my lips, my eyes darting down to where I know the scar is. The scar with a tattoo of a sunflower.

"Where have you been for six weeks?"

"At my sister's. With Sam, Rachel, and Lik. It's been rather annoying. I couldn't wait to come back to you."

I shake my head, barely believing how composed he is right now. "I tried to kill you, Nate."

"You tried to kill me because you wanted to go back to our daughters. Trust me, I would have done the same."

I push his hand away from my knee, frustration building inside me. "If you knew about them, why didn't you just give me back my freedom like I asked?"

His hand comes back, holding tighter this time. "Because

I thought pushing you would lead you to telling me the truth. Because I became obsessed with you, and because I am standing my ground: You are not free. You are mine."

"But—"

"Just because I don't keep you chained to the floor doesn't mean your leash is any longer than it was in the last few months, do you understand? I want you. I want my daughters. I want the warmth in my chest when I hold you in my arms, and I want to take care of the three of you. Don't mistake my need for you as a weakness. If anything, it makes me more dangerous than I've ever been, because I didn't use to care about what happens to the people around me."

He digs his hard stare in mine, and I welcome the shiver that travels down my spine. "I care what happens to you and those girls. So, you're not going anywhere, little sunflower."

"I want to live here. On the North Shore. In this house," I tell him adamantly.

"Then we'll live here."

My eyebrows rise in surprise.

"And I want to come and go as I please."

"You will, as long as you always come back."

Excitement brews within me. What kind of madness has taken the both of us that being told he'll never let me go is making me dizzy with anticipation?

"I want an equal part in your business." My lungs seize with an exhilaration I can't control. "Burn the prenup and let me run your empire with you."

"I told you I wanted you to rule by my side, even if it's hell we're ruling."

"Fine."

"Fine?" His eyes narrow on me, his lips pursing. "Just like that, you're mine?"

"Just like that? You kidnapped me and forced me to marry you, asshole."

He chuckles. "True."

"One last thing." My voice lowers, a warning sharpening my tone like a knife ready to pierce his heart. "If you ever hurt my daughters—"

"You mean *our* daughters."

"No." A heavy silence falls in the room. "I mean mine. The babies I held, the little girls I raised, the treasures who own my entire heart. If you ever hurt my daughters." I put my hand on his chest delicately and press where I know his scar is.

He hisses through gritted teeth, but he accepts the pain.

"Then I won't miss, Nate. If you have to remember one thing I say, remember that."

He nods sharply, carefully peeling my hand off him.

"I understand. But I would never. And if I did, which would be entirely accidental, you wouldn't have to do anything. I would rather take my own life than hurt them. Baby, if you thought I was protective before," he chuckles, quirking an eyebrow, "you just wait."

Pride warms my belly, sending sparks to my chest and putting a smile on my face. "I'll allow that level of protectiveness over them."

"Good." His hand on my knee slides up, and that gesture only sends electricity to my lower stomach. "Now I have one last request to clear the slate. I have done my share of questionable things to you, and you killed me and hid our daughters from me."

"Is that how you want to put it, then?"

"Yes."

"I think it's bold of you to request one last thing after you took everything from me, but go on."

His gaze scans my entire body before he pulls away. He stands up, reaches inside his pocket, and takes out a small plastic packet with two pills in it.

"Show me you trust me." Waving the packet between us, he looks down on me with all the power he has over me.

I retreat, plastering myself against the sofa. I'm not liking where this is going. "What is that?"

"This is a mix of diphenhydramine and diazepam."

"Diph—diphpen—"

"Diphenhydramine. It's a sedating antihistamine. And diazepam is the type of anti-anxiety meditation that makes one lethargic. It always depends on the person, of course. But I think the mix of both will do the job."

My eyes bounce between the packet and his face. "You want to drug me?"

"No"

My heartbeat relaxes. "Oh," I chuckle awkwardly. "For a second—"

"I want you to drug yourself."

My eyes widen. "Are you insane?"

"Yes, certified. And you know that. So take the pills and let's get this over with."

"I am not *drugging* myself for you. I am not taking some sort of sleeping pills when I know you're capable of anything."

I try to get up, but he pushes me back down. "You like it, Kay. You like it when you're helpless and when I can do *anything* I want. And I know what goes on in that pretty head of yours. You're Kayla King, how could you possibly ask for anyone to take control over you when you're the baddest and the strongest. You think there's no other way to enjoy what you like but by being forced. That makes you wet. Fuck, baby, it makes you melt like a puddle at my feet."

My heart accelerates, my cheeks flushing, but mainly, relief floods me. I have never been understood in this way.

"That's what I'm capable of doing, little sunflower. Forcing you. That's why we fit so well sexually."

He opens the pack and pinches the two pills between his thumb and forefinger before putting the empty plastic in his pocket.

"There are other things that link us, like the way you understand me despite me not understanding myself. And the way you need to be protected, because no one ever did that for you. But *animalistically* we match because I'm a hunter, and you've always wanted to be prey."

He leans over, putting a hand behind me on the back of the sofa, and showing me the pills. Right in front of my face.

"The girls. I can't."

"I will be sober. I would never put us in a situation where they can't be taken care of should an emergency arise."

My heart is beating so fast I can hardly breathe. Short bursts of air come in and out of my lungs, waves of excitement. This is what I've always wanted. Nate has only ever made me feel exactly what I yearned to feel. The lust we share is specific to our brand of fucked up. Victim wants killer to slay her so deeply she won't be able to do anything to defend herself.

A shiver courses through my body.

"Will you hurt me?"

"I will do everything you love."

"And...I won't be conscious?"

He lowers his head, skimming his lips against my nose, going down to my mouth.

"You will be awake, barely, but you will be too lethargic to defend yourself. It'll be a haze, almost a dream. Like that time I brought you back to my bed after leaving you in the basement for the day."

I bite down on my lower lip when he kisses my jaw, his tongue darting to my skin. A sigh leaves me and my shoulders drop.

"Open your mouth, little sunflower. And let me make you feel good."

I forbid myself to think any further about this, and I open my mouth.

He pulls away, only enough to watch me. "That's it. Show me your pretty tongue."

I hesitantly extend my tongue, blinking up at him.

"My beautiful wife, offering herself to me." He puts the pills on my tongue. "We'll start with these. You'll like it, Kay. If you want more, I'll give you another one. But *only* if I feel it's safe. Alright?"

I nod.

"Good girl. Now swallow for me."

I close my mouth, and his palm comes to cover it. My throat is suddenly feeling tight as I dry-swallow the pills. He drags his palm from my lips to my chin, then to my throat, following the pills as they go. All the way to my chest.

And then his evil smirk appears. It spreads and spreads until he looks like the devil himself.

"Would you like to be my little slut for the night, sunflower? I've missed you."

I drag in a sharp breath. I've never been scared of death, but just like anyone else, I know danger when I see it. I know a flame will burn; a knife will cut. I know lethal beings when they stand right in front of me.

But when did I start wanting to touch the fire and let it consume me? When did I start needing the feeling of a blade against my skin? When exactly did I realize it is a necessity to give myself to Nate and let him destroy me in the most beautiful, enthralling way possible?

"Yes," I rasp. "I want to."

Something resonates low in his chest, and he keeps watching me over the next few minutes. He tells me delicate orders, like *"undress for your husband."* and *"spread your gorgeous legs for me. Show me what belongs to me."*

I do. I get naked and open my legs to show him my pussy.

"Touch yourself for me."

Pressing two fingers to my clit, I circle gently. I bring them to my entrance and drag wetness back up, making a mess of my nub. He encourages me to keep going, tells me I'm beautiful, irresistible.

"Carry on," he says. "Until you can't anymore."

I'm panting, bucking my hips and pressing harder. I don't understand what he means for a while. But slowly, it gets harder to control my hand.

As my muscles become heavier, I'm struggling to hold my head up, so I let it fall against the sofa. My hand slips, and I can't get myself to lift my arm again.

"Nate," I mumble, my chest rising and falling to a steady rhythm.

"Yes, little sunflower?"

"I..." My vision blurs, and I blink. "It's str—strange." Words are harder to push out now.

"How? Describe it to me."

"It's h-hard to talk," I slur. It's such a complicated task to articulate.

I startle when I feel his hands on my thighs. Or I think I do, but I didn't really move at all.

"What else?" I feel him move, sense his voice below my head, like he's kneeling before me, but when I try to lift my head up, my muscles refuse to obey.

I blink slowly, the ceiling my only sight.

"My body." I sigh when he kisses my inner thigh.

"What about it?" he murmurs against my skin, sending thousands of explosives over my nerve-endings.

"I c-can't move."

"If you try really hard, you will. Just slowly."

"Aahh..." Only a mumbled noise leaves my lips. It's nothing compared to the way I feel, to the pleasure I need to express as he starts licking my wetness.

How can I feel him pleasuring me so precisely when I can barely feel my own body?

He plays with my clit for what seems like forever, and I writhe under him, but I can barely move. I'm so relaxed that I feel like I'm in another universe.

The sofa swallows me, and my hand languidly travels to his head. I can barely grip his hair; it feels like water through my fingers.

"Oh god, N-nate," I moan.

His whole head moves to the rhythm of his wet tongue against my even wetter pussy. The man has a gift for eating pussy, there is no doubt about that.

My shivers of pleasure should turn into shakes, but my muscles are too sedated to follow, so when I come apart on his tongue, it feels like an out-of-body experience. Like I'm floating in a sea of pleasure but slowly drowning.

Pulling away, he helps me sit up. I can feel my arousal

dripping down my inner thigh. He lifts my head by putting a hand at the back of it, and he kisses my lips hungrily.

The taste of myself makes me moan into his mouth. I'm not really controlling my reactions anymore, letting him guide my body into a sense of supreme pleasure.

"I could eat your greedy cunt for days, wife. You are truly addictive."

His words only send another wave of satisfaction through my body.

"Now that you're completely relaxed," he growls against my mouth, "let's play."

42

KAYLA

Flames - Tedy

My heart skips a beat, and I blink up at him when he pulls away.

"P-play?"

"Yes. Let's see what it takes to make you mine completely."

"I'm yours," I mumble.

A satisfied smile tips the corners of his mouth.

"Then let's test it."

He picks me up, holding me close to his chest as he walks to the bedroom. Depositing me on the bed, he caresses my entire body. From my hair to my cheek. My mouth to my throat. His fingers explore my chest, my breasts. They stroke my nipples, the nubs already hard from the barbels I've kept there.

"My good little wife kept her piercings. You couldn't stop thinking about me, could you? I bet you played with them when you touched yourself remembering the way *I* touched you."

I nod my agreement.

His hand surfs down my stomach, cups my mound, tickles my clit.

"Stay here, pretty girl. I'll be back."

It's not like I can move much anyway, but the second he leaves, I do find the strength to touch myself. Slowly, I dip the tip of my finger in and out of my pussy. That's not how I would usually do it, but I don't feel like myself tonight. I'm desperate for something to fill me. I want to clench around a hardness inside me.

"My, my. I left a naughty slut without supervision."

My head falls to the side, and Nate has never looked so imposing as he does standing next to my bed right now.

"Do I have to teach you a lesson?"

I'm smiling. I think I am. And I nod my head languidly. "Yes," I rasp. "Teach m-me."

"Teach you what, baby?" He takes off his t-shirt, throwing it to the side, and his jeans and boxers are next. "To behave? To not touch yourself when you're not allowed? Tsk, what a silly little slut you are."

I shake my head as much as I can when he straddles me. "To belong to you," I slur. "Make me. F-force me."

The mattress dips, his hard dick against my stomach.

That's when I see the kitchen knife.

"Teach you how to belong to me," he repeats. "That would be my pleasure, little sunflower."

He brings the knife to my throat, and the consciousness of the danger is here, but somehow, not the reflex to defend myself. My hands slowly come to rest by my head, and I follow my instinct of letting him do whatever he wants.

"You look so beautiful like this. So helpless. You're such a pretty victim."

My eyes flutter closed, and they take forever to open again. "I could kill you," he murmurs.

And I'm not even scared of it.

He drags the knife down and presses the tip in the hollow of my throat.

I whimper when he cuts my skin. It's superficial, but in my state, I feel like everything is enhanced.

He lowers himself, licking the blood from my skin, and drags it up my throat, painting me crimson. Straightening, he drags the blade down to my nipples, pressing it against each piercing he put there, then to my stomach, and shifts down my legs to access my pussy.

"Have you ever been fucked with a knife?"

A pit opens in my stomach.

"N-nate..."

"I want to put the hilt of this knife inside your pretty cunt. Aren't you desperate to feel something inside you?"

Wetness floods my pussy in response.

"You don't need to answer," he chuckles. "I can see it very clearly. Lie still."

He spreads my legs, settling between them rather than on them. "What a beautiful cunt you have, baby."

He brings a hand to my jaw, presses to the sides of it, and forces me to open. "Keep your pretty mouth open for me, will you?"

And then he presses the hilt of the knife against my tongue. "Suck it. Make it wet for yourself."

My tongue curls around the object, and I suck it into my mouth. I do it for as long as he keeps it there, and I'm panting when he finally pulls it out.

"Very good. Relax, baby. I'll make you feel good."

I startle when I feel the handle against my entrance. "W-wait."

"No."

The simple word makes me yearn for him even more. And when he pushes in, a cry of pleasure leaves my lips. He goes slowly, dragging moans out of me, making me needy for the knife. I clench around it, trying to keep it inside every time he pulls it back.

"I can see what you're doing," he chuckles. "Who decides the pace, pretty wife? Who takes control of your body?"

"You," I sigh desperately.

"That's right."

He keeps going, making me writhe. Slowly in, slowly out. A little deeper, right at the edge of my entrance.

"Oh, Nate," I cry out, feeling myself lose control. "I'm gonna c-come."

"Is that right? Are you going to come with a knife inside you? Are you going to come from me playing with this pretty pussy however I want?"

He does it again, pressing in ever-so slowly.

"Y-yes...yes..." And when he pulls out, I explode from the madness. Stars flash in front of my eyes, my head falling to the side and my back curving.

"That's my girl. Keep coming." He moves again, going harsher, stimulating me with only the hilt thrusting inside me. It's deeper now, his movement unforgiving.

"F-fuck."

"I'll be fucking you with this knife until you give me another orgasm, Kayla. So work that pussy against it."

I try my best to obey, but my muscles refuse. "Fight against the lethargy. Show me what a desperate whore you are. So desperate even those pills can't stop you from dragging pleasure out of this."

With a grunt, I fight against my body. I push up,

thrusting my pussy until my entrance presses against his fist. He's holding the knife in a way that ensures I can't cut myself. His hand is protecting the blade, so that must mean he's holding some of it, cutting himself.

"That's it, good little whore. Come, baby. Come again for me."

I reach a high so blinding my mouth opens to cry out, but it's silent. I'm squirming, fisting the sheet, uncaring of what I look or sound like as the wave of fire engulfs me.

The knife leaves me, a whimper pushing past my lips as it retreats. And suddenly, Nate's palm is on my mouth, covering the entire lower half of my face. It smells coppery and it's slippery too.

He's bleeding.

I want to tell him, but he's pressing too hard against my lips. "I'm discovering a new passion, little sunflower. Bleeding for you."

My nostrils flare as I inhale through my nose.

"Lick me. Feel the way I love to hurt for you."

He eases the pressure, and my tongue darts out, licking him shyly at first. But he's right. It's erotically addictive. So I explore further, putting my tongue flat against his palm before I bring it back into my mouth.

He growls, low, barely able to contain his hunger. "I want to sacrifice myself for you," he rasps. "I want you to shoot me if that's what you need. I want to bleed and know that it's at your hand."

Putting his palm on my cheek, he brings the hilt of the knife to my mouth. "Taste yourself."

This time, I open my mouth eagerly, sucking the knife in.

"I need you so much it hurts, Kayla."

His voice resonates everywhere within my body. And

LOLA KING

it's not even that he sounds desperate. He's not good at expressing things through his voice. But he pushes the hilt to the back of my throat, spreading his blood on my cheek. When he presses his hard cock against my slit, I feel it.

I feel how much he needs me. Mainly because I need him back.

He rolls his hips, sliding his dick between my nether lips and against my clit.

I moan around the knife, and he finally pulls it out of my mouth. "You're incredible. So perfect for me. All I want is to be perfect for you in return. And then..." He thrusts, teasing me with his cock. "Then you'll never leave me, will you?"

"I w-won't," I rasp. It's difficult to keep my eyes open, my body hard to control, but I still feel all of him. I still feel his desire for me. All of me.

"No, you won't."

He throws the knife to the side, wraps his hand around my throat, and smiles at me.

"What a beautiful wife." He uses his other hand to line himself up with my entrance. "Now scream for me, baby."

He thrusts deep inside me in an unforgiving push, and as he does, he presses his palm against my mouth. Yes, maybe screaming isn't such a good idea right now. I hold on for dear life as my body has no choice but to take and take what he gives.

He only fucks me long enough to bring me back to life, but not enough to make me come again. Instead, he pulls out, kneels up, and brings his cock to my mouth.

My jaw hangs open, and he pushes inside, slightly grazing against my teeth. His hand fists my hair at the top of my head, and he forces me to take him in, lifting my head and fucking my mouth.

544

I gag around him, spit spilling past my lips.

"Good little wife taking her husband's dick down her throat. Keep going."

He doesn't give me a choice anyway. He thrusts harder, making me choke on him and the taste of me. He pulls out as violently as he pushed in. Now covered in my spit, he drives into my pussy again.

For a minute, I don't feel like anything more but an object he uses for his pleasure...and I fucking love it.

"That knife is not as thick as my dick, is it, baby?"

Lazily, I shake my head from side to side, barely able to.

"And you've taken my dick in your ass before, haven't you?"

I nod this time, but that's even harder to do.

He pulls out, grabs my hips, and flips me around. "I'm going to put you in the exact position I need. Don't you worry."

Spreading my legs far apart, he drags my hips back until my ass is in the air and my cheek rests against the soft sheets. I don't have the strength to push myself up, and I just fold with my head on the mattress.

"Atta girl. Don't move."

I hear him search through my bedside drawer, but my brain doesn't even try to register what he's looking for. I only understand when I feel a cold slickness dripping between my ass cheeks.

"Nate," I groan. He's not actually thinking of putting that thing in my ass, is he? "D-don't..."

"*Don't* is not a thing between us tonight, baby."

Was it ever a thing between us anyway?

He starts with his thumb, like every time he fucks my ass, and that brings enough pleasure to relax me. Then come two fingers, the delicious scissoring, a new depth.

While he does that, I feel the blade against my ass. He cuts me, and I press my mouth against the mattress to scream this time. I'm too quick to realize he's cutting into the scar I already have of his initials.

"Who's your sun, Kayla?"

"You are," I moan. "My sun."

But when his hand leaves me, and I feel the pressure of the hilt, I try to move away from him.

"Fight me, and I'll make it hurt in a way you *don't* like."

I whimper into the sheet and give up. I prefer when he has his way with me anyway. He pushes in, caressing my lower back at the same time.

"I'll like it if you cry. Don't hold back."

Those words lift a weight off my chest. And when the pleasure joins the discomfort of him pushing the hilt of a knife inside me, a sob escapes me.

"That's it, baby. Let it all go. Relax your body, give your mind a break. Give it all to me."

He fucks me slowly, and I let pleasure engulf me. Tears fall as I moan, and I even beg him for more.

"Slowly," he says. "You're pushing back. Don't hurt yourself."

Am I? But I need him so much. Doesn't he understand that?

A cry passes my lips, some unarticulated words pleading for more. He accelerates, but he's careful not to break me. It's barely enough for me. I'm craving the pain, crying out my need for it.

And when he pulls out, I sob some more. "Please, Nate... More."

"Shh. I'll hurt you now."

He grabs my hips and thrusts inside my pussy with a force that pushes me into the mattress.

"You want to hurt, baby?" His dick hits my cervix, and I cry out.

"Fuck...pull b-back."

"I don't think so. You're going to take every single inch of my dick like you begged to, and I want to hear you thank me for it."

He fucks me hard, fast, mercilessly. And I do exactly what he asks for. I thank him as I hurt. I thank him as I drown in pleasure, and I thank him when I come around his dick.

With his hand at the back of my neck, plastering my cheek to the mattress, he drives into me with a desire to make me his.

He comes with a grunt, pounding roughly before slowing his thrusts to a slow roll of his hips. And I take it all.

"That's my wife," he growls as he pulls out.

I try to roll to the side, but his hand cups my pussy right away, and he holds me in place with the one at my neck. "Keep it in." Whatever little cum is already spilling out, he pushes it back in with his fingers.

"Nate," I groan.

"Don't waste my cum, Kayla."

I sigh, and I could swear it sounds loving.

Eventually he has to let go, and I roll onto my back.

"Are you alright?" he asks, leaning over me. I nod as much as I can, and he kisses my lips gently.

My eyelids are too heavy to keep my eyes open.

"Sleep, little sunflower. I'll take care of you."

"You will?"

"I always will."

. . .

I can feel the warm sun on my skin, but it's a hard task to open my eyes. I force my eyelids open, only to realize I'm alone in bed. Something woke me up. I think it was the sound the front door makes when it closes.

Last night comes back so quickly, my heart drops to my stomach. I shoot into a sitting position and look around.

The girls.

Throwing off the covers, I jump out of bed. I'm in my sleep shorts and a tank top. Did Nate do that? Something stings the top of my abdomen, and I lift my top as I open my bedroom door.

I have to squeeze my eyes shut and look again as I freeze on the spot. A tattoo. There's a freshly wrapped tattoo just below my boobs. Exactly the same place as where Nate's sunflower tattoo and scar are on his body.

And then a detail comes back. His hand pushing more pills into my mouth after sex.

He drugged me.

He tattooed a fucking sun on me.

I walk into the girls' room, worry eating at me when I don't see them. I can't help but jog down the hallway, and when I storm into the living room, panic grips my chest.

They're not here.

What was I thinking? Letting him *drug* me with the girls in the house. Just because I felt I could trust him. With my life? Yes. I know with certainty Nate would do anything for me. But he just met the girls.

I hear an excited shriek coming from the kitchen. I run there, wanting to see my daughters like nothing before.

"Again!" Lia screams.

The smell of salty bacon and the sweetness of pancake batter hits me. Nate is topless, only wearing his jeans from yesterday, his countless tattoos on display against his golden skin. His muscles bulge as he holds Lia in one arm, propped on his hip. Stepping to the side, he keeps her away from the stove, and extends his other arm before flipping a pancake.

She shrieks again, clapping her hands. "Again!"

"Well, we have a whole stack ready. Don't you want to eat it before we make some more?" The way he says it sounds like he's pointing out the obvious. We will have to work on that.

But Lia doesn't notice. "Ooookay," she drawls, pretending it's a chore to eat pancakes.

"Are you hungry, Livie?"

Livie is sitting at the table, her back to me like the other two. She's simply watching them.

My heart swells, skipping a beat when I realize Nate includes her like I do. Even if she doesn't reply, he insists on talking to her anyway.

He turns around and finally sees me. "Good morning, little sunflower. Did you sleep well?"

The corner of his mouth tips up, and I clench my teeth. "You tattooed me."

He nods, putting Lia down in her seat next to Livie. He kisses me, his hand cupping the back of my neck, and smiles against my lips.

"Actually, Sam did. He finished the tattoo during the night, but I couldn't sleep so he stayed until I fed him some pancakes."

"Is that why you drugged me even more?" I whisper-hiss, making sure the girls can't hear. "So you could *tattoo* me?"

He goes back to the counter, finishing two plates, and puts them in front of the girls. The pancakes have eyes and a smile made of blueberries on them, and they are covered in maple syrup.

"I did it because the occasion presented itself, and it might never again. It looks beautiful, by the way."

And weirdly, it doesn't even bother me that much.

"It's insane." But I smile as I say it.

"Insane is my middle name."

"My name is Celia!"

I look down at my daughters and realize that, for the first time ever, Lia didn't scream my name when I entered the room, and Livie didn't run to hide against my legs.

As if they're in a completely trusting environment with Nate.

"So, baby," Nate starts as he goes back to the stove. "Should I put a smiley face or a frown on your pancakes?"

I run my tongue against my teeth, my hands going to my daughters' shoulders.

Livie lets her head fall against my forearm, and Lia bounces on the spot. "Mommy likes pancakes. Right, Mommy? Pancakes. Yummy. Yummy pancakes."

I take a deep breath, feeling like this is the decision of my life, and Nate looks at me expectantly too, like it was a trick question.

Do you want me? Do you not?

I swallow thickly. "A smiley face, my sun."

A smirk appears on his face. The cat who got the cream is standing right in front of me in my kitchen.

"Good answer."

43

KAYLA

die first - Nessa Barrett

We have some options, Mrs. White. Doing a diagnosis for autism spectrum disorder is one of them, but Livie might just be taking her time. Her hearing is good, and she can certainly express herself in other ways. Some children choose not to talk for a long time.

I can't stop running those words in my head, over and over again. Three weeks after Nate officially moved into my house on the North Shore, he suggested taking Livie to a child psychiatrist. It's the kind of doctor I could have never afforded before, but Nate said we don't have to worry about that now, and he wants to make sure everything is okay with her. I had started whatever tests I could afford around the time she turned one. I already knew she had no life-threatening illness, no disability. That her hearing was fine too.

My daughter doesn't want to talk, and we will accept her the way she is. We will take it one step at a time.

"Livie," I say to her as I drive over the bridge that leads

back to the North Shore. "Mommy promised you a popsicle if you were good, and you were so good with the doctor. Should we stop by the shop?"

She blinks at me and taps her knee once. I believe that's a yes, then. She never really had a thing. Tapping her knee doesn't specifically mean yes, but she does refer to that part of her body a lot. If it was a no, she would have just ignored me.

Nate stayed at home with Lia. I left him to deal with the tantrum of asking why Livie gets to spend alone time with me, and I promised her I would have 'Lia time' with her too.

I hold Livie's hand as we walk into my local shop. She's already dragging me to where she knows the freezer is, and that's how I know I was right. I take her into my arms and hold her as she chooses the popsicle she wants.

"Should we get one for Lia?"

She leans over again and takes the exact same one. The yellow one that tastes like lemon.

"Are you sure?" I chuckle. "Is that the one Lia likes, or are you trying to get two for yourself?"

She drops it and goes for it again, grabbing the pink one this time. Strawberry.

"I think that's more like it." I get her the second one anyway because she's been extra good. I can give it to her another day.

As I wait, a familiar voice calls my name, and when I notice Emma, a smile spreads on my face. Who knew I'd ever feel that way toward her.

"Hi, Li—" She stops herself, looking at my daughter in confusion.

"This one's Livie," I tell her.

"Hi, Livie!" she exclaims. It's been weird being friendly with Emma.

She still works for Nate, which technically means she works for me, but we don't talk about that. She's at the house often, plays with my daughters, and we've bonded over many things in the last weeks.

"Are you alright?" I ask, looking at the tub of ice cream in one hand and the pack of beer in the other. I pay for my stuff and wait as the cashier rings hers.

She sighs. "Just another useless date that went to shit."

"Shitty dates don't usually get you down like that."

She gives me a lopsided smile. "I just had a huge argument with Billie." She huffs. "I love her, but she keeps trying to make me leave this place, this life. She doesn't understand that I'm not like her. The North Shore is my home. It's a shitty home, but I feel good here. Especially now that, you know, NSC and the Kings are not at each other's throats too much anymore."

She pays for her stuff, and we head out. "She hasn't been back since things have been better. Maybe you should tell her to come."

"She's been traveling for her fights. But fuck, you're right, it's been weeks. We always argue when she hasn't been here in a while, but this one was bad. I think when we don't have the outlet of hitting each other, she gets really angry and upset."

She looks away as tears sparkle in her eyes. "She told me not to talk to her until I was ready to leave 'the criminal life.'"—she quotes with her fingers—"behind. Which is bullshit because I won't. She hung up on me."

Letting go of Livie's hand, I look for my car keys in my bag.

"Do you know what it sounds like?" I ask in total honesty. "It sounds like she loves her sister and she's worried for her."

Emma looks down at her plastic bag and nods. "Yeah, I think so. It would be stupid to stop talking just because we're both so stubborn."

"Uh-huh."

Livie pulls at my sleeve, and I feel her impatience. I squat next to her, open her popsicle, and give it to her. "Here you go, sweetie."

I just bought us a few minutes.

"Are you doing anything tonight? You should come over. We'll distract you better than beer and ice cream."

She bursts into a laugh. "You just want me to make my spinach and ricotta stuffed chicken, don't you?"

"Emma, it's so good. I can't get enough of it."

A car driving into the lot at full speed cuts off our laughter. Instinctively, I move my body in front of Livie, putting her between me and my car.

"What the fuck, asshole!" Emma screams.

But I know something is wrong when their tires screech to a halt right in front of us.

"Get in the car," I say as I drop the popsicles and open the door in a split second.

I pick up Livie, ready to take her with me on my lap to not waste any time, but I'm already too late. Two men jump out of the back, balaclavas covering their faces, and they point guns at us.

"I've got my kid. I've got my *kid*!" I bark, turning back to them and putting a hand on her head. "Don't hurt her!"

But they're not here to kill us. I know that because we're

still breathing as they walk toward us. They could have just shot and got back in the car.

A hand flies to my hair, dragging me back. "You're coming with us," the male voice orders, bringing his gun to my head.

"Wait! Wait...let me put her down. I'll come, just don't hurt my daughter."

He doesn't give a shit. He pulls me harder, and I'm forced to drop Livie in a clumsy way, mumbling, "Go to Emma," as she falls out of my arms. "Go to Emma, sweetie," I try to say in a reassuring voice.

It's hard to keep a calm tone. He's hurting me, pulling me so harshly that I stumble backward. Livie doesn't move, but Emma is taking her hand, pulling her away.

We're already at the car, and the one holding me is dragging me inside. The other turns around to get in, and Emma uses that moment to pull out her gun.

In a split second, the man holding me aims...and he shoots.

The bullet lands right in her head, and she falls backward to the ground.

"Emma!" My scream burns through my throat, piercing my ears. "No, no, no!"

He lowers his gun toward Livie, and I freeze. "Please, no. Please, please, please. She's just a baby..."

Tears stream down my face, my entire body shaking. He holds for a second that seems an eternity, then finally puts his gun away.

The door shuts, and I stare at my daughter as they start the car. I watch helplessly as I'm driven away, and she's left in a parking lot with my friend's dead body next to her.

"Livie!" I yell desperately. I'm hitting the window with all my strength, but there's nothing to do.

A hand comes from behind me while he still holds me by the hair, and he presses a rag to my mouth and nose.

I try to shake him off, to no avail. The smell makes me gag, the product stinging my already watery eyes.

"Livie!" My scream is muffled anyway, and my lungs burn from whatever is on that rag.

As my eyes close slowly, the last vision I have is of my daughter staring back at me, the lemon popsicle dripping down her fingers.

44

NATHAN

Unstoppable - The Score

"Angelica," I say flatly as I open the front door.

In the living room, Lia is dancing in front of the new screen I bought just a few days ago. She asked for a big TV, so I got her a big TV. Kay was mad. Every time I do something that improves her house, she's mad. But I'm not going to have my daughters live in the same shitty house she grew up in, no matter how nice Caden tried to make it look. There will be improvements because I said so. Or because my daughters said so. And also, because I manage to do them behind my wife's back before she can stop me.

Plus, Lia calls me Mr. Daddy now instead of Mr. Nate. The girl can ask anything she wants in the world. I'll get it just to hear her little excited voice saying, *"Thank you, Mr. Daddy."*

"I need money."

For a second there, I was so lost in my thoughts, I almost forgot Kay's mom was standing on the porch. If she thinks she's going to be invited in, she's about to get a brutal awakening.

"And you're telling me that because? I thought you'd gone back to West Virginia already."

She shakes her head. "I need money," she repeats.

I narrow my eyes at her. This woman is incredibly irritating. I take a step outside, almost closing the door behind me to make sure Lia can't hear anything.

"Angelica," I say calmly. So calmly I make sure it's threatening. "While I was in prison, I sent you five thousand dollars every single month for almost four years. You remember why, right?"

When she doesn't answer, I explain it to her like I would to a child, since she's got the mental capacity of one. "It was to spend on my daughters. To take care of them, and to keep your mouth shut. I did it when I wasn't even sure they were mine. Just on the off chance that they were, I wanted them to have everything they needed. Where did that money go?"

She shrugs, looking away. "Spent'it," she mumbles.

"Well, you didn't spend it on my girls, evidently. Did you?"

"My boyfriend has problems. Debts. It's an illness. I used it on that."

I shake my head. "Tsk, tsk. Why would I pay for your boyfriend's addiction?"

"I took care of them!" she shouts in my face, angry from not getting what she wants.

I straighten and roll my shoulders back. "You did the minimum you should have done. You never took care of your daughter. What do you want for finally acting like a decent person? A trophy? More money? You left your own daughter with the man who raped you. You left when you knew he hit her, hurt her."

Rage rises within me. It's so different from the usual void I feel that I can't keep control of it. I step into her personal space, towering over her.

"You left hoping if he had her, he wouldn't come for you."

Her eyes widen, and she stumbles back. I'm going to assume I hit the jackpot there. So I keep going.

"You didn't even tell her I knew about Lia and Livie. You should have been on her side, not mine, just because I gave you money. Now, how about you leave before I kill you and make it hurt. And if I see you in the vicinity of my wife or my children again, I will hurt you beyond repair. You'll live, but it'll be a pretty fucking miserable life."

Her lips pinch, wrinkles creasing around her mouth. "I don't know what she sees in you."

I can feel my face twisting in disgust. "What? Compared to what you left her with? I'm going to guess safety, protection, comfort."

"You're a madman."

"And what better thing in life than to have a madman completely and utterly in love with you? Ready to do anything to keep you happy and safe? Leave. It's your last chance to do so in one piece."

I watch her retreat, running back to a rundown car. It's going to be a long drive home for her.

I'm about to head back inside, when a police car stops right in front of our house. Captain Martinez walks out, his eyes on me as he opens the back door. His expression isn't pleasant, but I can't pinpoint what it is. Bad news. If only I had Kayla to explain people to me right now.

559

He helps someone get out, and my stomach twists painfully when I see Livie. She's as silent as usual when he takes her hand and walks her to me. I'm already stepping down the porch, striding toward them. Livie lets go of Martinez and runs to me, so I welcome her in my arms, picking her up.

That's when I notice the blood splattered on her clothes. And it looks like it was on her face too, but someone used a wipe on her.

My sharp gaze snaps back to Martinez.

"I was called to a murder scene by the convenience store on Sycamore Road."

My arms automatically tighten around Livie. I take another step toward Martinez.

"Emma Scott got shot in the head."

I look down at Livie's clothes. Emma's blood.

"My wife, Martinez," I hiss. "Where is she?"

His mouth twists as he hooks his thumbs into his belt. "Disappeared into thin air."

There are a few seconds of silence as we just look at each other. I'm not speechless, simply trying to control my sudden urge to brutally murder a cop.

My wife...is gone.

Gone.

How am I meant to control the fury starting to boil my blood? It burns my veins painfully. I feel it from my heart, all the way to my wrists. Something *hurts.*

"What do you mean, *disappeared*?"

"She's gone."

Gone. I'm going to make him choke on that fucking word.

"Then why aren't you looking for her?" I try to put Livie

down, but she tightens her hold on me, so I give up right away. "I want the CCTV from that shop."

"No CCTV. The only witness was Emma and your kid who don't talk." He points at Livie with his chin.

"Don't talk about my kid." With that out of the way, I add, "There's an ATM right in front of the shop."

He shrugs casually. "No CCTV."

Alright. So the man has been bought.

"You want to hide things from me, Martinez? Are you forgetting who I am?"

"What you are is someone who's been weakened by family in a matter of months. And you're not as scary as the men who got your wife, believe me. I'll be staying out of that one."

He turns around, walking back to his car without a fear in the world. My phone rings, timed perfectly with his exit. It's an unknown number.

"Nathan White." The Russian accent confirms what I already know.

It's not Viktor Volkov, the head of the Wolves, because he speaks perfect English, but it's someone in his entourage.

I wait patiently for the man to give me more information. It's an art to control dread when it's already spreading within my entire body. My head twitches, and I hold Livie closer to me. As if she's the one protecting me.

"What a pretty wife. Very pretty."

It takes all of me to not threaten him. To not lose control completely. I still need more info.

"Too bad you will never see her again."

I take a deep breath, my nostrils flaring, and calmly ask, "What do you want?"

Because let's face it. I will give them *anything* to get Kayla back.

"We don't want anything."

He chuckles, having the time of his life. "We only teach you lesson. Bad things happen when you steal business from the Wolves. Now your wife works for us. Beautiful body. Good money. We keep her alive until she pays back all the money we lost from you trying to take over us."

I hear him speaking away from the phone, clearly to someone else. "Say thank you to your husband, sweetheart. All this is because of him."

She doesn't, of course. All I hear is a dull sound and a whimper from her. Something that sounds like pain and despair. Something that tears down my sanity, that liquifies and blackens my blood.

"Goodbye."

He hangs up on me, and I stand still for a minute, looking at my phone, my mind completely empty but for the delicious rage poisoning my heart.

Well.

It's time for a massacre.

I glance at the people around the table. I'm back in my Stoneview Mansion because I needed space. When you prepare for war, you need room to think, and I was suffocating in Kayla's house. Mainly because it smells so much like her. Because everything there is what forged her, who she is. I need away from everything that weakens me if I want to think straight.

Only the people I know I can use to find the Wolves are

Lawless God

around this table. Sam, of course. But also Rose and Lik because my sister spent two years with the Wolves when *she* was kidnapped by them. There was nothing I could do when it happened to her. I was stuck in prison. But Sam and Lik got her back in the end, and that means I can get Kay back too. The three of them have priceless information about the organization.

Elliot, Ethan, and Jade are here too, because I need people who will be almost as desperate as me to get her back. Which brings me to Caden, her brother. He's standing still, his gaze lost in the void as his fiancée cries silently into his arms. I don't think he realizes how hopelessly she's holding on to him. He looks like he's envisioning slaughtering the men who took his own sister. Good thing they're the same who killed Emma.

Xi stands next to them, strong arms crossed over his chest. He tried to console Billie, but Caden pulled out a knife. He and Lik don't look so well. I assume that tends to happen when you lose your stepsister so suddenly.

Two of Emma's trusted men are here. Logan and Nino. The former is here to be supportive of Emma's relatives, and the second deals arms. Meaning, he's been in some circles the Wolves have frequented.

I stand at the head of the table, taking a breath before I talk. Sam observes me like I'm a ticking time bomb. He's absolutely and undoubtedly one hundred percent right.

If I don't find Kayla soon, blood will spill. Scratch that. It will flood the fucking streets.

"Listen to me. I am not looking for an all-out war, some business deals, or to shoot every single Wolf you see on sight. I need everyone to act smart. We are not looking around blindly. We want something that will link us to

563

whoever was in that parking lot. A witness, a video. I want the car that took her. I want people who could draw me their exact faces and point them out in the crowd of a Taylor Swift concert, am I clear? Because *this* is the only lead we have right now. The Wolves are masters at hiding, and we won't get to them any other way. Find the people who took Kayla. They will lead us to where they're keeping her."

I turn to Logan. "Where is your little computer genius? I want her to hack the CCTV from that shop and the ATM right in front of it. Cops are refusing to help. Martinez kindly told us there are none, when I know for a fact both have cameras."

Logan shakes his head. "Tamar had to travel back to Morocco with her mom. Death in her family."

"I'll find someone else. In the meantime, get the laptop from my office. We'll get you on the dark web. I want you to scan every single..." Oh, this is going to hurt coming out. I let out a breath. "Every single sex trafficking website."

I turn to Ethan, Elliot, and Jade. "You were staying with a Wolf for a while, weren't you?"

Jade's eyes dart to the brothers before coming back to mine as she nods slowly. "Stanislav."

"Go to his house," I tell her boyfriends. "Tell me if he's there. That's it. Do not go in yet."

"He lives eight hours away."

"Then you better get going."

They're up in a split second, and I'm on to Sam.

"Their old compound. The one you'd found."

He shakes his head. "That place has been empty for a long time. They moved."

"I don't care. Lik, check it. Sam, I want you outside Vue Club." The club the Wolves own on the South Bank of

Silver Falls will surely help at some point. "The second I have a face, you can look for them there. *No point* in trying to get anyone else to talk. And leave Aaron Williams if you see him. It'll show our hand too soon, and those puppies would rather die than spill out where their compound is. Most of their soldiers don't know anyway."

I look around at who I have left. "Xi." He separates from Billie, taking a step toward me.

I'm surrounded by people who hate me. I've threatened them, the ones they loved. I united the North Shore and forced enemies to work with each other. But Kay has been taken, and the Kings have too much respect and love for her to not try to get her back.

And Emma is dead, so NSC wants their revenge. That means Xi might hate me, but he's on my side right now.

"What is it?" he asks, voice low. There's a rasp in it from the sadness that's attempting to choke him.

"You've got dealers in the area Kay was taken. Talk to them." I don't wait for his answer. I know he will.

"Any suggestions?" I ask the room.

"Martinez?" Sam suggests. "He didn't want to talk, but I'm sure we can make him."

I shake my head. "Martinez is dead."

My best friend cocks an eyebrow at me.

"I tried to hold back, Sam. I really tried." The fucker should have talked. I would have let him live.

I scan the room and stop on Kay's brother. "Caden."

His eyes shutter over to me like I just woke him up from a dream. I get it. He's probably the only one who comes near how I feel right now. His eyes look exactly like Kay's. It's unsettling.

I look him up and down, catching the sight of Billie's desolated form, and I deem he's got enough on his plate.

"Get your shit together," I simply say. "Your fiancée needs you." I pause, feeling like I need to say the rest out loud for myself rather than him. "Don't worry. We'll find her."

A snort catches my attention, and I turn toward Nino sitting right next to Logan.

I cock an eyebrow at him. "Problem?"

"Kayla was taken by the Wolves. You're one hell of a delusional fucker if you think we'll find her. And if we do, believe me, it'll be too late to get her back in one piece. It already is."

A silence falls over the room. Even Billie turns to him.

I slide my hand inside my suit jacket, pull out my gun, and shoot.

The bullet lands in his skull, and he blinks, swaying before falling forward, smashing against my table.

That doesn't help with the heavy silence.

I turn to everyone else, looking into each of their wide eyes. "Would anyone else like to raise an issue? No one? Good." I press myself forward, my thighs against the table. "Because they took *my fucking wife!*" I slam my gun flat on the table as I roar.

It makes them all startle, and I get it because I don't scream often. It must be a shock to all of them.

"Now if you think I'm not ready to annihilate every single motherfucker who gets in my way of finding her, *think again.* No one sleeps, no one *breathes,* until we've found her. Get that in your heads."

I turn to my sister, not containing my threats anymore. "Try Jake again." My useless brother has been refusing to see me since I've gotten out of prison, but he's not staying out of this one. "Tell him I'll slit Jamie's throat if he doesn't show up."

Just as I finish talking, the door to the room opens, and small steps sprint to me.

"Mr. Daddy, I want waffles!"

"Oh my god," someone gasps, running after her in a mess of blonde hair and a pink dress. "Lia, come back here. I told you not to go in there." Alexandra Delacroix, Xi's sweet girlfriend, looks at me with wide eyes. "I'm so sorry... she's so quick."

Rachel stands by the door, holding Livie in her arms, and making sure to stay out of the room when she notices the body. They both insisted on being here, but their significant others categorically refused to let them in the room. Maybe they understand why now.

Lia is already climbing up my leg, and I pick her up quickly, forcing her head away and making sure there's no way she can turn to see Nino's body.

I walk out of the room, holding her close to my chest. "And we're having waffles for dinner," I conclude to everyone before closing the door.

I'm heading back down the stairs after putting the girls to sleep, when Billie finds me. I'm not sure where Caden is, but everyone still here is in the kitchen, so he might be there.

"You didn't give me anything," she says. Her eyes are red, her face puffy.

I can't share her pain. Not only because I can't empathize with her, but because there is too much anger in me. Mainly, there's too much hope. Her situation is irreversible. I know I will find Kay. I have to.

"You're grieving," I tell her. "That's plenty enough."

"I want to avenge my sister, Nathan." She shakes her

head. "I—We..." She drags in a breath, her bottom lip trembling. "I told her I didn't want to talk to her anymore. I told her to not call me until she left this life. I was so mad at her and now..." A sob bursts out of her, clearly uncontrollable. "And now she's gone. My sister's dead and the last thing I said to her was to stop talking to me. I *hung up on her.*"

I put a hand on her shoulder, trying to be comforting. But there's no warmth emanating from me. No reassurance. I can't offer those things. She's come to the wrong guy.

"I'll avenge Emma," I say simply. "You do what you can to make peace with it."

I don't think that helps, but I have to keep moving forward. Billie is stuck, and I have to find the love of my life before a pain greater than hers enters my life.

I walk down the hall, nodding back to my guards who say hello to me. This house is a fortress. This is where I should have kept my wife and daughters. Where no one can get to them. Safe.

The front door opens, and my guard Enzo comes in.

"Boss," he says. "Someone here for you."

He steps to the side, and one of the million weights piling on my shoulders falls off.

"Would you look at that. He finally flew too close to the sun."

I grit my teeth, wanting with everything I have to attack him back. That's the kind of relationship we have. But I hold back, stay still. And I think he understands I have no intention of keeping the animosity going, so his tone changes.

"So I heard I'm an uncle now."

My brother Jake doesn't offer even the hint of a smile,

but he's here, and that's all that matters. He even brought Jamie.

"You are. They're sleeping." I look at their tightly joined hands. He's holding her like someone is going to snatch her away. "Were you too scared to leave her alone at home?"

"So one of your guards could go threaten her while I'm here? She stays by my side."

Jamie huffs, pulling her hand away.

"I insisted on coming. In case you both forgot, I have my own experience with people I love being taken away by the Wolves," she explains. "Hi, Nathan. I'm sorry about what happened. But just so we're clear, your threats did nothing. I'm the one who convinced him to come."

I nod. It's a good thing she's here. She will be helpful if my brother gives me a hard time.

She looks up at Jake from her petite form. "Come on. Let's get to it. Time is precious."

You wouldn't guess Jake and I are brothers if not for our identical eyes. He's bulkier than me, slightly shorter too. His hair is the blackest black, like Rose, whereas mine is a dirty blond. The twin's skin complexion is a little darker than mine too. Despite my chiseled jaw, my features are softer than his. I'm the kind of predator that'll lure you in to kill you. Jake is the kind you'll know to stay away from. Well, apparently, Jamie didn't.

I lead them to the kitchen. Caden and Billie are somewhere else in the house. I sent Lik away earlier, but Sam is back from his first stakeout at Vue Club. Everyone else but Rose and Rachel have their own tasks too.

Jake goes to his twin right away, hugging her tightly before saying hi to Rachel and Sam. Jamie follows, and they all turn to face me. Jake takes his laptop out of the backpack he brought and opens it on the kitchen island.

"Do I want to know what you did to piss off the Wolves?" he asks, looking down at his screen.

My brother isn't just a pretty face. He's a computer genius who became a millionaire by selling apps to companies. If someone can retrieve that CCTV video, it's him.

"I took ownership of the hotels they used to wash most of their money. It also happened to be the place they used for their sex trafficking. They held auctions there and occupied some of the rooms all year long as a luxurious brothel."

Jake looks up at me and cocks an eyebrow. "Is that what you're using those hotels for?"

I feel my eyebrows pinch. "Will you stop wasting my time?" I snap. "Of course not. I'm washing my money there. Using the hotels as a hub to receive stocks from my suppliers. I don't deal in humans. Now fucking get to it."

"Alright." He focuses on the laptop. "Let's find your wife, I guess." Tapping on the mouse pad, he types for a few seconds and says, "Where was she when they took her?"

After I tell him, he spends twenty or so minutes typing on his laptop, muttering nonsense to himself, and huffing like an old man. The longest twenty minutes of my life. I keep pacing around the room, aware of Sam's gaze on me. He knows I'm bound to explode at some point.

"I'm in," Jake says suddenly. My ears perk up, and I practically sprint to his side of the island. Rose comes too, standing right beside me.

He's on a server that has hundreds of videos from a

security camera. They're the same thing, the parking lot of the shop where Emma got shot and Kay taken.

"So that's the shop one. Was it today? Around what time?"

I nod. "Just after lunch."

I lean closer, my eyes squinting as he goes through the dates.

I'm coming, little sunflower. I'll find you. You just hold on, please. Hold on for me.

He finds today's videos, scrolls through the different times, and my heart freezes, turning to stone.

"It's gone," Jake murmurs. "It's been deleted. Let me try the ATM."

He does the same thing with the ATM's server.

"Deleted," my brother says.

"No." I push him out of the way, scrolling through the videos. "No, no, no."

I open one video, then another. All the ones for today. The CCTV goes from an empty parking lot at twelve p.m. and the next video is of the cops at the crime scene.

"I can look into anything near this shop. Is there another place that could have security cameras?"

"There's a gas station not far. Another minute by car."

My brother nods. "Let me find it. If they went that way, we might be able to see their car."

The gas station has multiple cameras, even one facing the road that watches all the cars go by. But at that time of day, even in that small town, there were at least twenty cars that went by. How am I meant to know which one it is? I watch them one by one. Jake even zooms in as much as we can. Nothing tells us if Kay is in one of those.

I spin around, turning to my sister. I don't want to do

this. I didn't want to bring up moments that almost killed her, but I have no choice.

"Ozy," I rasp. Her eyes widen when she understands what I want. She takes a few steps back.

Sam is onto me right away. "No. Nate, no."

Rachel follows, taking my sister's hand. "She doesn't know anything. There's no need to talk about it."

"Ozy, please. You must have seen something. You must have heard things. Places they hide. Safehouses. A different compound. I'm begging you."

The Wolves held my sister for almost two years. Why? Because she's the one who shot Vladimir Volkov. The same man I was accused of killing and sent to prison for. We were all there that night. Vladimir was holding me at gunpoint for the same reason the Wolves and the Cosa Nostra have always fought. Territories, businesses, money.

My sister shot the head of the Bratva Wolves to save me. There was more than Kay's testimony that sent me away. Because that night I took the gun from my sister and put my fingerprints on it. I spread my blood on the murder weapon. There was absolutely no way I would ever let it be linked back to her.

But the Wolves had a different idea of justice. A few months later, they took her, and before I could find her, I was arrested.

She shakes her head. "I'm sorry. I never... I was never awake when they moved me. The compound where I was held...it was destroyed."

"Enough." Sam puts his gigantic body between my sister and me. "You are not bringing back traumatic memories. Not when they are useless and even less when your sister worked so hard at getting better. I'm putting a stop to this for the night."

He turns to the two women behind him. "We're going home."

"I'm sorry," Rose repeats, and I can see how bad she feels. It's written all over her face.

"It's okay, Ozy."

But when I turn to leave the room, fire spreads throughout my veins. It's destructive, and unable to stop myself, I act on it.

Before I know what's happening, everything that was on the kitchen island is wiped away, thrown to the floor. And in less than a minute, my kitchen is destroyed, plates shattered, the oven door broken, appliances wrecked.

There's chaos in my head, and all that roars out of my mouth are the same three words.

"Where is she?" Something else is destroyed, but all I see is Kayla's body being used by other men. Men who want to break her. All I hear are her cries of pain.

"Where is she?!" I scream again. Something isn't right inside. It hurts. My heart is hardening, so stiff I wonder how it can even beat.

"...stop." I can barely hear her voice. My sister. She's trying to reach through the fury. "Please, breathe."

It's her hands flat on my cheeks that start to bring me back. I don't want to hurt her. She forces me to look at her, her eyes digging into mine. "We'll find her." I try to shrug her away, but she keeps me still with a soft hold.

"We'll find her," she repeats. "Nate, if I survived the Wolves for two years, Kayla King can too. She's as tough as they come. They won't break her. They can't."

I grunt something that sounds like an agreement through my panting breaths.

"We'll find her."

My shoulders sag. "I can't name it," I croak. "It fucking hurts."

Her eyes bounce between mine. "Name what?"

Kay would get it. My little sunflower would look at me, unimpressed, annoyed that I'm such a lost cause. And then she would help me. She would help me name it so I can process it.

What do I feel, little sunflower? Name it.

Helpless, my sun.

45

NATHAN

Woke Up A Rebel - Reuben And The Dark

"Daddy, I want Mommy's waffles. The waffles. I don't like, Daddy."

I sip on my coffee, taking my time before talking to my daughter. I'm leaning on the counter with Livie in my arms while Lia plays around with the food on her plate. She loves my pancakes, but when I make waffles, she prefers Kay's.

Because she associates waffles with her mom, and she misses her mom. So they're not good enough.

"Daddy, where's Mommy?"

Every morning, Lia asks me the same question. She asks for waffles, tells me she prefers her mom's, and then uses the occasion to ask where she is. And every day, I tell her the same lie.

"She's visiting Nanna, but she'll be back soon."

Three weeks. I've been lying to my daughter for three weeks. Lia just calls me *Daddy* now. Because I'm all she has.

I would have her call me Mr. Nate forever if it meant getting Kay back.

"Daddy," Lia insists, but there's been less energy in her in the last few weeks. Her voice isn't as excited anymore. She doesn't shriek with happiness like she usually does.

And Livie... She doesn't talk, but I know she's seen things that must have traumatized her forever. She's even less communicative than usual. She always ends up running from her room to mine during the night, seeking comfort in my arms. All I can do is hold her and hope for the best.

I put down my cup of coffee, then scratch the beard I'm sporting from not taking care of myself. I'm barely a shadow of the man I was weeks ago. How am I meant to live when I've not seen the person who makes me feel alive?

Lik found nothing at the compound where they had rescued Rose. Of course not. They told me it had been abandoned. Xi's dealers weren't at the scene when it happened. Logan found nothing online and stopped after he saw traumatizing stuff. Stanislav's house is empty. Elliot and Ethan broke in. There's no one there. Jade explained she didn't think it was his main place, but more a vacation home, which he obviously isn't using in the winter. I have nothing. No leads, no clues.

All I do is send Sam to watch Vue Club every now and then—but he hasn't seen any familiar faces around there—and spend my days scrolling through sex trafficking websites, hoping and not hoping that I see Kay on there.

"Daddy?"

Lia's little voice brings me back. "Yes, honey?" Kay calls Lia *honey* and Livie *sweetie*. I make sure to do the same.

She looks at me with her wide blue eyes, and her lower

lip starts trembling. "I miss Mommy." Her pout pinches the second she's finished talking, and she's done holding herself back. Tears start streaming down her face, triggering me into striding to her.

Livie's hold tightens on me, clearly sharing her sister's sentiment. Her nails dig into my shoulder, leaving little crescents in the tattoo there.

Lia jumps off the island stool, and I squat to take her in my arms. "Don't cry, honey," I tell her as I straighten up. "Mommy's okay." She has to be. "She'll be back soon. I promise you." I kiss her head, and then Livie's. "I promise both of you."

What is wrong with me? Making promises I might not be able to keep. Kay is out there, suffering, going through things I refuse to even imagine. I have no way of finding her. Fuck, I'm as lost as these two little girls, and I dare to make this promise?

But what else? There's no other option. No life I live without Kay.

I hug them for as long as I can without breaking down. And when I feel myself on the brink of holding on to my straight face, I pull away slightly.

"Who wants to dance while we wait for Uncle Lik? You love that song Alex showed you, don't you? What's the name?"

Just like all the other days, Lik is going to come around ten to watch the girls while I lose myself down the rabbit hole of trying to find their mom.

"Style!" Lia exclaims suddenly. "Yes, Daddy! I want to dance. Dance!"

I put them down, taking their hands.

"Let's go."

If someone had told me when I kidnapped Kayla King

that I would be dancing to Taylor Swift's "Style" with our two daughters months later...I would have laughed in their faces.

But here I am, watching Lia run around, hopping with her arms waving above her head. Livie holds my hand, and I make her spin on the spot before bringing her back to me.

She giggles and my heart melts into a puddle. It's so rare to hear anything out of her, that I do it again and again until she's rolling on the floor from laughter and Lia is tugging at my tracksuit, asking to do it with her too. I do. I enjoy the only moment of happiness I've felt in a while. A few songs later, we're all exhausted. Except Lia, of course. She keeps running around while I sit down on the floor and Livie comes on my lap.

She sits facing me and presses her favorite tattoo on my body with her little finger. The sunflower.

"Oh, sweetie," I sigh. My heart threatens to break, barely held together by the beautiful eyes of my daughter looking up at me. "The things you must have seen. I wish I could get inside your little head and erase them."

Taking her other hand, I add, "Now is the time you surprise all of us by talking, sweetie. Maybe even show us you're some secret genius who remembered the exact license plate of that car. Something crazy like that."

She blinks up at me, staying completely silent, and then goes back to pressing the tattoo representing her mother.

An hour later, I've changed into jeans and a t-shirt, and Lik has taken over looking after the girls. I walk into my office, stopping on the spot when I see Caden King sitting at my desk. He often comes with Ethan, Elliot, and Jade. They all want news I can't give them. They're all here right now, the three others sitting on the leather sofa.

Caden doesn't waste a second.

"I contacted the men from the Wolves who used to deal me arms, like you asked." His flat voice reminds me of mine, and I wonder if I always sound so empty.

"And?" I ask as I close the door. "What did they say?"

"They said they didn't even know she'd been taken. They don't deal with humans, only weapons. They also said they wouldn't tell me if they did because Kayla King deserved what happened to her after betraying the Wolves and marrying the man who killed one of them with his bare hands."

I stop by my desk, the same daily disappointing feeling washing over me. Every time I think of something that could get me closer to her, it leads nowhere.

"Which reminded me," Caden keeps going. "That it was a marriage she didn't even have a choice in." He puts his hand on the table, holding a gun. "That she would have never been a target for the Wolves if it wasn't for you."

He points the gun at me, but I stand still.

"Cade," Jade says quickly. "This is stupid."

"You're frustrated," I add, as if I could know.

"That's an understatement."

"Whatever it is you feel, I feel the same." I lean closer to him. "Do you want to act like an idiot and kill the man your sister loves? The twins' father? So what? So when Kay is finally free, she can hate you with all she has?"

His head tilts to the side. "You're driven by a hope that will lead nowhere. They got her. They've had her for three weeks. If we ever get her back, she won't be the same. And that's all because of you."

I clench my jaw, so infuriated I could snap his neck. And yet, I keep it in. "Do you think I don't know that?"

He straightens his arm, and the only reason I'm not

ready to be shot by yet another person with the King last name is because I don't want to leave my daughters behind. Because I know, deep down, I will find my wife and bring her back.

I just don't know when.

The sound of the door opening startles us both, and when Caden's eyes go behind me, he hides the gun right away.

"Daddy!" Lia's voice is not excited. It's as angry as this little spitfire can get. A lot.

Her furious steps run toward me, and she pulls at the hem of my shirt even though I'm already turning around.

"You said Mommy is with Nanna!" She puts her little fists on her hips like Kay does when she's angry at me. "Livie says she's with the men!"

"Livie talked?" I ask, shock lowering my voice.

"Livie no talk," she answers like I'm stupid. "I understand Livie. And she says Mommy is with the men in the white car with the horse. You lied, Daddy. That's bad. Mommy said lying is bad. You lied."

"The white car with the horse?" I repeat. I fall to my knees, taking my daughter's hands. "Is that what Livie saw? Did she say Mommy was in that car?"

"Yes," she insists, her face pinches as she shows me how mad she is at me.

"A Mustang," Jade says right away. "She means a white Mustang."

"Or a Ferrari?" Caden asks her.

She shakes her head. "Ferraris aren't exactly ideal to kidnap someone. It's got to be a Mustang."

Emotions surge inside me. "Thank you, Lia," I say, giving her a kiss on the head.

"You lied, Daddy."

"And that's really bad," I confirm. "But I'll make it right."

I grab my phone right away as Caden takes Lia with him out of the office.

"Jake," I say as soon as my brother picks up. "Check those gas station videos again. We're possibly looking for a white Mustang."

Of course, he was already on his laptop. "Give me a sec." I hear him typing for what seems like forever.

I crack my neck, feeling my eye twitch. Come on.

"Found it."

"What?" After three weeks of bad news, my heart can barely take a good one.

"A white Mustang drove past the station a couple of minutes after the time the CCTV stops in the parking lot. I've got a license plate. ADC 3358. It's a New York plate."

"Holy shit." My mouth drops open, and I have to shake my head to bring myself back. "I need you to find this car. Hack the highway cameras, every single one. I don't care. Just tell me where it went. And find out who this car belongs to."

I hang up on him, realizing Caden is back now. "This is still far from finding Kay," he says. "It's just the car that took her."

I come face to face with him, barely a few inches away.

"Listen to me. I have had a part of my heart ripped away by the Wolves. I could barely survive the first day; I don't even know how I survived three weeks. But I will not stop looking for her until she is found. If it's not with that car, I will find the man who owns it and break every single one of his bones until I get information. If that doesn't bring me to her, I will burn every single fucking house down in the state of New York until I get my hands on my wife. Do you understand? *I am not stopping.* Not until I get her back."

I observe him for a few seconds of silence before adding, "So are you with me or not?"

All he gives me is a nod, but I'll take it.

By the evening, once I've read to the girls and put them to bed, I've gathered everyone again. Because I know today is the day I find Kayla, and I need all of them to do so.

Fuck, I even laid out an arsenal of weapons on the long table in my dining room.

I'm coming. Don't worry. I'm coming.

We've all been waiting silently, as Jake is still typing on his laptop. I can't stop scratching my beard, pacing, playing with my gun. It has to happen. It has to be now.

"The car belongs to a man called Bogdan Vasiliev."

My sister's head snaps up from her phone.

"What?" Blood drains from her face, and that makes my heart kick into gear.

"Do you know him?" I ask.

"He—he was Aleksei's right-hand. He must have taken over human trafficking when Aleksei was killed."

Jake speaks again, bringing my gaze back to him. "I lost them between this exit, and that one." He points at two points on a map. "There's no exit in-between so I'm not sure where they disappeared. And the two are ten miles apart." He shakes his head. "There's nothing else I can do."

"There's a place Bogdan would mention in passing," Rose says. Rachel stands behind her, her hands on her shoulders. "But I have no idea where in the country it is. It...it could lead nowhere. I always assumed it was just some bar or something."

"The name, Ozy," I snap, my patience wearing thin.

"The Nightcap."

Jake is already on it, typing it on a map.

When the location pops up, my stomach drops. It's right along the highway. Between those two exits.

My head snaps back up, and everyone understands because they're already standing. Sam is packing weapons on his body, Lik copying him. Xi, Ethan, Elliot, Caden, they're all grabbing guns. Some to avenge the dead, some to save the living.

"What the fuck do you think you're doing?" I look at Caden grabbing a gun from Billie.

"Packing to kill the men who murdered my sister."

"Little Bee," he chuckles. "Am I going to have to tie you up to this chair to stop you from doing anything stupid?"

I don't listen to the rest, realizing this conversation is happening at two other places in the room. Ethan grabs Jade's gun while Elliot points at the oxygen bag she carries everywhere. It's a tiny thing, and she seems to barely ever use it, but I believe it's just in case.

"And where will you take your little break when you need to breathe?"

"This is bullshit," she snaps back. "I don't even need this thing anymore. You're the ones who insist I take it everywhere. Kay is like a sister to me. You can't stop me!"

My gaze lands on my sister and her three partners.

"You misogynistic fuck," she barks at Sam. "Give me that." She's trying to take back the gun he just snatched out of her hand. "I can aim better than all of you combined. My brother is suffering from this. We're talking about people who hurt me. I get to go!"

I take a step back from the mess, checking my gun has ammo by undoing the magazine and sliding it back.

I'm almost there, little sunflower.

46

KAYLA

Soldier - Tommee Profitt, Fleurie

The door to my bedroom slams open, banging against the wall from the force, and Bogdan stomps in. His gigantic frame makes me retreat on the twin bed, but I don't get off. If I do, he'll tie me to it. I learned that pretty quickly.

I only leave this room when they allow us to use the toilets and shower. Every day, a handler comes in, tells us to get naked, and takes us to the communal bathrooms. We use the toilet, brush our teeth, and shower in silence, not allowed to talk to each other. I think it's more than once a day because the girls need to shower often. But I couldn't say how many times.

I haven't spoken to anyone but my own handler and Bogdan. From what I understand, there's one handler for four girls. Because this isn't just my life now. It's the life of all the other women the Wolves took from the streets for sex trafficking.

Bogdan said I was young and beautiful enough to be put in their *luxury* auctions. That I could have had a better life if I'd been bought by some man there. *"Maybe even a prince,"* he laughed that day. But this is my punishment for Nate stealing the place where they used to hold those auctions. Now I get to stay in what they call the *"dirty brothel."* Wherever this place is.

On my first day, I broke the nose of my handler when he tried to put his hand between my legs while I was showering. That earned me the beating of my fucking life. Reminded me of when my dad didn't care if he broke me beyond repair or not.

But I'm not stupid. I did that on purpose. Because if I'm black and blue, they can't make me work. Even if this is the dirty brothel, they can't offer a broken whore who won't be able to satisfy their client.

I don't know how much time that bought me. I have no idea how long I've been here. There is no window in my room, and it smells damp enough that I know we're underground. All there is is a chest with all types of worn-down lingerie and a mirror leaning against the wall not far from it. A twin bed with an overused mattress, a thin gray blanket, and a single flat pillow. Oh, and a bedside table with a lamp that shines a red light and a drawer full of lube and condoms. How kind.

Without the sun, I've been unable to tell how many days I've been here. They bring small meals to my room, but they don't come at regular intervals, and the food never indicates if it's meant to be breakfast, lunch, or dinner. They do it on purpose.

And it works. I'm completely lost. All I know is that it's been long enough for my bruises to heal and for the swelling on my eyes to disappear. Even the cuts from their boots stomping on my stomach are gone.

I'm as good as new, and I know that's why Bogdan is here today and not the handler. He's the boss in this place.

He throws a sandwich wrapped in plastic film at me, and it bounces against my chest, falling onto my lap. I'm wearing what the girls wear if they're not with a client. A large gray t-shirt and some even larger gray sweatpants. That shit falls off my hips every time I try to stand.

"You look good, twenty-three."

I feel my face twist when he calls me by my number. I understood every girl here has no name, just a number, when I heard them call them before showers. They check we're all there every time we're taken out of our rooms.

Say nothing, raise your hand, keep your eyes down. That's what the girl standing right next to me said on the first day. She's twenty-two.

I heard her cries coming from the other side of the wall that same day while I was recuperating from being beaten up.

"You'll finally be able to start bringing us some money," Bogdan says. "You've already got two bookings for today. But the numbers will go up. People love fresh meat."

With a churning stomach, I stay quiet, sitting on the bed, avoiding his gaze by looking at my lap.

"Get up. Let me see what I'm selling."

I fist my sweatpants, refusing to let them slip down as I stand up next to the bed. I keep my eyes on the floor, not trusting what I'll do if I look at him.

"Your husband has stopped looking for you."

My heart squeezes painfully, a noose tightening around my throat.

That's not true. That's not true. That's not true.

I look down at my left hand, Nate's initials carved into my skin give me a sense of safety. If he was mad enough to do that, I know he won't leave me behind. They somehow let me keep my rings, maybe to remind me of why I'm here. I will try to sell them to a client. Tell them they're his if he gets me out. I'll fucking try anything.

"Until a week ago, I was told he was out of his mind. He was doing everything he could." He shrugs. "I guess he gave up because there's no more news from him. Nathan White has stopped looking for you, twenty-three."

He's trying to destroy your hope. But he will come. Nate will save you, and he'll bring you back to your daughters.

I try to imagine Lia's laughter and the way she calls my name. I think of how tightly Livie holds me when I carry her. I remind myself that, no matter what, Nate always finds me. He'll bring me back home. But my thoughts are cut short by Bogdan's voice.

"Undress."

My gaze snaps up. His hardened black eyes are on me. That man had his nose broken before. I can see that. And in a suicidal move, because I would rather die than have him sell my body, I punch him.

My fist flies to his nose, knowing it must be fragile from past hits. Blood splatters, and he brings his hands to his face as he stumbles back.

"Fucking bitch!"

He's back on me in a split second, wrapping a mighty hand around my arm and throwing me on the bed. It creaks under my weight as I land on my front.

"You think I'm as dumb as the other ones? That I'm gonna beat you up so we can't use you?"

I scream when he grabs the hem of my sweatpants, dragging them down my legs. He rips the oversized panties they gave me, and I kick back.

But then someone else runs in. The handler.

"No!" I scream as he presses a hand at the back of my neck and one on my back, keeping me flat against the mattress.

Bodgov spreads my legs violently, then my ass cheeks. "No, please! Please, please..."

Tears explode from my eyes when he spits on me.

"Fucking dry slut," he growls. "I bet you regret hitting me now, huh?"

"I'm sorry," I sob, unable to prepare myself for what I'm about to endure. "I'm sorry. Please, don't."

My entire body recoils in disgust, but the second I feel him lower his jeans and his naked hips between my legs, I fall silent.

It's almost like I can feel my soul leaving my being, the out-of-body experience completely unreal. Something is about to happen to this poor woman held down by two men, and I feel sad for her. There's nothing I can do to help her.

Nate isn't coming. And I'm never going to see my girls again.

I'm never going to feel my husband's arms around me, strong and grounding.

I'm never going to feel the taste of his lips on mine. I'm never going to get to name my feelings to a man who wants to listen to me. Who wants to understand me. Who wants to protect me.

A commotion brings me out of my bizarre state, and I crash back into my body.

He's not inside me. He's letting me go. They both are.

Gunshots.

There are gunshots down the hallways. And screams.

I sit on the bed, using the momentary break to pull up my underwear and sweatpants. When I look up at Bodgov, his eyes are on the door, his pants still down as we hear doors being burst open and women screaming.

It's getting closer.

Bang. Aaah!

Bang. Aaah!

It's everywhere. All the doors, multiple at a time. They slam open. *Bang. Bang. Bang.*

Sometimes it's accompanied by a silenced gunshot. *Pop! Pop!*

The two men look at each other, finally reacting. Bogdan glances around the room. His gun must have fallen off when he was trying to rape me.

The handler puts a hand on the gun at his waist.

"What the f—"

He's cut off when my bedroom door opens.

Pop! Pop! The handler falls.

Pop! Pop! Two more bullets, Bogdan is next.

And there stands the devil who caused this madness.

The tall devil with hair that always reflects the sun, blinding your senses. The devil with the eyes that draw you in and the smile that promises nothing but chaos.

And chaos he caused.

Nathan White lowers his gun and smiles at me like he's facing an angel for the first time.

"Little sunflower." As calm as the sea on a beautiful summer day.

My eyes fill with tears at the look of relief on his face. Heart exploding in my chest, my brain hardly believes that he did it. He found me.

"My sun," I cry out.

I jump up from the bed, stumbling over my feet, and fall into his arms. He takes me in, in that exact protective way that I love and long for. That gets me addicted, that calms my heartbeat and heaving breaths in only a few seconds.

He lifts me up, and I wrap my legs around his waist.

"Are you alright? Did they hurt you?"

I shake my head. They did hurt me, but none of it matters now that he's here, freeing me, giving me life again.

"I'm okay," I sob. I run a hand across my nose, sniffling. "I'm okay. You're here, and I'm okay."

He chuckles into my neck, his embrace tight and soothing. "I'm starting to see where Lia gets all that repeating from."

I burst into a laugh, still crying, finding it hard to believe this is all over.

"You found me," I whisper against him, holding him tighter.

"My little sunflower, I will always find you."

We walk out of the room together. It's a massacre. All the handlers are dead, and the women have run out of the building.

"Where are we?" I rasp.

"In the underground of a bar called The Nightcap. We're in New York."

I nod, taking the information in as he leads me by the hand, going over dead bodies. "How long?"

"Three weeks." It comes out strained, like it hurts to say.

"Is that why you have this horrible beard?"

He chuckles, turning to me as we keep walking. "Yes. But now that I feel alive again, we'll shave it off."

I smile at him. "The girls. How are they?"

"They miss you. And Lia calls me Daddy." There's a smile in his voice. I wonder if that's another feeling we could try to name.

"Of course she does. You're her dad."

We climb stairs that feel like they go on forever, and when we finally get to the top, my mouth drops open.

Everyone is here. Everyone. Nate's enforcer, Sam, of course. But Rose and Jake White are here too. I can already imagine what happened. Rose wanted to come because she will always have a vendetta against the Wolves. And because no one can tell her what to do, her twin had to follow to make sure she came back in one piece.

The people from my crew are here, Ethan and Elliot. I can't help the tears when I notice NSC is here too. Xi and Lik came, and I know why. The Wolves didn't just kill their boss. They killed their stepsister.

Caden is here. My overprotective little brother who must have been suffering for weeks.

And Billie. With blood splattered on her clothes and face and a gun in her hand. Tears mix with the crimson on her cheek.

"Billie." I run to her, taking her small form in my arms.

She lets me, her shoulders sagging before she wraps her arms around my waist.

"I'm sorry," I cry. "I'm so sorry. I couldn't do anything."

She shakes her head in the crook of my neck, trembling words stumbling past her lips. "It's not your fault."

I take a deep, staggered breath, and tell her something I hope will help her. "She was going to call you. She wasn't mad at you. I promise. She loved you so much."

When we step back from each other, Caden takes me in his arms.

"Tell me you're okay," he rasps in my ear, his voice weak.

"I'm okay. I'm not hurt." I pull away slightly, my hands on his shoulders. "I'm okay, Cade."

He nods. "I'll kill them all over again, Kay. Again and again."

I shake my head, chuckling. "Once will do."

I step away, nodding at the others as Nate comes to wrap an arm around my waist.

"Let's take you home, little sunflower."

I probably take the longest shower of my life once we're home. The girls jumped on me the second I walked past the door, and now they won't leave the bathroom. Lia is talking a hundred miles an hour, gushing about dancing and reading with Daddy, how his waffles are disgusting, and that he gives the second-best hugs in the world after Mommy's.

I'm holding Livie in my arms, and Lia is in Nate's, when we walk into the dining room downstairs. Everyone is with us, spread around the long table, and eating from the countless Chinese takeout boxes.

I stand at the end of the table, my husband wrapping his free arm around my waist.

Everyone turns to us, and I take them all in one by one. Sam, Lik, Rose, and Rachel sitting together at the other end.

Caden and Billie not far. Alexandra sits on Xi's lap as he forces a dumpling into her mouth. Jade, Elliot, and Ethan share two chairs for three. The closest to us are Jake and his fiancée, Jamie.

One person is missing. Emma Scott, head of NSC. My enemy who became one of my closest friends just because some psychopath went a step too far and she felt bad for me.

Tears come to my eyes. The emotions are too raw to handle.

"Um...thank you," I choke past the tightness in my

chest. "All of you. I... I don't know how I could ever repay you."

"Nothing to repay," Xi says casually. "NSC and the Kings are one now. We're here for each other."

It means everything coming from him. The man who thought he'd leave it all behind and still came to help rescue me.

"So, you're back in?" I ask.

He's about to answer, when his girlfriend cuts in with a stern tone I didn't think she was capable of. "Only for emergencies."

Xi wraps a hand around the back of her neck. "Only for emergencies," he repeats, looking at Nate this time. I feel him nodding next to me, agreeing to that statement.

"We're family, Kay," Elliot adds. "Always."

I nod, wiping the last tear falling from my eyes with the back of my hand.

"Don't cry, Mommy!" Lia exclaims. "Don't cry!"

"They're happy tears, honey," I tell her. "Mommy's okay."

I grab the can of cherry soda in front of me. The fridge was full of them. Nate kept adding to them, even though I wasn't here to take them out.

I raise it in front of my completely improbable and dysfunctional family.

"To Emma Scott," I say. "May she rest in peace."

Everyone else raises their drinks, repeating the name of the woman who fell to the hands of our biggest enemies.

"So, what now?" Caden asks.

They all look at Nate and me, expectant. What now, that we spent our entire lives hating each other, running our broken town? What now, that we all own it as a unified family? What now, that the world outside keeps spinning while we recover from the loss we suffered and while I heal from the fear of never seeing any of them again?

What now?

My husband and I stand tall at the head of the table. Our hands fall side by side, and he grabs mine tightly as we hold our daughters.

"Now, we keep on living."

THE END

EPILOGUE
NATHAN

Teeth - 5 Seconds of Summer

Six months later...

My phone rings, and I huff to myself when I see the number. This is going to be painful.

"Mrs. Caldon." I fake a polite voice when I pick up because one of the twins' parents has to.

"Mr. White, your wife has threatened another parent when she came to pick up Olivia and Celia today."

I pinch my lips, trying not to burst into laughter. The head of the Stoneview preschool always has a bone to pick with my North Shore wife. Even when she doesn't threaten anyone.

"Please." She sighs desperately. "You're a reasonable man. I am begging you, speak to Mrs. White."

Mrs. White. I will never get tired of hearing it. Technically, Kayla is Mrs. White-King now. But no one ever thinks of the second last name. She still hasn't changed the girls' name, but I'll get there.

If only Mrs. Caldon knew when my mask falls, I am the least reasonable between Kayla and me.

"I will. As soon as she gets home from pickup. Thank you for calling."

Just as I hang up, I hear Lia's excited voice passing the door. "Mommy is a super mommy!"

She runs to me, hugging my legs.

"Hi, Daddy."

"Hi, honey." I take her in my arms, giving her a kiss.

Kay walks in holding Livie's hand. Livie has that little smug look on her face she gets when she's happy, and Kay has put her most innocent expression in place.

I walk to both of them, give my other daughter a kiss, and cock an eyebrow at my wife.

"Where's my kiss?" she asks, her pretty lips pouting ever-so slightly.

So tempting, but I have to stay strong.

"Only the girls who didn't cause trouble get a kiss. What did you do?"

Livie giggles, and Kay has to hold back a smile. "Nothing."

She tries to walk past me, but I grab her arm.

"Kayla. I got a call from Mrs. Caldon. Heads of preschool usually only call about the kids doing something bad. Not the moms."

"Suzie's mommy said to Mommy that Livie can't talk."

I narrow my eyes at my wife. "That's it?"

"It's the *way* she said it," Kay huffs. She shrugs me off, taking Livie to the kitchen, so I follow.

My little chatterbox keeps explaining the story to me anyway as we sit both girls at the kitchen island.

"Mommy took Suzie's mommy to the side, and then Suzie's mommy apologized to Livie. Right, Livie? She apologized. And then I saw Suzie's mommy crying in her car. She cried." She takes a deep breath and repeats, shaking her head. "She cried in her car."

"Kay," I growl, turning to my wife. "Is this what you're showing the girls? Really?"

"Mommy is a super mommy."

Kay smiles innocently at me. "I'm a super mommy."

"Don't," I huff. "What did you tell her?"

She shrugs, pulling snacks out of the fridge for the girls. "I told her how I"—she waves her hand in front of her throat—"the last person who made fun of my daughters. That I made it last for hours. I was very specific."

"What? Who was that?" I ask curiously. I didn't know about this.

She starts cutting strawberries for the girls, and I grab two plastic bowls, filling them up with the grapes Kay put on the counter.

"My dad's girlfriend. Long before you came back from pr—your vacation."

We haven't told the girls about me going to prison yet. Maybe when they're older, we will, but then we'd have to say that Daddy doesn't do bad things anymore. And that would be a lie. Daddy runs a criminal organization with Mommy. Better to keep it to ourselves for as long as we can.

"That was stupid. Not your dad's girlfriend. Suzie's mom. Stoneview talks. Rumors spread."

She shrugs. "You would have done worse. No warning, I bet."

"Of course I would have. But I would have been *discreet*. Mrs. Caldon wouldn't have called you to tell you I"—it's my turn to wave my hand in front of my throat—"Suzie's mom."

"Suzie is not nice," Lia jumps in.

"What?" I snap my head toward her. "What did she do? Do you want Daddy to talk to her?"

She shrugs. "She pushed me once."

Kay and I both turn around from the counter, facing our daughters.

"She pushed you?" I repeat, my voice lowering. "Where does Suzie live?"

"With her mommy."

I narrow my gaze, a million ways to kill the entire Suzie family running through my head.

"Nate. Do not hurt that family," Kay jumps in.

"What? Why? Suzie terrified my daughter."

"She is *not* terrified. Lia, honey. How do we help Daddy with how we feel?"

"We name it," she says proudly. "How we feel."

"Tell Daddy how you feel about Suzie."

Lia shrugs dramatically. "I don't care."

"See?" Kay says. "She doesn't care. Suzie doesn't scare my tough daughter. Don't worry."

Later that night, Kay catches me on my laptop in bed when she comes back from reading a story to the girls. She's getting so much better at it and she loves to show off her progress. Her speech therapy has really been helping.

I'm going through the family names of the people in the girls' preschool while on the phone.

"Surely, you can find the address with their full name. I have an email address."

"*Nate*," my brother yawns on the other end of the line. "*For the last time, I will not look up this family's address so you can go commit a murder. Now let me sleep.*"

He hangs up on me.

"Nate," Kay hisses. "We said no."

She slams my laptop shut.

"She pushed her," I answer simply. "I won't hurt the child. It's not her fault her parents are terrible. I'll just kill the—"

"No."

I huff, running my hand against my face. "Fine. But if little Suzie ever hurts Lia or Livie again—"

"She won't. Come on. No more thinking of killing that family."

She puts the laptop away and turns back to me, taking off the only thing she was still wearing. One of my t-shirts. My eyes take her in, especially the tattoo of a sun. She's so mine.

"I see you trying to distract me from the topic."

"Is it working?" She straddles me, pulling my boxers down and rubbing her wet entrance against the ridge of my dick.

"It certainly is," I growl, as I feel myself getting hard. "Keep going."

She wraps her arms around my neck, but I put my hands at her waist and switch our positions. I grab the back of her thighs, pushing her knees to her chest.

"I'm not feeling very patient, little sunflower. If you want to play, you have to play hard."

I press against her entrance, making it hurt as I push in. She whimpers, but I feel her wetness double.

"I know your body by heart, baby."

That night, I fuck my wife like she loves. I make her my little slut the same way I always do. And when I come inside her, I press my fingers into her pussy, pushing my cum back inside as always.

"Nate," she laughs. "I am *still* on contraception. I renewed my shot, remember?"

"Stop renewing it, then."

She looks up at me, her neck stretching to watch me between her legs. "What?"

"Get off contraception. Give me another kid."

"I—" She stops herself, the gears turning in her mind. "You want that?"

I nod. "I want another. And maybe another after that. And again. I want the house full of proof of our love. I want mini versions of us taking over the world."

She giggles, and I lean over her, kissing her lips.

"What do you think?"

"I don't know about a ton of others. But one more, yes."

"Really?" My heart swells, my fingers tingling. I press a hand against her cheek. "You want another baby? With me?"

She nods, biting her lower lip. "I want another baby with you."

I kiss her again, taking her words in directly from her mouth. "We'll work very hard on this."

She reaches to grab her phone. "Should I set the alarm for 4:15 a.m.?" she asks.

I shake my head, taking the device out of her hands and putting it away. "They're gone, little sunflower. All we're doing now is waking you up in the middle of the night for no reason. Just because you're used to it and it reassures you."

She licks her lips, hesitant. "Are you sure?"

"I'm sure, baby. No more night terrors. Because you're safe now. You'll always be safe with me."

And this is a promise I intend to keep until the end of days. Not only for Kay, but for our entire family. I will always keep them safe.

ALSO BY LOLA KING

All books happen in the same world at different times

STONEVIEW STORIES

(MF, bully):

Giving In

Giving Away

Giving Up

One Last Kiss (Novella - includes spoilers from Rose's Duet)

ROSE'S DUET

(FFMM why-choose):

Queen Of Broken Hearts (Prequel novella)

King of My Heart

Ace of All Hearts

NORTH SHORE STORIES

(interconnected standalones):

Beautiful Fiend (MF, enemies to lovers)

Heartless Beloved - (MF, good girl/bad boy)

Delightful Sins - (MFM, enemies-to-lovers)

Lawless God - (MF ,enemies-to-lovers)

HOLIDAY NOVELLA

Merry Christmas From Daddy to Little One

ACKNOWLEDGMENTS

First and foremost, thank you to Caden, Billie, Xi, Alex, Elliot, Ethan, Jade, Kayla, and Nate. You guys might be fictional, but you have changed my life for the better. I have learned and healed through you...and yall are fucked up.

I would like to express how thankful I am to my readers for following the journey of all the characters who live on the North Shore.

When I decided to write an entire series about people who live in a broken town and who had been broken by life... I did not realise how much I would fall in love with them...and to everyone who has fallen in love with them too, well, thank you.

Thank you my King for your support and love. This one was a tough one...thank you for staying by my side. Thank you for drying the tears, for the calls, for picking me up and driving me to your house and rolling me into a burrito. Thank you for the dates when I needed to get out of the house, for booking the restaurants...thank you for being the best book boyfriend.

Thank you to my beautiful girlfriend, Jess. Needless to say this book is the one that burned me out and you were always there to take care of me. And that care package...I'm still emotional about it.

Thank you to Lauren, Ratula, Kat, and Mackenzie for helping me shape this book and make it the best version it could be.

Thank you to the amazing ladies from VPR for all your help. To Valentine, thank you for your support in this entire North Shore Stories journey. I know you're still mad about Emma (sorry?)

Thank you to my friend Natalia Lourose for your endless support and all the voice notes... We love voice notes.

Thank you to Alina May for hanging out with me during the Europe late nights/US mid-day and for the sleepovers across the ocean. You get me on a professional and personal level, and your help and support during the creation of this book means everything.

As always, thank you to my family for your support. You guys are the best and also the worst. I love you anyway.

Lots of Love,

Lola

3090496BR00360